A MEMBER OF
THE FAMILY

A MEMBER OF THE FAMILY

A Novel

Susan Merrell

HarperCollins*Publishers*

HarperCollins books may be purchased for educational, business, or sales promotional use. For information please write: Special Markets Department, HarperCollins Publishers, Inc., 10 East 53rd Street, New York, NY 10022.

FIRST EDITION

Designed by Elliott Beard

Library of Congress Cataloging-in-Publication Data

Merrell, Susan Scarf.
    A member of the family : a novel / Susan Merrell. — 1st ed.
      p. cm.
    ISBN 0-06-019280-1
    I. Title
  PS3563.E7426S24   2000
  813'.54—dc21   99-34923

00 01 02 03 04 ❖/RRD 10 9 8 7 6 5 4 3 2 1

For Jim

Being thus arrived in a good harbor, and brought safe to land, they fell upon their knees and blessed the God of Heaven who had brought them over the vast and furious ocean, and delivered them from all the perils and miseries thereof, again to set their feet on the firm and stable earth, their proper element.

William Bradford, *Of Plymouth Plantation*

Affidavit by Adoptive Parent or Prospective Adoptive Parent

I, __DEBORAH B. LATHAM__, certify that I am the adoptive

parent/prospective adoptive parent of a child, __MIHAI CĂLDĂRĂRI__,

on whose behalf I have filed or will file an I-600 (petition to classify orphan as immediate relative) according said child status as an orphan as defined by Section 101(b)(1)(F).

I have read the statement above and I am aware of the vaccination requirement set forth in Section 212(a)(1)(A)(ii) of the Immigration and Nationality Act. In accordance with Section 212(a)(1)(A)(ii), I will ensure that my foreign adopted child receives the required and medically appropriate vaccinations within 30 days after his or her admission into the U.S., or at the earliest time that is medically appropriate.

Signed this ___10th___ day of ___JUNE___, ___1993___, at
___3141 Main St. Sagttubo, NY 11963___.

Deborah Latham
(Signature of Parent)

Subscribed and sworn to (or affirmed) before me this ___10th___ day
day of ___JUNE___, ___1993___, at ___3141 Main St.___.
My commission expires on ___9.25.99___.
_B. M_
(Signature of Notary Public or Officer Administering Oath)

PART I

I

"MOMMA?"

"Yes, Honey."

"You know who's stupid?"

"Don't say that word, Michael."

"Mrs. Doroski's stupid. That's who."

"Michael."

"Momma?"

"Yes, Honey."

"You heard when Daddy said about George Washington?"

"What about George Washington?"

"When Daddy said about George Washington wore *dead* people's teeth? From dead soldiers? They took their teeth even though they were dead? Remember?"

Deborah Latham glanced in the rearview mirror. Michael was grinning excitedly. "Yuck. Why were you talking about that?"

"His teeth, gross, it's cool. Mrs. Doroski's stupid. She says George Washington had wooden teeth."

"That's what I learned in school, too," she said mildly. "Maybe Daddy got it wrong."

"Mrs. Doroski is stupid."

"No, she's not. Don't say that. It's rude."

Deborah Latham's toes were cold; she should have worn sneakers instead of sandals this morning. Fall, as always, had arrived surreptitiously. Temperatures dropped overnight. In a few days, autumn hues would erupt on both sides of Sagg Road, and the sand at Gibson Beach would be chilly under her toes.

She loved autumn; her husband yearned for it. Chris Latham, born and raised in Sag Harbor, detested the honking horns and broken beer bottles that were all he noticed of tourist-filled summers. He lived for Labor Day, when Main Street quieted and he knew the name of every strolling window-shopper. To a certain extent, Deborah had to agree with him: Although Sag Harbor in summer was picture-perfect, it was only during the other three seasons of the year that the village was a pleasant place to live.

The biggest problem with this autumn was that Michael Latham didn't want to go to kindergarten.

"I don't like school," he said now. "And I don't want to go."

"Michael, Honey, lots of kids don't like it at first. Caroline clung to my legs so hard I had to carry her into the classroom. For at least a week. But look how much she likes it now. She runs out to the bus every morning. You have to give school a try."

"I did. I already did."

"I mean a real try, not just a few days. Really give school a chance."

Parked back here, across the playground from the building, Deborah couldn't hear shouts or giggles, or the thundering pound of feet up and down the three flights of stairs. Michael was silent, staring out the window at the last few stragglers running into the brick elementary school. She thought, *I can actually feel his resistance; he's glued to that seat like a war protester. And I won't carry him in. I couldn't.*

"Hey," she said softly. "If I tell you the story again, quickly, will you walk in with me? Give it another try?"

He eyed her.

"Come on, Michael. Please."

Although his lips were tight and unyielding, he nodded. "Okay, I guess."

Deborah Latham had told this story so many times over the last three years that when she opened her mouth, the words arranged themselves effortlessly. "Back when you were just a baby, a long, long time ago, you lived halfway around the world, in a country called Romania, a beautiful country with mountains and white sandy beaches and tall trees in ancient forests. The land was beautiful, but the people were very poor. They had difficult lives, with little food to eat. There were lots of problems there. And many people could not afford to keep their own children, to raise them, even though they loved them very much. Your mother tried very, very hard to keep you. She worked hard and struggled and took wonderful care of you. She was a good, good mother. But there was a terrible accident—you should never be scared of that kind of accident again, because it will never happen to me or to your father."

Michael sighed happily, settling back in his seat.

"And you were sent to live in an awful place called an orphanage. Do you remember it?"

He shook his head, no.

"You really don't, do you?"

No, he shook his head again, vehemently. No.

Thank God for that.

"Well, you were there for about a year, a little longer, but you didn't have to stay. You were lucky. Because we knew Viorica and she found you, and when she saw you, she just knew right away."

"She knew right away," he repeated dreamily.

"Yes, Sweetheart. She could tell how special you are and how right you would be here. With us. She saw you belonged to me and Daddy, and to Caro."

"Did you already love me, even then? Did you love me?"

"We didn't even know about you, Silly! But Viorica came back to America as quickly as she could, and she said, I found a child, a little boy, and he should belong to you."

"And even though you and Daddy hadn't thought of having me, and didn't make me in your body, you still wanted me."

"You remember that part."

He nodded.

"The minute Viorica told you, you looked at Daddy and he looked at you, and you nodded at each other, and you turned back and said to Viorica, 'Of course we want him, as fast as we can get him,' and Caro said, 'A baby brother, for me!'"

"That's right, Sweetheart. And then we met with the social worker from the adoption agency, and she came and looked us over a million times, and we worked with the Immigration Department, and filled out so many papers you can't believe it. After a while, we found a great lawyer, and she helped us so much. Then, before you could say hinkety blink . . ."

"Hinkety blink!" He giggled.

"That's right, before you could even say that, there you were at the airport. And I'd been so busy getting things together for you, and I was so nervous, that you wouldn't like us, or that there would be some mistake, and next thing I knew I saw Viorica carrying you off the airplane. And my heart just flew across the waiting area and got stuck together with yours."

"It did?"

"It did. I hugged you so hard, and I was crying. I couldn't help myself."

"I remember!"

"You couldn't, Michael, Honey. You were only eighteen months old."

"I remember. I do."

"And then I was your mommy, and Daddy was your daddy, and Caroline was your sister, from that day on."

"And you love me?"

"And I love you."

"Even when I'm a bad boy, you still love me."

"That's right, even then."

They were silent, companionably so, watching the pure absence of movement—not even a brush of wind fluttered the stillness—across the long grassy stretch of the playground.

"Even when I fight with Caro, you still love us both the same."

"I still love you both the same," she repeated obediently.

"Even when I mess up, you still love me."

"I still love you, Joker. I always will."

"And Daddy, too?"

"And Daddy, too."

"And Daddy, too?" he asked again.

"Yes, Silly. Daddy, too. Caroline. And Grandma and Grandpa, and Aunt Michele and Uncle Sam, oh, everybody. You're part of our family, Silly."

"I'm not a bad boy, really," he offered.

"Of course not. What makes you even say that?"

He unlocked his seat belt, sliding down the length of the seat to lean forward and lift the door latch. "I can walk in myself."

She opened her own door. "I know that, Michael. I just like to walk you in. Keep you company."

"I won't get in trouble. I promise."

She opened his door, leaning in to help him out. "Listen," she said, grabbing him gently by the shoulders. "I trust you. I just like to walk you in. I like to be with you. That's all."

"Thanks, Momma," he said, taking her by the hand.

"You're welcome, Sweetheart," she answered, blinking her eyelids rapidly.

Inside, the halls were deserted. "What time is it?" Deborah muttered, freeing her hand from his to twist her husband's watch around on her wrist. "Oh my God, we are late. And today's the first day your class starts going to Morning Program with the rest of the school."

"I can go."

"No, Honey, I'll take you. It'll be fun. Lots of mommies and daddies go. You'll see. We can wave to Caro over with her class."

He shook his head, planting his entire body stubbornly. His sharp chin protruded downward, and his eyes glared at her midsection. She knelt. Even shifting him toward her was tough; he'd rooted his feet into the floor. "Michael, Sweetheart, look at me."

He only did it because he had no choice; she could feel no warmth, just resistance. "What is it?" she asked softly. "What's bugging you about school?"

He shrugged. His sweater was misbuttoned, she noticed with surprise—after all, she'd done it up herself—but she held back from reaching forward to correct it. "What is it?"

He shrugged again.

"Is it the other kids? Has someone been mean to you?"

He shook his head, no.

"Honest?"

Another head shake, more vehement. *No.*

"Where's that smile of yours, then? Where did it go? Where's my Wonder Boy?"

His lips twitched, just the slightest bit. She pulled him closer, hugging his thin frame to her own. His heart beat with such ferocity she could feel it physically when they hugged, and it always made her draw him in more closely. He was her miracle snatched from the dark door of hell. "Hey," she said softly. "Help me out here!"

"Momma." His arms snaked around her neck. His head turned to rest on her shoulder.

"You were so happy about starting kindergarten, remember? The shoe store? Your sneakers? Remember? And getting the same teacher Caro had?"

"She's mean."

"Caro?"

"No. Mrs. Doroski."

"I'm sure she isn't mean on purpose, Michael, Honey. Maybe you misunderstand her. She just wants you to know the rules of school. It's different from home."

"I know. It's not that. She gets mad at me for stuff."

Deborah Latham drew back to look her son more fully in the face. "Michael, Sweet, you know you like to get your own way. We both know that. But there are eighteen kids in your class, and they all have to get an equal chance."

"It's not that," he protested.

"You can be very charming, my little man, and maybe you get your way at home sometimes when you shouldn't. But home is different from school. Home is me and Daddy and the two of you . . ."

"And Mina."

"And Mina, but she won't be coming that much anymore. Now that you're in school, she'll just come when Daddy and I go out to the movies or to dinner."

"She'll still come to see us, she said she would! And she said in the summer, it would be like always. And Viorica said so, too."

"Don't get so riled, Michael! Of course we'll see them. Mina's not just a baby-sitter, not after so many years. And Viorica's our friend. But when children grow up and start school, things change. And it's not bad, it's good. You'll see."

He sighed, his body so still that only the smallest whisper escaped him.

"Change isn't always bad," she repeated. "Look, you came here to us, and that was good, wasn't it? You have to believe that we are always, always going to take care of you. Even when you're six feet tall."

His eyes widened. "Me?"

"Yep. You. I promise. I swear. I double swear. I pinkie swear. I'll even double pinkie swear."

He smiled reluctantly.

"We only want what's best for you. We want you to be our happy boy. Who knows how to read and write and do his numbers, and all kinds of things you'll begin learning this year. It's just the beginning, Sweetie, just the very start. And school is so much fun if you give it a chance."

He didn't believe her, not a bit.

"Don't you have drawing time, isn't that fun?" she tried again. "The art room is a thousand times better than our playroom. Did you see how many colors they have?"

He turned toward the main door as if he thought of escape, replanting his body a solid half-turn from his mother so that only a limited profile was visible to view. "She doesn't like me. I can tell. She's mean."

"Mrs. Doroski? That's impossible."

He shrugged, turning more fully away. His shoulders rose and fell, once only, and then he said, "Everything, she gets mad at me. If a kid cries."

"How . . . are you sure? She's not like that. She was great with Caro. She was . . . why, Honey, why do you say that?" Deborah Latham, who had been squatting next to Michael, lowered her knees to the linoleum-tiled floor in order to look him in the eye.

"A boy broke pencils. She said it was me. It wasn't! It wasn't!"

"What boy? When? Yesterday? What was the other boy's name?"

He shrugged again. "I don't know."

"What did she call him? Was it Ryan? Or Billy? Or Kevin?"

He nodded. "Maybe."

"If Mrs. Doroski really believed you'd done something bad, she'd have talked to me so we could all help you together."

He brightened slightly. "She would?"

"Oh, yes, she would. Of course she would."

A long silence. Finally, Michael looked at her directly. "I'm not like them," he said.

For a moment, she couldn't find a way to breathe. He was so young, just five years old, and he had already been through so much. "I'm not like them either," she said stoutly. "Sooner or later, you'll find out that being different is good. I'm special, and so are you."

He swallowed and his eyes abruptly glowed with excitement. "Jason won't play with me. He said I come from Monsterland, where bats kill people. And suck their blood. With fangs. Do they? Do they?!"

"Come on, Honey. Let's go to Morning Program." She reached out a hand, and he took it excitedly.

"Mom," he said, "'cause if they do, I'm going there sometime. To see the bats with fangs. I'm gonna bring one back with me. Like a pet."

"That trip will sure use up a lot of allowance," she said amiably.

His shoulders sagged.

"Maybe Mina knows, about the bats. You can call her after school."

"I'll call Viorica. She goes back all the time. Maybe she can bring a bat for me. Maybe she can take me with her sometime."

Deborah tousled his hair. "You can call her. I think Viorica's on the road, though."

"Oh, okay," he said, hopping forward in an enthusiastic burst, his sneakered feet dancing along the mottled linoleum. "That's okay then. I'll call Mina."

As they neared the gym, she said, "I'll talk to Mrs. Doroski. I'll do some scouting around myself, but I'm sure it's all fine. I really am. Mommies know these things. Okay, Champ?"

"Okay," he said, dashing back to pull at her hands. "Let's go."

"I love you," she said softly.

His eyes, shining up at hers, gave a fully satisfying response.

The noise in the gym was deafening: row upon row of chattering, screaming, laughing children, ages ranging from kindergarten through fifth grade. As they entered through the double doors, the sound seemed to swell. For a moment, Deborah thought she might panic; she had the notion that all the faces were turned directly on them: angry faces, irritated faces, unwelcoming faces. All those eyes and noses and teeth, those long arms waving, blurred before her. And every single one some mother's beloved genius, some father's future baseball star.

"Mrs. Latham?"

"Oh. Oh, Mrs. Doroski! It's so . . . there are so many children here today!"

Rose Doroski smiled. "It just seems that way. The third week is always sort of wild. One of the other teachers said there's a full moon. Can I take Michael over to our section? Or are you staying this morning?"

"I thought I'd hang around, that is, if you have a moment before the children go up to the classroom. I have a quick question for you."

"You know, I think it might be better if we met after school. If today is convenient, of course. I'd like to have a conversation with you, as well."

"You would?" Deborah asked.

"Oh, yes," Mrs. Doroski told her. "I really would."

Michael tugged at his mother's hand. "I told you!" he said, and then he turned, dashing across the gloss of the gym floor to the area where his fellow kindergartners sat. Even Deborah could tell that several children from his class were squeezing tightly together so there would be no free room on the bleacher with them. She didn't want to observe it, but she had no choice. It would have been impossible to miss.

Mrs. Doroski touched Deborah's arm. "This afternoon, at pickup time?"

"Yes," Deborah said, smiling automatically. "I'll see you then."

2

THE MEETING was scheduled for three o'clock, but the call came just before noon. It was the school nurse, saying, "Nobody's hurt, Mrs. Latham, but there's been a problem. Would you be able to come over to the elementary school?"

Deborah had been standing in her basement darkroom when the phone rang. For the first time in nearly three years she had tried to talk herself into cataloging old photos. It would be a step toward working again. She knew she should be ready; with both kids in school, she had no excuse.

Jumping back into the station wagon was such a relief that she didn't ponder the summons. A formal obligation; someone needed her. Nobody had been hurt; Maureen had underscored that several times in her gravelly voice. Why was it that so many nurses smoked? Any decisions about Deborah's own professional future could be postponed for another day.

The playground was packed with children, running and laughing, huddled in play, chasing a soccer ball across the grassy lawn. It was such a cheerful sight on such a beautiful day that Deborah was smiling as she entered the building and trotted up the stairs.

It wasn't until Mrs. Bennett's secretary jumped up from her desk that Deborah's pulse began to thrum. "Come on, Mrs. Latham, this way," the secretary said, hitting a chair in her eagerness to lead the way to Linda Bennett's office.

And Deborah, abruptly, understood why she was there. *Oh, God,* she thought, her chest tightening. *Why didn't I expect this?*

Rose Doroski stood just inside the office door; Linda Bennett was kneeling, holding Michael, but when he saw his mom, he threw himself toward her, rolling across the floor. That ugly red sweater was open, its sides flapping loose, its back panel pulled and gathered all the way to his neck. The silk-screened black Labrador on his T-shirt had crumpled up on one side. It was caught under his right elbow so that the dog's snout disappeared—just the dog's damp eyes and Michael's heading toward her. His body arched and lengthened until he was at Deborah's feet, grabbing at her legs. She squatted, taking him in her arms.

Mother behavior was taking over. She knew herself to be curiously calm, deflated really, her movements relaxed and fluid. Against her neck, Michael's forehead fit with a warm, damp thump. Now he would draw his arms around her; he always did.

"Michael? Michael, Honey? Are you okay?" she asked quietly.

He began to scream, a stream of gibberish emerging from his open mouth. What had they done to him? Deborah drew him in, glaring up at Rose. And that was when she saw the gash swirling across Rose Doroski's forehead. Blood and dirt speckled Rose's blouse. Was that a sneaker imprint? Her shirt was ripped, just above the right breast.

Linda Bennett stepped forward, extending her right hand. "Good afternoon, Mrs. Latham. I'm glad you came so quickly. We've been having a problem with Michael. He's been hurtful, to himself and to others."

Michael's arms tightened around his mother. She couldn't have taken Linda Bennett's hand if she'd wanted to.

Linda straightened. She wore such high heels Deborah couldn't imagine how she maintained her balance. "What happened?" Deborah asked. "What happened here?!"

It was Rose who answered, far from calmly. "I had to carry Michael in, kicking, from the playground, after a fight! I couldn't believe it, one five-year-old pounding at another with fists! Screaming!"

Linda Bennett turned to Rose, frowning slightly.

Rose didn't see; she was clearly too agitated. "I ran over to them, and he looked up. Michael looked up. He saw me coming! His face was all twisted and furious; he was yelling! He saw me! He didn't stop, oh no! He reached out and grabbed some pebbles—he actually hurled them at me! At my face! A teacher! Here! Look!"

She'd pulled him up, Rose said, untangling him from Jason Stall. It had been a struggle to get the boys apart, even though she wasn't a small woman. Jason sprawled on the ground, his belly quivering with sobs, his plump cheeks mottled red. Even in the air, Michael's arms and legs flailed, kicking in jerky, rigid spasms.

He'd screamed, Rose Doroski said, and when she imitated the sounds, Michael looked up with interest. He had screamed, "Nooo! Nooo! No!! No!!" His fists had pounded on Rose's chest and arms.

Deborah Latham could feel herself smiling. She didn't want to. If anything, she wanted no expression on her face, but her lips kept pulling apart, dry and forced. Watching Rose Doroski was like watching a cruel mime at work. Rose had seen this, Rose had done that. Rose had picked him up, Rose had carried him in. No wonder Michael didn't like her.

Michael's breathing sounded harsh and agitated. He gulped several times, and she thought he might break in and defend himself, tell what really had happened.

"Finally, I twisted him away from me, got him so that he was kicking the other way! The children, the other children, were staring so, they were terrified!" Rose said. "And I got him inside the building. He was making the strangest noises, I couldn't understand him at all, like those sounds he just made. And I ran past the main office and yelled for them to use the code, you know, the emergency code! And that's when he ripped my shirt, here!"

Inside the principal's office, Rose had placed him down. She'd kept a hand on each wrist; he was a really strong kid and he was straining to get away, but she held on firmly. "Stop," she had told him. "It's time to calm down."

And then he'd stamped on her foot. She'd held on tight even then. If she hadn't, he'd probably have run out of the room. She'd said, "You're really angry, Michael. What are you doing? What are you feeling right now?"

But he only snarled again, attempting to free his arms. That was when Mrs. Bennett walked through the door. "And then, of course, you got here," Rose finished, nodding at Deborah.

"I don't understand," Deborah said stupidly, casting around for what would be the right words to say. She couldn't focus, not on Michael, not on the other women, not on the story, not even on the cut on Rose's forehead. For some reason, the only thought she had was how oddly different Rose

Doroski's body was from Linda Bennett's. They were the same size, small women both, but Linda was built like an elf, and Rose's upper body was formidable. No wonder she'd been able to hold on to Michael. Linda, on the other hand, seemed so fragile that the regulation fire door loomed in menace behind her.

"It wasn't easy to get him quiet," Linda Bennett said. "He was very upset, kicking and lashing out."

Michael, on the floor, began to kick again, banging his head angrily, emitting another series of screeching sounds.

"What is he saying?" Deborah asked, but of course, no one could answer her.

"I think I should take him home," Deborah said.

Linda moved toward the door. "No, it's not a good idea. We've really got to calm him down first. He needs to know he can't—we won't—he needs to know this can't happen here."

"What can't happen here?" Deborah stepped toward Linda and the exit, completely disregarding Michael's presence at her feet. He rolled slightly, rubbing his arm where her sneakered foot caught him.

"Oh!" Deborah exclaimed, kneeling at his side again. He was, for the moment, quiet, his breath coming in ragged gasps.

Linda knelt also, putting a hand on Deborah Latham's arm. Michael started gulping air, huge gasps of air, a high whining sound threading through each inward breath. Before Linda could speak, the door opened with a bang, clipping Deborah's back.

Michael jumped to his feet. "Daddy! Daddy!" He lunged for his father, grinning widely, his white teeth bright against his gums. "Daddy!" he said again, and he slapped both arms around his father's knees, hugging him and laughing in giddy, joyful peals.

Deborah gasped. Rose looked shocked, and Linda Bennett rose to standing. Chris Latham didn't look any less confused. He bent at the waist, stiffly, and patted his son's back with a cautious, almost dainty, air.

A few minutes later, Rose walked Chris and his son down to the nurse's room. Michael was tired now, it was obvious, and Rose watched as Chris helped his son onto the couch. Chris sat down and the boy leaned into him immediately.

"You know, if the nurse can let us sit here a while, I think it would be good," Chris said calmly.

"I can stay with him," Rose said. "Don't you want to talk with Mrs. Bennett?"

He glanced toward the window, then back to her. "No," he said. "Actually, no. I'll stay with him. Deborah can handle that conversation. She'll tell me. I think I'd rather sit now, with the boy. If there's anything, I'll call Linda—Mrs. Bennett—about it."

Rose nodded. She asked if anyone wanted a drink of water, but neither of them appeared to hear her. Michael seemed to be struggling to stay awake. Chris held his son under his left arm, and patted the boy's leg with his right hand. An automatic gesture, this, Rose could tell; looking at Christopher's face, it was hard to imagine what he was thinking.

Rose had always considered Chris Latham to be her physical type. Out of reach, but definitely not out of her fantasies. He was a man of average height—he had to be at least two inches shorter than his wife—with a sturdy frame and short-cropped hair. Back in high school, he'd been pretty close to the cream of the crop: good-looking, smart, a jock.

The thing about Chris Latham was that even though he was cool, he wasn't a jerk. He was the kind of kid who said hello to everyone in the halls; he helped with homework; he wasn't rude or mean or full of himself. Once, when Rose had been trudging home after school, laden with a bag of costumes she'd agreed to iron before the upcoming dress rehearsal for—what was it? *Babes in Arms,* she thought, but she couldn't remember anymore—Chris Latham had pulled up in Anna Downing's slick old Chevy and offered her a ride. Everybody knew about Anna's car; they called it the Golden Goddess. Just getting in it—with Chris's hands on the wheel, and her getting to pretend for ten whole minutes that he was hers—oh, it was like being transported to heaven, a gift from above she'd probably thought about once a day for her entire life. Rose's fantasies about Chris Latham were most likely shared by 90 percent of the girls who had been at Pierson with him, but he didn't appear to know it, or court it, or care. He was, and this was widely agreed on, a truly nice guy.

Chris Latham, like Rosie's husband, Steve, was the kind of person the other villagers cited when they felt as if the summer people looked down on them. He'd gone to college and become a dentist. He was successful, kind, known to mix in both worlds. Folks liked Chris Latham for a lot of reasons, Rose guessed, but the most important one was this: Chris Latham remembered where he came from.

Rose knew that Chris Latham was a touch higher up the social scale than Steve Doroski. First of all, Chris's wife was "from away" and clearly different: You could tell she'd come from money. Still, she was friendly and didn't lord her background around the way some people did. So many of the newcomers saw the village as a blank slate they were more than fit to write on, but she seemed to see what the locals did, to understand how the old Sag Harbor had been glorious.

Caroline, the Lathams' daughter, was special as well. She was one of the brightest children Rose had ever had in her classroom. A tall, pretty child with black curly hair and a sweet smile, Caroline had come into kindergarten already reading. Musical and mathematical, she'd been one of the rare children the school might have considered skipping directly into second grade. Her parents had nixed that idea, though, pointing out how quiet Caroline was and how easily she might be overwhelmed by older children. Her mother had been concerned by how few friends Caroline had, just two other little girls, but Rose and Linda had reassured her that Caroline was, while extremely smart, a very normal child. Other children liked her, even though she didn't mix that much. One of the pleasures of having Caroline had been that she was influential; that year, almost the entire class had come out of kindergarten reading.

Of course Rose had been delighted to learn she would have the Lathams' son, Michael, in her classroom. He was a bright child, like his sister, and extraordinarily verbal. When Rose made her home visit to meet him, he used words she'd never heard before from a child his age. His mother explained that he was very sensitive to nuance; his vocabulary seemed to expand every day. And his drawing skills were amazing. His mother proudly brought out page after page: Her five-year-old son could reproduce a horse or car with the sophistication of a sixth grader. Rose Doroski had expected to have a banner year with him.

Boy, had she been wrong. Every single day of the last three weeks, she had been forced to face the fact that Michael wasn't adjusting well at all. He'd been rude and dishonest; he'd been rough and disruptive; and she didn't have the faintest idea how to reach him.

On the first day of school, even, she'd headed for Linda's office to confess that she was already sure he was the one child who might defeat her. Linda had been supportive, of course—she was always such a good friend—but she'd been surprised, Rose could tell. She hated to feel she was letting Linda down. After today, though, she was truly at wit's end.

God, she felt sorry for Chris Latham. With all his kindness, all his decency, his generous soul, well, he also had the burden of this horrible kid to bear. It showed that even the most besilvered lining had its cloud.

Michael Latham truly was a curse. Poor Chris. He certainly didn't deserve it.

3

YEARS BEFORE, a young mother had insisted to Deborah that all parents treat their children basically the same. Of course, children don't see it: Younger kids think the older ones get all the freedom, older kids think they never get a break. In fact, the kid's age had everything to do with how he or she was treated. At the time Deborah had been living with a Columbia grad student—a Marxist historian who later distinguished himself by marrying a circus acrobat—and she had been so far from the making and management of young children that she accepted the notion without question. The same woman also told her that the only require-ments for a good marriage were liking the same kinds of food and going to bed at the same time, another idea she accepted without a qualm.

Later, during her own pregnancy, she and Chris had assured them-selves that equity would be a watchword in their home. Chris hadn't thought he wanted children, not at first. What he told Deborah was that he wanted her for himself, and though she knew that to be true, she also suspected he was uneasy about becoming a father. He'd barely known his own dad—the elder Latham had dropped dead of a heart attack while cleaning the basement, only days after his son's twelfth birthday—and maybe some part of him connected becoming a parent with loss and death. Later, when Chris acknowledged he was ready to think about children, Deborah believed he had come to trust her, that he felt their relationship to be safe and solid. She wouldn't dream of testing these notions aloud, of course. Psychobabble made him roll his eyes; he got so much of it from his patients he often complained he should get therapist's wages on top of dental fees.

It wasn't until baby Michael came to live with Deborah and Chris and three-year-old Caroline that there was an opportunity to take out the concept of equitable treatment and polish it for daily use. What she saw then—what was so clearly true, so far from high concept, so laughably obvious—was that what one child needed had little to do with what another did. Caroline wanted to be hugged, all the time, as an infant. Her soft body molded to her mother's as if the memory of the womb was never far from her. But Michael, from his earliest time with them, took an embrace like medicine, holding himself warily until it was over. Both of them needed their hugs—in equal measure, and perhaps this was what that long-disappeared friend had meant—but they couldn't possibly have gotten equal treatment. With Caro, affection came unthinkingly, as easily as breathing. Michael had to be chased and cornered: He needed love so desperately that his impulse was to run from it. Sometimes, after grabbing an unwilling Michael and forcing his stiffened torso to mold itself against his mother's, she would want both to giggle and to cry.

She couldn't love them equitably, although her love for both was so infinite she couldn't claim she loved one or the other more. Caro needed softness, to be approached seriously and calmly, the way one might proffer tidbits to a fawn. And Michael, oh, what did he need? As mercurial as an ancient god, the boy demanded freedom and fealty. Sometimes it seemed as if he never would believe in them, that the hurts he'd endured before knowing them had scarred him irrevocably. But each time she entertained this notion, however fleetingly, he would seem to feel it. He could read the sagging of her shoulders with an accuracy even Chris never had acquired. Michael always seemed to know when he had pushed her too far, and he would come to her then with a drawing he'd made of a mother and child, or to point out a bird in the yard, or to ask for her help in tying a sneaker. Those moments were flush with a kind of loving gratitude she'd never, ever felt from anyone else.

He took more from her than Caroline ever had, and what he gave back was sweeter for being harder won. Did she treat them the same? Was she equitable and fair? She doubted it.

Was she doing her damnedest to give them what they needed? Would she lay down her life for either of them? Was her love steady-eyed and strong? Yes. And yes. And oh, yes. She knew it. Of all the questions she'd ever considered in her thirty-seven years of life, these were by far the easiest to answer.

4

IN HIGH school, Linda Danniger's brother Eddie had been one of Chris Latham's best friends. Five years older, Linda had had little to do with any of Eddie's crowd. They were all such babies, really, and so satisfied with the world around them. Not her; Linda Danniger hated the Harbor the whole time she was growing up. Sag Harbor was death in life, with all the worrying over money, and planting beans and peas, which always stayed too long on the vines because there wasn't time to pluck them off. They were too busy cleaning and cooking, she and her mom. Linda felt like an unpaid servant, while baby Eddie and his pals ran around like cocker spaniels, nipping and barking and bothering the entire village, never having to pay the slightest consequences. Never even having to pick up his own room. It wasn't fair, and all because their mother figured Eddie'd be supporting some woman all his life, so why make him soil his hands now?

Back then, Eddie had all the luck. But she had always known she was heading away, and she did, all the way to Columbia Teachers College, to return mid-island triumphant after a dozen years and be hired as principal of the elementary school she herself had attended! Of course, it had been in the other building back then; now the lower grades had their own school, and she was running it! Someone else cleaned her house and washed her clothes, and she bought all her beans at a farm stand. What a victory for the Danniger girl; she knew that was what the locals still called her, even though she'd been Linda Bennett for nearly twenty-five years.

Down in Virginia, working for the IRS, Eddie hadn't cared enough to return to Sag Harbor after their mom died, and he certainly hadn't cared when his sister put the family house on the market. He'd been mildly intrigued, however, to learn that Chris Latham had bought the place, and even more interested to find out that the house brought top dollar. He had, he assured his sister, thought the old rattrap would end up falling to the ground before somebody took it off their hands. When Linda repeated for the nth time that things were different in the Harbor now, that there was lots of money around, there had been a brief silence and an adenoidal breath on the other end of the line.

"Suckers everywhere," Eddie Danniger had said, finally. "Old Skinemandcheatem Sag Harbor lives on."

It was odd for Linda Bennett to be sitting across from Deborah Latham, knowing Deborah most likely slept in the same bedroom that Danniger elders had occupied for six generations. Mrs. Latham was so tall, distinctly un-Danniger-like; even Eddie was only five foot eight. But this one's head probably scraped that low archway between the master bedroom and the dressing room upstairs, the one that led to the new bathroom. Had the Lathams renovated the place, opened up that arch? They must have; how else would a beanpole like Deborah Latham get in and out of that bathroom?

It was as if Linda Bennett held a secret, a piece of intimate information about how Deborah probably lived. Telling her that she'd been raised in that house, however, would be a kind of crossing over into the personal that was utterly inappropriate under these circumstances. She couldn't do it. Later, however, she could mention it to Rose, remind her about the old days. They would definitely need to debrief after everything that had gone on this afternoon.

Linda began as gently as she could, merely saying that Michael's difficulties today were an escalation of a situation they'd been aware of since the beginning of September but were hoping to see ironed out as he grew used to school.

"It's been three weeks—it's only been three weeks since school began! How can you already have him pigeonholed like this?" Deborah Latham cried. "It's not fair!"

Linda's office was cheerful, painted a robin's egg blue, and her walls were lined with books. Her desk, Linda knew, was out of control, all cluttered with notes and reports and letters going in and heading out, but the table at which they now sat was a highly polished oak, its circular expanse marred only by the presence of the Kleenex box from which Mrs. Latham was liberally drawing.

Linda Bennett's gentle voice could take on an edge. Some days she felt as if that sterner voice was the only one she ever used at school; other days, of course, she floated home after watching her fifth-grade classes slaughter another school in Spelling Bee or sitting in on a first-grade play. Thank heavens running a school wasn't all crime and punishment; most of it, in fact, was fairly rewarding. It was only during incidents like this one that the atmosphere in her office turned sour; sometimes she fancied she could even smell the unhappiness, an acrid combination of nervousness and coffee in the grown-ups, of Chee-tos and bologna from the kids, agitated stomachs and angry minds emitting imaginary fumes.

With Deborah Latham, though, she had a different feeling, the sense that the mother was challenging her, that she didn't respect the authority of the office Linda Bennett held. Deborah Latham didn't like it that someone from her family stood accused of wrongdoing. She resented it, that was obvious. Well, she wasn't in charge here. "We've been worried from day one," Linda said. "We've felt we had to watch him closely."

"Why didn't you tell me? I could have talked to him," Deborah said angrily. "I don't think it's fair. Caroline had such a wonderful experience with Rose Doroski, and now, well, I can't understand why she's picking on Michael. He's making an effort, he's not holding back! Remember Caroline, how quiet she was? You never complained about her. In fact, when we were concerned last year, you were the people who told us that there was nothing to worry about!"

Mrs. Bennett nodded. "It was different. She played with other children. She made eye contact. She didn't defy us. Or break the rules."

"Look, I know he's very verbal, but maybe he understands less than you think. He's so bright it may make it difficult—I mean, English is his second language. He's not necessarily as fluent as . . . as Caroline, or, or . . ."

"We know how bright Michael is," Linda said. "It's very clear."

"Well," Deborah began, leaning forward aggressively. "Well, maybe his intelligence isn't being dealt with properly. Maybe he isn't being stimulated enough. I don't like to criticize Rose Doroski, but I cannot imagine why she doesn't see how very important it is to keep Michael active and engaged."

"Mrs. Doroski has been extremely involved with Michael's progress, Mrs. Latham. She has been quite industrious and quite concerned. I can't fault her in the slightest."

"Look," Deborah began again, her voice rising. Without breaking eye contact, Linda Bennett lifted one hand from the table and then dropped it lightly down again, a trick she often used when a slight jolt might lower the level of an upcoming outburst. "Look, I don't like to say this, but, well, but . . ." She paused, finishing in a rush: "He's different, don't you see? He's from halfway across the world! He doesn't always understand our ways!"

"That's not fair, Mrs. Latham. He threw stones at a teacher, hard enough to draw blood! That's quite unusual behavior for a five-year-old from any country!"

"He's not being treated fairly and he knows it. I completely understand why he might act out a little." Deborah Latham's hazel eyes glittered; she had stopped crying. Her cheeks were flushed. Small circles of red had started to appear across her forehead and neck, blotching even the skin at her collarbone.

"Mrs. Latham, I have to object. In these first three weeks, he's already demonstrated utter disregard for the rules of our community. He's shown little respect for the other children. He's thrown sticks at his classmates. He won't wait to come down the slide; he just slides into the child in front of him. He pushes. He runs on the climbing structure . . ."

"This is idiotic! He has a lot of energy. He loves sports, to be outside, he's exuberant!" In the hallway, two second graders clattered past, giggling loudly. Mrs. Bennett glanced toward the closed door and then to her lap; she'd been playing with her wedding ring. She put both hands on the table, spreading the fingers wide. Mrs. Latham placed hers on the table as well. Both women kept their nails clipped short, a fact that surprised Linda Bennett. She'd expected Mrs. Latham to have well-manicured, polished nails. The large silver bracelet cuffing Mrs. Latham's wrist was intricately crafted; later, the principal would describe it to Rose Doroski and wonder if it had been expensive. Because she had known Rose Doroski since childhood, had baby-sat for her years before, Linda Bennett would also confess that Deborah scared her slightly. She wasn't intimidated, not that—or not precisely. Sure, Deborah was pretty, more than pretty, and she seemed so smart and calm, utterly calm, on the surface. It was something else, and Linda Bennett couldn't quite put her finger on it.

"My own heart was pounding, just sitting across from her," Linda would admit. "Like she could have snapped at any moment." Rose would nod, eagerly, as if any small detail might justify her dislike of

Michael. Both women would fall silent, listening to the muted murmurs of Linda Bennett's secretary at her desk outside the door, handling the phones with practiced ease.

This mild foray into character assassination would make neither woman entirely comfortable. Blaming Deborah Latham did not lay the matter to rest. She was a mother, after all. In that role, she defended her son without question. All kids are hard to raise, even the good ones, and no kid is always good. Parents defend their children because they never lose sight of what is good in them, not even when they should. Linda herself had done a decent share of it, particularly when her older boy hit adolescence.

She'd never admit it, not even to Rosie, but while she was talking with Mrs. Latham, Linda Bennett had found she had to tamp down what could only be called feelings of empathy. It had been tempting, and frankly would have been easier, to offer friendship. As an administrator, though, she had the other children's welfare to consider as well.

"You know, I have Mrs. Doroski's classroom journal," Linda Bennett told Michael's mother. "I can show it to you. So many incidents are worrisome. See here, where she's written that he knocks down whatever he builds with blocks."

Deborah Latham sniffed, as if such a notation were petty and small-minded. She tossed her curly hair so that Linda Bennett, for more than a moment, regretted having recently shorn her own hair to such a neatly cropped cap. Mrs. Latham's frame, while long, was also slim and quite graceful, so that she could easily manage to shrug one shoulder, tilt her head, and raise her eyebrows while leaning back in the chair and crossing her feet at the ankles, the kind of posture a skeptical executive might choose during a junior employee's attention-grabbing but ultimately pointless presentation.

"It may not sound like much, in and of itself," Linda said. "But there's more. He's a very talented artist, and yet he only paints with the color black. Look here. Let me unfold this. Look at this painting, all these big, somber strokes. He worries us. We're worried for him. And the other children find him disturbing."

"Look at those sleeping animals. He's such a skillful painter. So he's not typical, that's obvious. None of you understand him, because, because . . . maybe you're just not used to someone from another country. Maybe that's all it is! His ways are different. That's all it is."

Linda sighed. "Mrs. Latham, you must know that we have children here from France, from Mexico, from Trinidad. We have a Russian boy in the third grade. And we've had other children from Romania and China and Thailand, from all over the world. We are used to difference. That's certainly not what's making the other children uncomfortable. This morning he struck another child with his fists."

Mrs. Latham flushed, the rosy stain on her cheeks filtering down her throat and spreading across the long line of her neck. "Where's that boy? How do you know what happened, who said what to whom? You're blaming Michael automatically." Mrs. Latham's fingers were long and pale; the thumb and middle finger of her right hand kept grabbing the same lush brown curl from just behind her ear, pulling it straight and allowing it to spring back to bounce against her skin. Each time, Linda Bennett had to will herself not to follow the curl's progress—bounce one, bounce two, bounce three, and pull.

Linda Bennett placed a forefinger against her right nostril. She was going to sneeze. September was always a terrible month for her; between the start of school and the flowering of ragweed, she was often so exhausted it was an effort to think clearly.

"Rose Doroski saw the whole incident," Linda said, "and so did the playground monitor. The school nurse spoke with Jason Stall, the other child. He described what happened, as did other children who were present when the fight began. The child says he was standing with some friends when Michael walked right up and started to hit him."

Deborah Latham's pretty mouth twisted into an odd rosebud. Lines appeared around it, six stern, irritated thorns. Even then, a dimple played just to the left and slightly above her lips. Those fingers, heading up to pull at her curl, were trembling slightly. Nevertheless, her voice was firm. "So you believe him?"

"He disturbs reading time. He can't sit still."

"He's so quiet at home, so self-sufficient. This makes no sense. And he's charming with me, very loving and sweet. He and his sister don't get along too well, I know, but . . ."

"Mrs. Latham, I know you were supposed to meet with Rose Doroski this afternoon. And I know what she wanted to discuss with you. But I decided this morning to make an appointment with you myself, to speak with you and your husband. I'm very concerned about Michael because of a separate incident, something that happened earlier today, during the children's story time. The children are supposed to make up their own stories; it's Mrs. Doroski's way of encouraging creativity and building self-esteem. She usually gets such sweet stories from the children. This morning, though, when it was Michael's turn, well, Mrs. Doroski asked him to stand. He said no at first, which isn't a big deal, lots of the children do, particularly in the beginning of the year. But then he changed his mind, and he stood up in front of six other children. He looked pleased with himself; Rosie, I mean, Mrs. Doroski, said he looked proud. He said, 'Here's my story. I killed my other mommy and made her dead, and now I'm going to do it again. I want to cut my mommy's head off. I like blood.'"

Deborah Latham gasped. "You're making that up!"

Linda Bennett shook her head, smoothing the pink silk of her shirt, tucking it more tightly into the band of her gray skirt. She turned to the next page of Rose Doroski's journal. It was blank. "I wish I were."

"That's impossible."

Mrs. Bennett smiled gently, shaking her head again. "I'm sorry. It happened this morning. Before, before all this . . ." She gestured toward the window, to the playground where the voices of happy children could still be heard. Unbelievably, the lunch hour was still going on.

"Adoptive children often have difficulties like this—people blame them for being different," Deborah Latham said, sitting straighter, her voice suddenly stiff and formal. "You pin a label on a child and decide to give up on him, and you have no right. It's just the beginning! Our family works so hard to help him. We've tried to accommodate, to show him love and make him welcome, to make up for the horrible beginning he had. I guess I was wrong to think you would understand. I shouldn't have told you he was adopted. You misunderstand him completely."

"Mrs. Latham, I think . . ."

"He's five years old," Deborah Latham said. "You can't give up on him. I won't. I don't care how difficult you make it. He's my son."

"We have no intention of giving up on him. We'll try everything we can. We will. I'm going to go to the school board for authorization. We'll hire an assistant to stay in the classroom with him all the time. We've done this before, on occasion, and it's usually quite helpful. We can see how that goes. If he can get used to being around the other children, can start to take part in classroom activities without disturbing the normal order of the day, then we'll start cutting back on the coverage. The goal is to make him a part of our community, but we all—Mrs. Doroski and I, everyone here—we think he's going to need some help accomplishing that goal. He needs an ally of his own here, a friend, I think."

"Well, when you put it like that," Deborah Latham said, slightly mollified. "I just don't want him treated differently. Singled out. My husband won't either. We want him to be treated like all the other kids."

"My brother Eddie went to elementary school with your husband," Linda Bennett said, reaching one hand across the table to take hold of Mrs. Latham's. "I know him, and I like him, and I like Caroline—and you. And this school will do everything to take care of your son and make sure he feels welcome here. He's had a rough start, Michael. He had a tough time early in his life, but we'll probably find that he's a good little boy underneath it all. Children are good, by nature. We'll help him find that place in himself, what was lost. We'll help him. We're going to help him."

Deborah Latham's wrist bent, her hand waving skittishly, dismissively. Her rings clattered against the oak table. "It would be nice," she said softly, "to feel as if someone else was on my side."

"There aren't sides here," Linda said, aware that in some sense she was fudging a truth. "We are on the same team. It was good that you told us about Michael's background, about his mother and the way she died, about the orphanage in Romania. It's better that we know."

The silence inside the office was enhanced by all the noise outside on the playground, the clattering of feet, the giggles, the occasional shouts: Hey gimme the ball! Gimme the ball! Linda Bennett, not for the first time, considered how many mothers and fathers had sat in just this way over the last six years and wondered how many of them thought she had failed their children. She hoped she'd done as good a job as she felt she had; she had really tried. In a certain sense, she hadn't raised her own children as well as she had raised this community's kids. She hadn't given up and she wouldn't—not with anybody's kids and certainly not with Chris Latham's.

"We'll help him," Mrs. Bennett said softly. "We'll do everything we can."

"I would hope so," Deborah Latham said. "It's your responsibility."

Later, when she was alone in her office with Rosie going over this conversation, Linda would recall how she had wanted, more than anything, to tell Deborah Latham off at that moment. But of course she hadn't. Instead, Linda had tightened her grip on Deborah's hand, pretended she hadn't seen the single tear, ignored the pink cross-hatching that riddled the whites of Deborah's eyes, and repeated, "We'll help him, Mrs. Latham. I know we will."

"We'll help him," Linda Bennett had said once more, suddenly recalling that Chris Latham himself had been an orphan of sorts. Her throat prickled with a tickly dryness that spread across her cheeks and up her scalp, an inexplicable sprouting of apprehension. This feeling she dismissed almost immediately, long before her afternoon chat with Rose Doroski. "Honestly," she said, "We will help Michael."

"That's all I'm trying to do," Mrs. Latham said, tightening her hand, making a fist under Linda's gentle fingers. "I keep thinking I can get in there, inside his head, that if I could only change the way he sees us, I could change the way he acts. He's had it so rough, I guess I want him to get a break now and then. I don't want him to keep paying for what he couldn't help."

"Neither do I," Linda Bennett said. "And I mean it."

5

"HOW THE hell can any man respect himself, can't even tighten a gasket, and makes jokes about me in the next room—does he think I'm so dumb I can't hear him making fun of me?" Gus Emerson stormed into Martin's office at least once a day ranting like that, or he had back in the old days when he worked for Dunn's Plumbing. Martin Dunn actually missed Gus's ranting, though he'd never admit it to a soul. It had been a comfort, something regular to expect. How many times had Martin explained that the more Gus resented the summer people, the more trouble he'd have with them? How many times had Gus stormed back out of the office, snorting like a horse?

Funny how back then, Gus just didn't get it. He used to hate the summer people with their fancy houses and the way they always seemed to be laughing up one sleeve at him and shortchanging the bill down the other.

Three decades later, of course, Gus would perfect his hayseed act and become plumber to the stars, leaving Martin's plumbing company in the proverbial dust. That hatred of the summer folk had served him well, driving him to a level of material success Martin never even dreamt of. Martin wasn't envious; he didn't want money. Seemed like that was all anyone else cared about. Martin didn't hanker after what the summer people had. He didn't hanker. He was as good as any man, good enough to hold his head up wherever he went, even when it seemed hard to.

He was a creature of the Lord's, and he yearned only for His approval.

On earth, he already felt anointed. The Dunn family's calling cards had long been printed for posterity. Martin Dunn's great-great-great-great grandfather was one of Sag Harbor's most prosperous whalers way back in the mid-1800s. Joshua Dunn hadn't been thought good for much until he made his way across the water from Rhode Island with a small bit of capital he'd scraped up by promising his own father he'd not return to Narragansett Bay. Once he found himself in Sag Harbor he turned out to have a kind of dour flair for awakening in his fellow man a spirit for adventures he'd never dream of taking himself. By 1849, Dunn had managed to amass a respectable whaling fortune while only rarely getting his feet wet. Even though he took in a thousand dollars in profit from almost every voyage, he gave little to his community.

Unpopular with both peers and family, Joshua Dunn spent most of his time alone, mulling over the ins and outs of Sag Harbor life in excruciating detail. His diaries, scrawled in leather-bound books now so fragile a rough hand picking them up for inspection might destroy an entire volume just by squeezing too hard, were in a box in Martin Dunn's attic. The journals detailed the crewing of the boats, the storing up of hams and dried apples, of soap and mustard and, of course, whiskey, for each trip. Joshua's diaries revealed, also, a bent for storytelling. There were tales inscribed there that could alter common perceptions about the course of life in the village, but scholars had never been given access to the books and never would. They belonged solely to the Dunns. In fact, nobody but Martin knew they existed.

In the 1850s, as the whaling trade declined, Dunn allowed his ships to be used as slavers. Often those vessels transported humans from the Canary Islands to Cuba, reappearing in the Harbor without evidence of illegal deeds. He was never caught, and his riches continued to accrue. He died unrepentant, an ill-loved but very wealthy man.

Martin Dunn hadn't visited the books much since he read them through in the early 1950s. He thought about their contents a great deal, however, and he was fully conscious of the glory of his lineage. He'd always intended to pass this private knowledge to his son Jack. In fact, the night of Jack's high school graduation, back twenty years before, was the last time Martin squeezed his heavy haunches through the attic door to check on the books. He'd gone through the entire presentation in his own mind a thousand times, he bet. He knew exactly how he'd escort smiling Jack up the rickety stairs. What ceremony he'd make of unlocking the tiny door under the eaves! What a bond the books would make between them!

But of course, it hadn't happened, had it? On the morning following Jack's graduation, he was dead.

Now Martin might not ever see those volumes again. His waist was too big around to fit through the crawl space into the attic, and had been for years. Unless he dropped a good hundred pounds, he'd never revisit the fortune in maritime history that lay hidden behind some old rolls of drapery material in the house in which he'd spent his entire life. It didn't matter, though, because he carried those books in his heart, with everything else he treasured: God, the memory of Jack, and a love for his village and its history.

Sag Harbor's was formerly a story of whaling and adventure. Even stay-at-homes learned trades associated with whale fishery, from sail-making to coopering to blacksmithing. More recently, Sag Harbor's tale was of factory labor—almost a century of sheet metal work and watch-making, later the manufacture of parts for an ill-fated module used on one of the Apollo flights—followed by the ultimate evolution into a mythological community of artists and writers and theater people whose love for the green hills and blue water and sandy beaches, as well as the simplicity of small-town life, spawned paintings and plays and novels that couldn't fail to make the entire community proud, no matter the color of their collars. Pride, of course, led to bragging, and bragging to an ever-increasing influx of visitors, transient or committed, some of whom eventually chose the Harbor as their home.

Martin Dunn thought tourism was a trap; it was impossible to miss the way the visitors altered the very fabric of the town, even as they celebrated it. Not just Sag Harbor but other quaint villages in Suffolk County had felt the tug between the lure of tourist dollars and the ensuing resentment of what those dollars had brought. In the 1970s, Sag Harbor was merely a beautiful blue-collar community snuggled just outside the twin dramas of Southampton and East Hampton; by the mid-1990s, Sag Harbor had begun to suffer all the pains of overgrowth and overpopulation a sweet little village could manage to endure. Graffiti appeared on cars and walls; teenagers bought drugs beneath the Ferry Road bridge; a car company wanted to rent the entire village for a weekend-long product promotion; and more and more of the locals became prosperous, raking in tourist dollars at upscale boutiques, as well as by maintaining swimming pools, installing alarm systems, landscaping, and building, building, everywhere.

Scores of summer visitors moved their families from Manhattan to Sag Harbor, wanting to raise their children in a more benevolent environment, wanting to enjoy the slower pace of life, wanting to be the kind of people who lived in a country town. Some of them had the gift of happiness; others lacked it altogether. Most of the out-of-towners felt like locals long before they actually were. Even the poorest of them used their money rather than hoarding it, acting as if a rainy day would never come. The dollars floating around the community seemed to waft through the air sometimes, there were so many active green bills.

And the locals—those lifers whose commitment to the area was bred in the bone like marrow—the locals didn't always see that living was tough all round, that one can be as unhappy with plenty as one can be without.

Martin Dunn counted himself lucky to be the kind of person who understood that injustice and difficulty were sprinkled on all of human-kind with a generous hand. Not for him any measure of envious griping; he shouldered his burdens and counted his blessings, few as they were, and he knew, above all, that on the Day of Judgment he would be found to have been an upright and decent man. His reward would come.

Like Job, he had paid and paid without complaint, and though he hadn't felt much bliss in his life, he regretted little. When it came to happiness, he couldn't fathom the order of who got it and who didn't, but then he hadn't given the topic much thought. When it came right down to it, he didn't much care.

Martin Dunn guessed he was as good as any other man from Sag Harbor, or East Hampton, or even from away. Locals, out-of-towners, summer people, transients—who were they anyway? As far as Martin could tell, they were all pretty similar: two-legged beasts with minds and hearts and brains, yearners and strivers, the curious and the bored. Not much to pick between the lot of them, no matter where they came from.

Funny how all along Martin Dunn had known that most folks were close to identical.

Gus Emerson, on the other hand, took upward of half his life to real-ize that underneath it, most folks just wanted to believe themselves bet-ter than their neighbors. And what Gus did with that understanding, well, that was truly amazing. Gus played the New Yorkers for fools and didn't mind humiliating himself in the process.

Martin Dunn could never have done that. He simply couldn't. It all came back to those books in the attic, he supposed. Those books told him he could hold his head up side by side with the New Yorkers or Gus Emerson or anybody else. Martin Dunn was a giving neighbor and a decent citizen, and he knew it, and he hoped the Lord knew it too. For the one sin Martin couldn't shake, and really didn't want to, was his pride.

6

SHE LIKED to listen to talk radio all the way there and back, losing herself in the concerns of Diane Rehm or Terry Gross, often fading out totally, soothed by the endless lull of intellectual discourse. It wasn't unusual to arrive at the parish hall parking lot unsure of what topic the show had covered, what celebrity guest had been interviewed, how many miles she'd covered, or even how complex the traffic had made the drive. Often, pulling up at the yellow stuccoed building, her car taking its place in the lineup of mud-splashed station wagons, she'd realize that the last moment she actually recalled had been on Montauk Highway heading west, just before Water Mill, as she rounded the curve where a plant nursery displayed its autumnal wares: the flowering kale, Montauk daisies, and unsold perennials that would soon be piled into compost to make space for Thanksgiving decorations and then Christmas trees.

Today, the sky was the blue of children's plastic toys, dotted by fluffs of high November clouds. Squinting in the sun's glare, Deborah Latham didn't see the woman at first: a peasant, squatting at the side of the road, swathed in black from head to foot. She was rocking, or so it seemed, her heavy frame keening in prayer, swaying devoutly, utterly out of place along this most urban stretch of Hamptons highway.

As Deborah drove closer, she realized that it was a small sturdy man, probably Mexican, glowering under an unnecessarily heavy black parka. That made much more sense; he must be waiting for the bus to Southampton. Around Tuckahoe, there was a huge, mostly illegal, immigrant community. He was probably on his way home after a long night's work restocking shelves, washing dishes, or cleaning offices.

In another twenty feet, she knew with certainty that it wasn't a man; she had been right the first time. She passed, no longer aware that she was driving, staring at what was actually a small blonde woman seated cross-legged on the graying, close-cropped grass: fine-boned and fiftyish, huddled for warmth in a navy blue sweatshirt pulled high over her ears, obscuring all but the front of her very chic haircut. Was she waiting for a handsome husband to swing past in the family Range Rover? Had she escaped from some swanky mental institution? Had she sprained an ankle while jogging? Or was she a poet, looking for inspiration?

The possibilities occupied Deborah Latham for the remainder of her drive to Hampton Bays, along with musings about her daughter, Caroline, thoughts that drifted through her mind as pleasantly as the high clouds drifted in the cool November sky: grace notes, purely soothing— more than decorative but far from simply palliative. Well, in fact, precisely that: By her very existence, Caroline Latham made the world not only beautiful, but right.

Even with Caroline, though, it was possible to lose oneself in worrying, to fear whatever forces were at work within her, to wonder at her very nature. Deborah, who had been athletic, outgoing, and fairly sure of herself all her life, could hardly fathom where such a shy pixie had come from. And so bright—Deborah had never been dumb, not at all, but she had never been nearly as smart as her daughter was. And she had certainly never deferred the way Caro did, had never been sweet or quiet or peaceful. Deborah—like Michael, she supposed—had been the angry thorn in her parents' sides. She had never made things easy for them. Maybe that was why she understood Michael so well, knew what made him tick.

But it was easier to talk about Caroline, even with the adoptive mothers' group in Hampton Bays she tried to attend weekly. Those women had all adopted Eastern Bloc kids; they knew what she was going through better than anyone. All through the early fall—ever since Michael's "shadow," Mrs. Nowicki, joined him at school—Deborah had faithfully gotten into her beat-up station wagon every Thursday morning, propelling herself westward as if the journey, and the meeting, might lead to some sort of absolution.

She was fond of those other mothers. They were shipboard pals, so serious about their children, so tolerant and good-humored about each disastrous setback. Deborah had always seen herself as a survivor, and she was proud of her strong spine, but these women kept rolling with punches she couldn't fathom enduring.

"Michael's a cakewalk compared to some of the things I hear here," she once said, and Pat and Wendy and Jane and Nell had nodded in agreement.

"Your problems are nothing," Pat said. "I had Thomas in the ER again last night. He beat his own face on the floor till it bled, practically broke his nose, and why? No reason. At least nothing he could come up with."

"It's fascinating, isn't it?" Nancy McLean, the social worker, intervened swiftly. "Don't you find it amazing how the situations, the problems, that bring each of you here are so different? Thomas and Michael, and Angela and Cindy, and Bradley, each with such unique issues. It makes one realize that they all are individuals, not cookie-cutter problems."

All the mothers turned toward Nancy. She was usually a sounding board, accepting and practical. Today, though, her normally calm voice had an undercurrent of tension, and she was leaning forward uncomfortably in the plastic bucket of her orange chair, her silver braid swishing forward to brush her lap.

"I wanted to show you this," she said, "because if you are anything like me, someone you know is going to hand you this article in the most disingenuous way, and you are going to be as angry or confused or hurt as I was, when my husband's sister did just that the other day."

She was holding up a long, two-column article from the *New York Times*. Deborah could see the words of the headline in bold type: "Rise in Adoptions that Fail."

Deborah, shocked, asked, "Why in hell did your sister-in-law give you that?"

Nancy shrugged, flipping her braid back. "I would like to talk about this without crying," she said, "so I will only say that what appears to be sufficient reward to me, and to my husband, for the work we've put in raising our daughter—well, obviously, some members of my extended family do not agree that the effort is worth it."

"I saw that piece," Wendy offered shyly, shifting her feet backward so that her heels slipped out of the flattened backs of her grimy sneakers. It was November, and she wasn't even wearing socks, Deborah saw. A fragile, late-fortyish woman with a perennially hunched-in posture, Wendy hadn't even managed to pull her blue shirt all the way down in back. It was as if she'd thrown it on in such a hurry that she didn't notice how the fabric had failed to unroll. The T-shirt bore a picture of two giraffes and a monkey, and the logo "Long Island Game Farm." Deborah hadn't heard Wendy's voice before, not once in the last six weeks.

Wendy continued, "I thought it was interesting, I mean, that the percentages are so high. And that the older the child is, the more likely the adoption is to fail."

"I disagree with so much of it," Nancy said, clipping her words with angry emphasis. "I find it hard to believe that these children are being labeled as having attachment disorder. What about the parents? Maybe they don't have enough love to give. Think about that." She glared around the room, so that Deborah, at least, felt a twinge of guilt.

Nancy continued: "But I wanted to speak to you about a doctor in Connecticut, a researcher who is studying adoptees from Eastern Europe. He contacted the agency, asked us to spread the word. He's doing brain scans, using a machine called a PET scan . . ."

"That's why Angela isn't potty-trained at six, I should take her to obedience school!" Linda interrupted. Everyone laughed, and there was a general recrossing of arms and legs. Even Wendy giggled softly.

"He's looking at brain development, trying to see whether children who've endured the early neglect ours have, well, he wants to see if the brains of our kids are similar to those of other children, raised under more usual circumstances."

"Are you going to do it?" Deborah asked Nancy. She already knew about this procedure; Chris had learned about it during an Internet search. He was so fascinated by the idea that he had contacted the doctor himself. She'd been too ashamed, though, to tell the others about what she'd learned.

"No," Nancy said, letting the ragged end of her braid lift slightly and fall with the decisive shaking of her head. "I'm not interested. But I thought you all should know. The climate for our kids is changing. You should be aware."

Oh, God, these others, her friends, what they went through. Her problems were nothing—how about Pat and her son, Thomas? How about Wendy, whose daughter Cindy didn't know her own address, or care, and would walk off with any stranger who smiled at her? How about Linda, whose six-year-old daughter hadn't yet taken her first unassisted steps? Learning to read was so far down Angela's list as to be unthinkable; she was still struggling to feed herself with a spoon.

When Linda cheerfully told the group about how Angela's surgery had failed to produce the expected improvement in her hips, about how the little girl would have to endure at least another six months on crutches, Deborah wanted to stand up and scream: "Don't you hate them for the way they kept our children stuck in cribs, for the lack of love, the lack of exercise, the lack of human kindness? That they had little food, I can accept that, but the cruelty of denying what is so easy to give, what every child needs—fresh air and love—don't you hate them for that?"

Linda and the others—Nell, Wendy, Jane, Pat—would have stared aghast at such an outburst. They were burden-shoulderers and pragmatists, multiple mortgagors who never sweated about right and wrong, who wanted more than anything simply to help, no matter the cost. It would have been their mantra, had anyone thought to assign them one: *no matter the cost.*

She knew what each of them would cheerfully answer: "I can only think how wonderful it is that I have Angela, or Joe and Cindy, or Bradley, or Thomas. I'm thankful, that's what I am." And then with a sturdy laugh: "We always manage, don't we? No matter how tough things get."

They felt that way, Deborah could tell. They were able to focus on the minutia of daily life and ignore the enormity of the long term, just as regular mothers did. They felt the way she felt when she watched Caroline on the playground, standing at the edge of a group of children but unwilling to make the move that might spur her into their play. *What was Caroline afraid of? Why was she so shy?* Those were the questions Deborah could have mulled over endlessly in a group of mothers, but there was no group for easy, bright children with few friends. And this group, devoted to the salvage and upkeep of mothers with extraordinarily difficult children, was too determined even for her. They liked to solve problems efficiently, timing their emotional outbursts, their ragged litanies of complaint, even their reports of incremental successes, to end with the ninety-minute session. They hugged one another and cried together and shared the names of doctors and therapists and lawyers. It was addictive, but some part of Deborah never did let go and join them fully. It was as if she knew, had known since the first few months after Michael's arrival, that acknowledging the problems too fully would mean she was losing her grip. And once she couldn't hold on anymore, couldn't keep her family together, she was frightened of what might begin to happen.

Nobody in the group was even remotely aware of this, of course. If anything, the adoptive mothers leaned on Deborah. She was the one Jane telephoned whenever her resolve began to flag, whenever Bradley did something so rotten Jane began to doubt she could survive.

In a call just a few days after that meeting, in fact, Jane reported what happened when she and her husband had gone out to dinner. When they came home, the idiot baby-sitter they'd hired told them Bradley had been playing alone in his bedroom the entire time. She'd had her Walkman on, Jane supposed, otherwise how could she have missed the fact that Bradley had gone to the basement and taken out his father's electric drill and then drilled a few dozen holes in his bedroom wall? Six-year-old Bradley had the idea he was going to rewire the cable so that he could have a television in his room, Jane told Deborah. "I'm sure he could have done it, too," Jane said, tears and laughter at war in her voice.

Deborah, who was alone in the kitchen after dinner, finishing the pots and wiping down the counters while Chris helped each kid with a jigsaw puzzle, said, "Are you going to make it?"

There was a silence on the other end of the line. "You heard Nancy McLean, didn't you? What she said, you know, about disruptions, in the meeting last Thursday?"

"Yeah. Of course."

"I was surprised how many adoptions break up," Jane said quietly.

"Me too. What was it, 10 percent for kids as old as ours? That's a huge number. I love how infant adoptions are practically always successful. Nobody ever finds them too tough. Did you read the article when she passed it around? The writer said adoptive parents over-romanticized what older kids would be like. Hah. This is about as romantic as hot dogs. I never thought of it as romantic. I wanted to help a child. I wanted to help him. I knew it wouldn't be easy."

"Yeah."

"Can you imagine, though, the idea of just sending your kid away, like he wasn't a person?"

"I know. I've never met anyone who did it. What happens to those parents?"

Deborah tried to laugh, a kind of half snort, half chuckle that emerged more from her nose than her throat. "They probably sleep at night, and go to the movies, and hang around with normal people," she joked.

"Yeah," Jane said.

"In the article it said they were all too ashamed to talk about it afterward, how humiliating it was to feel they'd failed."

"I can't imagine," Jane said. They were silent. On the other end of the line, Deborah could hear Jane breathe in and then out, a long sigh, and then the sound of water running.

"You cleaning up?"

"No, sorry. Running a bath. John's outside with Brad. I needed a break, I'm just so wiped out."

"Yeah." The silence went on longer, Deborah wiping down the counter for the second time. Outside, a dusty black Mustang sped by, tinted windows rolled shut, the bass thunder of music pounding.

Eventually, Jane asked, "Why the hell did she bring it up?"

Deborah squeezed the sponge into the sink and turned, leaning the small of her back against the oak countertop. Her T-shirt was spotted with water stains. The room, though, looked neat enough to close down for the night. Except the fridge: It was so covered with Caroline's schoolwork and Michael's drawings that she would need to weed through the mess and store some masterpieces soon. She was too tired tonight, though. Deborah shrugged, as if Jane on the other end of the line could see her. Then she said, "I think Nancy wants us to admire ourselves, you know? For the way we've stuck it out despite what the kids have put us through."

"It's funny," Jane said softly, "I don't often let myself think of the possibility, do you?"

Deborah stood taller, away from the counter, straightening her shoulders so the blades came together across her back. "I don't let myself at all," she said.

"Never?"

Deborah's throat was dry. She tried to swallow, then cleared her throat, raising only the smallest amount of saliva. "We've had him for three and a half years, Jane. Would you get divorced if John went through a tough time? It's not realistic to think you can ever have things perfect, is it? This is what life has dealt us, so we deal with it."

"My sister Nora," Jane said, "she's the same way. Her kid is Romanian, too, really difficult, worse than Bradley. He keeps getting kicked out of schools, and God knows what else. She gets mad at him, of course, but she'd defend him to the death. Nora says what you do. She's going to stick by him no matter what. Sometimes, I, well, I . . . well, I doubt myself."

"Michael's my son," Deborah said stoutly. "Anybody who could take in a child and then—what? Send him back like shoes that go out of style?—is worse than someone who never got involved in the first place."

In the next room, Michael made a piercing sound, almost a cat's wail, that arched suddenly and then disappeared, leaving a louder silence behind it. Chris began to read. Michael wailed again. Chris began to read more loudly, the syllables of *The Cat in the Hat* now becoming audible, his voice speeding up. He was trying to forestall something, Deborah could tell. She heard a thump, and then another—two, three, four times.

Chris resumed reading.

"You're right," Jane said.

What? Deborah thought, her focus lost.

"You're right," Jane said once again, more firmly. "I'm sticking with Brad, no matter what happens. I won't give up."

She had talked Jane over the river Styx. It was mildly elating. Deborah's fingers, still damp from the sponge, left a watery streak on her skin when she rubbed her forehead. In the next room, Michael coughed, a harsh, rasping sound that came faster and began to sound obviously forced. Chris began to read even more loudly, his voice rising irritably. The raspy coughs grew louder.

Deborah walked toward the French doors at the back end of the kitchen, phone tucked between right shoulder and ear, left shoulder rising as well, neck arching. *How had the salve for Jane's difficulties been so easy to come by?*

Chris kept reading, his tone more insistent and firm; Michael coughed and sputtered. In the foreground, her voice high and shy, Caroline began to cry.

"And I'm not taking him to a brain specialist either," Jane said. "What's the point? How come Nancy keeps wanting to get us involved in things that single them out? I want Brad to be normal, a regular kid."

Chris was sending Michael to his room. A loud protest, then a silence, then the sound of feet stomping up the stairs and another rasping series of coughs. Michael's door slammed, and Deborah heard the squeak of springs as he threw himself onto his bed.

"Are you there?" Jane asked.

"Oh, sorry, I thought I heard something," she said automatically.

"Are you okay?"

"Yeah," she said, shaking her head vigorously. Outside, only the sparrows were left; the other birds had already headed south for the winter, she supposed. "It's the paperwork that kills me," Deborah said. "All the reports and articles and prognoses and recommendations. I did all that stuff in the beginning, saw the psychiatrists and the lawyers, the special teachers and the behavior specialists. It helped, sort of, but then I realized I kept seeing the same thing over and over again." Deborah laughed, picturing the endless series of reports from a string of experts, each one claiming to have discovered that Michael was bright and friendly, that he suffered from an inability to control his anger, that he was an enormously gifted artist who could channel his artistic talents and use them to conquer his angry, aggressive behavior. "That's when I decided I would try to make it on my own. Nobody knew anything I couldn't figure out myself just as quickly."

"But the PET scan guy, the brain specialist? Are you going to do that?"

Deborah paused, hardly wanting to admit it. "Yeah," she said, eventually. "I mean, we already did it, in September. Almost two months ago. It was the worst."

It had been, in fact, so horrendous that Deborah couldn't fathom how to tell Jane or any of her other friends from the adoptive mothers' group. She didn't want to admit aloud that there were people in the world who thought the way Dr. Silver did.

Dr. Silver had not looked at them with any compassion. Of course that was what was always missing, but with Dr. Silver it was more extreme, as if he simply didn't see that they were human, much less special: Deborah and Christopher, truly decent and concerned parents; seven-year-old Caroline, growing more silent and resentful with each trip, each set of questions focusing yet again on five-year-old Michael instead of her, never a real interest in her.

Dr. Silver had been one of the few specialists who didn't wear glasses, oddly enough, and yet his focus had been the most myopic. "The child will be injected with a radioactive compound—a tracer labeled with an isotope—and then we'll be able to watch as the tracer is processed in his brain. He'll have to keep very still inside the machine— that's why we strap them down. And then we'll have quite a nice picture of what's going on in the child's brain, why he's having some of the problems he's having. I imagine parts of his brain have completely atrophied, that's what we so often see with these foreign . . ."

"Hey," Christopher had said, jerking his head toward Michael and Caroline. The children were making no pretense to be occupied by other thoughts; both of them were staring at Dr. Silver, eyes wide and fearful, skin far paler than normal. They'd chosen chairs next to one another, surprisingly, and now Caroline reached over and took her younger brother by the hand. He let her hold his palm between her two hands.

Deborah could hardly hear the doctor's words. Instead, her ears were filled with another sound, the memory of the sobs that sometimes exploded from her son out of nowhere, the way he would throw himself onto the ground—at the supermarket, in front of the television set, in the street on the way to the playground—kicking his feet and hammering his fists as he shouted an unrepeatable series of sounds over and over again. It wasn't Romanian; Deborah had asked Mina to listen and was assured that it was simply a series of random noises. That hadn't surprised Deborah, because when Michael first came to them at the age of eighteen months, she'd purchased a set of Romanian language cassette tapes by mail. She had hoped Michael would find the voices reassuring. She'd hardly been prepared for his reaction the first time she popped a tape into the car cassette deck on the way to pick up Caroline from nursery school. Michael had been safely strapped into his car seat, gazing cheerfully out the window, and the minute he'd heard the first words—*Servus! Numele meu este Ion! Ce mai faci?*—he'd bolted upright, throwing his head back and pounding his legs in fury against the back of the driver's seat. He'd been kicking so hard, she'd hardly been able to pull over to the side of the road. It wasn't until she ejected the tape that Michael calmed down.

When they got home that afternoon, she placed the entire box of tapes at the top of the coat closet, out of sight and, she hoped, out of mind. Crayons and paper, pastels and paints—those were the things her son needed. That was it. She had learned that day to avoid Michael's past, that the focus had to be on amalgamating the little boy into the easier, more comfortable world the rest of them inhabited.

Of course, it had taken time to truly understand that lesson. Deborah wanted to help her son, and so did Chris. They had read widely—adoption manuals and therapeutic guidebooks. They had listened to the experts as long as they could. From the first visit with dry, practical Nancy McLean, the rangy social worker who handled their home visit, they had been more than willing to ask questions and seek assistance. Nancy had hooked them up with the adoption psychologist Rita Hofstadter, rabbit-toothed and freckled on every visible part of her body, an unlapsed Freudian who insisted that two-year-old Michael's traumatic past could be worked through in play therapy. She didn't care how long it took, she insisted, refusing to read in anyone's eyes that time was of the essence; each day with Michael was harder, not easier, than the one before. It wasn't that progress was slow; rather, the changes seemed to proceed in a negative direction. Michael's anger and frustration escalated. Dr. Hofstadter applauded the release of emotions, and Deborah, who in theory supported this notion, found that in practice she couldn't bear it. She hated sitting outside in the waiting room, imagining Dr. Hofstadter's empathetic grin, the way she must sit cross-legged on the floor with Michael, her pudgy belly folded in upon itself, grabbing at her T-shirt so that it draped her form without self-consciousness, demarcating years of ice cream rewards and lonely dinners, plates heaped with pasta to serve as ballast for the solitary reading of some culturally significant magazine.

Dr. Hofstadter emerged from her office with Michael. Her lips trembled with glee, drawn thin around those notable teeth. It was as if she wanted to shutter them but couldn't stretch her mouth sufficiently to do so. "He micturated!" she announced proudly, pointing at a damp spot on her skirt.

Deborah looked up eagerly, placing Dr. Hofstadter's copy of the *Atlantic Monthly* down on the sofa. "What's that? He what?"

Dr. Hofstadter brushed Michael's brown curls with a loving hand. "He micturated!" she repeated.

"What is it? Is that a word? You don't mean he peed?"

"Why yes, he did! It's such a good sign! He was willing to let go, in my office! I see such potential for movement here!"

Bowel movement, Deborah thought to herself. "Well, that's great," she said calmly, turning to Michael. "Are you ready to go? I mean, shall we leave?"

Michael nodded mutely. His cheeks were flushed, a deep rose staining across the cappuccino of his skin. When he turned to Dr. Hofstadter as if to meet her eyes in a silent good-bye, the therapist leaned down and took him by the shoulders. "We had a good session today," she said. "I'm very pleased."

Michael spat, not even taking the time to draw a deep breath or gather further saliva from his throat. He simply spat, directly into Dr. Hofstadter's face, droplets landing on her nose and the lid of her right eye, a single drip beading her pale eyelashes and dropping onto her turtleneck.

"Michael, stop that!" Deborah grabbed his wrist, pulling him toward her.

"No!" Dr. Hofstadter didn't even bother to wipe her face. "No!" she repeated, with a grin so huge her gums showed in all their pale pink glory, a grin so enormous it unfortunately brought the big bad wolf to mind. "Don't you see? This is real progress!"

Deborah restrained the desire to burst out laughing. The doctor was endearingly foolish to look at in the best of circumstances, all folds and rolls and freckles, her hair tangled down her back, her skirt stained so completely that even its gay floral pattern couldn't hide the accumulation of children's "breakthroughs." Her heart was certainly in the right place—her tolerance beyond believable, her desire to help undeniable.

"You know," Deborah said, clutching Michael's wrist with a firm hand, "I just realized something important. I suddenly knew, without a doubt, that behavior matters to me. I appreciate what you're doing. I think you deserve enormous credit for what you're trying to do. But for me, it doesn't matter. If a wife kills her husband, it doesn't matter to me what he's done. It's still murder. To me, you can't just go around saying that horrible behavior is okay because it's progress. It isn't. It's just bad behavior. If he peed on you, he did something wrong. If that's a breakthrough in your terms, I don't think we're in agreement as to how to help him. I'm sorry."

Dr. Hofstadter, still kneeling on the floor as if she and Michael were peers, began to bring her heavy form to standing. She opened her mouth to say something, but Deborah shook her head, lifting one hand like a traffic cop.

"No," Deborah said. "Honestly. Thanks for trying. This isn't going to work."

In the car, Michael stared out the window without a word, his small hands resting calmly on his snowsuited thighs. A tiny smile played on his mouth, just the smallest hint of something that might have been victory. "I'm sorry, Baby," Deborah whispered, reaching back with her right hand to pat his thigh, still steering with the left. In the rearview mirror, she saw his dark, unreadable eyes shift to meet hers, and then shift back, staring out at a field covered in snow, its fall-sown crop breaking the surface, swords of toppled grasses straining to stand erect despite the snow's restraining weight. It was so easy to forget that he was only two; those eyes seemed to know everything. She found it hard to believe there was anything he would be unable to understand.

By the time they got home, Dr. Hofstadter had already left a message on the telephone answering machine. Her tone as somberly dire as she could probably ever make it, Dr. Hofstadter warned that the family was prolonging its difficulties by refusing to free Michael to face the issues of his past.

In reporting on this, Deborah didn't tell Chris about the message; she'd known what he would say. Chris didn't really believe a therapeutic examination of Michael's past could help. To Chris, only the present and future mattered. He couldn't be bothered fretting over what came before; that was a waste of time and energy.

Dr. Bram, the family therapist, came next, the year that Michael turned four and Deborah could no longer scratch up any children to play with him. Short, compact, and friendly, Dr. Bram saw Michael's problems as a weakness in the family system, a weakness he could shore up by reframing his problems as family issues. Chris had hated Dr. Bram with such passion that, after three visits, he insisted they not return. "I can't explain why," Chris had admitted, "but that man irks me so much I have fantasies of throttling him."

"You don't mean it?!" Deborah asked. "I like him." It was true, Dr. Bram reminded her a great deal of friends of her parents, people she'd known since childhood. He was practical; his goal was to help them efficiently and without a great deal of self-indulgent dredging-up of the irrelevant. She wanted to continue seeing him.

Dr. Bram's practice wasn't limited to adoptive situations; he worked with all kinds of families in difficulty and he responded to the reduced family party without even a blink. He did ask where Chris was and if they should wait for him, and when Deborah said he wouldn't be coming, Dr. Bram simply nodded.

Close to the end of the session, just as Michael and Caroline were clearly becoming restless, Dr. Bram stood and walked toward them. Deborah and the kids had been sitting in a neat line, politely attempting to avoid the mention of Chris. Now, as the doctor approached, Michael shrank back against his mother's shoulder, pushing his head hard against the bone of her upper arm. His ear pulled at the cotton of her red sweater, dragging it so that the seam under her arm dug into the skin of her armpit. She shifted, and he shifted again, his ear landing on precisely the same area with the exact same pressure.

Dr. Bram reached over the boy to release an audiocassette from the tape player on the spindle-legged table behind the couch. "Here," he said. "Here's the tape of the session. Tell your husband he should listen to it. He's part of the family, whether he comes to therapy sessions or not."

"I can't do that," Deborah said, holding the tape limply, her arm still outstretched as if Dr. Bram might take it back into his possession.

Dr. Bram put his hands into the pockets of his faded blue jeans; he was well fleshed, and just the first joints of his fingers could work in easily. When he pulled his stomach muscles in, the effect was so visible that Deborah had to shift her eyes away, looking instead at the neatly polished toes of her black cowboy boots. Chris had given them to her only a few days before, an advance birthday present he'd brought home and placed on her side of the bed without flourish. The boots were low-heeled and beautiful, an intricate series of swoops and swirls tooled into the leather by a local artisan, a patient of Chris's who had begged to give him a pair of her expensive boots in exchange for a new dental crown.

Michael and Caroline dissolved into fits of giggles.

"Quite a belly, huh?" Dr. Bram said good-humoredly, letting his muscles go slack so that his stomach bulged over the waist of his jeans again. "I can make my teenaged daughter lose her mind by doing this in public."

Deborah put her hand on Caroline's head, weaving her fingers through the gloss of the black curls.

"Tell him," Dr. Bram said with a calm note, an insistently calm note, "tell him it's the parents who have the most potential to help their children. Not the experts, the parents. There's no therapy to match what a parent can do."

Deborah stood, stepping forward across Dr. Bram's soft blue carpet. He smelled like oranges. His curly Vandyke of a beard, mottled gray and luxuriant, only served to emphasize the lack atop his head. His pate was ruddy and smooth; perhaps, she thought, he actually polished it.

"He won't do it," she whispered, leaning down to speak directly into his ear. The children, behind her, were still as royal guards.

Dr. Bram lowered his voice to match hers, although it wasn't clear why. He certainly didn't appear to care whether the children heard his words. He said, "It seems as if there has to be an Other in your family, an alien, someone who does not fit in. Have you noticed that?"

He is an alien, she wanted to say, jerking her head toward Michael. *He isn't from here, he doesn't think like us, he isn't one of us. We want to make him change, we don't deny it. Help us to become normal. Make our family regular. Please.*

"Your husband wants so much to be an outsider, to be separate from the rest of you, to force the family to function without him even as he remains in charge. It's not so atypical, for a man, I mean." Here the doctor's eyes crinkled slightly, as if he were amused by this quirk of his gender. "We run across it frequently, therapists do, in all kinds of families. I will say that."

"That's ridiculous," she said reflexively.

Dr. Bram's gray eyes studied her.

"He's uncomfortable, that's all."

Michael, on the couch, coughed quietly.

"He's excluded himself, hasn't he?"

She looked down, at the flecking on the shoulder of Dr. Bram's polo shirt. It matched his eyes. His gaze, though limpid, was honest. Were he not so unattractive, she might actually find his looks appealing.

"It happens all the time," he said, taking a half-step back. "In lots of families, like yours and also very different. Don't give him so much power. Why can he step in and out of the family circle? Why isn't he required to help? He's so powerful that the rest of you can't stand up to him?"

"You can't possibly be going by any rule book, saying this kind of thing to me," she said weakly.

"You think that coming here is rejecting him," Dr. Bram said softly. "It isn't. He's rejecting you."

Deborah stood even taller, towering over the doctor with rigid back and shoulders. She could feel a nerve twanging in her neck, the same one that had gone into spasm several times when well-fed baby Caroline had still needed carrying but had grown too heavy for extended lifting to be comfortable. "Michael," she said stiffly. "We are here to help Michael."

"You're a family," Dr. Bram said. "He doesn't have the problem. You all do."

Chris was so furious when Deborah reported this conversation that he called Dr. Bram's service right away. The doctor returned his call in less than ten minutes, almost as if he'd been waiting for it, but when Chris began to tear into him, all Bram said was that he couldn't talk to Chris except during the family's regular therapy session.

"I'm talking to you now," Chris insisted, red-faced and furious, fist clutching the receiver, pushing it against his ear. Dr. Bram had only sighed on the other end of the line.

"I'd love to see you, with your family," he'd repeated. "There's no reason to run from therapy, not if you want your situation to improve."

"Then listen . . ." Chris began again.

"Next Tuesday, I will," Dr. Bram said. "I hope you'll be there."

By Tuesday, however, even Deborah had come to see how obnoxious Dr. Bram had been. There was no reason to see a therapist as insensitive as that, she agreed. Besides, they were really doing fine. Just fine. And if they all pulled together, the way Chris wanted to, why, things would only get better.

Chris was bound and determined to prove they could manage their son by themselves. Once, in the middle of folding their plain white towels into long thirds, and then in upon the center into thirds again so that she could stack them neatly in the linen closet, she'd had the uncomfortable idea that perhaps Chris wasn't simply *against* therapy, perhaps he was actually frightened of it. Closing the closet door, she stood for some moments, listening to the low humming of the refrigerator and the angry calls of blue jays exploring the empty bird feeder in the backyard. What did he think a psychologist might discover? What could some expert recommend that would be so awful?

From the first, she had wrestled with a sense that Chris was holding back, that part of him wasn't eager to love Michael, no matter how successfully the boy was "fixed." This was a feeling she didn't seem able to shake; the first—no, the only—emotion she had ever had regarding her husband that she honestly felt unable to share with him.

"What could possibly bug you about Dr. Bram?" she had asked when Chris had originally announced he wasn't returning.

"I just don't like him." Chris's expression was sulky, his shoulders sloping, neck lengthened forward so that the weight of his head pulled it even farther down. All he could possibly be regarding were his sneakered feet on the clean oak floor. He looked, she reflected, as uncomfortable as one of the children caught taking red licorice from the pantry closet before dinner.

She shrugged, a kind of *well, it's not such a big deal, I can't understand what's bugging you* kind of gesture.

He shrugged in return, finally meeting her eyes, one eyebrow cocked in embarrassment, and said, "He's just so damn sure of himself, so sure he knows all the answers and we don't. But he only sees Michael for fifty minutes on Tuesday and Friday. How the hell can he know him? I don't buy into what the guy is selling. Snake oil, no more, no less."

It wasn't as if they didn't want to help Michael. They wanted, more than anything, to settle him down, let him fit in, calm him. And each intervention had its effect, but not what the experts planned: They did grow steadily less ignorant with each exploration into their son's lack of self-control, but none of the discoveries had been positive. At best, each move, each doctor, each choice had come to seem a further theft of Michael's possibilities. Was defining his anger as biologically set in stone likely to make life easier? Was injecting him with a radioactive chemical any worse than some of the other horrors he'd already endured? Wasn't the fact that her children had sat hand in hand in Dr. Silver's office proof positive of the fact that Michael could make connections, that he did love his big sister, that the violent incidents would diminish in intensity and grow less frequent in the years to come?

Mina's cousin Viorica certainly believed that to be the case.

"He is adjusting," Viorica had insisted just days before, nearly two months after Michael's little incident at school. "Many of the children I bring here do not make half the progress Michael does. Remember he was swaddled and left in a crib for so many months. Remember how crooked his leg was at first? It straightened out by itself, no doctors. You worry the wrong way. He needs love, not more doctors. He barely knew his mother or his father. You are being naive, I think, to want there to be no problems at all."

Deborah had been alone with her and Michael, sipping mugs of tea for warmth, watching him race about the backyard kicking a ball. Both women had marveled aloud at how remarkably graceful and fast Michael had become. "I certainly understood there would be problems," Deborah said now. "Of course there have to be. It isn't the learning difficulties or the fears that I mind. I knew he would grow slowly. I knew it wouldn't be easy. I expected all that. I feel I can teach him. But with Caroline, he's so rough. She's older and stronger, and still he hurts her so often. He hits her when she's in his way. He kicks. He twists her arm so hard she has red marks an hour later. And as he gets older, well . . ."

"So he hits his sister," Viorica said, shrugging. "My brother hit me too. Brothers do that."

"I had a sister, no brother, so I don't know. But the way he gets angry, his rage is so—so huge. It's terrifying. I honestly think he could hurt her terribly."

"Don't worry so much," Viorica said. "Let him be a boy."

"Christopher thinks he's too rough with her, too," Deborah answered, drawing the sides of her black cardigan across one another, hugging the edges tightly to her stomach, arms snug under her breasts. "It's cold out here. Do you want to go in?"

Viorica shook her head. "I've got to get going," she said. "But you Americans, you have big hearts and good intentions, and still you don't want to know where these children have come from. You want to make it all better right away."

"That's not true, that's not true at all!" Deborah cried. "I'd do anything to help him, anything. He's my son. But Caroline is my daughter and I have to think of her, too."

Viorica shrugged again, picking her worn shoulder bag up off the picnic table. She pulled the barrette off her dirty-blonde hair, shook the strands free and quickly combed through it with her fingers before refastening her ponytail. "You like things easy here. It's what you're used to," she said, shaking her head back and forth before kissing Deborah brusquely on both cheeks.

"She thinks we're spoiled," Deborah complained to Christopher that night. "But he *is* hard. He's harder than other boys. Otherwise, why is it that nobody wants to play with him? It's not as if the other mothers are knocking our doors down asking for him to come over. It can't be normal boy stuff—people are scared of him."

Chris was in the bathroom, the door ajar as he brushed his teeth. The children were long asleep, and Deborah was in bed, propped up on three fluffy pillows. "When I was growing up here, things were so different," he said.

"I know, you've told me." Deborah rolled her eyes and grinned.

"I'm an old man," Chris said. "I'm thirty-eight years old; I guess I've got a right to repeat myself." He smiled at her in the bathroom mirror, then curled his lips, pretending to sneer. She waved one hand lazily in mock salute, then sank deeper against the red pillows.

"Go on, Old Man. Let's hear it."

"Seriously, Deb. It was different. Families hung together, the neighborhoods were safe, you know all that. Think what this community did for me, growing up without parents. I wouldn't have survived without all the kindness and warmth extended my way, not just by the Gastons but by everybody. That's what's so confusing about all the crap with Michael. Maybe it's prejudice; after all, I was a Harbor boy from the start, and he's about as foreign as they come. Maybe times have changed. It's like the whole community is angry at us because he's so different. We're the ones under attack all the time. Rosie Doroski got mad at us when he acted up in her class. He's different, so he has to be handled in a different way, but she won't see that. He doesn't fit in and I did, I guess."

"That's not what they say," she agreed. "They act as if he's the problem. They won't admit they don't want to give him a chance."

He pulled on a T-shirt, then moved into the dressing area, rooting in a drawer for shorts. He went back to the bathroom. She waited, expecting him to answer. Eventually, she sat up and pulled one of her three pillows from horizontal to vertical in order to lean back against it, sitting higher.

"It's more than that," she said, running her hands nervously over the smooth surface of the quilt. "The rest of them band together blaming us, it's incredible. You don't get to see all of it, you're too busy looking into people's mouths and telling them to floss, but I get it every single day. Dropping him off, picking him up—dirty looks left and right. And it isn't as if your old high school buddies are any nicer to me than anybody else. Sometimes I wish we could move, just so your old girlfriends wouldn't treat me like I've brought a monster into the village."

"My old girlfriends? My old girlfriend, you mean, and there's just about nothing Cynthia Stall doesn't roll her eyes at these days. But Jason Stall is her nephew, the kid Michael fought with. And Cynthia said Jason was waking up with nightmares for days. The kid didn't want to go back to school. He was scared he'd see Michael, that it would happen again."

"When did you talk to Cynthia?" she asked sharply.

He picked up his toothbrush, looked at himself in the mirror, and replaced the brush in its cup. "I see her around," he said. "She's a patient, you know."

Deborah was silent.

What he didn't want to admit was how Cynthia had looked outside the pizza parlor only that afternoon, her once bright blue eyes flat and cold with fury. She had stopped him, holding her own daughter without regard for the way the little girl pulled at her mother and tried to loosen her wrist. With her other hand, she'd held onto Chris's sleeve, as if she knew that he might turn and walk quickly away.

She stopped him to complain, to wonder aloud about why Deborah had never called her sister-in-law to apologize for Michael's attack on Jason. "Who does she think she is?" Cynthia had demanded furiously. "Who? What kind of woman doesn't care enough to find out if the other kid is okay? What kind of cold bitch is she?"

And Chris had been speechless: The vehemence of the attack, the clear "us versus them" quality of it, had knocked him off his guard as surely as if she had punched him out of the blue. He'd stood for a moment, blankly, wanting to find something to say that somehow kept him in the middle, that didn't deny her the right to be angry but still defended his choice of family. He'd stood, and her breath hot against his cheek was an ironic reminder of other times, years before, when they'd been even closer physically than this, when touching her skin had been as normal as brushing his teeth or writing with a No. 2 pencil. His head was so empty the only thing he was aware of was the absence of thought. All he could think to do was leave, and so he did. A coward's move, he knew. A natural for him. Walking down Main Street, back to his office, away from Cynthia's stiff-fisted, straight-backed rage reminded him sorely of other, equally craven gestures he had made.

"Speaking of monsters," he said to Deborah, "did Mina tell you Viorica's thinking of returning to Romania? Permanently, I mean."

"How can that be? I spent the entire afternoon with Viorica; she never said a word!"

Christopher shrugged, tilting his head to meet her eyes in the mirror. "Viorica works in mysterious ways, her horrors to perform. Your guess is as good as mine."

"She's not that bad, really. And she loves Michael, which has to count for something. She must have decided not to do adoption services anymore. That's weird. She's so devoted to the orphans, how could she bring herself to quit?"

"If I understood Viorica, I could control the world. That woman hasn't made sense to me since the day Mina brought her to meet us." Chris turned off the bathroom light. He walked through the dressing area, his head just brushing the air space they'd freed by removing the arch the Dannigers had built to separate the two rooms more formally. Chris sat down on the edge of Deborah's side of the bed, next to her outstretched legs. "Maybe she's finally starting to face the fact that Michael isn't the easiest kid in the world. Maybe she's getting out of the business because she sees how much trouble she's caused us."

"Hardly likely," Deborah said dryly. "But Mina loves her; that's a point in Viorica's favor, isn't it?"

"Well, they're family, and from the same part of the world. That has to be . . . ," Chris began.

"I know, I know," she interrupted. "It's just so odd, the way Mina is so sweet and open, her whole life is written on her face, and Viorica—I just don't get what's going on inside her head."

"I don't trust her. It's a gut thing."

"Well if it weren't for her, we wouldn't have Michael," Deborah said.

"Yeah," Chris agreed, and when they looked at each other, brown eyes into hazel ones, for the first time each knew that the other had indulged in the same damning, horrible thought. Neither Deborah nor Christopher said another word out loud that night, and when Deborah reached over to pick up her book, Christopher merely slid to his own pillows, turned toward the window, and closed his eyes. It seemed as if he fell asleep quickly, his breathing consistent and relaxed. Deborah, on the other hand, sat bolt upright in bed, eyes moving across the lines of her book as if she comprehended what she was reading. Every thirty seconds or so, she turned another page, inhaling in a short, sharp breath, hardly blinking.

"Was it useful? The brain scan? What did you learn?" Jane's voice on the phone that evening was high and excited, slightly envious, as if she'd just learned the Lathams had embarked on a miracle cure she hoped to take herself. But the healing waters of Dr. Silver were not what Deborah had imagined them to be. She couldn't lie about it: Dr. Silver, with his myopic stare and pinched mouth, had taken away her hope.

Before Dr. Silver, she had assumed the losses to be worth the gains. Like the tornado that had popped up one summer almost from nowhere and sped down Montauk Highway, destroying hedges and hundred-year-old elms, ripping the roof off at least one stodgy Victorian home, Michael was leaving damage in his wake. They'd always understood this, had always known this was the cost of fighting for Michael's future. But the good doctor's blow had been expertly complete; Dr. Silver had been picking through human wreckage for years, and he knew the difference between detritus and the seeds of possibility. Betting on Michael's chances for becoming a functioning citizen, a man able to maintain relationships, he assured them, was akin to buying fool's gold. Nevertheless, he wished them all the best of luck.

Deborah turned back to the sink, staring at the warp of her reflection in the mica that the dark night made of her windowpanes. Her hair, curling wildly around her head, took on the glinting kitchen lights and made a sweet, pale halo around her face. "No," she said softly, resolving not to return to the adoptive mothers' group again. "No. I wouldn't do it. Useless at best. It really wasn't worth the bother."

7

"I'D NEVER blame you for Jack's death," Martin Dunn had said to his wife Alice, back more than twenty years before. She knew it couldn't be true. Martin blamed her for just about everything: for the way the wind blew up and over their hill, depositing huge mounds of dried leaves right at their doorstep every October, and for the way the grout kept peeling and cracking around the tub.

Blaming his wife for most things was Martin's greatest skill, she guessed, and always had been. She was used to it. She wore his blame better than most of her clothes. It had lasted longer than any fabric ever could, never stuffed forgotten in the back of a drawer, unfaded despite life's required washings. How she knew he blamed her had to do with the way most news went between them, never spoken in actual words. They were silent, most of the time, now that the boys were gone, but Alice guessed she knew exactly what her husband was thinking. After forty years, how could she fail to?

In the week after Jack's death, veins had cross-hatched the whites of Martin's eyes. Someone else might have guessed he'd been crying day and night. The truth was that Martin never did shed a tear, not once that entire time. The most Alice ever saw him do was wipe the back of his hand across his forehead, smoothing down his eyelids along the way. Was that grief? Not her kind.

During the long days of calling hours, thanking the endless stream of neighbors for their cards and cakes and all those generous trays of lasagna and chicken, he'd been so polite and thoughtful she'd wanted to kick his shins. Not a single person walked through the door he hadn't offered coffee to, or thanked as if that particular gesture could make all right again. He'd looked at pictures of Jack people brought by; he'd joked about some of the fool things the boys had done, like climbing up to the Danniger's attic and spying on girls at a sleepover. She'd seen him smile and chuckle and shake his neighbors' hands, both hands at once. *It was Martin to a tee,* Alice thought—*he lived life on the outside.* She herself had barely been able to lift up from her chair. She'd just sat there, mutely, tears running down her cheeks so endlessly her dresses wore dark patches.

That entire mourning week she'd gone through so many kinds of thoughts: hating Anna and Des for being alive, hating herself for ever letting her boy grow up so he could die, and finally, long before the last casserole came through the door, coming around to put the pure fire of her hatred exactly where she thought it belonged. She recalled words Ellie Emerson had said years before, back when the boys were still small. "Martin's really smart, I know, and he's got a heart big as a cantaloupe," Ellie had said. "Seems like he understands everybody's point of view on everything. I never saw a person more eager to forgive. Funny how he rides *you* so hard, though, like you can't do a thing right and nobody else has a fault at all."

Alice had been frightened of Ellie at that moment; how dare she realize such a thing? Until that comment, it had never occurred to her that Martin's disdain was visible to anyone else. "I don't mind," she'd said offhandedly, and Ellie's response was the worst.

"That's what Gus says," Ellie said matter-of-factly, making it completely clear that she and Gus had chatted about Martin and Alice. Alice feared that thought so much she banished it, erasing the conversation from her brain whenever it threatened to surface. At that time, Gus still worked for Martin; how dare he criticize his boss? Or was he defending him? Either way, it was awful.

Ellie hadn't bothered to say more, thank the good Lord. Later, when Jack died and Des left, and Gus quit to start Sagg Plumbing, Alice had wondered what else the Emersons talked about. She couldn't bear the way her thoughts ran.

It was Anna Downing's car Jack died in. Some fluke of fate had been all that kept her safe that night; she and Jack were usually inseparable. The next morning she'd as much as admitted it, oddly shamefaced, standing awkwardly by the couch as if Martin and Alice might be angry at her for remaining alive.

"Part of me wishes I'd been with them, like maybe I could have changed what happened," she'd said, "but then I get so mad, thinking about Des, and how much I wished Jack would stay away from him. I know Des is yours, too, and I shouldn't say it, but Jack never did any-thing wrong, anything dangerous. Never. Not unless Des was egging him on. I get so mad," she'd repeated, not looking up at either of them, fingers pleating and flattening the hibiscus flowers on her silk skirt.

Alice couldn't help noticing that Anna's nails were painted and shaped; the thought intruded that Anna might have been given the mani-cure as a kind of pick-me-up gift from some friend or another, and that notion was incredibly irritating. Later, of course, she would remember that Anna, too, had graduated from high school the day before.

Martin hadn't been quite so heavy in those days, twenty years earlier, but he'd had a certain amount of trouble negotiating his way out of a deep armchair even then. What he tended to do had to have been learned at his plumbing company, a way of projecting his voice from deep down in his throat so that even his mildest comments sounded like statements of doom.

"We don't see that Des could have done anything wrong," he'd proclaimed, and no one had answered, even though that so obviously wasn't true. Otherwise, where was Des that morning? If he'd gone to jail, they would at least have known where he was. Where did Des go in the days after? Who fed him and kept him in the weeks and months that followed?

Truth was that in the twenty years since Jack's death, jail was the only place they ever did hear about Des showing up. About six months after the accident, Des was booked on a breaking and entering charge. Martin refused to go up to Riverhead to see him, and Alice didn't drive, so that was that. They never did hear from their adopted son again.

She didn't think Des was dead, she prayed he wasn't, but even so, it was his room she'd started putting the foster children in two years after Jack's death. That was when Martin called Social Services to tell Miss Lilley they'd be willing to have some children again.

The children arrived with regularity, and she bathed them in the same tub and potty-trained them with the same rickety step stool. The little boys ran back and forth in the fenced-in yard for hours, like ani-mals, and the little girls made cookies using her grandmother's recipes.

When they cried at night—and they all did, but usually not for the first few nights, not until they felt safe enough to let a tear slip down a bony cheek—she would sit up in bed just like Miss Clavell and quickly tuck her long gray hair into a bun using the mother-of-pearl clip she favored. She'd head down the hall to the room Des had used, the one she'd always called the babies' room, even long after they'd decided Des would stay and be a real-life brother for Jack.

Over the years, the monthly stipend had gone up, and the information coming from child welfare was less complete than it used to be, but she didn't much care. She knew what to do.

She had a Xeroxed list of questions from a now-retired caseworker that helped to organize information on each foster child, from the youngster's legal status, to visitation plans, to what medications he or she was on. She filled out that same questionnaire for each child, and she noted allergies and behavior problems. She made sure doctors' visits and shots and dental appointments went like clockwork. She sat quietly in her living room every few weeks, watching one mother or another kneel, sobbing, in front of a toddler. Alice averted her eyes politely until the mother sighed and said she had to be going. Then Alice made ready to grab the screaming boy or girl in her fleshy arms, holding the child as the mother's boyfriend's motorcycle gunned backward down the high driveway.

By now, there were so many children that Alice couldn't keep their names straight anymore. Instead, she called the two-year-old who didn't speak "Blondie" because she hoped that one day the little girl would be as giddy and dizzy as the cartoon character. There was a dark little infant she called "Ramon" because she remembered a man from church with that name, years before, who'd jump-started Anna's gold Impala once when the kids got stuck at the beach.

The words to use with them were always there, automatically, whether they cried or grew hungry or angry or confused. She could help the little ones to feel safe and not be scared or baffled by all the changes. That was no different than it had been, before Jack and before Des. But what she couldn't do, anymore, was to care about the children's tears, not the way she used to. She could look into the big, pleading eyes of a little girl whose stepfather had burned her on the stomach and arms and back with a lit cigarette, and she could say, "Come here, Honey, let me put some salve on that, you'll feel so much better," and the little girl would come to her, grateful for the love she appeared to be giving. The odd thing was that all their hurts couldn't reach down to her heart, not anymore. She wondered if, since she'd gotten so fat, that stupid muscle had been buried too deep to reach.

She drove the kindergartners to school, and she took them home. She washed them and fed them and held them. She baked with the little girls and told the little boys to go out in the yard. She read to them. Some of them were cute, and some were winning, and some were bright. After a few months, or six, or perhaps a year, each one moved on to a loving, permanent home. When they were gone, they were gone.

She'd never let another child stay. She was sure of that.

And then one evening during Bible study, Martin had pushed his chair back from Ellie Emerson's sturdy oak kitchen table and crossed his thick arms across his thicker belly so that each hand almost found its way into the opposite armpit. He'd taken off his glasses and put them down next to his glass of iced tea, and leaned forward so that the folds of his white shirt creased onto the table—looking for all the world like he had a set of ladies' breasts, Alice Dunn thought, and then she blinked twice, hard, to banish the thought.

Couples sat across from one another at Bible study, in the same seats they'd had for thirty years: Alice across from Martin; Ellie across from her husband, Gus; Nan Downing across from Otto. The Downings' daughter, Anna, was married now, living happily in Schenectady. Alice hated having to smile when she looked at pictures of Anna's children. Ellie and Gus hadn't had any kids, never wanted to; they were fine the way they were. And Alice and Martin, well, they'd lost the ones they had, hadn't they?

That night, Martin leaned back from the table and put one arm across his big belly and then the other, and then he leaned forward again. Jack had been dead for twenty years, and Des had been missing for nearly as long, and what Martin said, staring straight across the table at his wife of forty years, was this: "I've been thinking about how the Lord sends trials and tribulations to us as a kind of honor. I mean, I believe losing my boy the way I did has to mean the Lord has plans for me in the life everlasting. And I've been thinking if I'm to be rejoined with my son, I almost cannot wait. And I certainly wonder if the good Lord means to let my son sit face to face with the woman who brought that snake Des into the garden that was our home."

"Me?" Alice whispered.

He nodded, smugly. *Yes.*

Ellie Emerson's faucet leaked, *plink, plop*, into the sink, *plink, plop, plink, plop*. The butter cookie Alice had been chewing caught in her throat with a dry, pointed edge, but she could not cough, couldn't bring herself to make a sound. Alice's face was white. Her mouth drew tight, into a little circle.

The other men, Gus and Otto, looked down at the table. Gus pushed his glass forward so that the cubes of ice clinked and settled. Otto chuckled awkwardly.

Alice said quietly, "I think maybe we should speak with the pastor."

Martin raised his eyebrows and shrugged. "Fine for you," he said. "But what will I get out of it?" He raised his glass and took a long draw of iced tea.

Ellie Emerson tapped her nails on the table, her eyes sparkling with puzzled excitement. When there was something Ellie didn't understand, she'd work double time seeking out the facts she wanted. That thought scared Alice, who couldn't bear the thought of fending off Ellie's grueling examination. A flush rose on Alice's cheeks and began to spread hotly, down her neck. In the lamplight, her dumpling skin glowed with a pink sweetness.

Martin, generally a man of punctilious behavior, gave a loud, self-satisfied belch. Elbows wide and chest puffed, he patted his stomach. "Well, that's that," he announced. "Probably best to call it a night."

8

"DON'T GO," Michael said softly, one thin wrist stretching out from underneath the Power Rangers quilt he'd found by himself in a catalog and come excitedly to show her. He was never the kind of child who wanted things in a greedy or accumulative way, although he hoarded what he had under careful, orderly management. She almost always gave in when he asked for toys or coloring books or even those awful bed sheets. There were fundamentals she would never be able to give him no matter how hard she tried, so if a toy or other such thing might be a step toward making him whole, she would try it.

Mostly he wanted paints and crayons, plastic soldiers, and jigsaw puzzles. He didn't play like other children and never had. His soldiers never spoke or fought; he piled them up, end to end, so that the silent feet of one fit neatly inside the molded rifle arm of the next, placing them in even rows, inside boxes, in bags. He could define order from a very early age, and he excelled at puzzles, could manage very complex pictures and pieces at three and four years old.

Even at two, when he had been with them only six short months, his play had had an intensity, a private, self-sustained quality, that other parents remarked on with envy. Liz Glennen, whose son Whit played side by side with Michael until the middle of the year that the boys were four, who had been the last mom to staunchly try to make things work when Michael's temper tantrums had driven all the others away—even Liz used to joke that Michael would probably end up drawing technical plans for NASA or repainting the Sistine Chapel solo.

He had all the trappings of a loner: thin-skinned sensitivity coupled with a natural emotional distance, an ability to amuse himself for hours. His responses to new situations and people were crude and off-putting, and one could read that as a natural unfriendliness. Deborah thought that was far too simplistic an explanation. He was frightened, she believed, and he resisted new circumstances because he'd already endured so many of them.

"Don't go," he said again.

"You okay, Sweetheart? I can sit with you for a while, until you fall asleep."

She smoothed the garish quilt up, tucking the edges under his pillow. "Those are rabbit ears, young man. They'll keep you cozy all night long."

"Momma?"

"It's bedtime, Michael. Time to go to sleep."

"Please, Momma?"

"What is it?"

"Sit with me."

"I said I would, Michael. Now close your eyes, it's bedtime."

He shut them obediently, squeezing them so tight she knew they'd be open again in a moment. She sat next to him, stroking a hand lightly down his face, smoothing his eyelids shut. His breathing slowed.

As she began to ease herself off the bed, his eyes popped open. "Momma?"

She sighed. "Yes, Honey."

"Stay with me, Momma. I can't sleep."

The laundry wasn't going in tonight, nor would the dishes get done anytime soon. She sat back down obediently.

"You're my own momma," he said softly, placing his small hand on top of hers.

"Yes, I am, Michael," she answered, the words catching in her throat. "And you are my own boy."

With all his problems, he had always been such a wonderful gift. From the beginning, they'd had flurries of pride and pleasure in helping a child in such dire need. Not even Caroline, who'd been almost four when her brother arrived, not even she would forget the wan and scrawny boy who'd been delivered into their life by Mina's cousin Viorica.

How could Dr. Silver understand what they'd already done for Michael? The good doctor's message was that it had been pointless to have tried so hard. But it was only Dr. Silver's opinion, and he was not a parent. He could chart numbers and graphs all he wanted, and he would never understand what Deborah did. She was sure of it.

To think back on that first day! The living room was decorated with bright red streamers and a huge, hand-lettered sign saying WELCOME HOME, MICHAEL! As she'd pulled into the driveway with Viorica and little Michael, oh, back then not Chris or Deborah or their own bright, beautiful daughter could fathom the possibility that the gift they were giving this unlucky soul might not reap only the most fantastic rewards.

And when the car drew up to the door! Caroline had run up and flung herself toward her mother in glee, shouting, "Where is he? Where's my brother!? Let me see him!" Not for her, not then at least, had there been any resentment. She'd been thrilled beyond belief at the thought of Michael, proudly telling all her friends at preschool how a new brother was arriving from halfway across the world to be saved and have a happy life with her and her mommy and daddy. Now, here was little Michael, finally arriving, and Caro was beside herself with joy and then, abruptly, puzzlement.

"Hi, Little Boy! Hi, Brother! Can't he say hi? Make him talk!"

Mina, Caroline's baby-sitter, had been so sweet with her charge that afternoon, making sure to give her lots of attention. She had even brought a big-sister gift, a sweet-faced doll Caroline could change and feed and play mommy with. While Caro was oohing over her new baby doll, sturdy Viorica had calmly lifted Michael out of his seat and placed him by his new sister's side. He was so small then, not even twenty pounds and already eighteen months old, with the oddest greenish-yellow tint to his skin. That was probably the hepatitis, Viorica whispered to Deborah and Chris. The bald spot on the back of his dear little head might have been funny if it hadn't been so sad.

"It's from the crib," Viorica had explained to them. "He never grew hair there because he was always lying down." Viorica had brought him from Romania; she was the person who found him in the orphanage and talked to Christopher and Deborah about him. Viorica worked tirelessly on behalf of the Romanian orphans and had brought dozens to the United States in the years since she'd emigrated, but Michael was the first child she'd placed with a family she knew personally. It was a reflection of her feelings about Michael, she said, that she'd come to talk to her cousin Mina's employers and plead the little boy's case. The Lathams had responded just as she'd hoped they would, and now, months later, Michael was theirs.

Of course, he must have known they were good angels and that he was saved, but in his first hours he simply didn't have a way to show his appreciation. He didn't smile as he looked around the comfortable, sunny living room, even when Deborah knelt to take him in her arms. He was happy, everyone could feel that, but to show it he opened his lips a mere millimeter—smiling was a skill he'd never learned.

There was so much he couldn't do back then: Michael couldn't chew; he didn't know how, even though he had seven teeth. He couldn't walk or eat with a spoon or talk. He just scooped cereal with his fingers and stared at his new family with those big, big eyes of his, and after a few days, Caroline shouted, "Mommy, Mommy, come quick! Michael smiled at me! He did! He did!" It was as if Pinocchio had turned into a real boy before her very eyes.

The first therapist, the one the agency recommended, had said it might be better to think of Michael as an adolescent, with all his moody unpredictability, his random, inexplicable bursts of neediness and rejection. They hadn't seen Rita Hofstadter for long, but Deborah hadn't forgotten that simple comment, had isolated it as a stroke of genius in a sea of inanity.

For so long, it seemed that Deborah was getting through. Even now she couldn't suspend the possibility, couldn't bring herself to give up. He had always wanted Deborah to love him. He had wooed her from his first months, with his huge eyes and unexpected grin and those seemingly fragile fingers reaching for her.

It was natural to want a mother first. She would love him, and he would learn to love her, and from that, he would become familiar with how to love. And then his father would begin to reap the reward, and Caroline, and then the world. It still seemed so clear.

It wasn't that life had been so much easier in Caroline's first days; it was just that the issues were different. She could never pretend she and Chris hadn't fought constantly in those first few months of Caroline's infancy, bickering about a whole range of irrelevant topics that later seemed to come down to which of them was giving up more for the other, for the good of the family. Chris would come in from work, and before he could say whether he wanted a beer or to go for a jog, Deborah would snap, "Can you say hello to your daughter?"

As if a seven-month-old baby, asleep in a portable crib, really noticed. She'd never admit it, but even Deborah knew that.

"Give me a second, I just walked in the door. I'm tired."

"And I'm not?" She had a way of looking at him, in those days, with a kind of fury that turned her huge hazel eyes narrow and nearly black. He didn't want to look at her, she could tell; she could feel his lack of pleasure in her, and it made her all the angrier. He didn't appreciate the difficulties or the tedium, she knew. He had no idea how endless the days were, how little there was to fill the time. She loved her daughter with every ounce of her soul, but think what she did with her hours: changing diapers, handing toys to Caroline and retrieving what she threw, watching her learn to sit and laugh and babble, spooning applesauce and cereal into her eager mouth. It was all wonderful, and yet it was grueling in a way almost impossible to describe. Deborah could sing "I've been working on the railroad" forty times in a row without sating her daughter. She folded endless loads of laundry, spent hours pushing a stroller through a landscape that had once seemed provincial and sweet and now only seemed a lonely path between diaper changes. Chris got to go to work, to speak with adults, to expect his dinner without planning what it might be. He got to shower without interruption. He had no idea.

They couldn't get out of these exchanges; they were so tired it seemed as if nasty, barbed sparks contained all the passion they could muster for one another. And then, one morning at breakfast, Caroline started to cry.

Deborah picked the baby up out of the high chair, and lifted her T-shirt just enough to ease one breast out of her bra. Caroline latched on and began to nurse, one fist stroking her mother's skin, the other tucked tightly against Deborah's neck. She made a low humming sound as she fed.

Deborah was silent, watching Caroline. Chris said nothing, his eyes first on his daughter and then on his wife, and then, suddenly, he began to chuckle in a shamefaced way, wiping at the inner corners of his eyes with thumb and middle finger. His fingers were long and delicate, square across the tops. They bent easily, hinged with graceful precision. Whatever they touched, his fingers seemed to caress, from dental instruments to baseball bats to his own forehead. His chuckle twined through Caroline's nursing hum, startling Deborah into looking up.

"What?" she asked uncertainly.

"You're a good mother," he said.

She reddened, glancing down at her daughter and then up, meeting his eyes fully in a way she hadn't in months. She shrugged, but she was flattered.

"It's hard, isn't it?" he said softly. "You work hard at it."

She shrugged again and then she nodded.

"I'm sorry, I really am."

"Me too," she admitted. "I don't want us to end like this."

"End?"

"You know, to just slink out of love." She was not avoiding him, her eyes direct and open, her expression far from angry. If anything, she was feeling relief. It had been so long since she'd felt seen by him that she had almost forgotten how delicious the feeling was. She allowed herself to smile at him, a real smile, and he grinned, for just a moment letting affection flicker between them. His gaze fell to the long fingers of his left hand splayed uncomfortably wide, his wedding band not yet dulled; after all, it had less than three years of wear.

She said, "To find ourselves together just because we *had* loved each other."

"I don't want that," he said. "And I hate all the fighting. I don't remember this, any of this, from my own growing up."

"It's okay though. It's better than, you know, than the dull roar of nothing," she said. Caroline blinked. She said, "Gaa!" and glared as the nipple slipped from her rosebud mouth. Her coloring was intense: black hair, blue eyes, white skin, pink cheeks and mouth. She could have been the model for Walt Disney's Snow White, except that she was prettier, far prettier. Even strangers stopped to comment on it. One small hand waved and slapped down, onto her mother's breast, as if to command it back into service.

"I hate it," he said. "Us, when we fight, I mean."

"I can tell," she said. "That makes it hard. I don't like seeing you angry."

"You could have fooled me," he said dryly.

"Well, look," she said. "It's better than not talking at all."

He stood up and walked to the French doors, as if such a comment were easier to consider with his back to her. Caroline made a gurgling sound in Deborah's arms and sighed, settling lightly into sleep. Outside, high overhead, one could see the thin stream of vapor made by a jet heading east, to France perhaps, or Italy. The low growl of its vibration sounded briefly, and then Chris opened his mouth. He closed it.

Deborah said, "It will get better, you know. But only if we talk about it.

Only if you're willing to fight. If you swallow everything you want to say, we'll end up like everyone else around here, no different. They all thought they were special when they started, that they knew real love. It wasn't just us. The gift isn't feeling love, it's making it last. If we want to make something more than most people have, we need to do a little more."

He turned to her, his brows drawn tight as if he were trying to puzzle out her meaning.

She leaned toward him, the child's cheek hot against her bare breast. She said, "Everyone starts out special, every couple. You know. But it fades away, not the way passion ebbs and flows, the way friendship does. And all the men end up watching TV, and all the women end up in the kitchen, and I don't want that. I don't want that. I'd rather be alone."

"That's ironic," he said. "You aren't ever alone anymore. She's always with you. I'd have to line up and buy a ticket."

"That's it, isn't it? It bugs you." She was squeezing Caroline harder than necessary, and the little one squirmed jerkily, waking. She lifted her head to nuzzle Deborah's neck, for all the world as if an additional nipple might be hidden there.

He turned back to the window, shrugging. "No," he said. "It's nothing."

His back was broad, the white fabric of his shirt pulling against his shoulders. He wasn't an extremely big man, but he was strong, and the musculature of his back was better defined than his irregular involvement in physical activity might suggest.

Eventually, he curled his fingers into a ball, pounding once and then again on the doorjamb, his eyes half-shut, his shoulders slumped low to curve in, the way a child might protect a treasure found on the beach or the last chocolate egg at Easter. When he finally spoke, his voice was soft and even. "I'd have liked a mother like you," he said. "For myself, I mean."

Deborah's cheeks flushed. Caroline, who had slipped back into sleep with her lips still tight on her mother's nipple, now suddenly arched backward, burping and pooping with a matched set of explosions. Without pausing, Deborah's hands slid down Caroline's back and around, turning the baby so that she rested vertically, nose against her mother's neck. Deborah rehooked the bra cup, pulling her T-shirt down.

"I'd do anything for her," she said. "I really would."

"So would I," he agreed, but the way the words came out was unwilling, practically ungracious. As she studied him, he laced his fingers together against his chest.

"I mean it," she said softly. "I remember how big grown-ups were when I was little. And I thought they knew everything, my parents, I really did. I believed in them like they were gods. They could fix people, and they always took care of me when it mattered and let me down when I had to learn how to handle myself. I mean, I was lucky, as busy as they were, they really paid attention to me and to my sister."

"I envy that, too," he said, and then he straightened. "I'm tired," he said. "I'm going to take a run."

"Look," she said, and she was pleading for something, although she couldn't tell if he knew what it was. "I'll protect her, at any cost. I mean it. She'll not be let down."

"Great," he said absently, already over at the door to the living room. He tapped one finger against the wall. "That's good. That's great."

Close shaves were part of marriage, and they'd made it through their share of them. Happiness was so clearly within their reach that she knew, even then, that they would always be able to find it.

At bottom, she had always believed that nothing ever really went wrong if one was willing to stand up and fight, to expend a little extra energy. She could still feel the possibility of contentment, even now. She had always been, and was still, a true believer.

Even now, she could picture happiness without half trying: Saturday morning at Mashashimuet Park, a picture-perfect family-sized playground in the center of the village, where Caroline stoically worked at pumping on the swings, running from one swing to another and down the row, and then over to the other swing set, the one where the seats were too far from the ground to be climbed on, where she would fling her stomach down onto the green rubber belt and lift her arms and legs high up in the air, proclaiming, "I'm flying! I'm flying!" Caroline giggling; Chris chuckling, delighted by her glee; Michael smiling. And she, Deborah, so certain of her own competence, her own strength, the integrity of her choices . . .

Of course Michael, technically no infant at eighteen months but still so underdeveloped, had to be carried from the baby swing to the playground carousel, but he was already starting to smile, to coo with pleasure when they lifted him onto the rough wooden platform and helped him to hook one fist and then the other to the metal spokes. Caroline would run over and throw herself, cross-legged—*splat!*—onto the platform, easily grasping one spoke and then another, smiling up at her parents with such utter trust. Then Chris would motion to Deborah, grinning, cocking an eyebrow, and he would drawl, "Hop on, Pardner. I'll take you folks for a spin."

She would, too. She'd jump onto the platform, curl down easily between her two lovely children. Grinning up at her wonderful husband, she'd never close her eyes, not once, not even when he got them spinning so fast her stomach felt the rickety old carousel waffle and grumble as it gathered speed, not even when the clouds started to blur and Caroline's loose, vibrant giggle came from both behind her and in front—even then Deborah would want to take it all in. She loved them all so, she loved them all!

There was joy back then, and pride, and already such a sense of accomplishment. Oh, what they had done! What they were going to achieve! It wasn't bliss; it was dogged diligence, but of such a sublime nature! Later, she knew, when they looked back on the work they had undertaken with Michael, on the sacrifices Caroline had to make, on all the loving effort they were expending, well, she knew they would all agree it had been worth it. She knew it.

And Chris, his leg muscles tightening with each wide step, his back curved away from them as if his torso were a sail filling with air, his arms stretched forward to push them all around and around and then around again, dizzy with glee, proud and in charge—if she was the glue, he was the power, she couldn't deny it. He kept the portrait together solely by strength—by painting the walls, mowing the lawn, by nailing two-by-fours wherever they were needed. And what she knew and had to give, and what he knew and had to do, why, they were unbeatable, a couple for the textbooks.

Deborah's promise, the way she'd vowed to protect Caroline at any cost, had not been forgotten. Not by her, certainly, but not by Chris either. He'd reminded her of it at the strangest times, for example, when Viorica first mentioned Michael to them, and Chris's eyes had lit eagerly, knowing his wife was strong enough to mother anyone. He had turned to her in faith, believing in her power to heal. Chris had trusted her. She knew it. He had allowed himself to believe in Deborah, in her ability to love without doubt or fear. He himself might not feel that way, but he admired her so. "I know you can pull off the impossible," he had said, and even when Michael gave them difficulty, when he defied them or spat at Caroline or threw food or kicked a newly planted lilac out of the ground, Chris still turned to her for the longest time, believing that his wife could make it all right.

"Daddy love me?" Michael would ask at three years old, scampering after Chris, pulling at the leg of his khaki pants.

"Mommy love me?" he would ask Deborah, pulling her head down to his, so that her cheek rested on his cheek, brown hair mixing with black on his garishly decorated pillow.

"Daddy love me, Daddy? Daddy?"

And "yes," and "yes!" and "yes!"—so many times they'd said the words, and given the hugs, and sworn fealty and commitment, and vowed never to change. They did love him, they told him, watching to see light jump in the matte sheen of his eyes, to see the glint of true belief. They did love him, they did.

"Mommy love me, Mommy?"

"Yes, Michael, you're my son. Of course I do. I love you."

"Daddy love me, Daddy?"

"Yes, Michael, I do. I love you."

Chris had certainly not denied love. He had hugged the boy and played kickball in the yard and taken him on little father-son outings to the boatyard and the hardware store, or down to the firehouse to check out the fire trucks. This wasn't what Michael was after, however. No matter how many times Michael asked the question of his father, it was his mother's answer that really mattered.

It was Deborah he wanted, Deborah whose company he would insist on every night at story time. In the beginning, they had read the children stories together, moving the kids to their own bedrooms as sleep began to overtake them. But after a few months of evenings when a hardly toddling Michael pinched his sister, or took the book she asked for and ripped the pages, or simply lay in bed kicking so hard that nobody could concentrate, Chris suggested that they read one-on-one with each kid on alternating nights. On nights when it was Caroline's turn to read with Deborah, however, Michael would become inconsolable. He wanted his momma. And he wanted her to himself. Once in a while, rarely, he would ask for his father, but before Chris left the room, he'd always need that last hug from Mom.

And she would always give it to him, staying as long as he wanted, coaxing the near-black curls away from his eyes, smoothing her hand down the length of his skinny arm, rubbing his pajama'd bottom through the bedclothes. When he slept, his eyelashes lay like hatch marks against his warm skin, and his breathing was calm and even. But his mouth never loosened; his lips never dropped apart defenselessly. The way his fingers would clutch at her when she stood to slip from the room told her that he never really slept soundly, never could accept her leaving him, not even for a moment.

Often by the morning he would have slipped quietly down the hall and into his parents' bed. She'd wake to find him curled like a snail inside her own curved shell, his breathing matched exactly to hers, right hand resting on her wrist. Chris, behind, snored peacefully, his bottom nestling hers as if the only two people who existed were she and he. Michael, shifting against her stomach, seemed to have a similar notion.

She couldn't give up on him, no matter what Dr. Silver said. She couldn't. All the passion, the loss, all the vile memories roiling around in him would resolve in peace. If anything, her hope was flaring stronger these days, thriving in a place beyond the pettiness of circumstantial evidence, determined to prevail.

So often, it would be Michael, not Chris, who nudged her softly in the morning. "Momma! Mom!"

"Wha? Shh, Daddy's sleeping. What is it, Honey?" That moment of floating—the bridge between sleep and waking—was perhaps the biggest sacrifice she'd made by choosing to mother. Unlike so many other changes wrought by parenting, she couldn't quite put this one away. Each morning, wakened by him or his sister, she quite consciously had to quell a sense of loss. She cautioned him again. "Shh."

"Listen!" he whispered, lowering his voice obediently.

Outside, birds twittered to one another, an endless sweet conversation. No cars, no airplanes overhead, just the light flutter of leaves and the constant calls and chirps. High tweets answered by high tweets, chatter by chatter, deep-throated chirp by deep-throated chirp. "Hear that?" Michael whispered.

"Yes, it's beautiful, Honey."

"No, listen," he said. "No one ever chirps at the same time. Can you hear it? All those birds singing and nobody ever talks at the same time."

She smiled, stretching, flexing her feet under the summer quilt. "That's true! Wow! The things you think of," she murmured affectionately, drawing him in for a hug. "You are so smart."

Michael never completely relaxed, not even with her. His heart never seemed to stop pounding with tension she was sure was born of fear, and yet, as she held him, she could feel his yearning for softness, his joy at briefly believing himself loved by her. She could feel it. She knew it was there. She could feel it pulsing through his back like blood.

A sweet little boy was in there, and she was finding him. No matter what any fool expert claimed to know.

9

THERE was a single beggar who used to skulk the streets of Sag Harbor, an unwieldy crone with close-cropped hair who usually wore a magenta sweatshirt and spent her mornings requesting dollars from any friendly soul who had the misfortune to meet her eyes.

In the beginning, when Deborah first moved from Manhattan, she frequently handed change or a bill to the woman, generally as they passed one another by the bench next to the bank. That had been in February and March, but it had taken until early in the fall for Deborah to get up the nerve to ask the woman if she'd like to be photographed. It wasn't that Deborah was shy about such requests; it was simply that relationships in Sag Harbor seemed so intricately filigreed. The constant intertwining of connection had the effect of tying one's hands; anybody might be related to local royalty, throned or fallen from grace. The possibilities for giving offense loomed in alarming permutations.

But the beggar had seemed pleased, flattered really, at the thought of being photographed. The guarded expression on her face gave way to an enthusiastic grin, revealing a carefully maintained set of teeth at absurd odds with the fragrantly overworn sweatshirt and sneakers. "Sure," she'd said eagerly, and for a moment Deborah doubted the woman's sanity and her own wisdom as well. The woman smiled wider, and those pretty teeth effectively alleviated any concerns. The whites of the woman's eyes were pale pink and so flushed with broken veins it was impossible to tell what color her irises were. What a thrill it would be to try to capture the light so obviously flickering in the woman's soul. Not often was she granted access to such an interesting subject so easily; she had to think it boded well.

"When can we meet?" Deborah had asked eagerly. The very thought of exploring this woman's face with the camera lens had a quality of inevitability, as if such work would automatically justify whatever impulse had brought her out to visit the East End of Long Island less than a year before and grabbed her almost without warning, compelling her to give up her New York City apartment within a week and haul an entire van of possessions to a town she'd barely even seen before. She'd not regretted the move, not a bit, but she hadn't been remotely close to understanding it before this moment. Now, in front of the Apple Bank for Savings, she knew precisely why she'd come to make Sag Harbor her home.

The woman leaned forward as if she were willing to offer herself to the camera right then. Her curly gray hair was neat but filthy; in another setting, she'd pass for a farmer's wife coming in after an arduous day in the fields. "Name the time! Name the time! Take my picture!" she said, and Deborah nodded happily.

"Do you want to meet at Long Beach?" she asked.

The woman's face fell.

"No, no," Deborah said, quickly. "Any place you like. I don't know Sag Harbor that well. Is there any place you think would be good? That has special meaning to you or is very beautiful?"

"How about my house?" the woman said.

Deborah imagined a weather-beaten cedar shack in the woods around Barcelona Neck or a cave out by the bluffs. "Great," she said. "I'd love it. When's good for you?"

As significant negotiations take place, it often seems that even the atmosphere slows around the bargainers, snaking them together and setting the rest of the world apart. Perhaps other people were walking up and down the street that afternoon; they had to be, but Deborah didn't register their presence at all.

The woman's name was Faith, she said, and Deborah giggled before she could stop herself.

In the ensuing silence, Deborah, embarrassed, felt she had to offer something and so she said, "How about now? I have my camera, everything, in my Jeep. Parked just across the street. I could give you a ride home."

Faith shrugged, the way Deborah had expected she would earlier, when initially asked to pose. "Okay by me. Let's go."

Her house, in a typically Sag Harbor twist of expectations, was extraordinarily large and beautiful, one of the old whaling mansions on Main Street. It was impeccably kept. "Do you live here alone?" Deborah asked, her chest constricted in an odd combination of envy and pity.

"Yeah, I don't mind though. My mother lived here, and my grandmother and my great-grandmother, and her mother too. All my sisters, three of them, we lived here together, and now they're all gone. Papa's gone too. I don't mind though. This room, the living room, see those chairs?"

"They're beautiful. That fabric—I've never seen anything like it before."

Faith nodded, face flushed with pride. "Papa brought that cloth back with him, from one of his trips. It was woven in Thailand; it's very unusual. He traveled all the time. He had the bug. All the men in our family always did."

"Were you—did you marry?"

"No," Faith said, shaking her head. One dirty hand reached out to stroke the orange and indigo weave on the chair. Each of her fingernails was broken into sharp, awkward points, a set of weaponry she didn't appear to realize she was sporting. "I never had much of a taste for leaving home, and the four of us, me and my sisters, we had such a nice life together. It was so nice," she repeated, her voice trailing sadly.

"Your sisters, then, they've . . ."

"Yes," Faith said. "All of them."

The garden made more of a metaphorical match to what Deborah had imagined she would see, wild swooping unpruned bushes, tree limbs fallen and left in place to decompose among a tangle of purslane and lamb's ear and wild roses and vines. It was so extraordinary she could imagine a wealthy South-of-the-Highway landscape client requesting just such an unkempt paradise on purpose. "Here," she said, the syllable an explosion of air, all praise without embellishment. "We'll shoot some out here, if that's okay."

"Whatever. I don't mind," Faith said, and then she stopped short, grinning as if struck by an enormously appealing notion. "Hold on, I'll be right back," she said, waving one dirty hand in farewell. If an elderly woman in torn sweatpants can scurry like a squirrel, that's what she did, scampering back inside, leaving the French doors open behind her.

Deborah wandered around the yard, pausing to step carefully over a decomposing isosceles triangle formed by a half-fallen elm tree wide enough to have marked more than a century in this yard. She picked up a tangle of pink-flowered vines for closer inspection, inadvertently pulling a handful out by the roots. "I'm sorry," she said softly, even though there was nobody around to hear.

A blue jay squawked fiercely at two squirrels who were hovering below a cracked bird feeder. He wasn't going to share, the bird informed them royally, and then he dove threateningly a few feet toward his supplicants. The squirrels backed up, turned, and scampered off in separate directions while the blue jay, fat through chest with pride and sunflower seeds, returned to guard duty on the branch above the feeder.

The yard wasn't large, by any means; certainly such a huge house would look even grander on a palatial lot. She turned, Pentax in hand, sheaves of pale flat grasses switching at her legs. Even without squinting she could see shot after shot crying to be taken, pictures on all scales, from the tiniest sculpture of pistil and stamen to the majestic arch of willow branches twisting down and around toward the banks of the bay at the very edge of the yard. The dock teetered nearly into the water, a small rowboat lightly tugging at the thick rope knotted around and over one crooked pier. It was glorious!

Deborah felt rather than heard Faith's return, shifted around to greet her, and gasped. "My God! You look wonderful!"

"They were my great-grandmother's clothes, all of them," Faith said shyly, pulling the heavy brown silk taffeta skirt through the grasses. Her hair, caught severely in a matching band of silk, no longer obscured the high plane of her forehead or the neat lines of cheekbone and eye, an amphora-like shape regal enough to make an Egyptian princess proud. Around the hem of the skirt, two thick rows of darker brown embroidery shimmered in waves as she stepped.

"Why do you—I mean, why don't you, I mean . . ." Deborah shook her head, confusion and pleasure flitting across her face. Faith smiled back, her watery blue eyes meeting Deborah's warm hazel ones with frankness.

"Why don't I act like Faith Henry of Main Street, Sag Harbor?" she asked, her tone gaily self-mocking. Her fingers, the nails crooked and torn although she'd made an attempt to clean the dirt from her hands, stroked lightly, caressing the stiff expanse of her skirt.

"I guess. Yes."

Faith began to turn, catching one side of the skirt and then the other in her hands, twirling round and round, a lovely, innocent smile playing across her face. Her eyes moved from Deborah to the shuttered windows on the second floor of the house, and then, as she turned, to the blue water lapping up to the willow's roots, and back to Deborah and then the house and then the water, and around yet again.

"Why?" Deborah called to her. "Why ask for money? What do you need it for?" Without thinking, she was shifting the f-stop and the focus, imagining the light, framing what she would see if the camera were at her eye. Her hands, held low and steady, couldn't help themselves.

Faith began to laugh, still turning, her left hand now free and held high, as if an imaginary partner were appearing. She turned, faster and faster, until Deborah thought to call, "Careful, take care now!"

"I am. I do! I always do!" The sky above was blue and clear, the air just slightly crisp in the way that only fall days can be. One lone cloud hung overhead, a huge, vain cumulous puff hovering as if to protect only Faith, who continued to twist and circle, her skirts flattening the tips of the tall grasses.

Despite herself, Deborah lifted the Pentax and began to shoot. "You're beautiful," she called, meaning it absolutely. "You really are!"

Faith circled, throwing her head back so her neck lengthened and lost its creases, her smile growing fuller and more ecstatic as she turned and swayed. Deborah shot frame after frame, drawing closer in on Faith's face, the utter purity of Faith's glee, the bliss of found innocence. "This is wonderful," Deborah called. "Wonderful!"

Faith grinned, turning faster. As her hands rose higher and her legs swung around, she fell, hard, onto the ground. Her right arm reached out to soften the fall but failed to, caught completely as it was in a heavy fold of ancient brown silk. Her head hit against the half-dead elm tree Deborah had crawled over earlier, and her eyes rolled back briefly before closing.

Deborah dropped the camera and scrambled over to Faith's draped form, tripping over a stump hidden in the grasses but recovering her balance before she hit the ground.

"Hey. Hey, Faith. Are you okay? Are you okay?" She touched Faith's face. The older woman's skin was warm and she was breathing. A trickle of blood escaped the side of her mouth. Deborah had seen many people hurt in her life; her parents were emergency room physicians and she'd spent a great deal of childhood time staring at wounded and broken body parts while waiting for a shift to end, but today she realized she'd never before been in a position of responsibility around an injury. She was aware of a numbing sense of panic, a kind of tingling fear that made it utterly impossible to think clearly. She sank to her knees and tried to straighten Faith's skirt, pulling yards of heavy cloth from beneath the other woman's body, turning her over in the process.

Faith opened her eyes. "Wow."

"You fell."

"Yeah. I haven't danced in a long time." Faith chuckled. When she opened her mouth, a well of blood slid over her lower lip and down the front of her dress. "Damn."

"You're bleeding," Deborah said. "Should I call a doctor?"

"No, I don't think so. I broke a tooth clean out of my jaw, that's what it feels like. Can you drive me down to Chris Latham?"

"Sure," Deborah said. "Who's he?"

Thus it was Faith Henry's fuguelike dancing that brought Deborah and Chris together. To say they became lovers the moment they met sounds idiotic, of course, but it was true. Neither Chris nor Deborah failed to notice the intensity of that first brush of hand against hand, Chris running down from his second-floor office to help a daunted Faith and her heavy dress up the stairs. When a pot finds the only lid that could ever truly seal him close and right, even a fool has to know it.

"What happened?" Chris asked, and then, before Deborah could begin to explain, "Who are you?"

She opened her mouth again, not sure if he wanted to know about her or about what had led her to Faith, but he had already turned away. He was assisting Faith into his chair, as gently as if she were a bride crossing a threshold, murmuring something into her ear that made her giggle weakly.

In the light of Christopher Latham's office, Faith's age showed more clearly than it had even through the camera's eye. She had to be in her seventies, her solid cheeks and arms the result of a lifetime of activity, not the decades of drinking Deborah had previously supposed to be the cause.

"The right lower incisor, that's odd. You must have hit the decks in the strangest way. What were you doing, dancing through the trees in that weird old yard of yours?" Chris teased, flicking his white mask down so Miss Henry could see he wasn't serious.

Deborah gasped. "How did you know?" she asked. "She was. That's exactly what she was doing."

God, the woman was beautiful. He couldn't quite keep his eyes on her; they kept slipping away as if it were too intense to let his eyes meet hers. Every time he looked away, though, he had to look back. She was tall—he could see that—and her shoulders were strong and her arms lean. Her skin was clear and pale, and her long fingers were so white playing nervously in the brown of her hair he couldn't bear to look at them. He wanted to take her hands and still them, covering them with his own. And her eyes—they were huge and green-blue and very serious, but he imagined she could laugh. He looked up at her again and down at Miss Henry, and he wanted to say something, but all his breath was caught right at the base of his throat and he felt sure his voice would squeak like a teenager's, so he just half-shrugged his shoulders and tried to smile.

She leaned against the doorjamb. His office was plain and white, the only decoration the huge picture window revealing all the beauty of the bay and the Ferry Road bridge outside. Sails dotted the water. From the distance, even speeding cars seemed to trundle over the bridge, one after the other. She imagined this was what he looked at all day, the view part of what made him seem like peace just to be near.

Her last lover had been a stock analyst, the one before him an assistant professor of history at Columbia, and the one before him a photographer like herself. She'd met them all with a certain sense of fate, of knowing she would love them; she'd always had an instinct for the inner resonance that drew people to one another. This time, though, it was grander, because of this village where they were and who he seemed to be. He was fine to look at, his frame well proportioned and his eyes dark and sad. There was something else, though, so fundamental it couldn't be seen. She didn't know exactly why this resonance, this vibration between them, was occurring at quite so high a pitch, but it was exhilarating. As in the earlier part of the morning, expectations and assumptions were twisting up into themselves in an extraordinary fashion today.

"'We wonder how the fly finds its mate,'" she whispered. He was cleaning Faith's mouth with a soft cotton cloth, but she could tell by the stilling of his hands that he had heard. His hands were elegant, long-fingered and graceful; even though he had Faith's blood smeared on his thin rubber gloves, she could tell that being touched by him was going to feel extraordinary. "'The moral is that what we seek we shall find, what we flee from flees from us.'"

Chris put his right hand on Faith's shoulder gently, straightening to look at Deborah. "'And hence the high caution,'" he said softly, "'that since we are sure of having what we wish, we beware to ask only for high things.'" He started to laugh, uncomfortably. "You like Emerson."

Deborah shrugged, putting her hands in the pockets of her jeans. It was hard to look at him; she felt as if everything she was feeling showed when their eyes met. "Not particularly. I mean, yes, but not really. I like poetry more, you know, Whitman, Dickinson, Poe. Emerson's so convoluted, and his poetry isn't very good, I think. But I love the essay on Fate, I read it in high school, and I've never been able to forget that part. I don't know, I don't know why."

"You studied literature in college, didn't you?"

"Me? No." She laughed nervously. "I didn't really go to college. But I'm kind of a big reader."

"I never quote poetry at anyone," he said. "Honest."

"Me neither," she said, grinning. "I don't know why I started."

Faith laughed aloud. "I do," she said. "But then I'm an old spinster lady."

Deborah closed her eyes. When she opened them, they were both smiling at her. Faith's head was twisted to look around the back of the chair. With the tooth missing, she looked even more like a beggar then she had earlier in the morning. Deborah started to wave one hand in farewell, forgetting that it was in her jeans. She lurched forward and immediately began to blush.

God, Chris thought, *my God.* He couldn't stop smiling, couldn't remember what he was actually supposed to be doing. His skin felt warm; a small bead of moisture was already trickling down the small of his back. Under the white coat, of course, it wouldn't show.

"I better go, I guess," she said. "If you're okay."

"Yeah," he said. "I'm fine."

"I'll never get this tooth replaced if you don't get out of here," Faith said, straightening around to face toward the window. Chris, his hand still on Faith's shoulder, flushed a deep red, up from the base of his neck to his cheeks and across his forehead. The red mottled and paled almost as quickly as it had spread. He patted Faith twice. He looked down at her, gave a start as if he'd just remembered she was there, and said, "Oh."

They were silent, all three of them, for a long moment. Deborah turned toward the door and then back again. "Hey," she said to the back of Faith's head, just visible above the top of the chair. "Seriously. Why do you beg?"

"I don't know," Faith answered, pulling the brown silk band off her hair without turning. Chris could see she was tired. "I don't know," she said again. "It's just something to do."

Deborah had made her living from fashion photography, but her interest had always been in faces and forms, particularly those of lonely older women: the worn, played-out souls who hung on without reason or encouragement no matter what life dished out.

They could be found almost anywhere. She'd first seen such women as a very young child, waiting in the emergency room for her mother or father to be done with a shift. Her parents, so focused always on the utter tragedies that brought patients to them, were repelled and perhaps offended by her need to see the victims as even marginally virtuous. To Deborah, however, many of them had been holy, simply because they'd survived.

She'd first held a camera at the age of fourteen, a gift from her mother and father before a family trip to Colorado and New Mexico. When those rolls of film were developed, Deborah's shots were all of wrinkled Acoma Indian women sunken to the sandy earth in front of their homes, statues seated before low tables displaying rows of hand-built painted pots.

"You didn't get any photos of the pots," her twelve-year-old sister, Michele, said. "Or me and Dad and Mom. It's a whole roll of old ladies' faces."

"I know." Deborah had shuffled through the pictures, ashamed and elated at the same time. She'd caught something, she could feel it; some mystery about how to live could be explained by these women and what their eyes revealed. The whites, so pure against the deep milky brown of skin, the searing near-black of the irises, the wisdom in the striated series of seams that had clearly been more serious than laugh lines—she had known without doubt that studying such women was what she was meant to do.

And she hadn't been swayed.

"Deborah is downwardly mobile," her mother had sniffed, hardly joking, when Deborah told her parents she had no intention of accepting admission to Vassar or Yale, but instead had decided to head for the photography department of a small New York City technical school, a place where learning about Chaucer or theoretical physics was utterly inconceivable. "She could go anywhere, do anything with her life, and she thinks she's discovered the secret of the universe in some drunk's face."

Her father, even angrier, had turned from the kitchen, stomping outside to their deck, where he spent the next half hour silent, staring up at the March sky despite nearly a foot of snow dampening and then freezing the lower portion of his gray trousers.

Over the next months, her parents had come to her and alternately begged and threatened, citing their interest in her future, the need to know and be prepared for all kinds of careers because of the arbitrary nature of fate. Deborah had understood their point of view, until they told her they wouldn't underwrite even a portion of her photography education.

At that point, seventeen and not very brave, she began to pack, engaging in a game of chicken that escalated so rapidly that she left home, believing the rift to be permanent, within a matter of twenty-four hours.

Her parents hadn't been proven wrong, either, for Deborah's photographs had hardly taken the world by storm. She'd made a respectable living; the silence and strain that separated her from the rest of the family slowly healed over and, once Christopher entered the picture, disappeared. Christopher couldn't tolerate the notion of a family divided, and Deborah loved him too much to belabor the issue. She'd been old enough to make up her own mind at seventeen, although she understood that most seventeen-year-olds aren't. Nobody could have known she'd be able to work her way through school without parental support, make a small career and ultimately a happy marriage, without any of the backup most young adults rely on. She didn't resent their abandonment, not any more, but she liked that it was clear she'd survived without them. She'd made her point and certainly didn't have to be stubborn or pigheaded. If it mattered to Chris that there be harmony, well, she could certainly respect that desire.

After all, he was the most reasonable, caring man she'd ever known, and he loved her for who she was. After years of being an outsider in her own family, she'd finally found a kindred soul.

First meetings aren't always so portentous, of course. One's breath is rarely ripped out and then returned in a rush of joy. To be granted such a gift once in a lifetime is more than enough to ask; if, a decade later, the joy persists, well, one has to feel unusually grateful.

After Deborah and Chris became a couple, they saw Faith Henry occasionally, out of gratitude more than anything else. She was a strange old bird, but that wasn't what kept them apart; Deborah had rather liked that side of her. The truth was that Faith's views about a lot of topics were fairly reactionary: She disliked Jews and Blacks and Catholics, and she thought that people worried a heck of a lot more than they needed to about pollution, because God would take care of all the cleanup that needed to be done on his great green earth, a point of view that Deborah saw as overtly incorrect but virtually inarguable. After a time, even though she'd brought them together, it became easier to avoid Faith or to wave in a friendly manner from the opposite side of the street. It certainly didn't make sense to give her spare change.

The following spring, Faith had a stroke while sitting in one of the gaily covered chairs in her living room, drinking English breakfast tea. Her body wasn't discovered for several days, not until the mailman mentioned to one of the local cops, a buddy of his, that he hadn't seen Miss Henry puttering outside in a week or so.

When they heard, Chris said he wished they hadn't dropped Faith. Deborah was surprised at how quickly one can move from being self-protective to being cruel, and wondered if Miss Henry really had been hurt by them. The last time they'd seen her, she'd complained of terrible pains in her legs and arms, and told them she'd been dreaming of an old dog her father had loved, a huge black Lab who'd guarded their property in her childhood. "She was so happy for us, though," Deborah said. "And she was really sweet, but she was crazy. She really was."

Chris didn't remind Deborah of his mother's death; he couldn't. But he was thinking of her. He kept failing older women, one after the other, it seemed to him. The thought was too lunatic to say aloud, so he shook his head quickly and asked Deb if she was up for taking the canoe out with him.

"Of course," she said, and she ran upstairs to get a sweatshirt.

Nevertheless, both Lathams thought about Faith Henry often, not without guilt but mostly with pleasure. Years later, when they told their children the story of their courtship, the part about Faith was always the most romantic to tell. Even when they were furious at one another because of some trifling domestic incident, or because of something far more real, the way rages tend to be after a decade of marriage, the thought of Faith Henry dancing and then falling amid the tangled vines of her garden never failed to make Deborah reach over and touch Chris's shoulder, or Chris lower his lips to kiss the soft hair on top of her head. Faith Henry had brought them together, and, no matter who she'd been, they couldn't help but think of her as an angel, or even a magician.

10

CALLING a homeopath's number was pretty close to an admission of despair, and Deborah knew it. All the way over to Emma Hollander's pretty Madison Street cottage, Deborah had forced herself to take deep, calm breaths, aware of how crazily her heart was beating.

She couldn't quell the notion that Emma Hollander might know exactly how nervous—how utterly skeptical and, at the same time, how completely credulous—she was. If Emma was a crank, she would know Deborah to be a potential sucker, because the truth was that Deborah wanted above all to believe, to divine with certainty that homeopathy was the magic bullet, the secret weapon that could truly change the odds for her troubled son.

The basic idea was that by identifying precisely what was troubling Michael—by acknowledging the entire spectrum of his unusual characteristics, from his small size to his verbal skills, his preferences in food, his sleeping habits and preferred positions, his aggression and his solitude—one might discover a precise remedy. The remedy, arsenic or chalk or one of a host of other substances diluted until it was barely a memory, would activate his own immune system to begin healing itself. Although its proponents cited two hundred years of precise documentation to support their beliefs, homeopathy still seemed a somewhat flaky concept to Deborah.

Consulting a homeopath was not something she would talk about at home. Chris and, particularly, her parents believed dogmatically in the facts dispensed in their medical training. Her father felt strongly that Michael should be put on some Prozaclike drug. Hadn't he said so time and again? Hadn't he cited study after study, showing that such drugs worked miracles with difficult, temperamental children? Even Deborah's mother, who tended to distance herself from parenting issues, thought Michael could benefit from a little pharmaceutical assistance.

"It's age-related," Deborah insisted to Chris. "Their entire generation uses drugs for everything. They can't sleep, so they take a pill. They want to lose weight, they take a pill. They don't feel alert, they take a pill. My father would rather take five thousand different heart medications than start exercising, and he knows the benefits of changing his diet, but does he do it? He smoked well into his seventies, and she still reeks of tobacco nine times out of ten; if that isn't typical of doctors I don't know what is."

Chris smiled, rolling his eyes heavenward. Nonetheless, she could tell his sympathy wasn't completely sincere. He couldn't quite bring himself to dismiss the idea of using medication with Michael. Frankly, since Drs. Hofstadter, Bram, and Silver had each suggested consultations with a prescribing psychiatrist—and Eric Booth, one of the Sag Harbor shrinks they knew socially, had recommended such a course as well—it was hard to deny that the shared opinion of so many experts might be valid. Was it such a terrible idea, really? Drugs might quiet Michael, cool his temper, tone him down a notch.

"It's just that I keep hearing about kids who are totally zoned out by drugs or who say they feel really weird, not themselves," Deborah said. "And I think doctors prescribe these things too fast, when the kids are still growing. Who knows what effect it would have on his development? He could end up with health problems or fertility problems, or whatever. Cancer, maybe."

"You have no basis for saying that, Deb. Nobody knows the facts. The studies don't show long-term side effects."

"It's unjust and immoral, and I won't even consider doing it," she said, her lips tightening into a pencil-thin line.

"A lofty statement," he said, his tone clipped. His hands made a soft *slap, tap tap, slap, tap tap*, alternating palm and fist against the kitchen tabletop. She had finished the dishes. Now she scrubbed the sink with cleanser, wiped down the counters, and turned, her shoulders squared stiffly.

"You make me sound . . . ," she began, and then she shrugged, trailing off. She turned to lay the folded dish towel on the drain board.

"Well," he said, tapping more quickly with his knuckles on the table. "Well, sometimes, you state things so strongly. If I didn't know you, I might, I mean, I might think you were shutting off ideas that didn't fit into your picture. You keep damning one part of the equation and not the other. You sound so certain, angry even, don't you ever think maybe . . . " He stopped. His fists swiped each other nervously, knuckles brushing knuckles with a dry whisper.

"That's crazy," she said. "That's crazy! You're the one who won't consider alternatives. I'm not saying I'm against the idea of medication, not absolutely. I'm just not so sure I want to write off other possibilities. I'm not going to say there's absolutely no chance that some other kinds of interventions might be less harmful, and maybe have fewer side effects, and even help him more. You're pretending to be open to alternatives, to other ideas, but you aren't! You aren't at all!"

Her voice was rising; she could feel a sick kind of pleasure surfacing in her belly, a self-righteous anger that even *she* knew wasn't fair.

"Okay, okay," he said.

"Don't patronize me! Don't act like you agree, like you just want to calm me down!" *She was not going to cry. Wasn't he being unfair?* The rage was physical; she could feel anger rising, creeping up her throat like some foul meat she'd been unable to digest.

"You go too far out on a limb sometimes," he said, hunching over, his elbows pressed hard into the oak table. He couldn't even look at her.

"That's not fair!" she cried.

He shrugged. "I'm just telling you how it seems to me. The question is, can Michael be made to fit in this community, in this family? And what are you willing to choose to do to make that happen? You say it's a moral choice. I guess I think it's a practical one."

"How can you be like that? So calm! As if he is just anyone, as if he doesn't matter?"

He stood up, his chair scraping against the worn oak floors. He pushed the chair in neatly, placing his hands on the back, side by side. "When you say things like that, you end all argument," he said evenly. "Because you make it sound as if caring for him can only go along a certain set of guidelines that you've put together. We're different people. We have different ideas and see different things. I would like Michael to be happy *and* calm. I would like him to make his way in our family, in Sag Harbor, in the world. I would like all those things. But I refuse to close my eyes to the very real possibility that he's had too hard a life already, that maybe he will only survive, not thrive. You know as well as I do that he's . . ."

Chris fell silent, his eyes closed. Even when he opened them again, it was in the way a housewife partially raises blinds in the early morning: He could gather information easily, without being revealed in the slightest. Deborah breathed shallowly, there by the counter, her shoulders stiff and her neck stretched in a kind of pelicanlike defiance. Her eyes were narrowed, her fingers busily wound and tangled through the dish towel; her chin, cocked out and toward him without sympathy, barely quivered. Her fury was numbing; she hadn't known she could feel this kind of rage, not ever, not even in the most passionate fits of childhood play. She detested him, coldly. She disdained every detail of her husband, from his nose to his feet. Should she allow herself to be close enough, even the scent of his neck would be as foul as the slime of garbage. He was hateful and she knew it, suddenly, with a beautifully translucent certainty.

"He isn't ever going to make us proud. You've got to know that," Chris began again. His fingers on the chair had stopped moving.

"So what? He's our obligation. We took him on. He's our son."

"I know that. I'm not denying that. When you talk to me that way it sounds as if you're in this alone. But you're making yourself alone, can't you see that? You are so determined to do this your way, to make up your own mind. You won't let me in; you won't let me help."

"You don't want to," she answered coldly. "You've already made up your mind. You've already given up on him. You think Doctor Silver knows more than I do about what's best for my little boy."

"You don't give me much of a chance," he said, ever so softly.

"What? What did you say? I can't hear you when you—oh, forget it," she said, raising one hand dismissively. She refolded the red and white checked dish towel into thirds.

"I said, you don't give me much of a chance. You only want me to support you. You don't want to hear my point of view. You really don't."

"That's ridiculous," she said angrily. "That's unfair."

"Have it your way," he said, and then he walked into the family room and turned on the television. In a moment, she could hear him begin to flip channels, short bursts of laughter intercut by snatches of portentous music.

She remembered how they had both been amused by Deborah's friend Elizabeth Bloom, how she had moved to Sag Harbor and slowly taken up various forms of alternative healing: first acupuncture, then yoga, then homeopathy and naturopathy. It had driven Elizabeth's husband, Les, nuts; he was an orthopedist, and he thought Sag Harbor's New Age bent was laughable. Daughter of doctors, married to a dentist, Deborah had thought it all pretty ridiculous as well. But when Caroline's best friend, Ada, made it through an entire winter without a bout of otitis media, a victory her mother, Elizabeth, attributed to regularly spaced dosing with echinacea and tincture of nettles, it was hard not to become at least mildly curious. The year before, both Caroline and Ada had wintered on antibiotics; the year they were three, however—the year before Michael arrived—only Caroline had gotten sick. By the time Michael crossed the threshold, Deborah had one foot squarely in the natural healing camp; she wasn't ready to give up on Western medicine, but she was sold on the use of herbal remedies.

Though Chris rolled his eyes occasionally, he didn't say a word in front of the kids, sometimes going so far as to encourage one of them to swallow the grassy drops of nettles or the sweet orangy drops of echinacea. When Michael's ear bothered him, Deborah would tie half an onion to it, using a headband of Caroline's, or she would warm a few drops of mullein oil or garlic oil and soothe the eardrum with that. The miracle was that it appeared to work. Even Chris couldn't deny it.

"God," she muttered, moving the dish towel back to the counter, trying to tune out the insistent shrill laughter coming from the television. He said she was too rigid, but he was the one who had walked away. He had left her alone. Who was really unable to listen to whom?

Deborah, Chris felt, kept embracing one cure after another like she'd found the Holy Grail. She was all impulse and enthusiasm, and, while he loved her for it, such behavior was far from realistic. She dismissed each failed effort with disdain, and then summoned up the same amount of zeal for her next blind leap. Deborah was essentially an optimist, strong-headed and good-hearted, a believer by nature. He, on the other hand, had seen more of the tragic, and he knew that reasoning and rationality were the only methods for coping with the worst problems. Gathering information eventually led to answers; Deborah seemed to shoot wildly, randomly, and while she was on occasion right, her lack of method irritated him. Her inability to compromise, her disdain for it, was equally annoying.

Chris believed in compromise. His history and his training called for spanning both sides of any question. He couldn't spurn alternative healing the way he used to; he couldn't dismiss the possibility that Michael's oddness might well be served by some unique, creative approach. But he also couldn't deny that medication might help.

In just the same way, Chris Latham also couldn't argue for or against adding parking spaces in the village; on the one hand, he wanted more patrons in the stores—he wanted his friends and neighbors to grow fat and financially comfortable—but he also wanted peace on the streets, to find his paper waiting for him at the variety store, to get a call from the tackle store the day the blues started running. When he and Will were young, they wandered all over the village, through the woods, down to the beaches. They went miles from Collins Street each day and were never surprised to find out that Eileen Gaston—and of course Chris's mother, when she was alive—had been keeping tabs on them with ease, through phone calls among the adults. They'd heard Eileen make the same kinds of phone calls to her friends, casually mentioning that Joey Stall was shooting his cap gun with that Backes kid, down behind the cemetery, that her own Joe had seen the boys not more than an hour since.

Of course, since Joe and Eileen owned Gaston's, pretty much everybody in town had to run by their place for milk or a pound of chop meat by the end of each day. Both by personality and by proximity, Eileen was an ideal conduit for information, taking in news and handing it out again as casually as she would press a piece of penny candy into a kid's palm when he called on an errand for his mom. Whether she was self-appointed or not seemed almost beside the point. When Chris read Steinbeck's *Winter of Our Discontent* in college, he couldn't help being infuriated by the portrayal of life in a village grocery. The Gastons loved their life: Joe and Eileen made a joy out of every day, running the same kind of store as depicted in the novel but with such passionate rectitude, such true kindness. It wasn't simply Chris, or Will, for whom they were home; in a certain sense, Joe and Eileen Gaston were the very definition of the word.

Chris had never paid much attention to how safe they all were, not when he was a kid, but now that he was a parent, he often wished he could re-create that aspect of his history. Not that he'd want to be as rock-bottom poor as everyone was back then, but he would like to see and feel such caring protection once again. To get that caring, he knew, one had to see a neighbor's point of view, to compromise a little. It bothered him that his wife couldn't seem to understand it.

Her parents didn't bother to be tolerant of Deborah's "New Age phase." It infuriated them. On one visit, back when Michael had been with them only six months, her father had actually pulled a medical bag from the trunk of his gray Coupe de Ville. His hands shook, even then. He'd been retired for almost a decade, and sometimes looking at the gray shadow that tinted his pinched mouth one had to wonder how many more visits he would have with his grandchildren. Deborah's mother, nine years younger, was beginning to forget things with such regularity that even respectful colleagues at the hospital were starting to tout the notion of her retirement. As they stalked in through the front door to plop the medical bag onto the kitchen table, however, both doctors evidenced a forbiddingly competent aura of disapproval.

"Mom, really! This is ridiculous! There is absolutely no need for this, and you have no right!" Fighting with her parents was so natural, Deborah barely had to breathe to begin.

Chris, who had been turned toward the counter and hadn't seen the Berlins enter, now reached for the pot of decaf coffee he'd brewed to welcome his in-laws. Even in her late sixties, Lydia Berlin still liked coffee—and secretly, a cigarette—at every opportunity. She worried about her grandchildren, but for herself, she expected immortality. "Hey, Lydia, hi there, Bud. Long drive? Coffee?"

"I want," Bud Berlin began slowly, pitching authority through each tremulous syllable, "to look at my granddaughter's ears."

Chris chuckled, stepping forward to throw an arm over his father-in-law's shoulder, to pull the older man slightly closer to the living room entry. Two-year-old Michael lay on the Oriental rug, carefully edging and shading the spaces in a Barney coloring book. He didn't walk yet, but a six-year-old might have had trouble imitating his skill with a crayon.

Caroline was dressing a baby doll, murmuring quietly as she pulled on white knit booties and tightened the blue ribbon that collared the doll's sweater. Deborah had put Dvořák on the CD player; it was the New World Symphony, and both children were following the music absently, with gently swaying heads and loose-ankled feet.

"Look at them," Chris said. "What are you worried about?"

"I don't like that natural medicine crap," Bud answered. "You don't know what's in those damn bottles, those tincture things you buy. It could all be water, or, or, soy sauce, or . . . worse," he concluded darkly, eyeing Chris while raising his voice so Deborah would understand that every syllable was meant for her.

She opened her mouth to snap at him, to say once again that she was confident the kids were doing well, that one had only to look at them to know this, but Chris spoke more swiftly, smiling at Lydia and proffering the coffee pot. "I always forget," he said cheerfully, "where Deborah gets that mild sweet temper of hers, until Bud walks in the door. Never did grumpy apple fall so close to tree. Coffee, Lydia?"

"I'd love it," she said, putting one well-manicured hand on her son-in-law's arm, flirting slightly, still certain of her attractiveness, although far from sure where her glasses or car keys might be.

"I'd still like to look those children over," Bud insisted.

"Fine, Bud. Have some coffee first. You've had a long trip. Sit for a minute."

He took the cup Chris offered, filling it almost to the top with half-and-half before adding a small amount of coffee. Pulling out a chair, Bud Berlin settled in at the table and took a large gulp. "At my age," he said, smacking his lips like a satisfied cat, "you can't drink too much coffee. Keeps you up all night."

"Oh, and half-and-half is good for you? Shows you don't have to be New Age to be an idiot," Deborah muttered, wiping down the countertop with short, angry strokes.

"What's that, Debby dear?"

"Nothing, Mom. Honest. It's nothing."

"I'll check those kids over later," Bud said firmly, all tremor absent from his voice.

"Dad. You weren't even—aren't even—a pediatrician." He exasperated her beyond belief. Sometimes she couldn't imagine how she had ever gone a day without being furious at her father; he was so completely sure of himself that she almost always felt unprepared in his presence. *Thank God Chris was nothing like him*, she had thought that morning. He might not approve of the methods she was trying; at least, though, he was open to the notion that anything was possible. A totally honest man, her husband wasn't stuck, like her father, on the idea that having the upper hand at all times was of paramount importance.

That visit had been only three years before. Funny, how she used to think her husband such a paragon of flexibility.

"So what? I may not be a pediatrician, but I know what I'm doing," Bud had said, chugging half his coffee-flavored cream with enormous satisfaction. He waved a hand in the air dismissively, then wiped his mouth with the back of it. "You think I don't know what I'm doing? After fifty years of doctoring, I can't check over a couple of kids? That's a hoot!"

"Have some more coffee, Bud. Want some?"

"Deborah, Dear, take me upstairs," said Lydia. "I've got some gifties for the kids I want to show you."

"Sure, Mom. Okay." Her parents had been present less than fifteen minutes; already Deborah was exhausted. It was going to be a long, long weekend.

Lydia drifted toward the stairs. Aging suited her beautifully; she was softer, kinder. Though she was less attentive, her grace was almost enhanced by the very absence of efficiency. *I adore her,* Deborah thought with surprise, the emotion rising up where just a moment before had been exhaustion and irritation. Such a rapid transition from one feeling to another—she nearly quelled the impulse to say the words aloud. Her mother turned and paused, lightly surprised, sweetly pleased. "Why, of course, Deborah, Dear. Of course you do. And *I* love *you.*"

With that, she started up the stairs, murmuring as if to herself, as if to finish a thought she was following, "'Oh, wad some power the giftie gie us. . . .'"

Deborah's mother, by that time, was already on her way to becoming all light and weightlessness: a fragile blonde, on the brink of elderly and yet a pixie, still blessed by extraordinary, if slightly unpredictable, intelligence and a smooth flirtatiousness neither of her daughters had quite inherited. Despite being a rarity—a female medical student in 1946— Lydia had allowed herself, with an alarming sense of legitimacy, to retain her femininity in a world unequipped to cope with her presence. When she had entered medical school, the only woman in her class, she had been given only the privileges and rights of a nurse. But she had not allowed that situation to remain static; she had never fought, never insisted; she had, as she had so frequently reminded her daughters, merely taken what was her due, for example, permanently annexing a patient bathroom so she need not change her uniform among either male doctors or female nurses and ignoring suggestions that she might like to "sit out" a particularly gruesome procedure or demonstration.

One story Deborah and her sister, Michele, had not been told until they were teenagers was about a day, early in medical school, when Lydia and her all-male counterparts were beginning anatomy studies. Three of her classmates, real humorists Lydia called them, her voice deadpan, decided to remove the penis of one of the corpses they were to dissect and to place it in the pocket of Lydia's coat. At the end of the afternoon, as Lydia shrugged into her raincoat before leaving, every male eye in the classroom had been on her. She'd placed her hands in her pockets, paused, looked around the room, and then, calmly removing the dismembered member from her coat, had asked, "Does this belong to one of you?"

In the startled silence that followed, the future Lydia Berlin tossed the penis onto the tiled floor and left the classroom. She was halfway down the hall before any of her classmates recovered sufficiently to laugh. After that, no one gave her any trouble, but she never allowed herself to become one of the boys. Odd, independent Lydia would have considered that a failure.

"No wonder you had no trouble getting hired in an ER," Deborah had exploded, laughing along with Michele. One had to admire Lydia; she was not a simple woman, nor a simply good woman, but she was more than interesting. She was compelling. Small-boned and tiny-waisted, she looked so fragile that her strength seemed even more clearly to be emerging from some internal rock.

On the other hand, Emma Hollander, the homeopath, was large and comforting. Deborah liked the way Emma seemed to own a room by filling it. She had come prepared to ignore certain aspects of the experience, had joked about an ancient crone in a musty tree house humming some New Age theme song, but Emma Hollander seemed about as normal as they come. In fact, when she came to the front door of her eighteenth-century cottage to greet Deborah, the two women were dressed identically, in faded blue jeans, neat white T-shirts, and black Converse All-Stars. Neither woman commented on this overt similarity in the first flurry of introduction and greeting, but at least for Deborah, it had been a relief.

"Would you like some tea?" Emma offered, stepping aside so Deborah could move into the white-wainscoted entry hall. An eight-paned window to the right of the door was so clean that sunlight sparkled there, tricking Deborah's eyes; it took a moment to adjust and see that directly before her was the stairway to the second floor. To the left was a narrow hall leading down to a large, sunny kitchen, the far wall lined by four sets of French doors. Out back, a still verdant lawn rolled down and around a huge holly tree, stalling at a whitewashed fence covered with red-berried vines of burning bush.

"How beautiful!" Deborah said, stepping closer to the French doors, now catching sight of a series of beautifully carved birdhouses lined up on ironwork poles with white stone bases, one after the other: a Southern mansion done in miniature, a red and white barbershop pole, an Empire State Building, a plaster of Paris cave dwelling, a clown's head with mouth agape, and several simple traditional birdhouses done in bold pinks and greens.

"Those are incredible!"

Emma moved closer. One breath and then a second came sharply. "Yeah," Emma answered. "They're pretty special."

"Did you do those? Make them, I mean?"

Emma shrugged.

"You did, didn't you?" Deborah's voice rose admiringly, but Emma had already turned again, making a wide, deliberate gesture toward a little room off to the other side of the kitchen. A soft shaft of light played on the planked oak floor just below the single step; dust, dancing in a single ray of sun, glowed and shimmered. "In there," she said. "There's my office. I don't drink coffee myself, it antidotes remedies. But I can make some for you."

"No. No, thanks. I'm fine," Deborah said, crossing one arm and then the other across her stomach. Even with the sunlight, she was chilly this morning; it was October, after all.

"Okay then. Let's get to it."

"Have you been doing this kind of work a while?" Deborah asked. "Homeopathy, I mean?"

"No," Emma said, and Deborah had the impression that she was slightly embarrassed. "I haven't." Her eyes were nearly round, with deep brown irises; the smooth white lids were ever-so-slightly larger, veiling now for protection.

"How did you become interested in homeopathy?" Deborah giggled nervously. "How did you ever even hear about it?"

"I've always known about homeopathy," Emma said. "It's one of the oldest forms of medical care there is, and it's so logical, I mean, the idea that the immune system can be stimulated to cure itself. You just give it a little jolt of whatever's bothering you. And if it works, it's really miraculous. It's too bad more people don't take it seriously."

Deborah giggled again. She really did feel nervous.

"Well," Emma said, more forcefully. "Let's get to it."

Just going over Michael's short life history took the better part of an hour. Emma took notes on a yellow legal pad, pausing only once to blink with myopic intensity when Deborah explained that her son's natural mother had been murdered, back in Romania, when he was no more than an infant.

"In his presence," Deborah said, "and he was alone with her for several days—her body, I mean—before they were found. I can't quite imagine what that must have been like."

Emma shook her head sadly.

"I suppose," Deborah said, "that I should tell you his father was the murderer, but I don't believe it was ever proved. I don't believe you should assume he has inherited some kind of evil streak. People assume that, you know. And they think that children from Eastern Europe, that with all their problems they have some kind of innate evil, some propensity to be bad. The media just skewers these kids. That isn't . . ."

"Oh, no," Emma interrupted. "I was just wondering how much your son saw, if he felt responsible in some way, as if he did it."

"He was an infant. He probably slept through most of the time he was alone with her, and cried. He had no idea what was going on."

Emma pushed her glasses higher up on her nose. They were red-framed, too perky for her by half. Her looks improved dramatically when she folded the octagonal frames and placed them to the right of her laptop computer. "Babies, very young children, leave their bodies very easily," she said.

Deborah's heart sank.

"No, seriously," Emma said. "That's why infants so often cry out when their parents are making love. They have more freedom than we do, aren't so locked in their bodies. I know it sounds strange, but it's quite well documented."

Deborah emitted a short, high giggle, then shook her head. She shifted in her chair, not wanting to say anything disdainful or rude.

Children aren't capable of separating themselves from what they see, Emma explained, so that part of Michael might feel he was killed during the murder and part of him might believe he was the killer. "He's emotionally ill, I suspect, because he witnessed this violent act."

Emma leaned back in her chair, put both hands on the desk, and smiled as if she were very proud of herself, as if she had completed the first part of an assignment she hadn't been entirely sure she could work her way through.

"He was in one of those awful Eastern European orphanages as well," Deborah said, forging onward. As long as she was there, she might as well go along with it, see what the homeopath might come up with. "And sometimes he tunes out so completely I can't reach him."

"He goes into stupors?"

"I guess. Yes." She nodded. "Absolutely."

"Alternating, you say, with periods of aggression and anger."

"Yes." It was so quiet in Emma's office, it was hard to believe they were on one of Sag Harbor's busiest streets. Even the ceiling fan did its work silently, and Emma's fingers, brushing the computer keys, barely made a sound. She was scrolling through lists called rubrics, she explained. For Deborah, the fact that Emma worked with a computer somehow vindicated this effort. She could tell Chris that the homeopath hadn't been strange at all, that there had been no chanting of birdcalls over a bowl of smoke.

Deborah sighed. Even when her house was quiet, she heard things—cars speeding past, an oak tree brushing against the second-floor windows of Caroline's room, a kind of sublevel electronic humming emanating from every appliance in the house—a combination of sounds that made it virtually impossible to think clearly. Here, one might actually be able to focus.

"Anything else I need to know?"

"No. I mean, yes. I mean, I don't know if it's important. It's probably nothing."

"Might as well tell me."

"No. No. That's okay."

"It's up to you, of course, but if you think it might be useful, that there's something else I should know . . ."

Deborah shrugged, looking down at her legs. She rubbed at the inner corners of her eyes with the first two fingers of each hand. "No, actually," she said finally. "There's nothing else."

Emma nodded matter-of-factly. She began to type again, her ringless fingers flitting over the keys.

Michael joined them for the second visit, but he didn't seem to take to Emma the way his mother had. They hadn't talked very long before he called Emma Hollander stupid. He turned to Deborah and said, "She's stupid, dumb. She's a stupid lady. I want to go."

Deborah blushed, leaning forward to take his hand, about to admonish him.

"Lots of people think this is stupid," Emma said calmly. "And maybe it seems that way to you, but you might be surprised. Sometimes it can be very helpful."

Michael shrugged. "You're stupid," he repeated.

"Okay," she said. "Think what you want."

Michael stood and stalked from the room. Deborah began to follow him, but Emma stopped her. "It's fine," she said. "I have what I need."

In a moment, the screen door slammed. He was out in the yard.

After working at the computer for several minutes in silence, Emma turned to the bookshelves behind her. She pulled down a series of books, some paperbacks with jaunty yellow and rose bindings and two old, heavy clothbound tomes that looked as if she might have bought them at a witches' yard sale. Eventually, she closed all the books, turned to Deborah, and said, "Anacardium. I'm sure of it."

"What's that? What do you mean?"

"It's the remedy I want you to try."

"But what's wrong with him?" Deborah asked apprehensively.

Emma Hollander explained that the Anacardium state develops because of unbearable inner conflict. She thought Michael might be shouldering deep-seated anxiety and grief because he saw himself as both killer and killed. "He's very vulnerable and needy, while at the same time he's angry and distant. Does he have any problems with his bowels?"

Deborah shifted uncomfortably. "Yes," she said. "He does."

"Well," Emma said with satisfaction, "stomach pain is quite a common condition with Anacardium individuals."

She pulled out the middle drawer of her desk, revealing an intricately divided space filled with small blue vials. "These," she said, picking out one of the vials. "One pill three times a day. Let it dissolve under his tongue. Try it for a month and then let me know how he does. This is going to take some time."

"Can it hurt him? What if it's wrong?" It didn't feel like medication, nor had what Emma described felt like diagnosis. Deborah could hardly take the vial from Emma's hand.

Emma shrugged. "Then he won't get better. We'll try again."

The pills, Emma said, were essence of the Anacardium nut diluted with ninety-nine drops of water and shaken sixty separate times. One drop of Anacardium to six thousand drops of water. There was no risk of poisoning or anything like that.

"Then what's in the pill?"

"Milk sugar and ethyl alcohol. One drop of the six-thousand-drop mixture on that sugar pill. Honestly, there's nothing to worry about."

"Well, then, how will I know if it's even working?"

Emma said, "You'll see him being easier in his life, like a weight has been lifted from his shoulders. He'll sleep well; his energy will be more balanced. He'll be more comfortable, and so will you."

"Okay," Deborah said doubtfully, not wanting to admit how ridiculous the whole thing sounded to her, wanting beyond hope to believe in it. She pulled out her checkbook and wrote a check for $55.50 to cover the consultation and remedy.

"Look, I think this is going to work. Just give it a shot," Emma said, pushing her chair back to stand up and walk around the desk. Deborah had the clear sensation that Emma was about to hug her.

God, Deborah thought, *I could use a hug.* Emma, though, seemed suddenly distracted by something she saw out the window. For a brief moment, Deborah thought of reaching toward Emma, but she didn't. She couldn't. She might start crying, hanging on for dear life to save herself from drowning in her own humiliating tears. She was not going to ask for that kind of help. She would make her way without it.

Outside, there was a *crack* and a loud *thud.* Emma paled. "Oh, no! Stay away from my birdhouses!" she shouted. Her sneakered feet, scurrying across the pale tiled floor to the open French doors, sounded like angry slaps.

I I

ALL THE truly wonderful building lots in Sag Harbor had been seized for generations by local families. The ranch houses they'd constructed were decorated with pale blue or yellow or white frosting, bordered by short-cropped, weed-free lawns and neatly tended mauve rhododendrons. Fences were frowned upon, unless shin-high and painted white to mimic the waist-high barriers that crumbled in front of the huge, shabby palaces that lined the town's Main Street. When they were boys, Chris Latham and his best friend, Will Gaston, had spent most dull summer afternoons perched on one rock or another at the harbor or ambling up and down Squid Row eyeing the mansions and quelling their envy by sneering at the way time was tempering the houses' grandeur. Even the most enthusiastic expenditure of manufacturing profits or investment returns couldn't mask the essential ungainliness of the huge estates. Walkways were so short they hobbled the giants they crawled up to. Once, when they were about ten, Chris had confided in Will that he thought the Stanton estate looked like an oversized basketball player with size seven feet. "You know what they say about guys with small feet," Will had responded, and then both boys had fallen silent, nervously contemplating the awful possibility of such a disastrous inadequacy.

Luckily, both Chris and Will ended up with normal-sized feet, although neither of them ever grew tall enough to play basketball professionally. When Chris was twelve, his father died suddenly, and his mother faded slowly for the next couple of years, never really behaving like a mother to her only child again. When Chris's mother finally slipped off to join her husband, the boy had been, in many ways, relieved. Now he could move the rest of his clothes, books, and photos across the street to the Gastons' house without being frightened of what his mom might think or hurt if she failed to notice his disappearance.

When his dad was alive, his mother had been a big, heavy woman with the kind of lips that never got thin or tense, not even when she threw her head back and guffawed. Chris had loved shelling peas with her and helping her to set the table, or at least he remembered it that way. He remembered how she'd always paid attention, taking his words seriously even when he was just mouthing off. Once, after an afternoon in the neighborhood during which he'd failed even once to excel at Capture the Flag or kickball or even Spin the Bottle in the Dannigers' basement, he'd yelled at her when she asked how the day had been. "Shut up," he'd snapped, placing a folded cloth napkin at his father's place. "Why do you always have to know? Why do you ask so many questions?"

"I don't . . . ," she'd begun, not moving from the stove.

"Don't bug me," he'd yelled, hardly understanding where the fury was erupting from. "Just don't bug me!" He'd almost said he hated her, but he didn't, not even then. He was ten or eleven at the time—he couldn't exactly recall now—but he'd had to stop himself from crying by squeezing his eyes tightly shut.

The silence in the kitchen had been excruciating: steam rising off the peas, the bubbling of the noodles in the heavy enameled pot, the aroma of breaded pork chops in the oven. He could hear and see and smell, and yet when he tried to turn his head to look at her, or move his lips to form an apology, or even raise a hand to wipe his words from the air between them, he could not move.

His mother's forehead was shiny, her cheeks pink, her lips pale and open. She brought her right hand up, the one holding the slotted spoon she'd been about to use again to stir the noodles, and she held it against her breast so that the spoon bowl rested on her neck, forcing small, fleshy dots to rise. A spot of water dropped onto her shoulder and spread in a quarter-sized patch across her shoulder.

"Chris," she said softly. "Please don't."

He'd not responded—in words, that is—but he'd carefully placed the other napkins out and finished setting the table. He'd politely eaten his dinner, cleared the table without being asked, done his best to wipe the incident away. He didn't want to think he'd hurt her, not then or ever. Later, after she'd slipped from life to sitting at their living room window waiting to die, he'd assured himself that almost any small cruelty would have wounded her: She was the most delicate of souls encased in the sturdiest of forms. He'd told himself that had she been a strong woman, she would have stayed whole after her husband died, would have found another reason to live, would have found the life pulsing through her son to be reason enough to go on. Chris Latham's mother, like the stately crumbling mansions of Squid Row, couldn't handle the abruptness with which circumstance—the wind, the time, an accident, an artery—could change the course of things. She looked big and comfortable and serene enough to endure, but the fact remained that she was as fragile as the little pig's cottage of straw.

The ranch houses, though—they were like cockroaches: tiny, perfectly formed, indestructible as hell. Maybe the eye didn't linger on the Gastons' place, maybe the laughter inside wasn't as deep and infectious as his mother's had been, but at least it had always been safe to call it home.

The Gastons had been good to Chris, utterly stable and kind, and from the time he was little more than twelve he'd considered them to be his true parents and Will to be his brother. He was grateful beyond measure for the way they had opened up their tiny rectangle of a home at Seventeen Collins Lane, how they had made over the spare room for him without fanfare, how they had never pretended the more elaborate old house across the street didn't contain a decade's worth of loving memories. They had been easy, Joe and Eileen, and they had been decent. If either of them had lived just a few years longer and been able to meet Deborah, he knew they would have been as proud of his choice as they had been of Will's. When Chris allowed himself to think about it, he knew he would never have struggled his way into adulthood—never have gone to college or dental school, never have met Deborah, never have had Caroline, never have made a life for himself with all its complications and derailments and worries, and all the decent parts as well—without the warm, loving hands the Gastons had extended so freely back when he was a twelve-year-old boy.

Michael had been so much better for so many months that it was possible to breathe easily now and then, to think of grabbing both kids and running down into the village for dinner at the Paradise or Conca D'Oro. They'd gone to see a Disney movie, as a family, one Sunday afternoon in late November, and Michael had sat on Deborah's lap while Caro leaned contentedly against her father. In the dim light, watching color and shape flicker on the huge screen, Deborah had been conscious mostly of her son's still weight. That constant irritating quiver of his thighs had disappeared; he no longer infected others with his tension. None of his limbs held the heaviness of Caroline's; when he leaned into his mother, she could feel his heartbeat even through the ribs on his back, but his weight always rode lightly on her thighs. And when she put her arms around him, hugging his thin form against hers in the dark, she could actually feel him start to smile, as pleased as she at how much calmer he had grown, how easy they could be with one another.

The Anacardium pills were simple to take, one small dot that melted on the tongue in less than a minute, three times a day on an empty stomach. The only problem came, a happy difficulty, some ten days after the treatment began: He was suddenly eating so much, she couldn't find a moment when his stomach seemed truly free of meal or snack. And he was growing taller and stronger before her eyes, stretching the limits of his sweatpants and T-shirts so that she was forced to lay in a new stock of clothing for him. And wonder of wonders! For the first time, she'd purchased jeans in size five; he could finally fit in the clothes meant for his age group!

She held onto the description Emma had photocopied from one of the less dusty tomes on her shelf. It was amazing how much of it was dead-on accurate: "The Anacardium state often develops in individuals who are living with unbearable inner conflict. Out of this internal strife come two strong and contradictory tendencies: inferiority and cruelty. . . . In other cases there is prominent hardness and anger or violence. Hardness and cruelty to animals or people. Desire to prove himself. History of abusive family. Weakness of memory. Fear of failure. Fear of someone behind him. Frequently fights or history of many fist fights. Absence of moral values. Sensation of a band around a single part of the body. Ulcer and gastritis with pains better by eating."

And from another book: "Wild, childish, expressionless. . . . Quivering pressure in the thighs; trembling of the hand and of the arm. . . . Torpor. . . . Disposition to take everything amiss, to contradict, to fly into a rage. Frequently screams loudly, as if to call to someone; so furious has to be restrained. . . . Sensation as if the mind were separated from the body. . . . Weakness of mind and of memory."

Even Chris, she told Emma giddily, even Chris had seen the shift in their son. "He'd practically given up hope, my husband had, things had gotten so tough. And now, it's amazing! How quickly it's working! Michael's been friendlier and calmer. His energy is more even. He's sleeping well. It's a miracle!"

Emma Hollander sounded relieved. After the incident with the bird-houses, she'd probably had her own doubts as to whether Michael was healable. Having him back at her office, his attitude unchanged, might have been difficult to arrange. But that was only Deborah's guess. All Emma now said was that Michael would always have his basic Anac-ardium issues to deal with; they would just become more manageable. And, she warned Deborah, things might get worse again, without notice. This would only mean he needed to be reexamined. "He's had so many difficulties that even though he's young, we may need to work on layers of constitution."

Whatever that meant. Deborah barely heard her. The truth was that the shift in Michael was so complete, she could taste victory. His devils had been beaten. She knew it the way she knew what Caro wanted for breakfast. He was her son now, fully hers. There was nothing bitter-sweet about this triumph, nothing at all.

In line with Elizabeth Bloom and her daughter Ada, waiting for Santa Claus to make his yearly appearance in the village, it had been hard to con-tain her glee about the changes in Michael. He'd finished his month of medication, and even without the pills, he'd continued to improve notice-ably. Watching all the children scrambling happily over a rowboat—a weather-beaten prop from a play the Bay Street Theatre Company had staged in its first season, years ago—Deborah confided to Elizabeth that she was thinking of calling the school, that even Mrs. Bennett would have to see how much Michael had improved, how unlikely it was that he still needed Mrs. Nowicki to shadow him in the classroom. "I mean, look at him, at his energy, the way he's smiling! He's playing with them, and no one is angry or scared or getting hurt. He's so obviously better!"

"He really is," Elizabeth agreed, calmly brushing Deborah's scarf back over her shoulder and straightening her friend's knit cap. "I'm so glad you called Emma. I'm so glad you took the leap."

Elizabeth's grin was even larger than Deborah's. She was pretty and blonde, extraordinarily sensible and matter-of-fact, and that grin of hers exposed a set of even teeth that could probably open soda bottles if she tried. Elizabeth was the only person besides her sister, Michele—and Chris, of course—that Deborah felt she could trust herself to lean on at all. Elizabeth was solid and stable; she knew who she was. Even with awful Les as her husband, the couple still added up to one of the Lathams' favorites—Elizabeth pulled enough weight for both of them.

Sag Harbor's Santa Claus was patient; he took his time with every child, and so it seemed hours before Deborah and her children inched their way out of the cold wind to enter his inner sanctum. Even inside the theater lobby, one often had to wait for another forty minutes, and so Santa's Helpers always provided cider and papered tables to color on, a distraction for eager children. Tinny Christmas songs cycled off the loudspeakers. Deborah hummed along, elated. This was one of the best afternoons she had had in years. And it got better.

By chance, Michael ended up coloring at the same table as Whit Glennen, and the two boys began chatting, not looking at one another, grinning off into the crowded layers of giggling, cookie-eating children, nudging with elbows and knees. Michael sketched the outline of a huge Tyrannosaurus rex in black crayon and then offered it to Whit, who began scrawling at the dinosaur in orange and red, disregarding the limits Michael had laid down. Michael threw his head back, laughing loudly. Whit joined him without hesitation. Liz Glennen wouldn't quite meet Deborah's eyes at first, and she hovered protectively about the boys, but after ten minutes or so, as everyone loosened jackets and removed hats, she seemed visibly to relax. Deborah's fingers and nose began to warm; she wanted to make her way over to Liz, but Elizabeth Bloom grabbed her arm.

"Don't," Elizabeth cautioned quietly. "Just let it happen."

Deborah itched to go toward her son and Whit, to make some comment to Liz, but she knew Elizabeth was right. She stood quietly, watching her children, feeling utterly relaxed and proud. Great, in fact. She felt great.

On Santa's lap, Caroline lost her shyness completely. Some other child had smeared a last bite of chocolate chip cookie on Santa's shoulder, and Caroline laid her hand in exactly the same place, leaning in so closely that Deborah wondered how the poor man managed to avoid claustrophobia. Caroline's lips moved eagerly; she had a whole host of requests to confide. She wanted toys, lots of them. She wanted to play the flute. She wanted to stay up late enough at night to watch *Sister, Sister* on television, which her mother never let her do, even though sometimes Mina would. She wanted an American Girl doll, either Samantha or Kirsten, she didn't care, and could she possibly get some doll furniture, too? And a cat, if Santa didn't mind. Maybe a gray one.

Santa was chuckling so much he could barely get a full "ho, ho, ho!" to emanate from the depths of his well-stuffed belly. His beard shifted as he winked, nodding toward Deborah. She wondered exactly who he was, which villager. Chris would know.

Caroline hopped down excitedly, turning to hug Santa one last time. She whispered something to him, and he said, "What?" She looked over at Deborah and then at him again, and her shoulders seemed to fall.

"That's okay," Caroline said, so quietly Deborah had to strain to hear the words.

Santa, his ears stuffed with music and white polyester curls, had trouble catching Caroline's words as well. "Ho, ho, ho!" he shouted. "Merry Christmas, Caroline!"

Caroline whispered something else, looking down at her bright red snowboots. Only Deborah saw her lips move, and then she saw her daughter buoy up again, visibly, in a burst of energy, waving so hard at Santa that she tripped backward off the stage. Deborah jumped forward to help her up. Michael took two cautious steps onto the stage, his eyes huge and serious.

"Ho, ho, ho!" Santa called, grabbing onto his belly with both hands. "Merry Christmas!"

It was Michael's turn.

He slipped onto Santa's lap and melted, molding himself against Santa's red flannel belly so that his own stomach curved outward, like the polished curves of a wooden sled.

"Hello, Michael!" Santa boomed. "Have you been a good boy?"

Michael looked toward his mother. She nodded, yes.

He turned back to Santa, nodding proudly.

"And what do you want for Christmas? Ho, ho, ho!"

Deborah's breath caught. Michael was shaking his head, back and forth, no. He didn't want a thing, he said.

"You must choose, Michael! Toys, books, games! What should I bring for you?"

He shook his head, no, eyeing Santa, his tiny mouth set so seriously that Deborah's heart twisted. She pulled Caroline in closer, against her thighs, and zipped her red parka, pulling the hood over the mess of her curls.

"Ho, ho, ho! That's not good! Every child wants something! Don't you want a sled or toys?"

He shook his head again, no. His belly arched up against Santa's stuffing. His legs hung so precariously that it occurred to Deborah that she should go over to them, help to straighten and lift him to a safer position.

"You must want something! Ho, ho, ho!"

Michael shifted against Santa's lap. No, he whispered. He didn't want a thing. Santa shrugged helplessly, looking toward Deborah, obviously amused at the contrast between her two kids.

Deborah saw Santa's look, at least she registered it on some level, but mostly she saw Michael. Santa couldn't hear what she heard, what she already knew to be true: She could hear his inner wishes, loud and clear. His forehead glistened. He was staring at his mother with a morbid intensity that reminded her more than anything of victims she'd seen in the emergency room—a scalded child; a bleeding, broken-legged teenager; an elderly woman dazed after a mild stroke—of the way one's very personhood could be stripped abruptly away and then as suddenly restored by the simple gift of being *seen* by someone, by feeling a touch of a hand or catching sight of a small smile, or even, under the best of circumstances, feeling the calming weight of another person leaning in with sincere caring, in validation of one's very breathing.

He glared across the room at her, panting in the unzipped parka he'd still failed to remove. He didn't want anything, that's what he'd told Santa. But his stare said something else, told how much he wanted just one thing. She had given him the first measure of peace he'd ever had. He feared the loss of it. All he'd known in his short life was change.

It was his mother that he wanted, guaranteed, now and forever. For Christmas, and at Christmas, and every day thereafter. Nothing more, nothing less.

Some things are too tough to say aloud. Surely Santa would understand and know what to bring this little boy.

Elizabeth, next to Deborah, began quietly to cry. It was hard not to join her, smiling through tears. In fact, it was impossible. Even Santa's eyes seemed to glisten a little more brightly.

On the way out of the building, neatly tucked into their jackets, clutching the coloring books and red-striped candy canes Santa's Helpers had tucked in their hands, the children paused to say good-bye to Ada and Whit. Liz Glennen shrugged a tentative yes when Deborah asked if she thought the boys might get together. All in all, victory.

There had been a cost, and they had paid it in full. It couldn't get much sweeter than this.

Later that night, just after ten-thirty, when the gibbous moon had painted herself huge and glowing against the pinprick lights made by millions of stars, Martin Dunn maneuvered the baby carriage off Collins Lane and down Squid Row, not eager to bring little Shane back home even now that he'd been strollered into sleep. The toddler's tears had dried nearly an hour before, but Martin walked on, not tired and yet not awake, thoughts totally at bay. His footsteps were quiet as whispers on the concrete pavement. He'd walked steadily for more than an hour and a half, and every joint in his legs would probably protest in the morning, but the night was more beautiful than any night had ever been. It was crisp and cold, and though the sky was free of clouds, the promise of snow smelled like tin foil in the air.

He was free of dishonesty and always had been; he'd never once in his life been swayed from the desire to behave according to his duty, even when the Lord had thought to test him. Any mistakes he had made, well, they had been natural mistakes for a man. The Lord would understand.

He had always been willing to endure any test, he truly had, and he had loved his family and his neighbors as best he could. But tonight, oh, the air was so rich with the scent of death freezing its cold fingers on all that bloomed so heartily all summer long, and the pale grass everywhere seemed to glow in the moonlight. He was alive! He was alive! *I don't want to die,* Martin thought suddenly, passionately. *I want to live forever!*

And so he walked on and on, from Peconic Avenue down and across to the old factory and on until he found himself back again on Main Street, where each of the big, beautiful houses cast its eyes upon him. Instead of telling him he didn't belong—and he did, despite what those reflections appeared to be saying—tonight the gaze of each window was cheery and approving, as if the estates had been awaiting his return. He had a right to be here. He didn't have to skulk down the street just because he wasn't basking in the spoils of a life devoted to capitalism. He belonged here as much as anyone: Dunns had lived on Squid Row ever since the late 1700s. It wasn't until his grandfather sold their home at the corner of Main and what was then Hunting's Hill that the Dunns had started slipping from village street to back street in such consistent retreat. Of course, Martin's older brother Eric had managed to dance his way back from irrelevance to one of the more elegantly understated mansions in Sagaponack, but Martin didn't quite fathom how this had happened. How had he managed to return himself to the grandeur of his heritage without appearing to break a sweat? When Martin thought about it, it usually seemed as if every move Eric had made had been blessed and every tiny step he himself had attempted had been blocked or thwarted by another test from the Lord. And yet, tonight, inexplicably, such injustice failed to matter. No bitterness marred his vision.

Every so often he could hear the startled scurry of a squirrel or red fox, or even the bark of a dog alerting its master to Martin's presence. The wind was cold and cruel, but to Martin it blew little puffs of sea air straight down Main Street from the wharf, caressing his face, caressing his neck, stroking his collarbone at the point where his shirt could no longer button, slipping down gently to brush across his heart. "Jack," he whispered, suddenly. "Jack." He stopped, forgetting the stroller, the sleeping foster child, even the tired bones in his own feet. As his dead son's soul wafted over him, Martin Dunn lifted his arms wide and up, so that his heart stretched forward in his chest. *If this is joy,* he thought, knowing that it was, and then he shouted gruffly, as if chastising one of his employees, "If this is joy," Martin Dunn shouted, "give me more!"

The ensuing silence was louder than his voice had ever been, and then a dog began to bark, and then another. A window lifted, and a sleepy voice yelled, "Who's there? Who's there?"

Shane, who had heard so much more and so much louder in his brief life, did not stir. Martin seized the handles of the stroller and began to push, shoulders shifting forward and head lower. The wind was making his eyes water. He'd probably sprained a toe, walking so far. Every bone in his feet ached like the devil, every single one.

PART II

12

DEBORAH'S parents had decided to remain in their Philadelphia suburb for their postemployment lives. Her father had already retired; her mother, for whatever reason, seemed unable to stop working and still made daily visits to the hospital, although her hours were severely curtailed.

Deborah's sister, Michele, was finishing up her doctoral work in psychology; she and her husband, Sam, had recently bought a home in Radnor, the town just south of the one the girls had grown up in. Sam managed money for a small group of wealthy investors, a job that made him alternately benevolent and unbearable. Deborah didn't like him; in fact, she couldn't quite fathom what had drawn her younger sister to him.

Up until this summer, it had generally been the four Philadelphians who'd shared a car up through New Jersey and across Staten Island to visit for major holidays. Deborah and Chris would rent a propane stove and a huge pot from the Seafood Shop in Wainscott each Fourth of July weekend. They'd take all the fixings for a clambake out to Albert's Landing and have a wonderful feast, then sit back in their beach chairs to watch the Devon Yacht Club fireworks, sated with clams, lobster, and corn. With so many grown-ups, the kids had been easy to handle at the beach. Even Michael, between his mother and his grandfather, had been able to sit through the fireworks without barking in fear.

This year, Michele had felt too sick to travel; her morning sickness seemed worse than Deborah's had been, and when Deborah tried to cajole her sister into attempting the trip, Michele only sniffed down the phone line before saying, "For country fireworks, they're pretty nice, but it's hardly worth driving five hours leaning out the windows to vomit."

Things had been so peaceful since Christmas, six months now; why shouldn't this trip be a pleasure? They had come through the other side of a long, difficult period, had proven themselves to have flexibility in the face of excitement and stability in the face of change. Chris had encouraged the trip. Even though he had to work, he felt the rest of them should be able to enjoy the holiday. Surely, even without his authoritative presence, the Lathams could risk taking their family show on the road.

Now, at nine o'clock in the morning, as their mother began to negotiate the rigors of the Belt Parkway, Caroline slumped in the front passenger's seat, her black hair curling down the door and in through the handle. Michael, in the back, was kicking his sneakered feet rhythmically, skewering his sister's spine. Caroline slumped further forward and to the right, sighing loudly, glancing over at her mother, who couldn't have been less aware.

Outside, car after car sped past theirs, commuters in T-shirts and those in suits, women with cellular phones tucked between bent head and shoulder. Deborah stared at the on-off flicker of brake lights on the car in front of hers, teeth clenched, hands tightly holding the wheel.

"Mom." The word exploded forth on the wings of a weary sigh.

"Not now, Caro sweet. Give me a minute."

"Mom. Mom. He's kicking me." Caroline's voice raised itself from sigh to whine and back. "He's kicking me, make him stop. Mom."

"Cut it out, both of you. Give me a minute, please, I'm serious."

His voice came sweetly from the backseat. "Momma?"

"Yes?"

"Are we almost there?"

She chuckled. "Not even halfway, Mickle Pickle. It's a long trip."

He kicked the seat roughly. "Watch it, Honey," she said. "That makes it hard for me to drive."

"I like to be home," he said, kicking again. "I don't like it there."

She decided to ignore his feet. "You haven't been there," she said. "Not since last summer. Remember their big yard? That's where Mommy and Michele used to play. And the swing set? It's just like ours. You'll have fun."

"I want a dog," he said abruptly.

She laughed. When she glanced back over her shoulder to grin at him, her eyes slipped past Caro's expression; the little girl's eyes were wary, her left fist clenched on the armrest, her right hand clutching the door handle.

"A dog? What brought that on?"

"Can I have a dog? Can I?" His voice was high and shrill.

Caro spoke softly. "I'm scared of Scupper," she said.

"Ada's dog? That little thing?" Deborah asked. "Why?"

Caroline shrugged, shifting to stare out the window. "I just am, that's all."

"Well, then," Deborah began. The traffic was growing thicker and far more challenging now that they were on the Belt Parkway. Perhaps a full minute had gone by before she realized she'd not finished her sentence.

She'd been thinking about Rapunzel, a big-eyed cocker spaniel that she and Michele had seen at an animal shelter with a friend's parents. Lydia and Bud flatly refused to entertain the notion of bringing Rapunzel home; they'd seen too many dog-bitten children in the emergency room, they said. Discussion over. Placid Michele had merely shrugged and given in; it was her tendency to avoid fighting City Hall at all cost. But Deborah had resisted, as usual.

She'd been twelve at the time and on the verge of young adulthood, and she remembered that she had believed most sincerely in those years that there was little she didn't know or understand about human nature. She felt herself worldly-wise and poorly used by her parents, an unpaid meal-maker and Michele-watcher, and she had taken it as hardly honest when her parents stated unsympathetically that taking care of one another was what people in families did, no matter their ages. She had wanted a dog to take care of—just a dog, not a sister—and she had wanted beyond anything to defy them. She would have bathed Rapunzel and fed him and walked him, all with fierce devotion.

She was capable of bottomless devotion, even back then, and so was little Michael, she knew. Silently, she resolved to find him the dog he wanted.

Just then, he kicked the back of Caroline's seat, hard. She shot forward with an abrupt thrust. The seat belt caught her, less than a foot from the front glass. Caroline's neck snapped up and back. "Oh!" she exclaimed.

"Michael! Stop that!" Deborah's tone was sharp. In the rearview mirror, she could see on his face an expression she hadn't seen for months, perhaps not since the previous fall. His lips were set in a tight line, and his glittery eyes were disingenuously wide. A flush was rising, visibly, up his cheeks, and when she glanced again, he had begun to smile. His entire torso seemed to lift, excited, from the seat, as if he might fly forward, released from his seat belt to scratch and claw at his sister with malicious pleasure. "Don't!" Deborah shouted.

He smiled at her in the mirror, grinned really, as if she'd misunderstood him. He stayed forward, however, not settling back in his seat. He seemed to grow taller and more purposeful, his spine lengthening. "I didn't do anything," he said easily. If he'd sounded resentful, or sulky, she'd have known he had kicked the seat on purpose. This way, it was impossible to be sure.

The traffic on either side was relentless, as if she might be assaulted, scraped, or overtaken by any car that passed. Even with her windows up, she could hear music blaring, then fading, from a succession of car radios.

Caroline faced forward, staring out the window without expression. She was cross-legged on the seat, her skinny legs white against the beige upholstery. When they'd bought the car, the salesman had warned them that beige was terrible with kids; it showed dirt and stained easily. The salesman had turned out to be right. When Deborah had Mina or Elizabeth Bloom in the car, she always threw a towel over the seat. Most of the juice and ground-in cookie and tar from sneaker bottoms would never come out, not even for a far more diligent domestic.

Caroline covered her ears.

Deborah reached over to pat her daughter's thigh, eyes still focused tensely on the road. "You okay, Caro Banana?"

Caroline shrugged, not even smiling at the baby nickname. She was crying, Deborah realized, little beads feathering from the edges of her eyes and flattening along the pale surface of her cheeks. Caroline shook her head vigorously, turning toward the side window. She drew her knees up to her chest and wrapped her arms around them. Her legs were dotted with scratched mosquito bites and patches of purple bruising, a child's badge of summer.

"Caro, Honey, what is it? Should I pull over?" Even saying the words frightened Deborah; until they were over the Verrazano Bridge, she doubted she'd actually have the courage to switch lanes, much less pull off the road.

"I want a dog," Michael said.

Caro's left shoulder shrugged higher. Her torso twisted toward the window, so that not even a glimpse of profile was visible when Deborah stole another quick glance her way. Around them, horns honked, mufflers failed, radios blared. Deborah could feel sweat gathering underneath her bra and down her belly, soaking into her T-shirt.

"A dog, Momma. Can I have a dog? I want a dog."

"Not now, Michael," she said.

"Momma. I want a . . ."

"Hush, Michael. I'm driving."

"Mom."

"One more word from you, Young Man, and all discussion of a dog will be over. That's final."

In the rearview mirror, framing Michael's martyred face, a grubby van loomed ominously. She tapped on her brakes to warn the other driver to slow down. He honked, leaning on his horn for an interminable stretch.

"Shit," she muttered. "Oh, shit."

Caroline emitted a sob, unsuppressed—a gulping, explosive sound. It startled Deborah, who turned in sharp dismay, hardly realizing that she was pulling the wheel to the right at the same time. The car in the next lane honked wildly, its driver rolling down his window to yell an obscenity. Caroline turned back to face forward, sinking low on her seat. Deborah hit the brakes again, knowing she was reacting badly, knowing even before it happened that she was about to be hit from behind.

Her heart pounded. Her breath was utterly tight, stuck in her throat. She would have closed her eyes as the impact came, but when it failed to—when all she heard was another series of indignant honks—she took advantage of a break in traffic to swing into the right lane and off the exit ramp.

She wasn't up for this. Something had slipped out of place, some part of the gear structure that had kept them all working so peacefully since last December. On a side street, after pulling into a bus stop on the wrong side of the road, she switched off the ignition and sat, feeling her heart pounding far too fast, trying desperately to get her breath. She shut her eyes, took in another deep breath and let it out. After the last few minutes, the street noise around them sounded quiet and friendly. She could feel her pulse beginning to even out.

Caro sighed.

Michael said nothing.

Silence. Deborah's eyes closed again. Blessedly, there was nothing to hear. She breathed out, softly, and then she heard it, a thud, and then again, and then that soft, rhythmic kicking began again. *Thud. Thud. Thud.*

"Michael."

"Michael!! Mom, make him stop!"

"Michael. Stop it now."

Thud. Thud. Thud.

"Mom!! Mom!! He stinks! Michael pooped his pants!!! Make him stop kicking me!! Mom!!"

Nosing toward her, the brakes of a city bus squealed in protest. The driver honked, leaning hard on his horn. As she scrambled to turn the keys, Caroline screamed again. "Momma! Look at him! Oh, gross! Look at him!"

Without turning, she already knew what her son had done, could smell his poop and feel the pleasure he had taken in smearing it; whether it was on the window, the seat, or on himself, she almost didn't care. *They'd been going along so beautifully; why had she dreamed of altering the easy rhythm they'd been enjoying? What kind of a fool would take such risks?*

"Momma! Momma!" Caroline screamed. The bus driver leaned on his horn.

If she turned, Deborah knew, she would see Michael grinning, but she wasn't going to look. She wasn't. Windows all the way down, and as fast as possible, she was heading home.

13

CHRIS LATHAM spent a great deal of time staring into the mouths of members of all of Sag Harbor's societal castes; in his sixteen years of practice he'd bonded and bridged and extracted something from nearly every jaw that had passed through the village. He was proficient at his job, and his hands were gentle. He had a way of setting his patients at ease with mild, sweet jabs of humor that almost always left even the shakiest dental patient chuckling as the saliva extractor began to gurgle. Occasionally, Chris would find himself musing lovingly over a particularly white and evenly spaced set of teeth, and even more rarely, he'd be drawn up into a kind of yearning for one of his more attractive patients, but such mild breaches of his affection for Deborah rarely lasted more than a few weeks and had never amounted to more than a pleasurable period of flirtation. Like fever, his fantasies grew humid and slightly painful, peaking in intensity just before the flush faded utterly away.

Chris often occupied the disengaged areas of his brain in refining his theory of the local caste system, all the while making molds of teeth, replacing crowns, filling cavities, irrigating gums, and, of course, staring out his picture window at the extraordinary view of the harbor below. Sailboats darted back and forth, motorboats zipped under the bridge toward the mild waters of the open bay, and every so often a pair of deer stepped gracefully across his parking lot. Chris's mind operated on two tracks as his hands pried an elderly woman's jaw open to examine more closely a potentially lethal leukoplakia. If she knew what he was looking at, her jaw would probably open so wide she'd never get to close it again. Poor Mrs. Dunn.

Chris figured there were four kinds of people in the Harbor these days. Basically, there were the "real people," those whose families had lived in the village since forever, who traced their roots back to the earliest settlers, and who continued to do variations of the work their families had always done: blacksmiths becoming plumbers; farmers becoming building contractors; fishermen becoming electricians; factory workers becoming irrigation installers. White and black; Presbyterian, Episcopalian, Methodist, Catholic, and Jewish—each subset maintained its own private world, yet the rhythms of each group's daily life were entirely in synch with those of the others. These folks hadn't changed in hundreds of years, or so they believed, but the world had changed around them, and lots of them didn't like that at all.

Chris didn't exactly agree that the locals hadn't changed: They'd gotten angrier in the past decade, even as they'd come to like how their lives were being improved by all the money the summer people shot at them so carelessly. What Chris thought was that lots of the locals had stopped liking the way they lived. It was a constant challenge, not to back down in the face of the aggressors. The summer people even drove that way, forcing left-hand turns into oncoming traffic, cars nosing five or six feet past a stop sign, for no reason, he suspected, except to make it clear that they could. One August morning, on Main Street, a Range Rover had backed straight out of a parking space and into Chris's car as he'd been driving past. The driver emerged in the most blasé manner, overweight and underdressed, but still supremely confident, utterly sure he was in control. He hadn't apologized, hadn't allowed Chris to say a word. "Hey Man," he'd interrupted. "No problem. Take this."

And he'd reached into the back pocket of his linen shorts, removed a money clip, and counted out ten hundred-dollar bills. He hadn't even looked Chris in the face, or extended his plump hand, or touched the grimy visor of his baseball cap—not the slightest gesture. He hadn't even checked for damage to his own vehicle. Worse, Chris had taken the money. He'd gotten back into his car and counted the hundreds again, hardly able to believe their number. The scratch on the passenger door wouldn't cost ten dollars in touch-up paint to fix, even a fool could see that. As he sat there, stunned, cars behind him began to honk. The driver of the Range Rover stuck his head out the window of his car and yelled, "Hey Man, get a move on, would you?"

Later, Chris wished he'd thrown the money on the ground and summoned a cop. He just hadn't had the presence of mind, as if the fat man's ability to end discussion served as a clamp cutting off any movement in his own synapses.

The summer people dressed so well and had such large parties and great cars, and they seemed to smile all the time. (Chris had worked on a number of those smiles and could attest to the fact that a great deal was invested in creating and maintaining those perfect teeth.) It was hard for Chris and his old friends not to compare themselves to these all-that-money-can-buy others. It was hard not to feel they were the losers, not because they actually were, but because the out-of-towners didn't even seem to see them, as if they weren't worthy of notice.

If anything, the summer people believed the locals were natives, in the classic sense of the word. To a Wall Street capitalist used to having his every desire immediately gratified, the plumber was a primitive being. Every time the plumber squatted down on his heavy haunches to squeeze his torso under the kitchen sink, the capitalist suppressed a smile, already fabricating the story of how the plumber's crack had revealed itself as he pressed forward and out of his faded blue jeans, so eager to find and repair the faucet leak. What they didn't know, but Chris did, was that Gus Emerson, the plumber, was chuckling to himself as well, hardly able to believe that this thousand-dollar-an-hour investor couldn't look under his own sink and tighten the valve himself. Why, Gus didn't even need a wrench for this job, but he'd thrust himself forward under the sink to cover the fact that he wasn't using it; otherwise, the poor city idiot would think Gus wasn't doing the job properly.

All the same, Gus, like Chris and almost everyone else, was jealous of the city people. Not because of the money they had, but because of the way they were so intent on enjoying their lives. When the first Bohemians came out to live—painters, poets, musicians—nobody in the village of Sag Harbor had envied them. They'd not altered the order of things. Gus could remember two lady writers who'd shared one of the Bulova houses back in the early seventies and called Dunn's because they couldn't get their tub to drain. Martin had sent him over. There'd only been one bedroom in that place, but Gus hadn't let that put him off the job. Those ladies were so wispy and sweet. He told himself they probably shared the bedroom to save money. They offered him tea, and he hadn't even let a smile cross his lips at the thought of drinking it.

When he handed them the bill, one of them, the shorter one, asked if he'd be interested in a painting by a friend of theirs, a guy named Kooning, and Gus had thought, *oh why the hell not,* and taken the ugly thing in exchange for the new drain filter, even though he knew Martin would dock him the money. Ellie had been a little angry about it. He'd lost that painting of course—stored in the attic, it disappeared like a leather glove—and when it turned out it could have been the making of them, Ellie had just shrugged her shoulders.

The Bohemians had looked like everybody else, though. They dressed as if clothes were for coverage. They weren't beautiful, and they were fairly quiet, and most of them were as intent on the regular rigors of their work as the locals were on theirs. It wasn't until later, maybe the last decade or so, that the city people changed, became mysteriously beautiful and so focused on their own pleasure that they destroyed the rhythms of daily life.

Once, when Chris and Deborah had gone out to dinner in the village, she'd put down her menu and asked the waiter for flounder. Chris had started laughing.

"What?" Deborah had asked, half defensively, half ready to be amused. "What is it?"

"Flounder," he'd said, shaking his head back and forth. There were gray streaks in his eyebrows, made visible by the romantic yellow of the candle flame. "It's junk fish to us. It's what we ate to survive. When there was nothing else, there was always flounder. It's hard to believe anybody would charge seventeen dollars for a plate of it."

"Well, it's what I want."

"Get it, then," he'd said neutrally. "What's the difference? It's just funny to me, that's all."

The restaurants catered to the city people in every way, serving wines and appetizers and desserts the locals would never think to demand. The boutiques on Main Street carried their preferences in clothing. "You know," Cynthia Stall had once confided as Chris fastened the paper bib around her neck, "sometimes I see someone on the street dressed so cool, and maybe six months later I see the same shoes or pants in a magazine. I can't figure out how they keep ahead of things like that."

Cynthia had been so beautiful herself, back in high school, that she could have worn a green plastic trash bag and stopped traffic. He remembered that she'd refused to wear panty hose when all the other girls switched from garter belts and stockings. She'd said she loved the way she felt when she wore them, and he'd never forgotten that. It was, he supposed, the most intimate fact he knew about any woman other than his wife, and occasionally, even now, without his intending it, he couldn't help musing about the mystery of it.

He hadn't known what to say when Cynthia confessed to feeling over-whelmed by the city people. Nevertheless, even he could tell that they held onto their looks while so many of his high school friends had failed to do so. He didn't know how that had happened. So many of the girls he'd known had grown pale and doughy; the boys had widened and coars-ened—if they hadn't drowned like Cal Stewart and Skippy Martin, or turned into a drunk like the Hughes kid, or crashed into a tree like Jack Dunn, or simply disappeared off the planet like Des Dunn. In truth, he didn't mind that Des had gone AWOL from Sag Harbor life; the very thought of his presence outside the bank or at the Corner Bar or in this office itself, oh, such an idea was unthinkable. But now here was Des Dunn's mother in the chair this morning, and he couldn't bear to break more bad news to such a chronically unblessed woman.

"Okay, Mrs. Dunn, you can spit," Chris said. "I'll be back in a moment." He was worried about her. In specific, he was bothered by a patch of wavy lines on the back of her tongue, a rare manifestation that in this particular presentation was likely to mean only one thing. He hated to believe it. Chris had known the entire Dunn family his whole life, not just Martin and Alice but Eric's family also. He'd known Jack really well; they'd played baseball and ice-skated and hung out together since elementary school.

Chris could only imagine what Alice Dunn had been through: one son in and out of jail and then disappeared, the other popped out of a convertible into a tree on his way home from a party the night of high school graduation. And on top of everything, Alice was married to Mar-tin. He hated to bring bad news to someone who'd already endured so much. He knew it was unethical to be silent; he knew exactly what to say under these circumstances and had said such things several dozen times before. Yet he couldn't bring himself to speak.

How could she possibly have these symptoms? As much as he dis-liked Martin, he knew him to be an upstanding, righteous man, or at least he believed him to be. And Alice herself was hardly a likely candi-date for drug use or extramarital sex or just about any risky behavior. It was fairly unthinkable and even more difficult to consider verbalizing. Chris didn't want to speak the words himself, couldn't bear to be the person to inform Alice Dunn that such a curse had come upon her.

He washed his hands again, as if that had been why he'd walked into the lab. Mrs. Dunn was resting back in the chair, hands folded peacefully across her belly, watery eyes focused on the gay sails of the boats fluttering out in the harbor. "It's something, isn't it, that view?"

"Yes," she said, and the grateful way she turned those pale eyes toward his made him certain he would not be able to say the words it was so clearly his job—and responsibility—to utter. Her skin was thin as crepe and soft to touch, and the way it folded down upon itself on the way into the collar of her flowered dress made him yearn to brush a finger along her neck. His own mother would be a good fifteen years older than Mrs. Dunn, he thought.

"That'll be it," he said, hating himself. "You might stop in one day next week, let me take a second look at the bonding."

"Thank you, Doctor," she said, and he reached down with his two hands in order to help her to standing.

"You're welcome," he said.

Alice Dunn looked down, smoothing her dress over her belly. "Give my best to your wife," she said, and she backed out of the room, eyes locked upon his in gratitude.

Deborah, of course, was a member of the third class of Sag Harbor citizens, what he and Will called year-round summer people. She'd moved out from the city some fifteen years before to focus on her photography and live, as she'd called it, "in the country." Now Deborah was a lapsed photographer at best, but she was a tireless member of the community. As much as he loved her, Chris knew that it was people like Deborah who'd probably done the most to destroy the fabric of life in Sag Harbor, imposing their city values seven days a week, twelve months a year. Chris knew that while the summer people might think he'd married up, the locals definitely believed the opposite. In their view, the year-round summer folk simply didn't get it, and their ignorance was making the village unbearable for all.

The fourth group of Sag Harborites, the immigrant population, well, Chris himself didn't pay much heed to people who complained they were taking jobs away from locals. The way the want ads in the newspapers looked to him, there were too many jobs to be filled, not too few. Column after column of advertising listed requests for housecleaning, baby-sitting, and landscaping work. He'd heard people complain that the foreigners strained the capacities of the food pantries in winter, when there was little work and money was tight. He hated to think of people in need. Back when he was young, everyone had pitched in so unquestioningly that such situations rarely arose. That was how the Gastons had taken him in; Chris saw giving to others as the only way he could repay that debt, and so he and Deborah donated food to the Whalers' Church weekly. In a way, he supposed that adopting Michael went to pay down his debt as well.

Chris walked down the hall to the bathroom, latched the door, and stood against it.

Then there were the day-trippers, of course, but they didn't count. Like the ranch houses that dotted the village, they were omnipresent and yet hardly worth a moment's consideration. Nevertheless, they brought in a great deal of money, spending freely in the gift shops, the restaurants, and the clothing stores. One had to have them, he supposed, although they rarely affected his life. Once every two or three years, someone slipped on Main Street and broke a tooth. If he wasn't too busy, he'd try to fit the person in, but those bills often went unpaid and he frankly didn't need the business. In the long run, he preferred not to acknowledge the true out-of-towners.

As he reentered the examination room, Rosemary bustled in to prepare for the next patient, efficiently whisking away the tools used on Mrs. Dunn, replacing her paper cup, wiping down the tray. She was smiling, her teeth the identical color of her white nurse's uniform, bright and slightly shiny. She was always smiling, he reflected, even when she thought she was alone.

"You're awful quiet today," she said, brushing past him into the lab.

He didn't move from the doorway, just shrugged his shoulders, which of course she couldn't see. She opened and closed drawers rapidly.

"You okay?" she asked, not looking up from her search. Whatever she was searching for wasn't in the lower cabinets, and now she stood, raising herself up onto tiptoes to try to reach the upper shelves. With her fleshy arms raised that way, he could see the mottled surface of her thighs: dimpled, veined, the imperfections visible even through her heavy stockings. He felt sorry for her, for the first time ever, despite her short, plump, cheerful nature and the way nothing ever fazed her—not her difficult marriage, her troubled adolescent children, her lonely efforts to forestall aging at the gym and at the Corner Bar. Rosemary Leahey had been sweet and perky at twenty-five, when she'd first come to work for him. She was just over forty now, struggling uphill every year and for what? He wondered. To find out what Mrs. Dunn shortly would, that the husband who'd treated her so badly hadn't simply been contented to live in uneasy, unhappy equilibrium?

There was something so appalling about the idea that self-righteous Martin Dunn had a seedy side. Chris almost couldn't bring his brain around to the notion. Why, if upright Martin Dunn could betray his wife and all his well-mouthed values, well, it was beyond hypocritical. Despite the many times Chris had found himself attracted to another woman, this chasm was one he hadn't dreamed of crossing, not seriously. He didn't consider monogamy to be a subject of pride. Unlike Martin, he'd never dream of flaunting his code of honor.

Very rarely did Chris Latham wish his father were still alive, that he might turn to his dad and feel the pleasure of allowing himself to go weak. Right now he would love to let his guard down just long enough to find out how he was supposed to feel. There was an entirely decadent side to life he had only rarely been invited to share with other men, and it confused him and titillated him and relieved him all at once.

He loved his life, his wife, his family. He so truly did. He even loved Rosemary Leahey and Alice Dunn and the rest. In truth, he wished them all happiness, the way he had long ago determined he wanted it himself. Sorrow and loneliness had given him no hidden pleasure. No surprise that he had sought contentment ever since; the joy was that he'd been able to find it. Deborah said he was lucky. Others who knew him and cared about him—Rosemary, Will—echoed the sentiment.

It wasn't luck; it was diligence. He worked hard at the arrangement of his life, and he could be extremely patient. Look how long he had waited for the right woman with whom to make his family. He'd been a determined boy, he knew, and he was very much a focused man. He didn't ask at random, and his needs didn't change. He only rarely made mistakes; recently he had realized that every time he moved impulsively, he lived to regret the gesture wholeheartedly.

Christopher Latham asked only a peaceful life: little change, few surprises, rare adventures. He needed his days to move naturally and predictably; he required it. He would do whatever was necessary to maintain the pace.

In the long run, he was sure, he would get his way.

"Throw me the shovel," Michael yelled, and Caroline chucked it up in the air and across to him. It was just past one o'clock on that same afternoon, and they were home again, cleaned up, and unpacked. There had been no damage to the car, only filth on Michael. Deborah supposed she had overreacted, but she didn't care. She was just so glad to be home again.

Mina was coming to join them shortly. For now, the children were digging their way under the deck, lifting wedges of dirt and grass out of the ground and placing them in a neat row, for replacing later, once the game was over. They were troweling to Australia, united in comfortable play. If anything, they were playing far more cooperatively than usual.

Deborah had the other shovel, the big one. She was moving yarrow plants into a big clump over by the swing set, so that the area up by the house could be filled with the twenty lavender plants she'd just purchased in town. It was too late by half for planting, but she thought if she watered every single morning, she might be able to give the lavender a decent start in life. They'd all been digging for half an hour already; she didn't care what the kids were doing, even though Mina moved to stop them when she first arrived. "It's the back side of the deck," Deborah assured her. "Nobody sees it. And they're having so much fun."

Mina seemed perfectly pleased to jump into the spirit of things. She slipped her blue flip-flops off and started to dig with a plastic beach shovel, pouring water wherever Caroline directed her to. Michael's little face shone with perspiration; the tight set of his jaw lifted his cheekbones and narrowed his eyes. Through the even lines of his teeth, the very tip of his tongue was visible, pressing stubbornly forward. Caroline, too, seemed to concentrate completely; neither child looked up when Deborah dragged the heavy green hose directly past them.

Once the yarrow was replanted, Deborah set a hose on the area, flooding it. Planting the lavender was a snap; the entire bed was already dug up and so it was just a matter of scooping piles of moist soil with her gloved hands, inhaling deeply to breathe in the sweet aroma and pressing firmly down with her palms to set the silver-stemmed bushes in place. She was done. But the July day was so cool and beautiful, so springlike, that eating lunch outside was required.

"Tuna fish, that's the answer!" Deborah said gaily, and when nobody protested, she went inside to begin preparing sandwiches.

She loaded a tray with tuna salad, bread, lettuce and tomato, and a pitcher of lemon slices in ice water. Pushing the screen door open with her foot, she called, "Come on, guys! Let's get to it!"

They came running, and when Mina insisted they go inside to wash their hands, neither child fussed at all. "Can I do that?" Mina asked. "Let me make the sandwiches."

"Okay, fine. I'll pour."

They worked in silence for just a minute, comfortable with one another, as familiar as family. Mina said quietly, "I wanted to tell you, to say, that I think he's doing so well. You must feel so good about what's happened. What happened today means nothing. All children have fights. Just like Viorica says."

"I hope so. I think so. I do," Deborah said. "I really do. Besides, it wasn't really the fight that threw me. I could have handled that. The driving was harder than I thought it would be."

Mina chuckled.

"And you," Deborah said. "You've been so helpful, so here for us. Coming over today like this, I can't thank you enough."

Mina shrugged. When her shoulders moved up, her blouse pulled at its buttons, gaping enough to reveal the small pink bow on her white nylon brassiere. She was too young to have skin that papered along the breastbone the way hers did. Each time Deborah noticed such an overt manifestation of the difficulties Mina had undergone, she felt a surge of admiration for the younger woman. She herself could never have survived what Mina had been through, she was certain of it.

"I've done nothing," Mina said. "He prefers Viorica to me. But I can see he's turned the corner for good. I can see it. Earlier, at Christmas, I hoped you were right. I didn't believe. Not even when your husband said he thought Michael was calming down."

"He does think so, doesn't he?"

Mina nodded. "Yes, I think so. But doesn't he tell you?"

Several flies danced over the tuna fish, the low buzz of their humming a counterpoint to Deborah's swift nod.

Mina cut a sandwich in half and then again in quarters. She moved that plate across the red picnic table and began to reach for a second plate. As she reached, her head brushed against a branch that hung too low, setting the leaves fluttering. "Oh!"

"Oh!" Deborah cried in response. "Are you okay?"

"Oh! Yes, I'm fine. It surprised me!"

They were silent. Inside, Caroline's giggle rose, high and friendly. Michael's voice, low and serious, answered.

"I still can't quite, I still don't really . . . ," Deborah began. As her voice trailed off, she picked up a paper napkin, unfolded it, and began to scrub at a small offering of gray bird doo at the edge of the table.

Mina said, "I believe it now. Honestly. Sometimes one can only be grateful, not question how things happen."

"I know, I know. I try to tell myself it isn't fragile, that it will only get better. But I still don't sleep, not always, not even when he does. And when things happen the way they did today, I have trouble reminding myself that all kids are bad sometimes. I have trouble remembering that not every problem is an indication of something horrible. I can't shake it, I guess. This fear."

"I don't feel it. Not anymore," Mina said stoutly, staring into her employer's eyes with a disarming level of confidence.

"Honestly?"

"Yes."

The phone began to ring. Deborah stood. A blue jay, in the tree above, gave a sneering call. "I'll get it," she said. "You start the kids, okay?"

Mina's nod, sturdy and calm, made the world feel predictable and right.

It was Lydia, on the phone, calling to check in, an unusually maternal action. It must have been quiet at the hospital. Deborah, atypically, began to complain, as if the relief of Mina trusting in Michael's new state gave his mother the freedom to say things aloud she'd never voiced before. "Oh, it's Michael, he's outgrowing everything," she complained complacently. "Chris will freak when he sees how much I've been spending."

"But why aren't you coming?" Lydia asked. "Your father didn't explain."

"Oh," said Deborah. "It's complicated. The traffic was terrible. We had car trouble. I mean, my car started to overheat, and when I pulled over, well, I parked in a bus stop. I didn't see. The sign. And the car was, well, I couldn't, by then." She was going on too long; she couldn't stop herself, like a dog who keeps digging at a hole long after the mole has disappeared. The dirt from the shovel handle colored the moisture on her palms; when droplets fell to the table, they were a pale, translucent gray. She had forgotten, she realized, to wash her hands.

"And you," Lydia said. "Now that the project of the boy is turning into regular life? When will you get back to work?"

Her mother could be so oblivious, thank God.

"I don't know, Mom. I can't imagine why you think I need to hurry. They're so little, still. I like being home with them."

"Well, Dear, I simply wondered, had the thought occurred to you that you might start taking your pictures again? I'm only asking. I'm only curious."

Amazing how quickly irritation could surface, even when she was doing her best to remain calm. Her mother was a button-pushing expert.

She tried not to let her voice rise, but the effort was futile. "Really, Mom. I'm perfectly contented! Not everyone needs to be running out to find meaning in the greater world. This is what I do. This is what I want to do! I'm happy taking care of them!"

Her mother sighed, a long, low exhalation that was all the more audible for the way it rounded down the telephone wire. "You know," Lydia said, "when you were little, you and Michele, I assumed if I was happy and satisfied, you would be, too. I thought you would learn from my example."

"But I did, Mom. I did. I want different things, that's all. I like my life the way it is. Especially now. You made your choices, I make mine."

"The problem is," Lydia continued, as if her daughter hadn't spoken, "that I never did feel satisfied enough with what I was doing, with how I was living. I guess I was never satisfied enough to feel sure the price was worth it."

"What price?"

The silence lengthened. Outside, the children's voices were suddenly audible, Michael's tone challenging and a little too loud, but nothing to worry about. Mina was out there, after all, and Mina felt sure it would all be okay. Mina was Romanian, like Michael, and she had seen him all along. If she felt today's incident was a tempest in a teapot, then surely it was.

Lydia seemed to be gathering her thoughts. "I don't know," she began eventually, her voice drifting.

"Mom? Didn't you like what you were doing? Weren't you happy at the hospital? Didn't you like your work?" Deborah asked. "You always seem so sure of yourself."

Lydia didn't answer.

"Mom?"

Lydia's clipped authority returned as swiftly as it had departed. "The appearance of contentment is an art form. Someone said that, it doesn't matter who. It's just a way of mine, a trick I do. It has nothing to do with what I feel, what I'm feeling inside. Amazing how no one ever seems able to tell. Amazing."

Her voice trailed off. Deborah, inexplicably unable to form an answer, knew only that she felt cheated.

Outside, there was a scream, and then a shout. "Deborah," Mina yelled. "Come quickly! Come now! Hurry!"

14

ALICE had been a little inconvenienced by the way she had to wait for Dr. Latham. He'd been over an hour late, and she had even thought of leaving, but now she was glad she had stayed. That nice Chris Latham was such a good dentist, and he never hurt at all. And he'd said he was sorry, he'd had to run home for something.

He had grown up so nicely. Such a pleasant dentist, and he seemed to be a devoted family man, too. As she drove, she ran her tongue over the bonded tooth, enjoying the smooth surface that had replaced a sharp, ragged edge. With no crag to explore for the first time in several days, her tongue settled back for a well-earned rest.

She'd intended to stop at Schiavoni's for a ham steak, but there wasn't a parking space and she didn't feel like pulling around behind Main Street and walking in the back entrance. There was leftover meatloaf in the freezer, and she decided to defrost it in the microwave. Martin would like that, especially with a good helping of mashed potatoes and buttered beans. If he came home, of course. Otherwise, she would probably eat both servings.

On impulse, Alice turned left instead of right at the end of town, heading over the bridge to North Haven. She steered the Buick carefully, watching for any flutter of movement that presaged a deer, and when she came to Long Beach, she pulled in. Earlier today, it had been warm and beautiful, but the temperature had dropped abruptly while she was waiting for Dr. Latham to return from his visit home. Now, at four o'clock, it was chilly, and only a few hardy groups of sweatshirted mothers and toddlers dotted the sand. The beach seemed narrower than normal this year, as if despite a paucity of winter storms, the Northeast wind had succeeded in herding the bay up and overland.

Alice turned off the engine and reached her left hand toward the door, allowing the fingers to drape over the handle, motionless. She didn't have the energy to lift her heavy frame from the driver's seat, couldn't even imagine why she'd thought she wanted to. *What did it matter, a fleeting moment of chill beauty at the beach? In a moment, just a blink of a moment, it would be fall, and she could dream of the humid summer left behind.* Alice closed her eyes, startled to feel water welling out of the inner creases. *Why was she crying?*

That sweet dentist, she told herself. Such a nice boy, a friend of Jack's, and such a pretty wife he had and such lovely children. They'd adopted a little boy, a dark one, from some foreign country. Alice imagined how affectionate their evenings were, what interesting subjects they addressed at the dinner table. Ellie Emerson cleaned their house, and she said Mrs. Latham was finicky about dust and insisted all the clothes be folded just so. Her towels had to be in thirds, not halves, so that no edges showed when the closet door was opened. Ellie said the little boy sometimes scribbled on the walls and that their house was hard to clean. Ellie said the boy was crazier than a three-dollar bill; he was trouble coming as sure as tomorrow's sunrise. Ellie said she thought Chris Latham was a saint.

Hadn't Ellie told her about something that little boy had done, back sometime the previous fall? She hated the boy, said he was the devil incarnate. What was it? Oh, he hit someone at school, Ed Stall's grandson. Was that it? Alice shook her head, as if she'd remember more easily once she joggled her brains around. She didn't pay too much attention, sometimes. Particularly to Ellie.

Ellie Emerson had no forgiveness. Alice hated to think the thought, but there it was. Those were the facts. Alice couldn't pay too much mind to Ellie's harangues about the Lathams. Just the fact that Ellie kept working there long after Gus's business success had made it possible for her to drop most of her clients told Alice all she needed to know. Over the years, Alice had figured out one thing about Ellie Emerson: If she didn't hate something about a person, that person was dead. Sometimes Alice wondered what Ellie Emerson said about her when she wasn't present; most times, she tried not to let her mind wander in such a direction.

She was thinking so hard, she didn't see the woman come up to her window, was startled when she heard the knock. "Mrs. Dunn, is that you? Are you all right?"

"Mrs. Latham!" Alice struggled to sit up higher in the seat, embarrassed at how she'd been caught, eyes shut, slumped over in thought. "I've just come from your husband!"

"I'm sorry to bother you; I just wanted to make sure. We . . . ," and here she nodded down at the sullen-faced five-year-old with her, "were heading back from the bathrooms, not that they're open, as we've discovered, but I saw you, and I, I'm sorry to bother you." Deborah was flushed; was she shy or embarrassed?

"You probably didn't think an old lady like me would be asleep, did you? You thought I'd died here, I bet!" Making such a joke, about herself, was hard to do, and Alice could feel that she was growing as red as Deborah Latham. Mrs. Latham's face twitched, a startled look that made the skin draw tight along her forehead. Alice never had been too skilled at making jokes. Nobody ever had called Alice Dunn funny, at least not to her face.

Deborah Latham was remarkably tall, Alice observed. Up close, she looked more like a giraffe than a woman. As Deborah peered in the window, Alice saw that her eyes were huge, a deep, yellow-speckled green, the color of the bay. Her lips and nose were slim and long. Wisps of pale brown hair blew forward across her cheeks, as if the clip that held her curls had been specifically designed to let a few locks escape. She looked, Alice thought, like the kind of woman who worked at looking like she never worked at looking good.

"And who is this?" Alice asked, gesturing toward the little boy.

Deborah stiffened slightly. "Michael," she said. "Come say hello."

He didn't look up. *Lord, Des had been like that, so unwilling to let anyone in.* "Hello, Michael," she said. Her breath was shallow, and her heart was beating far too fast. "May I . . ."

"Would you? We'd love it!" Deborah said at the same moment, and Alice couldn't tell if she meant it or not, but she wanted so badly to get out of her dented Buick and join them on the beach that she chose to believe the other woman. Mrs. Latham opened the door for her, and she heaved her left leg around and then her right and struggled up from the seat.

"You're fat." Michael said calmly.

Deborah gasped, opening her mouth. Alice couldn't imagine what Deborah might say, and so to be polite, she looked down at the little boy and said, "I know." Her tone was easy and matter-of-fact, purposely so. The moment passed.

Deborah was smiling at Alice delightedly, and Alice felt elated, as if she'd crossed over into the world of Them without effort, a move she'd never have imagined possible. She could tell Deborah liked her, a sensation that made her feel suddenly energized and important. It was a pleasure to listen to Deborah, to feel her words pour out so freely, a gift that easily shortened the manifest distance between them. A few feet away, Caroline and Michael scraped sand into a huge mound with their fingers, working side by side like a married couple no longer needing to exchange verbal information in order to communicate. The little girl had a neat white bandage over her temple. Maybe she got hit with something.

Deborah was saying, "And then, after maybe six months of it, our neighbor Ed Stall . . ."

"My husband went to elementary school with him over at Pierson," Alice interjected.

"Pierson? I thought that was just the high school."

"Oh, no, back years ago, when Martin was growing up, Pierson was the entire school, first through twelfth grade. Actually, it was that way during your husband's time as well."

"I thought Chris had told me everything about Sag Harbor. But I didn't know that," Deborah said. She shook her head back and forth. "I can't imagine this community so small."

"It wasn't that long ago. When my husband was growing up, that whole area over by Brick Kiln Road was just fields. He says those trees were only planted when he was in his teens. That was before I got here, though. Martin, my husband, he says you used to be able to see straight from the ocean to the bay if you stood on the right hills."

"That's odd," Deborah said, shifting slightly. "I'd have thought there were always trees there."

"I know. It seems funny. It seems more natural, with trees, I guess. But the truth is those trees were put there not by God, but by man. At least, according to Martin."

"Amazing."

Alice couldn't take her eyes away from Deborah. If she did, the spell might break, and they'd be strangers again. She liked Deborah, there was something about her that Alice truly liked.

They fell silent, watching the children. Caroline was seated at the very edge of the sand, so that her toes just avoided getting damp each time a wave broke. It was far too cold for her to be getting wet, Alice thought. Michael crouched behind his sister, his haunches so lean they were hardly able to draw the cloth of his shorts taut against his thighs.

"Oh," said Deborah, reembarking on her story. "So Ed Stall never said a word to me, not the entire first year we were living there, and I used to try so hard, I'd smile at him and go out of my way to greet him, and, really, no matter what I did he seemed really unfriendly. And you know his daughter used to date Chris, back in high school?"

"I remember," Alice said, feeling a twisting as if her heart were trying to wring itself dry. "I remember." She couldn't seem to get enough air in; her breath felt shallow.

"Are you okay?" Deborah asked.

"Oh, yes, yes." Alice's right hand fluttered forward. "Go on."

"So I thought, maybe Ed Stall hated me because he wished Cynthia had married Chris, but when I told that to Chris, he laughed like I'd said something completely crazy. So I don't know, I guess Chris and Cynthia weren't such a big item?"

"I don't actually . . . I can't quite . . ."

"I'm sorry," Deborah said. "Of course you wouldn't. I just assume everyone knows everything about everyone."

Alice couldn't tell, it seemed as if Deborah honestly didn't know. "My son," she said. "My son Jack and also Des, my other one, they were both in your husband's class."

Something was odd; she could see that Deborah knew it but couldn't put her finger on what it was. Alice's whole body felt suddenly off, wary, as if they'd gone from being potential friends to utter strangers. How could Deborah Latham possibly not know what had happened to her sons? They were friends of her husband's, close friends.

"Are they still here, your sons?" Deborah asked.

Alice, in the sand, felt almost as if she had been molded there, layer after layer settled like a craftsman's project at the water's edge. Her eyes barely flickered, the glow across her wrinkle-free features wavering not at all as she said, briefly, "No."

Deborah leaned back on her elbows in the sand. She closed her eyes and stretched her belly up, leaning back as if she could lengthen the warmth of summer across her entire body. "It's probably time to go," she said quietly.

Alice didn't hear her; she was too busy wondering why she'd stopped liking Mrs. Latham. Strange how quickly that had happened.

"I should pack them up," Deborah told Alice, her tone regretful. It was hard to tell exactly what it was she was already beginning to miss. "The kids, they're getting tired."

"You have nice children."

Deborah nodded. "Caroline's a breeze. A breeze. Michael, though, he can be difficult sometimes. Today's not been his best day, in fact. He's okay now though." She laughed and added, "I look like a good parent."

Alice took the comment seriously. "I'm sure," she said. "Just look at them."

Caroline and Michael did show to particular advantage in this July light, Caro's earnest features not merely unusual but actually beautiful when she smiled, as she was doing now. Alice wondered about the bandage on her forehead; it looked fresh, and there seemed to be a great deal of swelling, but since the mother didn't mention it, Alice decided not to ask. There was nothing she liked less than a person who asked about topics that were better left unexplored.

And Michael. Now that he wasn't sulking, he was adorable: petite and lithe. Familiar. His nose and mouth and eyes were hardly the same; it was just the way his feelings decorated his features that reminded her so of Des. Expressions fluttered over his face like light tempered through clouds; he was all emotion, energy turned human. He looked like joy, nothing more, and it lifted Alice's heart to see him. She loved little boys. Oh, she'd used to love little boys so much.

She was turning into a batty old lady, wasn't she? What had come over her, thinking thoughts like that?

When she looked up, Deborah Latham was watching her with that kind of patient tolerance that always reminded Alice of why other people liked Martin. It made her nervous. Alice said, "Ed Stall is a nice man. He goes to my church."

"Oh," Deborah said, as if she'd suddenly remembered what she'd been saying. "Oh, yes, Ed Stall. That's right. So let me just tell you what happened, then I have to take them home. It's been kind of a long day."

Alice nodded. She was watching Michael. He was a devil, that one. Look how he'd gotten wet all the way up even to his shirt, and his mother hadn't even noticed. He was careful, Michael, to get his way discreetly. Des, too, always managed to do that.

"So, one day, when I was about six months' pregnant with Caroline, one day Chris comes in and he says, 'Deb, you've got to keep your clothes on during the day,' which is ridiculous, it isn't like I spend the day in the nude; I simply walk around the upstairs when I'm getting dressed or putting the beds together or whatever, and I say, 'What are you talking about?' It turns out Ed Stall had been too embarrassed to say anything all this time, and neither Chris nor I had realized how close the little window at the end of their second floor hall is to our window, and I felt so embarrassed!"

Deborah laughed, but it didn't sound exactly right. Alice was startled by this story, but not because Deborah walked around naked; that was so obviously something she would do that it wasn't even a mild surprise. What made Alice uncomfortable was the immediate realization that Chris knew very well how close the window was between the Stall's house and the Danniger's old place. Hadn't Chris himself gotten caught with Will Gaston and Eddie Danniger and her own son Jack? Hadn't all of them gotten caught one night spying on Cynthia Stall and Anna Downing and a bunch of their friends at a sleepover, back in eighth or ninth grade? Alice remembered it as if it were yesterday, driving into the village to pick up her son and running into Joe Gaston who'd come to pick up Will and Chris. She remembered because she'd loved Joe Gaston utterly for his sense of humor, for the easy way he dealt with his boys. Martin, she knew, would be all over Jack as if spying on a sleepover was one giant step toward hell. Lord, she'd envied Eileen Gaston that day, she could admit it now. She really had.

There was no way that Chris Latham had forgotten about the windows that linked the Stalls and the Dannigers. In fact, buying the Danniger place and living there, he'd probably relived that evening a thousand times. Alice smiled politely at Deborah Latham, for all the world as if she'd enjoyed the story.

Deborah smiled back. Once again, her eyes gazed sympathetically into Alice's, friendship—or something—beginning to bloom despite the cards stacked against it.

"Let's do this again," Deborah suggested warmly.

Alice was surprised to find that she wasn't surprised. She'd somehow expected Deborah to say that. She nodded agreement. "I'd like to," she said. "I honestly would."

Deborah leaned over, with both hands outstretched. "Let me help you."

"Oh, you'll need a forklift to help me up," Alice said, but then she gave her weight into Deborah's hands, leaning forward awkwardly to come to standing. "Ewf," she gasped. "Thank you."

Up at the cars, Deborah was immediately occupied with the wiping of faces and the fastening of seat belts. Alice settled heavily into the Buick, and turned it on, gunning the gas pedal several times to make sure it didn't stall. The waves were larger now, and darker. The tide was rolling in, and although it was far from evening, the very faintest tinge of pink had begun to frost the July sky.

"Hey!" Deborah called.

Alice turned. Deborah's expression was awkward, half grimace, half smile.

"You must think I talk too much," Deborah called through the car window. "I shouldn't have told you that story!"

"That's okay," Alice said, suddenly ashamed for Deborah. "It's just talking."

15

---◦◦◦---

DEBORAH'S white Volvo station wagon was always clean on the outside. The inside, however, was terminally littered with cracker crumbs and discarded juice boxes, crayons, and prizes from goody bags at birthday parties: small plastic frogs, pink heart-shaped pins, candy wrappers. At one time, she'd tried to keep up with the mess in the car, but it rapidly became clear that it was impossible. The moment the floor was clean, a packet of graham crackers would be smashed into tiny pieces all over the tan carpet. "I'll sell the car when they're older," she'd joke to Mina, seeing in shared chuckles an absolution. This afternoon, though, the car seemed filthy and uncared-for, the mark not of someone who was easygoing, but of someone who was truly unclean. She shuddered as she turned right off the Ferry Road bridge and headed down through the village. Even though it was midsummer, many faces were familiar: first, Caroline's friend Ada and her mother outside the five and ten; then, their favorite waitress heading into the pizza parlor, and, in the next block, a local musician tending to his garden.

By the time she had pulled onto Madison Street, Deborah already regretted the impulse toward Alice. She couldn't imagine what had drawn her toward the older woman. Honestly, what could they possibly have in common? As the dear old houses lining village streets gave way, as usual, to the hideous old ranchburgers, Deborah's taut lips flowered into a wry smile. She shook her head rapidly, as if by doing so she could clear all thoughts of Alice: of her huge, damp vulnerability; her pale, watery blue eyes; her Buddhalike stillness. How could any woman let herself get that large? Alice Dunn's body had settled on itself on the beach, as if any place she ever sat in her whole life could be her last. And there had been that weird tension when Deborah mentioned Cynthia Stall. Maybe one of Alice's sons had been after the girl when Chris had snared her. Maybe Alice didn't like Chris as a teenager. Maybe, most likely, the Dunns were jealous of how well Chris had turned out, an orphaned village child who'd pulled himself up from almost nowhere and turned his life into something special. Deborah bet that the Dunn boys were sulky and unwilling employees of their father's plumbing business. Surprising that she'd never heard Chris mention them.

Chris really had done well for himself, Deborah thought. As she pulled into Pike's farm stand on the first southern stretch of Sagg Road, she caught a glimpse of the kids in the rearview mirror. They were both breathing lightly, eyes closed, slumped against the leather of the seats. Caroline's hands were on her belly, rising and lowering with the bellowslike movement of her stomach. The bandage wasn't visible right now, the way her cheek was turned against the leather seat. Any swelling seemed a trick of light. For the moment, the events of this entire, horrible day might simply be ignored.

Michael sprawled toward his sister, over the center armrest, jaw lifted and chin raised high. He looked as if he'd dropped into sleep by narcotic, his last desperate act an urgent need to cast his eyes upon Caroline, even though the dreamworld had obviously overcome him in the process. He must love her with an overwhelming fury.

It was true, Deborah thought, that the larger picture was unusually positive. Look what Chris Latham had done for himself, a miracle considering the childhood he'd had. Look at his beautiful children, his career. Even she, herself, was a wife not to be ashamed of. She'd certainly kept face and figure; she was bright and friendly, a warm and loving wife. He'd done well for himself, Chris had, and perhaps that rankled some of the people with whom he'd grown up.

Deborah let herself out of the car, nodded at the young woman tending the farm stand, and began to inspect the season's first batch of tomatoes.

"I ran into Mrs. Dunn, Alice Dunn, at the beach today," she told Chris later. He was stacking dishes into the dishwasher as she put away leftovers, wiped down counters, and swept Michael's spurned pasta from the floor. "We sat together. I liked her."

"Alice Dunn?" Chris didn't look up, simply kept wiping bowls and rinsing cups. He had his particular methods for stacking the dishes, and when he was teasable, she liked to ride him about his compulsiveness. Tonight, though, he seemed to have an edge. He'd completely ignored Michael during dinner, as if this might serve as punishment for the rest of the day's events. When Caroline whined that she didn't want to finish her pasta, it had been Chris who'd gotten irritated, his anger too great to contain.

Deborah hadn't tried to make conversation; after the children finished, she'd dispatched them to the family room and, soon after, helped them to bed. First Caroline, then Michael, each treated with the kind of careful consideration the circumstances so clearly demanded. Now, somehow, she and Chris would have to make it uneasily through the next two hours, until their own day ended.

"Yeah. Funny, she's a sweet old lady," Deborah said.

"Yeah. She is."

"I liked her. I thought I'd ask her over, sometime, for coffee."

A pause. Chris put two more plates in the dishwasher, then opened the cupboard, pulled out the Electra-Sol, and poured it into the two compartments, snapping each shut as it was filled. He replaced the detergent, shut the door, and turned. "Why?"

"Why what?" There were two sinks in the Latham's remodeled kitchen: his and hers, they called them. Chris's was for dirty dishes; Deborah's, down at the other end, was for filling pots with cooking water and washing vegetables. Now, she took the sponge she'd been using and rinsed it at her sink. "Why what?" she repeated.

"Well," Chris began. "What would you possibly . . ."

"I liked her," Deborah interjected. "It was just a feeling. I would think you'd be glad if I made a friend from here, someone besides the people I already know."

"But you have friends from here. You have Will and Peg when they come out, and Elizabeth Bloom and Glennen, what's her name? Liz? And all those mothers from the school. I just don't get it, you making friends with Alice Dunn. She's so, I don't know, she's so not your type."

"What's wrong with her? You like her, don't you?"

He shrugged. "Yeah, of course I do. I've known her all my life, though. It's different. It's not like meeting her, or . . ."

"Is it me? You think I'm a snob?" Deborah asked, her face flushed a pale pink. Her lips were tight and tense; he could see he was treading on thin ice.

"No, no. I simply don't see the pull toward certain people. She's a good woman who's had a terrible life, and I like her and feel sorry for her as well, but I cannot see one patch of common ground the two of you might be able to place your feet upon."

"You feel sorry for her? Why?" It wasn't that Deborah hadn't felt the pleasurable twinges of pity herself; it was simply strange for Chris to voice such a feeling.

"Her sons. You know."

"No," said Deborah. "I don't." Her back was to the counter now. She plucked at her white T-shirt, wiping the tips of her fingers dry on the cotton.

"They died," Chris said. "I mean, Jack did, back when we were just out of high school. Driving home from a party. I think Jack was bombed beyond belief, and Des was in the passenger seat sleeping off his own booze. Jack hit that tree by Peerless Marine, you know, the oak near Fresh Pond Road. Des was thrown clear out of the car, didn't even get a scratch. Jack ended up half through the windshield on the passenger side, crushed into that big oak tree. It was a mess. He didn't have a chance, died right there."

"Oh my God, that's horrible." Her heart was pounding, as if Caroline or Michael might die that way someday.

"Yeah." Chris pressed the dishwasher START button and let the soft electronic humming fill the silence. He hated to think about that night. Beyond anything, he hated to think about that night. Deborah sat at the kitchen table.

"And the other one, what's his name again?"

"Des."

"Des. Where's he?"

Chris shrugged. "Jail, probably. He's not exactly making his parents proud."

"Jail," Deborah said, breathing the word out almost as if it were an endearment. "For what?"

Chris shrugged again. "Oh, anything. Drugs, mostly, breaking and entering, DWI. Nothing big time, at least as far as I know."

"She talked about her sons," Deborah said. "She didn't say a word about this. And she seemed so nice, so honest."

He said, "Was Caroline okay up there? Did she need the painkillers?"

"Oh, no. She went right out, they both did. They were exhausted."

"Who wouldn't be?" he asked dryly.

She was silent. Outside, in the dusk, she could make out the form of a couple walking a dog. She could hear the jingle of its tags, the murmur of friendly voices. She put one hand to the half-opened window, laying her palm on a pane of glass until the ghostly shapes receded into the twilight.

Eventually, she said again, "That Mrs. Dunn seemed so nice, you know, so honest."

He sighed. "Deb, I've said it a million times. People here, they don't *talk* about everything. They just live their lives. Mrs. Dunn wouldn't bare her soul to some lady she met on the beach, particularly someone who's not local."

"But she seemed so friendly," Deborah protested.

"Not everybody equates friendship with confession, Deborah," he said.

"Don't sound like that."

"I'm sorry," he murmured, turning back to check on whether the dishwasher door had latched properly. Sometimes it failed to catch, and then the entire cycle would shut down after the first loud groan of its beginning. He opened the door and closed it, pressing the START button once again.

16

EARLIER in the afternoon, just after leaving the plastic surgeon's office and before meeting Alice Dunn, Deborah Latham had found herself thinking about men—another man—with enormously piqued interest.

It had been, somehow, impossible to return to the house. They'd pulled into the driveway, gotten Michael from Chris's car, and grabbed a couple of bathing suits for the kids to change into at Long Beach.

Their car trailed Chris's down Main Street. He was heading back to the office; some of his patients had decided to wait, and others hadn't been reachable when he'd gone running out so quickly. He was relieved to have the appointments, Deborah could tell. Whatever had gone unspoken in front of the plastic surgeon might otherwise have had to be said aloud.

Driving down Main Street, she noticed a very pregnant woman serenely crossing in front of Fisher's Antiques. The woman was of medium height, blonde, and well dressed; she walked slowly and carefully, and it was not her beauty but her expression that caught Deborah's eye. The woman's face was alight with confidence and calm, Deborah thought, ripe with a low-level radiance brought on by good diet and comfortable thoughts. Her spouse, on the other hand, trailed a few steps behind: a handsome man in walking shorts with a shell-shocked glaze over his features. He was protecting her, perhaps, dogging each of her footsteps as she sailed easily along. Although his face seemed calm, even bored, Deborah had the distinct impression that he was mentally parsing life insurance forms, planning for college savings accounts, considering how to put an addition onto their house. She was sure the man was over-powered by worries, perhaps leery of getting too close to the tall-prowed ship that formerly had been his adorable spouse, terrified at all the freedom he was leaving behind. He followed his wife because he wasn't quite ready to lead. She was growing up, and he was going with her.

The man's expression stuck with Deborah for the rest of the day, like a huge pill she'd tried to swallow but hadn't quite managed to get down her throat. The image of his face kept returning to her. He'd seemed so indifferent, so entirely absent, yet at the same time angry, tense, lost, and worried, that she pitied the pregnant woman her future.

At the time they met and fell so immediately in love, Deborah and Christopher had both been, in their ways, comfortable alone. If the village of Sag Harbor was Christopher's family, he hardly needed to do more than walk down the street on his way to work to feel as if he'd been in touch with what he loved. It wasn't really until Deborah came along that he gave in to the notion of needing one person in particular; when he did, he rapidly learned to need with a kind of furious constancy that both thrilled her and made her feel entirely safe. Until meeting Chris, it had been more in her nature to resent and flee from this kind of adoration; with him, it was perfect.

Leaving her first family in the abrupt way Deborah had, she had been fairly sure she would never find or make a true home of her own. She'd often laughed with her friends in the city about the very idea of it; why, she'd once known a woman who cooked all day Sunday in order to have meals for the week, and she'd made fun of the erstwhile home-maker behind her back. Ironic how she, too, had become focused on such seemingly little triumphs of organization and planning.

But her mother had never been a homemaker type, and her mothering had never been as constant and steady as Deborah tried to make hers. Lydia Berlin had been the beacon atop a well-placed lighthouse; her attention when focused was utterly satisfying and complete. When she'd shown up at Deborah's piano recitals, the fact of her presence made the air in the room alive and energetic. "I wish I had a mom like yours," other kids frequently told her. And she'd learned to roll her eyes skyward as if to say, "If you only knew." Because when Lydia's focus slipped away, as it so frequently did, its absence was excruciating. The only saving grace, the only feature that made the loss of love palatable, was knowing how rapidly the beacon would spin again, how guaranteed the glow of her returning attention would be. Her presence always more than made up for her absence; in effect, it erased it, so that years later, the mental portrait her daughters carried was of a mother who loved them completely.

Deborah had only understood this by knowing Chris. As she became more comfortable and sure of his love, not only was her sense of today altered, but also her understanding of the past. Perhaps this was why she had begun to spend time with her parents and sister with such pleasure; being part of her new family had shown her that her mother and father had had no malevolent intentions toward her; they'd simply done the best they could with the material they were given. Now, because she had to deal with both her children, she could see that the basic stuff that made up a particular child was not always easy to figure out. As much as her parents had failed her at some crucial junctures, she had failed them as well. She hadn't been the child they knew how to like. She hadn't fit in. And in leaving at seventeen, abandoning them in the way she did, she'd punished them so totally that erasing the distance even twenty years later was a constant task, the gentle cleaning and covering of an unhealable wound.

Deborah's sister, Michele, was the next to tackle the subject of the failed visit, her call coming not an hour after the kids were in bed, finally asleep. Chris was watching television in the family room, something he rarely did. She was sitting in the kitchen, staring out the open back doors, wondering lethargically when the screens would need replacing. In the bottom corner of the right-hand screen, a gash had appeared. For the moment, no mosquitoes seemed to be nosing their way in, but soon, she suspected, she would need to do something about the rip. When the phone rang, Deborah almost didn't pick it up, lunging for the receiver after the fourth ring.

"Hey, it's me," Michele said. "Mom said you hung up on her. She couldn't understand why you weren't coming after all. Is everything okay?"

Deborah glanced toward the family room, then turned, seating herself at the kitchen table with her back to the archway. She had already begun to cry. "I don't know," she said. "It's the kids. Michael. Don't tell Mom."

"I thought . . . you said . . . I thought he was doing so much better. I won't tell Mom anything. You know I won't."

Deborah nodded, as if her little sister could see. They weren't always intimate—months could go by when they didn't talk—but when they had to, they could broach most subjects easily. Now it seemed as if the only person she could confide in was Michele.

"He was going after Caroline in the car, hitting her. I couldn't take it, the yelling, and everything had been so great for so long now. I'd almost forgotten how bad he can be."

"Oh, I'm sorry, Deb, that's terrible."

"And then, well, when we got back here, he hurt her. He threw a rock, and it hit, above the temple. It's pretty bad. She had stitches."

Michele was silent. After a moment, Deborah said, "I can't take it anymore, not him, not her, not Chris." She was whispering. In the other room, the sounds of canned laughter were loud and aggressive.

"Chris?" Michele's voice was shocked. She loved Chris, everyone in their family did, and he could do no wrong in much the same way that Deborah herself had long been able to do no right. From her family's point of view, she was rebellious and independent, and he was warm and connecting. He'd brought Deborah back into loving contact with her parents; he'd been a good friend to his sister-in-law; and he'd been a pal to her husband. Chris's effect on Deborah had been of warming her up and bringing her home to them, a more loving and easygoing adult. Criticizing Chris was almost unthinkable.

"Chris. Yeah. Or Michael, it's the two of them. I feel so alone. Chris is giving up. I could tell he is, all evening. I don't know what to do."

"How's Caro holding up?"

"Fine," Deborah answered, surprised. "She's fine."

Michele's voice was soft and slightly wary. "Growing up with you, you know, rebelling right and left the way you did, sometimes I got kind of shut out of things, felt sort of lost in the storm."

"She's an oldest kid, not a youngest. She's fine."

"Keep an eye on her, Debbie. Don't make me come up there and take the hairbrush to you." The sisters had been six and four, hiding in a closet they'd decorated with towels and scarves of Lydia's. They were playing queen and princess, and when Michele's vain attempt to overpower the throne and become queen had failed, she attacked Deborah with her hairbrush. A palace revolt of limited impact, of course, although Michele still claimed it had political and historical importance, that without this uprising, Deborah might have grown up to become dictator of the no-longer-free world.

"Don't joke. It's not funny."

"I'm not really. I'm sorry."

"You know, in the beginning, when he first came to us, how I told you we'd have to go around all the time explaining him to everybody? He doesn't walk, but that's because of where he came from. He's small for his age, but that's because of where he came from. He can't use a spoon, but that's because of where he came from . . ."

"He doesn't talk, but that's because of where he came from." It was Chris, who had walked into the room quietly and now stood behind her chair.

"Oh!" She said, into the phone, "It's Chris."

"Do you want to go, call me later?"

"Yeah."

"Love you, Deb."

She pressed the OFF button on the portable phone and turned to face him. Gently, he touched her nose and then her eyes, closing them. She sighed, her shoulders relaxing.

"We're in a terrible place," he said softly. "I never thought we could be here."

She nodded. "I've never really noticed how few women friends I have here," she admitted. "Not until this past year. I never thought I could feel lonely, not with you."

He half-smiled, nodding and shrugging his shoulders at the same time. "I know. I tried to talk to Will, even; I called him at the end of the day, before I came home, but I couldn't bring myself to tell him what happened to Caroline. What Michael did. I couldn't bear it. Like I was betraying us."

"I hated coming back this morning," she said. "I really wanted to prove I could handle them. He wasn't even so bad, he wasn't. I just didn't expect it, not anymore. I thought it was over, and now, I don't know. I just feel so tired."

He put a hand on each of her shoulders, pressing gently. She turned away from him, placing one of her hands on top of each of his.

"Why did we do this?" he asked. "I can't remember."

One clear tear was still visible on her cheek. "I remember so well," she said. "I remember, I was just telling Michele, I remember how much we had to explain, how proud I was of what we were doing. I thought we could make a difference, that in our own small way we could help."

"I don't remember even making the choice," he said. "Did Viorica talk us into it? Did she force us to take him somehow? I feel as if I must have been crazy. I can't imagine having agreed to it."

"You loved him," she said quietly. "I know you did."

He shook his head vehemently. "I wanted to love him," he said.

In the silence, another burst of laughter emanated from the family room, where the television blared without an audience.

"I don't know why *you* did it," she said eventually. "But I did it for you. For where you'd come from and what happened to you."

He was surprised. "Did we never talk about this?"

"Yes," she said. "We did. And this is what I told you then. You honestly don't remember?"

"No," he said. "I don't."

"We could have had our own child, so easily," he said then.

She looked down at the table and then turned back to face him. "Do you want some tea?" she asked. "I'll put on the water."

He nodded. "Why didn't we?" he asked.

She stood, pushing the chair so that he had to move backward. Instead of sitting down himself, he went to the counter and hoisted himself up on it, his long legs dangling down. He put his hands first in his lap, then wrapped them around his belly to his back, then down on either side of his thighs, on the counter. He made a sound, almost a chuckle, and then he shook his head.

"We could have had our own child," he said again. "Look at Caroline."

"I know that," she said, placing the kettle on the stove.

"Were we being noble?"

"I don't know, I guess so. That was part of it. I never . . . it didn't . . . it didn't seem crazy then. And I don't regret it, not the way you do. I mean, we could have had our own, but he would have still been out there with nobody loving him and no home of his own. We made a choice. To help someone."

He nodded.

She said, "If we don't stick with him now, we'll destroy him."

He nodded. He looked down at his thighs and then up at her. "I hated your pregnancy," he admitted. She turned back to the stove, modulating the flame. "I love Caroline," he said. "You know that. But I hated you being so . . . so dual, so not reachable, so changed."

"So fat?" She was grinning, her arms outspread in mockery of her pregnant shape.

"No," he said. "It's not funny. It wasn't that at all."

He was confused, she could see, and she was furious at him on one level, wanting him to agree with absolute certainty that having become responsible for Michael there was no possible way to shrug off the burden, that to do so would be to deny his very humanity. But she was still so utterly drawn to her husband that when he looked up from contemplating his knees and gave a slightly shamed smile, she found herself standing between his legs at the counter and pulling his mouth down to hers.

At first he didn't want her to touch him, she could tell. His lips were tight and tense; he was thinking of everything awful between them, and this reminder of all the good came too rapidly, changed the climate too abruptly.

In a moment, though, his lips softened and his mouth began to move with hers, and then her arms went around him, and his around hers, and he drew her in closer so that her hips were pressed against his groin. His breath deepened, and she laughed softly in his ear. She nipped at his neck and up, at the lobe of his ear.

Under her white cotton T-shirt, his hands stroked her back and along the slight curve of her waist, sweeping up her ribs to cup her breasts. "You wear the best underwear," he murmured, and she giggled. "Is it the same below?"

She shook her head. "Not yet, but watch," she said, and he did as she twisted out of both jeans and panties at once. "Some things are hard to do gracefully."

"Graceful isn't the word for you," he said. "It's something better." He slid down from the counter, leaning against it as he wrapped his hands and forearms around her buttocks to pick her up and turn her around, so that her behind rested just on the edge of the counter, her head thrown backward. Eyes half-closed, she spread her legs wide, bringing an ankle up to rest on each of his shoulders. Her hair trailed back over bottles of olive oil, vinegar, and wine. Her nipples, thickened by Caroline's breast-feeding, jutted sharply up through her T-shirt. His breath quickened. He reached one hand forward to touch her right breast, his fingers caressing the nipple and then stroking the entire surface. He wanted to kiss her there, but he couldn't lean that far without altering her position—he was supporting her—and so he reached back to unzip his own jeans and tug them down enough that they could fall.

"Aaah," he whispered as he entered her. She could barely move her hips to meet his, balanced as she was, and he had to hold back not to come too quickly. Even now, even a decade after they'd begun together, that sometimes happened, a feeling of being overwhelmed by her, by them, by the very act of loving someone with such a direct and complete sense of freedom and openness. A danger lurked there, of needing too much, of caring and feeling safe, a danger he sometimes could even acknowledge but only in his own head, not aloud, not even to her. He paused, leaning away from her, consciously stilling his thoughts until he could go on more easily, concentrating on the pleasure and trying to placate the fear that way.

"Oh, God, keep going," she moaned, "keep going," and he did, and she did, and they moved together easily, familiarly, wonderfully, until first she and then he began to breathe even more unevenly and to grab onto the edges of the counter (she) and the smoothness of her buttocks (he), as the circle tautened and grew tighter, pleasure flowing faster and faster into a knot of pure joy and then diffusing softly, release.

He kissed each of her shins before lowering her legs and helping her to slide into a seated position at the counter. "Wow," she said. "I'm never going to feel the same way about cooking here."

"Me neither. I think maybe we've found a better use for this counter."

"Mmhmm."

The teakettle must have been boiling for some time now, with steam rising and clattering through the black cap that covered the spout. Chris pulled his jeans up before crossing the room to turn off the flame. From the family room, canned TV laughter continued to emanate in short, manic bursts. Outside, a lone car went by, its radio blaring.

"Can you close that window?" Deborah asked. "That smell, do you smell it?"

It was awful, actually, now that he noticed it. "When did that start?"

"I don't know," she said. "Just now's the first time I smelled it. What could it be, a dead animal?"

"I hope so," he said.

"Why hope that?" She jumped off the counter, picking her jeans and panties up from the floor.

"You're really beautiful," he said, watching her. "I feel as if I must have done something right I have no clue about, otherwise how could I have you? You're too wonderful for someone like me. I mean it."

She gave a half shrug, smiling. "You flatter me, sir."

"It's true," he said. "I love to look at you. I love to be with you. I love who you are inside. I know I don't say it much, but it's true. It really is. You're the best friend I've ever had. I don't know who I'd be without you."

"You're not so bad yourself, Christopher Latham," she said.

He gestured toward the window. "What a stench. I think it's the septic system, and that's an expensive problem. I hate to imagine how much it's going to cost."

"Chris," she said quietly. "I mean it. I love you."

"You'd better," he said, ruffling his hair and making a face like a crazy ape, tongue lolling out the side of his mouth. "You'd better," he growled, and he came toward her, leering and rolling his eyes, those beautiful fingers of his extended ready to tickle her until they both fell to the floor, giggling madly, locked in another, less heated, embrace.

They didn't discuss Caroline's injury, Michael's behavior, or Alice Dunn any more that night. It wasn't until Deborah began to sink into sleep that it suddenly dawned on her how obscenely personal Alice must have found the intended-to-be-amusing story about walking around nude in front of Ed Stall. How utterly inappropriate she'd been. The thought hovered, threatening to waken Deborah in an anxious tangle of embarrassment and shame, but then she let the realization vaporize—an act of will—and allowed herself to drift toward sleep. In the morning, she would let the shame in if she had to. For now, she was a mother of small children, and above all, she needed her rest.

Chris, next to her, was silent, his eyes closed. She was almost out when he sighed, exhaling a long, controlled breath that came close to a sob, waking her immediately. She turned to him; was he dreaming or worrying?

"You're thinking about him, about Michael, aren't you?" Deborah whispered, leaning across him so that her white cotton nightgown brushed his shoulder.

He stiffened. "Sleeping—talk 'morrow."

"Good night," Deborah said. She patted his hair, once, and turned to settle herself again in the darkness. In a few minutes, they were both breathing easily, bottom to bottom, backs and arms curved gently up and away from one another like swans' wings. From the bathroom came the low, even whisper of the toilet running.

Two doors down the hall slept Michael, his head swaddled three times round by his own hand, in a crocheted blue quilt, his thin legs tight together, tension visible even in the way his right arm stretched forward and up to keep a watchful hand on the quilt. Even now, close to four years after his arrival, he still feared the loss of his blanket in the night.

Behind the next closed door was Caroline's pink room, ornate with cabbage roses and flouncy pillows. A night-light cast a pale glow over the books and games and toys scattered everywhere. Her shades were pulled down. No stripes of moonlight danced across her bed, but an oak tree scratched outside her window as the wind forced one scrubby branch forward, *carr-ip*, *carr-ip*. Seven-year-old Caroline slept deeply, sturdy fingers clutching a baby doll she'd be ashamed to show her school friends during the day, one long arm protecting an equally shameful trio of stuffed cat, bear, and dog. On her forehead, just below the hair-line, a large square bandage was taped neatly, covering the first con-cretely visible wound of her brother's four-year term. If anyone had asked her, she probably would have said she loved her brother. She knew she was supposed to. She didn't like to think about the way things used to be. It made her too sad.

Even as she slept, her forehead throbbed. She knew how sad Michael made her mom, and usually she tried not to complain. She tried really hard. She was holding on as best she could. Although she didn't know the word, Caroline Latham was stalwart and determined to remain so.

In the car, on the way home from the plastic surgeon's office, she'd ven-tured, just once, to explain what was going wrong. It was only because she was so tired. Otherwise, she'd never have bothered her mom like that. She loved her mom. She loved her mom to be happy. But in the car, she had said, "I really hate Michael, I hate him. I do! And I wish he'd just go away."

"You don't mean that," Deborah had said absently, apparently focused on getting home without incident. Chris and Michael were in Chris's car, following behind.

"I do, Mommy, I do. It was so much better without him. You think I can't remember, but I can. I remember how nice it was, before. Can't he go back?"

Tears were no longer visible on Caroline's face, but the salt had left a powdery residue that blotched her cheeks.

Deborah rubbed Caroline's knee with her right hand. "He's your brother, Honey. What's going on is miserable for all of us, even him. I know it."

"That's not true. He doesn't care at all," seven-year-old Caroline said stubbornly. When the rock had hit her head, she'd fallen back and across the leg of the swing set, catching her shorts on the metal hook of the extra swing—her own fault, she supposed, because she'd tied the ropes around the leg to get the swing out of the way as she played. But even though her pink shorts had ripped, and her now-grimy T-shirt had a hole as well, the skin on her stomach was unscratched. She poked a finger through the tear in the T-shirt, rubbing her own skin thoughtfully.

"I know how difficult he is sometimes," Deborah said cheerfully. "I feel as if we're getting closer, though. He's going to be all right. We all are. What happened today was awful, but in the way that things get horrible before they get better. Don't you see? That medication he started last November, that the homeopath gave him? He was better when he took that. Maybe I'll call her again."

"You're wrong. He'll never get better. He's awful."

"Don't say that, Caro, Sweetie. It's going to get better. You'll see. Summer's here, the days are long, the beach is beautiful this year. It's all going to be fine."

"Daddy doesn't think so," Caroline said spitefully, looking over to gauge her mother's reaction.

"Yes, he does," Deborah said, and the tone in her voice was funny, almost like plastic snapping, a sound Caroline had never before imagined a person could make.

Caroline snorted.

Deborah glanced toward her and grinned. "Baby," she said, "I know it hurts something awful. I do. But things will get better, I promise you. Funny," she said, and paused.

Caroline waited.

"Funny," Deborah repeated thoughtfully. "But with that bandage, and all your black hair all tangled, you look like some pint-sized gypsy rebel from an Italian war movie."

Caroline turned to stare out the window. She was beginning to cry again.

Later, long after dinner and clean up, when her mom tucked Michael into bed, Caroline heard her ask him, "You're sorry, aren't you?"

He'd said, "Uh huh."

"You *are* sorry, aren't you?" Deborah had asked again.

Michael must have nodded, because her mom's footsteps sounded as she moved across the room and flicked his lights off. Those were the last noises Caroline heard out of his room that night, except the creak of his springs, just once, as he turned and sighed. He must have fallen asleep in ten seconds flat.

Caroline, on the other hand, couldn't find a comfortable way to rest for what seemed like hours. Finally, around the time when the quiet began to deepen so that only the leaves scratching her screened window made a sound, Caroline fell asleep. She didn't dream, couldn't. She slept on her stomach, one foot hanging so far off the bed it nearly reached the floor. Her legs were covered with a pale pink sheet that barely shifted under the rhythm of her breath.

17

"MY FAVORITE part of the Bible is when the lady eats the magic apple," Caroline confided to Mina at bedtime a few days later. Chris and Deborah had taken a rare night out together, heading to the movie theater in East Hampton.

Mina, startled, did not know how to respond, feeling at a loss largely because the barriers of language loomed higher whenever conversations like this one began. She was sure Deborah and Christopher had an agenda of their own where religion was concerned, but she could not believe they'd actually referred to Eve's experience in the Garden as an occult activity. Coming from where she did, from Braşov, a Romanian city just south of Dracula's Transylvanian lair, she had paid a healthy homage to lore and village tales all her life, yet her most sincere respect had always been saved for the teachings of the church. The stories of the Bible were the truth, and she had never considered Eve's experience in the garden to be other than fact.

At moments like this she hated the Lathams, wanted more than anything to work and live among people whose conventions were comprehensible. Deborah's long, slim legs, her eager eyes, her warm smile all served to confuse Mina. Her employer seemed the epitome of grace and sophistication, giving and kind—she had been extraordinarily good to Mina herself—yet, to speak of the events in the Garden this way had to be a kind of evil.

Having escaped from the very worst horrors of Ceauşescu's regime, Mina and her cousin Viorica often agreed that the Americans were incomprehensible. As rich and comfortable as they were, they were so selfish as well, so unwilling to think about the suffering of others. Why had freedom bred so many similarities to totalitarianism? Viorica's brother was smashed to death by club-wielding twenty-year-olds from the Securitate, fresh-faced villains who were warning her father to cease dealing in black-market goods—or to cut them in. Viorica was upstairs hiding in a closet, straining both to hear and not to hear as her brother shouted, then screamed, whimpered, groaned, and died. She could not imagine why the Americans thought so admiringly of violence, celebrating it in song and film. She had expected something else, having dreamed of this country the way Americans dream of lolling on a Caribbean beach, full of rum and shellfish and relaxed beyond measure. America had turned out to be confusing and sometimes frightening.

Viorica suspected that she and Mina imagined Sag Harbor to be more dangerous than it was, and sometimes she made such a claim aloud. Viorica suggested that the two of them were so used to being frightened that they found themselves in fear unnecessarily. On occasion, irritably, she had implied that Mina was surprised by America in ways that she, Viorica, was not. Viorica believed that Mina was weaker and more vulnerable, as if Mina's nervous system had been permanently altered by all her years of worry and skulking, and of living with the constant question of whether she had inadvertently committed an act that would lead to some awful retribution. As a result, Viorica wanted, no, insisted that if she returned to Romania as she intended to do, Mina would have to join her.

Mina didn't want to leave. For her part, she suspected that Viorica wanted to find America unpleasant, that as much as her cousin yearned to find happiness and well-being in the land of freedom and opportunity, the problem—the failure of America to conquer Viorica's discontent—lay in Viorica herself and not in some aspect of their situation. In fact, Mina herself didn't consider her overriding feeling to be one of fear. She was more disoriented than afraid.

"What's your favorite story from the Bible?" Caroline asked, head on the pillow, hands relaxed by her ears, eyelids drooping. The pink quilt was pulled up to her neck; only a neat white fringe of lace was visible. Her teeth were brushed, her eyes were clear, her black hair was neatly braided. The bandage, which Mina had just replaced, was a square inch of white cotton taped along each edge. Cutting the bandage to size had occupied Caroline completely; she seemed so engrossed in the mechanics of healing that the event itself no longer mattered. She was so lovely, so white, so smart, that sometimes Mina wished she had stayed small; when Caroline was one and two and three years old, Mina had felt securely in charge, but now she wasn't always sure who held the reins.

"I don't know," Mina confessed. "I never thought of picking one out that way."

"Come on. Really try," Caroline urged. Her instincts were all for category and organization; she couldn't conceive of anything, from the metaphysical to the most real, that mightn't resolve itself in a list, or in ascending order of preference, or with a winner.

"That's not the way I think about the Bible," Mina said. Standing, she began to fold Caroline's discarded clothes, separating out the still-clean T-shirt from the dust-speckled jeans, tying the socks together for washing.

"Try," Caroline said again. The solemn confidence, the smoothly royal bones of her cheeks, her arms resting on the pillow—such easy strength was confusing to Mina. How could a little girl be so commanding? Deborah always spoke of Caroline as shy and clingy, yet Mina had never found her so.

"Oh, I don't know, Caroline, I don't have a favorite," Mina said, and her exasperation came out as if she were angry at her seven-year-old charge, when in fact she was irritated at her own inability to feel solid and safe.

"You have to have a favorite, Miney," Caroline insisted, cajoling.

"Go to sleep, little Caroline."

"I'm not little, and I don't want to go to sleep. I want to talk. I'm not tired, not the slightest bit tired."

"Go to sleep. It's bedtime."

"Mommy lets me stay up, she always does if I'm not tired. She always does. Sometimes I even wake her up, if I can't sleep."

"You shouldn't do that," Mina said, shocked. "You should never wake someone up who's sleeping."

"Why not?" Caroline shifted on the pillow so that her two black braids spread away from one another. Her eyes were huge, expectant.

Mina sighed. "Oh, let me sit. I'll tell you a story my mother used to tell me when I was about your age."

"She's dead, isn't she?" Caroline asked.

"My mother?"

Caroline nodded.

"Yes, she died many years ago. I told you. It was just before I came to work here, with you. But let me tell you."

"Of what?" Caroline persisted.

"What what?"

"What did she die of?"

Mina shrugged. "Of death."

"That's what you always say. But when people die, it's always because of something. Everyone knows that."

"She died, Caroline. She wasn't young, and her life was very hard. She got sick and she died."

"Don't get mad at *me*, I'm just asking."

Mina smoothed the pink quilt underneath her fingers. Since she had lived in America, her hands had grown plumper. She made fists with them, leaned forward, and said, "My mother used to tell me that when you sleep, your soul leaves your body. If you waken a person too quickly, his soul might not have time to get back inside. That's why you should always be gentle when you wake someone up. Wake your mother up slowly, if you must, or let her sleep until she wakes by herself."

"That's silly."

Mina shrugged. "Maybe. Lots of people believe it to be true."

"You made it up."

"No," Mina said, "I didn't. Once, maybe a hundred years ago or a little more, there was a woman in my country who owned a very beautiful, very productive vineyard. She hired some men to help with the chores. One afternoon, it grew so hot that they all lay down outside, in the shade of a huge tree, to take a nap. When the men woke up, they were unable to get the woman to awaken. They shook her and called to her, and she didn't move. She just lay there like she was dead, with her mouth wide open."

"Maybe she *was* dead."

"She wasn't, though. One of the men had left his leather pouch at the vineyard by accident, so the next day he went back with a friend. The lady was lying there still as a stone. So the man picked up his pouch, and when he opened it up, a huge fly buzzed out and flew into the lady's mouth. She woke up immediately."

Caroline could hardly breathe, she was so amazed by this story. "So that was her soul, is that what you're saying?"

Mina nodded. "And that's how they knew she was a witch."

"Is that true?"

Mina shrugged. "True enough," she said. "That's what my mother told me."

Caroline said, "My mother doesn't believe in stuff like that." Her tone was doubtful, as if she wasn't sure whether it was Mina or Deborah who actually had it wrong.

Standing, Mina leaned over to kiss Caroline on the forehead. As she turned, she caught sight of Michael lying on the hallway carpet, listening. "You startled me, little Mihai! I thought you were asleep!"

Michael hissed, "Don't call me that. Don't ever, ever call me that!" His face was scrunched as the knot on a balloon.

Mina could not bear to see him angry; although they were merely compatriots, he felt to her like family. "Hush, Little One," she murmured, walking toward him, hands outstretched. "Hush. Let me put you back in bed."

"I can do it *myself*," he sneered, coming to his feet without taking her proffered hands. He was still somewhat small for his five years but far stronger than he appeared. His skin was a beautiful musky mahogany, against which the whites of his eyes glowed no matter what the season. He moved quickly, now, away from her, and inside her chest she felt a twist, as if this growing distance might wring her own soul dry.

The following evening, Chris, who had been out of sorts ever since his failure to promptly refer Alice Dunn to a doctor, decided to drive Michael to t-ball practice in Mashashimuet Park. Deborah was thrilled to be released from this particular duty and yet wary all the same; in the past four days, Chris had shown so little interest in Michael that she mistrusted his sudden offer. She helped Michael to tie his sneakers, and then she turned, about to speak.

"What?" Chris asked. He had his sunglasses on, and he stood by the door, ready to leave as soon as Michael was dressed.

Deborah, caught with her mouth open, simply advised Michael not to forget his glove.

"Huh? Oh, yeah," he said, and then he smiled widely at his mother, all those surprisingly white teeth revealed like a gift. "Thanks, Mom."

The two males were silent at first, Michael waiting for Chris to speak, Chris concentrating on the road. He wanted to say something to Michael, something fatherly, something not severe or angry or reprimanding. It was difficult to remember that this little boy was only five years old. One of the therapists they once consulted about him actually had Chris and Deborah lift four-year-old Michael onto a table. "Look at him, up there," Dr. Bram had said. "He's the center of things, isn't he?"

Deborah had nodded and Chris had half-shrugged.

"Who put him up there? Who made him so tall? Who made him so powerful?" Dr. Bram had a painterly point of a beard, mottled gray and slightly curly, that always seemed to be damp and dotted with crumbs.

Deborah had nodded again, mutely, already letting her eyes hood over. It was Chris who answered. "That's not exactly true," he protested. "Michael isn't simply our son. I mean, he's our son, now, but he wasn't always our son. And when he wasn't, he learned some ways of acting that make it difficult to . . ."

"I don't remember that," Michael interrupted, speaking so swiftly the individual words blurred together. It was as if he didn't want Dr. Bram to know he'd ever lived elsewhere, ever not rested safely with the Lathams.

Now the early evening air grew slightly chillier, and the light began to take on grayish overtones. Michael reached over to touch his father's wrist. "Hey," he said. "Hey, Dad."

"Hey."

"Want to hear a story Mina told me yesterday, at bedtime? About witches?"

"Sure," Chris said. "Sure." He turned right onto Madison Street. "Oh, shit," he said. "Excuse me." He pulled into a driveway and backed out again, now heading south. "I meant to go left."

Michael told his father all about the vineyard-owning witch whose soul was a buzzing fly.

"Wow," Chris said. "Witches." He laughed, turning right onto Jermain Avenue. They were only a few short blocks from the park. Suddenly Chris said, "That reminds me. There were witches here, at least in East Hampton. I forgot. We learned about it back when I was in school. There was this woman named Goodwife Garlick . . ."

"Garlic!" Michael giggled.

"Yeah, isn't that funny?" Chris smiled down at his son. "And some woman actually died, I don't know, this had to be two hundred years ago, and this woman Elizabeth Howell claimed that Goody Garlick had put the evil eye on her."

"What's that?"

"Oh, I don't know, like wishing something bad to happen to her," Chris said, retreating, suddenly remembering his son was only five years old.

"Like she'd *die*? Is that what she wished? That the lady would *die*?" Michael's cheeks were flushed, he was smiling widely, and Chris, for a moment, knew the boy to be his son, a sensation made odder because it so clearly revealed how rarely he felt Michael to be his. He felt warm, damp appearing under his arms and across his back, as if he had suddenly been caught embarked on a crime he hadn't even realized he was committing.

"I guess, yeah, or maybe that her cow would stop giving milk."

"That's a joke. Right? You made a joke?" Michael's smile was still large, but his gaze was slightly defensive now.

"Yeah, I did. Seriously, this Elizabeth Howell, she died. And Goody Garlick was sent over to Connecticut to stand trial for witchcraft."

"That was here, huh? That happened here?"

The car pulled into the park. "It was here. Now hop to it, there's your team."

"Aren't you coming?" Michael asked. "Aren't you going to watch?"

"I'll be there in a minute," Chris said. "I want to watch from here for just a sec."

Michael shrugged. "Okay."

His son's small form marched determinedly over to the pack of waiting children. Chris sat, not sure why he didn't have the energy or desire to join the other dads in sideline coaching. There was a scream, and then a second scream, and then a series of shouts, as Dan Crulley ran over to separate a wrestling mound of kids.

Chris opened the door and made to run toward the field, but it was too late. Dan had Michael by the neck of his T-shirt, and he was hauling him back toward Chris. "Hey, Chris," Dan said matter-of-factly. "You better watch this boy of yours or you'll be visiting him in jail some day."

"What happened?"

Michael said, sullenly, "Nothing. I didn't do anything. It just happened."

Dan chuckled. "Yeah, and I'm president of the United Nations. This kid just went after Steve Gray like he'd been lit on fire. This is the third fight he's got into since we started practices, and I'm not even mentioning bat-throwing or anything else. Hasn't your wife told you?"

Chris shook his head, no.

Crulley shook his head, as if in agreement. "That's funny. She was pretty upset two nights ago; that's when he threw the bat at her. I think maybe Mike here better take a breather on baseball for a few weeks. We've got no call for troublemakers. We're looking for t-ball players."

Chris didn't feel a thing, not angry, not cold, not even numb. Some hand came out and grabbed Michael by the arm, shoved him in the car. If it was his own, he couldn't tell. He just wasn't there.

In the car, Michael said, "Sorry."

Chris didn't say a word, couldn't say a word. He just turned left onto Madison and right onto their street and pulled into their driveway feeling as if some part of him was never going to come alive again. He couldn't even fathom what it was. He turned and started to yell. Later, Chris couldn't recall his words, that was the strangest part. He couldn't take them back as if they hadn't happened, nor bring them to mind to mull over. It was as if time stopped for a moment, allowing some inner truth-teller out and then forcing it to move on. It couldn't have been he who spoke. Impossible. Otherwise, he'd not have been able to forget so easily what he said, particularly when what he said was that anyone who acted like Michael couldn't possibly be a son of his.

"My parents died here," he'd yelled, "and every damn soul in this town did every goddamn thing they could to keep me alive and raise me up! And those of us who're trying to do the same for you don't have the slightest notion of how you could do such rotten, evil things the way you do. Why are you like this? Every day, hurting everyone, picking on kids you don't even know, drawing blood every single day of your life! People live and die here like decent people. They don't bring hell with them the way you've done! They don't!"

And then Chris started to cry, huge, aching sobs, like a woman might cry but never he, and all the while, Michael just stared at him, that small smile on his face, and after a minute or so, he reached one hand over and patted his father on the wrist. "Don't worry, Daddy," he said. "Don't worry. It'll be okay."

18

VIORICA had always been fond of Michael. His eyes had never been cold; when he stared he was genuinely curious. Children at the clinic where she found him were in marginally better shape than those at other hospitals, slightly better fed and more alert. She'd seen Michael eating a thick, warming gruel, and even seen him touch the matron's pale brown hair when she lifted him from the crib for Viorica to see. He was small and quiet, but his eyes drew her in, let her know that inside he was still alive.

It had been Viorica's mission to save these children from the arduous combination of hunger and boredom that constituted existence in Romania. She brought them by ones and twos to America, hoping that life in the New World would make them. In the beginning, she'd not tried to weed and sort them, believing that any child could and should be saved. In some sense, she'd rapidly been proven wrong. Many—no, most—of the children she'd handed over to expectant, loving hands had rebounded utterly from the dull deprivation of their earlier days. But she could now see that the few who hadn't adapted easily were poor choices from the beginning. Their eyes had shown it from the start, so blank that no amount of prodding or affection could ignite a warm light. One little boy she'd placed in New Jersey had stabbed his sister with a carving fork because she'd taken the piece of turkey he wanted from a serving platter. Another had been utterly, utterly unable to formulate speech, although there was no biological basis for the deficit. He'd refused to let anyone touch him, as if a touch could burn, and his parents had been heartbroken after three long years, finally acknowledging that all the love in the world could not reach him.

But Michael, to Viorica, was a dream child: sweet, loving, and amazingly resilient. His past had been traumatic, she knew from the *sora şefă,* the head nurse at Clinic No. 7. God knew Viorica's own past hadn't been so pleasant, and look how well she'd done. She hated the way the Americans acted like victims of everything, as if the most minor complications were huge and unbearable. Michael's mother had died in a violent manner, sure, but he was doing fine. Viorica knew with certainty that Michael was utterly superb, a smart, happy survivor. In a certain sense, he reminded her of her brother: It wasn't simply that they were both named Mihai, but also that the younger Mihai retained a quality of exuberance that wasn't entirely suppressed even when she found him, isolated as he was in that peeling, white iron crib in that dingy white-walled room. Her brother Mihai would have held on to life with the same sort of vehement insistence, she knew it, if only the Securitate jackboots hadn't robbed him so utterly.

It was after Ceauşescu fell from power that Viorica received permission to emigrate to America. She'd not intended to see Braşov again, not ever, but she'd found herself overwhelmed with the desire to go back and rescue children, so determined that she simply couldn't conceive of an alternative to this task. In 1991, she began returning regularly to Braşov to rescue children from the institutions. Working through private American adoption services, she'd placed at least a hundred children from Braşov and neighboring areas.

Short, sturdy, and rarely flustered, Viorica learned from her early mistakes, and over time, she developed a reputation for finding and facilitating the adoption of children who could only be described as of the highest quality. She stopped smoking as she began to make a steady income; in time, she began to feel herself to be more than five feet tall and a genuine hero. She streaked her hair blonde and wore nail polish and dressed in pale pastel suits. She had earned, and saved, a fairly substantial amount of money in the past six years, which was amazing considering she had little education and no experience when she arrived in New York. Mina hadn't done half so well.

Viorica was planning to have her teeth fixed before she returned to Braşov, but she didn't want to go to Christopher Latham. She didn't like him, although she didn't exactly know why.

"How can you not like him? He's so nice and handsome, and so good with the kids," Mina would ask, and Viorica would roll her eyes. She thought Mina had a crush on Christopher, and she thought that was ridiculous.

"He doesn't like Michael. He doesn't try hard enough. He doesn't understand what Michael needs." They were in the little kitchen in Mina's apartment, and Mina was making dinner, a vegetable goulash to be served over noodles. Mina was the better cook, always had been. She'd once boasted she could take any five items in a refrigerator and pull together a decent dinner, and as far as Viorica could tell, it was true.

"That's not true," Mina protested. "He likes him, he loves him. He's a father, that's what fathers do. Your father didn't spend as much time with Mihai, or you. I think Chris tries really hard." Mina paused and turned, taking a deep breath. "You know," she added slowly, "I have to tell you something. Something about Michael. An awful story."

"What? What?"

"It's terrible what happened. Michael, he hit Caroline over the head with a rock. She was hurt very badly. She had to have stitches."

"When was that?" Viorica asked sharply.

Mina's lank brown hair slipped forward to cover her eyes. She bent away from the steam, stirred the tomatoes, then turned back to her cousin, still holding the wooden spoon in her right hand. "I was there when it happened. Earlier this week. He was doing so well, but now, I don't know. And I'm worried about Caroline. It's hard for her."

"Who did the stitches? They went to the hospital?"

"Oh, no, they took her to a plastic surgeon in Southampton. She thought he was nice. He gave her a set of nesting dolls, like the ones *bunicul nostru,* our grandfather, gave us that Christmas years ago. Remember?"

"It doesn't make sense," Viorica said, shaking her head from side to side. She picked up the saltshaker and spilled some grains onto the table, rolling a few at a time under her index finger to spread them around. A few grains slipped up and under her cherry red nail, and she stuck her finger into her mouth, licking it clean.

"Why not? Why should he not have troubles? So many of them do."

Mina sat down across from her cousin, squeezing between the white enameled cabinets and the table's edge to take the only other seat. She placed an elbow on the windowsill to her right and tilted her chair slightly back to feel the brush of the breeze on her arms and cheek. She loved this apartment. It was so small compared to the Lathams' house or to those of the other two families for whom she baby-sat, but it was completely hers, completely clean and completely private.

Viorica, on the other hand, barely noticed surroundings. She could as easily live squashed on Mina's couch with a single drawer to call her own as in the most luxurious estate to stamp its feet up to the ocean in Southampton. She never seemed to measure people by what they had or owned but by who she instinctively knew them to be; of course, this was why she was so irritated at the implication that she had mismeasured Michael's potential.

"But he was so special, even Constanţa, the *sora şefă* at Clinic No. 7, talked about how many other people wanted him. He glowed with what a wonderful son he would be. He never gave them any trouble, and he never seemed to fade, the way some of them do. I just don't believe it. They complain about him too much, the Lathams. They make it hard for him."

"She knows you think that."

Viorica shrugged. "I don't hide it, why should I?"

"Do you want another glass of wine?"

Viorica nodded. "Why should I hide it?" she asked again.

After a moment, Mina said, "Because I work for them."

"This is America. You can have an opinion here."

Mina walked to the ancient gas stove, spoon in hand, but did not begin to stir.

"I said, you can have an opinion here," Viorica repeated, her voice rising. "You seem to think we are still not safe; I always notice it. If you feel so unsafe here, you should think about going back. At least there, the ways will be familiar to you."

"I don't feel unsafe. I think you do. You want to go back. You are scared. I think that's why you never sit down for a minute."

"I'm sitting *here*." Viorica gestured widely, her fingernails glittering.

"You know what I mean."

"I love it here," Viorica protested. "I love it more than you. That's why I bring the children here."

"You like the money. That's why you bring the children here."

"That's not fair. That's not true."

Mina shrugged. "Maybe yes, maybe no."

The evening sun was low and reddish warm, rays streaming through the oak-leafed limbs outside the kitchen window, casting a glow across the room even though it lacked a full hour to the sunset. Mina wiped her wrist against her forehead.

"But Michael isn't easy," Mina said. "He wasn't loved. It shows."

"I don't believe you."

"That's because *you* love him, but what does that matter? You love him a little, from a distance. You brought him here. You see him once in a while. You're fond of him, that's a better way to say it. He's very troubled. Stopping by every two weeks, you can't see that."

"That's unfair," Viorica said. "I do see him. I know him. He's a good boy. You're not there every day either. They could try harder, I assure you."

"Maybe, but I don't think so. He's not an easy boy. He hits, he yells, he spits. He hurt Caroline so badly she'll have a scar on her face the rest of her life."

"Boy stuff. I've told Deborah so."

Mina rolled her eyes, grimacing at her cousin. "You don't mean that."

"I do," Viorica insisted, her voice sounding tight, as if the passageway to her throat were constricting.

"They had to take Caroline for surgery! Oh, the blood! You can't imagine! The plastic surgeon couldn't even count the stitches, they were so many layers deep. And it wasn't the first time he hurt her, oh, no."

"He's been so much better. You've said so yourself."

"And now he's so much worse," Mina said, mimicking her cousin's harsh tone. "He hits his mother. He doesn't listen. Last year, remember? He was sent home from school for attacking other kids. He got thrown out of t-ball for fighting!"

"So?"

"And you know this, how the one time I tried to bathe them together—and this was years ago, back when he wasn't even three yet, and he was so little, it's hard to imagine—he held her under water like he wanted to drown her. She was five years old and scared, pushing back, trying to stop him, and he kept holding her. I had to pull them apart. He didn't even look like he cared when I hauled him out of the tub. Caroline was crying and crying, I could barely get her to sleep."

Viorica shrugged, elaborately. "You are rehashing old dirt."

"I'm not! He's gotten worse even than that! Worse! I can see him growing worse every day!"

"I see them playing together all the time. Kids do things like that to each other. It doesn't mean anything."

Mina slapped the dirty spoon onto the counter. "This isn't normal, I tell you, Viorica! I am the only person who will still baby-sit for them.

He has no friends. He's too mean, too rough. The children don't like him. If what you're thinking is that he's like your brother, you don't remember how it was. You are so wrong! You just don't know! Mihai was funny and sweet and brave . . ."

"Michael is, too," Viorica said. "You just don't want to see it."

"Believe what you want to believe."

"The mother listens to you," Viorica said. "Tell her he's a nice little boy. Tell her how good he is. Tell her to be patient. I'm asking you. Please."

"I can't. I thought so once, and I did, and I was wrong," Mina answered, flatly. "Now, I would be lying."

19

"I'LL TAKE him out," Martin said, removing squalling Shane from the shelter of his wife's fleshy arms.

Alice stared after her husband as he wrapped the little boy in his jacket and plunked him down into the stroller. Shane was quieter already, his ragged hiccups slowing.

"That's three nights in a row," she said, in the voice another woman might use to reprove a hard drinker stumbling in at two o'clock in the morning.

"It helps the boy sleep. I don't mind."

"But your bursitis—isn't it bothering your ankles?"

Martin lifted his shoulders slowly up and then down in a dramatic shrug. He shook his head elaborately, raising his eyebrows high. "Now don't worry about me," he said, his voice almost giddy to Alice's ears. "I'll be just fine. I can take care of myself."

She felt as if he were implying that she really didn't take care of him at all, a notion she utterly resented.

"It's your funeral," she said.

"That's right."

Out onto Noyac Road Martin strolled this evening, his head and shoulders straightening as if the very act of wheeling Shane could turn him

165

into cock o' the walk. Shane began nodding off before they'd even gone a tenth of a mile. As they passed The Other Stand, Martin thought about a night the previous summer when he'd stopped to buy corn and found the place closed. There had been a few ears of corn still left in the bin outside, though, and he'd reached in and taken them, not even pretending to leave the requisite dollar and ten cents behind. When he returned to the house, Alice said, "Oh! You got them. I'd have sworn they closed by six," and Martin didn't even answer her.

That was the second thing he'd done that he shouldn't have been proud of, maybe in his entire life. His first sin, of course, had been a few years before, when he'd made some visits to a fancy house up near Patchogue. He didn't like to think of those women too much, not anymore. They'd scared him just a little. They were no more interested in him than Alice was, not really. They wanted his money, he guessed, that's all. But, oh! Those girls knew what they were doing. There were five of them, and he knew them all, he supposed, knew their names and what they felt like underneath or atop him, but he didn't like to think about them as people. He knew they didn't think of him that way, so why should he? They could call him "Honey" and he could call each one of them the same, and it didn't matter a whit. The Lord knew he'd held out as long as he could, for years, really. The Lord knew a man was only human, that his needs were meant to be met.

He hoped the Lord knew that, but he wasn't sure. That was why he'd stopped visiting that place.

He hadn't done anything too bad for months after taking the corn from The Other Stand, as if waiting to see if there'd be any fallout, some awful surprise punishment sent from the heavens. There'd been simply silence, though, and slowly, throughout the spring, he'd embarked upon a series of harmless, minute alterations of the normal way of things. Nothing dangerous, or cruel, or overtly evil: material costs padded just that little bit, extra hours thrown onto a customer's bill, change not returned after a trip to King Kullen for a sick neighbor. Oddly enough, he'd felt prouder of himself each time he pulled off one of his tiny maneuvers. Very unlike him it was: Up until recently Martin Dunn had never, ever committed even the mildest of reprehensible acts, never even kept a library book out late or adjusted a nickel on his taxes. But lately, he'd felt seeping into him like a slow, unfixable leak a kind of joy bordering on elation bordering on pure, true happiness, and it needed sweet little pinpricks of risk to keep it trickling in.

Now he thought of taking a second mortgage on the house. Rates were way down, and he had the idea that perhaps that money could be used for something—some plan that was brewing way in the depths of his mind, so nascent an action that he couldn't even concretely formulate what it might be. All he really knew was that he wanted to keep it a secret. Alice shouldn't know, couldn't know; she'd just spoil things with all her fluttery little questions.

But Shane, as they walked along together, seemed to understand everything. The baby was so pure it seemed as if he'd merged with his foster father: Martin didn't even have to formulate words to know little Shane understood him. Still, it was nice to talk out loud. They strolled, the baby's eyelids slowly drooping, and Martin said, "You, Shane, are a good baby, an easy baby, a lovely baby. When my Jack was little, he was just like you, smiling when it was time to smile, crying when it was time to take a walk or have his diapers changed. I wish I'd taken him out like this. It would be something, a darn pleasure, to think about. A real memory. A showstopper."

While Martin spoke, Shane shifted into sleep, his shoulders rolling slightly forward, his puffin's tummy puffing out below.

They passed the Emerson's backyard, visible up the winding slope of Valley Road, and Martin leaned over to pat Shane's blanket into place. The breathing of a winded jogger became audible as he drew closer, thighs tight, sneakers thudding on the tarred road behind them. Cars whipped past only rarely on this July night, taking the curve so exuberantly that Martin was forced to veer off road each time. The lone jogger took the inside path without even a glance in their direction, forcing Martin and Shane further out onto the blacktop. *Why does no one say hello?* Martin wondered. *It isn't as if he truly didn't see us.*

Martin steered the hind wheels of the stroller up, directing it back to the ribbon of grass. In his buttock, a nerve abruptly seized, sciatica running like electricity down the top of his thigh. He stopped, breathing hard into the tops of his lungs, trying to force the air down farther, to his stomach. All his energy tightened around that rod of pain searing its way down his leg. He couldn't get the breath in, simply couldn't, and he determined to keep walking, slowly, as if a calm steady pace might unlock the fangs gripped on his nerve.

"That's Gus's house," Martin confided to Shane, his voice slightly faster and higher pitched than normal. "He used to work for me, for years he worked for me, ever since high school. Now he's got his own business. He doesn't want to be employed any more is how he says it. I don't care. I don't care. Gus Emerson's entitled to all the work he can scratch up for himself, that's how I see it. You know what, though? Even his own wife still calls me when her faucet leaks. Says she can't get out of the habit of it. I know Gus brags he's getting such fancy South-of-the-Highway work he can't find time for his own wife, that's what he tells everyone. I don't buy it though. The fact of the matter is there's no better outfit than Dunn's, and that's the way it's always been. Even now I'm slowing down, I'm still twice the plumber Gus Emerson is. It's a fact."

Shane clearly agreed, shifting slightly onto his left hip and beginning to smile in his sleep. His eyelids quivered; he was dreaming. The very air had grown calm for the baby's benefit, wind politely quelled, cars diverted onto other byways; the footfalls of the jogger were no longer audible. By the time Martin veered the stroller into the Long Beach parking lot, the runner's spandexed thighs were barely visible at the far end. Two seagulls fluttered up from the North Haven edge of the beach and headed toward Martin, curious about any food he might be interested in discarding. Beach plums, just beginning to send out their buds, reminded him, suddenly, of the way the beach had looked in his childhood. He was breathing better now, more evenly. His heart wasn't pounding. The pain in his leg seemed bearable, although he couldn't tell if he'd gotten used to it or if it was getting better.

Martin couldn't recall exactly when the first beach road had been put in, but he remembered hearing his father talk about the motorboat Mr. Gilbride used to have, with extra seats all along the rear and sides. For ten cents each, his father and his friends could hitch a ride straight across the cove to Short Beach. They would spend the day hunting for frogs, building huge sand castles decorated with clamshells and horseshoe crab carcasses. At some point, someone would remember the bacon sandwiches they'd brought with them, and then the day would somehow have disappeared. Mr. Gilbride was far too prompt: At four o'clock he'd pack up his hot dog stand and yell to the boys that it was time to go. They'd chug home, tired and completely contented, the day having disappeared without a care.

Those were wonderful, wonderful days! Martin's childhood had been equally idyllic, and he'd tried to show his own boys how marvelous their world was, he really had. He was positive. Surely they'd spent afternoons trekking through the gray powdery mud on the cove side of the beach, just as he had as a child. He could feel it now, between his toes, as if he weren't wearing his ratty old sneakers. That mud was warm talcum to the feet, and each footprint would stay so that he could imagine himself Hansel trying to lead the way back home. Beach grass fluttered long as banners, swishing his ankles. Did the beach plums grow there? He couldn't recall.

Oh, but the terns, he couldn't forget them! How they had hated Martin and his friends! How they had hated Jack and Des a generation later! The mud was where they nested, fragile eggs scattered in soft indentations in the dusky powder. Protecting their progeny, the terns had learned to resent visitors beyond measure.

"Eeeeeyew! Eeeeeyew! That was the sound they made as they dive-bombed us. We'd just laugh and laugh," he told sleeping Shane, who did not flinch. The seagulls, hovering overhead, fluttered their wings to lift upward slightly and then float back down.

He'd found Indian arrowheads on this beach and the most beautiful shells. He'd gone out on innumerable occasions with his brother and sister to collect the seaweed they banked around the house; that was the insulation people used to winterize house foundations in those days. Ah, it had been wonderful! Not easy like it was now, but not draining either. He'd had such energy in those days. The effort had always been worth it. That kind of work didn't take it out of you; it was just the way things were. Cold in winter. Hot in summer. It made sense. Martin missed gathering seaweed. He missed having adventures with his little brother, and he missed carrying his sister on his back all afternoon so his mother could get her housework done.

He was panting. He'd been walking too fast, and now the knife of pain down his leg and up his lower back had spread, radiating and diluting itself into a dull, bearable ache. The evening, instead of growing cooler, seemed to be heating up degree by degree. He stopped the stroller and stood, feeling a trickle of water inch down along his T-shirt from collarbone to belly.

He hadn't thought about his childhood in years. *God,* he thought to himself suddenly, *why does no one see me? Can't anybody look, or listen? I have nothing to show for all I've lived. Nothing at all. But I could talk if someone would listen. I really could.*

"Listen to me, why don't you? Listen! Listen to me!" He was screaming, his two arms lifted as high as his bursae would allow. His lungs were empty, his throat wide and dry. The wind, blowing from the north, kissed his back.

At that moment, the seagulls gave up on Martin Dunn and veered west toward Riverhead, wings undulating. It really was getting warmer. He shook his head, squared his shoulders, and began pushing the stroller forward. His left buttock was sore. Maybe nobody heard him because he had nothing to say worth hearing. If he weren't a man, he'd almost feel like crying.

The baby was still asleep when Martin finally arrived home, limping slightly. He had to struggle to get the stroller up the steep driveway and over the single concrete step without waking Shane. Inside, he abandoned the boy and sunk himself heavily into one of the two easy chairs. Alice, in the other chair, was watching a *Dateline* segment about a male nurse who made a habit of raping obstetrical patients after their babies were delivered. She nodded at him, turning back to her program.

"Can't you get me a glass of water?"

"Oh," she said, fluttering up from the depths of the chair as if she were a hundred pounds lighter. "I'm sorry. I'll get it now."

"And some ice cream."

"Ice cream. I'll get it."

"Okay."

They ate in silence, working through the ice cream stolidly, staring at the television screen. "Oh," Alice said. "I forgot. I'm sorry. Chris Latham called."

"Whaddid he want?" He blinked deliberately, as if he would have rolled his eyes heavenward but didn't want to do the work.

"Something to do with a leak in the bathroom. Toilet's been running, I think. He asked could you get out there tomorrow. He asked for you, not Paul or Joe."

Martin dropped his spoon into his ice cream bowl with a clatter. "Does he think I don't know how to run my own business? Does he think he can tell me who I'm going to put on a job? Just because he went to college and married some girl from away? Does he think that turns him into city people, makes him more important than anybody else? I remember him when he was too short to make Little League. I remember his mother sitting waiting to die. Two years she sat still as a stone not letting a soul help her live."

Martin's face was bright red, the words sputtering out his lips rapidly, as if at any moment the flow might dry up and cease. His fingers, in his lap, found one another and held on, flat thumb clamped down on flat thumb. Alice still faced the television; he couldn't even tell if she was paying attention. He had more to say. "I know where he came from, Chris Latham. He's a Sag Harbor boy. He can't tell me how to run my business. If he wants Dunn's Plumbing, he'll get whoever I think best. It's my business. I'll send who I send."

"Okay," Alice said, shrugging. "It just sounded like it was you he wanted."

Flattered, mollified, irritated, resentful—Martin didn't quite know which direction he wanted to head in, so he didn't go on. He put his lips together and held them that way, channel changer in hand. After a very long time, perhaps as much as five minutes, he muttered, "He didn't look different from the other kids."

"Who? Chris Latham? When the boys were small?"

"Yeah," Martin admitted.

"I know," Alice agreed. "I've thought that, too. It's funny."

20

"WHY DO you read that kind of poetry to them?" Chris asked. "It's morbid."

Deborah looked up, surprised. "It's Whitman, for God's sake. It's about Lincoln's death. Haven't you ever read 'O Captain, My Captain'?"

"Probably. I know I've heard it before. But they're so little to be hearing about people falling cold and dead, don't you think?"

The children were snuggled up on either side of Deborah, attitudes so relaxed and loving it irritated him. He couldn't recall ever sitting that way with his own mother, or with Eileen. The hugging he remembered was very conscious, used in greetings and departures and rarely even at that. He both admired and was repelled by the way in which Deborah was able to swarm over the family, a warm, enveloping mass drawing her strength from the act of loving. Bright monarch butterfly wings or glistening peacock feathers—her love had just such a dramatic quality of display, alternately gorgeous and vulgar, depending, he supposed, on his feelings in the moment. What made the least sense of all to him was how she seemed to be failing with Michael. It proved that love was not enough to atone for the past, or perhaps that Deborah's love wasn't real love at all. How else could they have found themselves in this place?

"What's that poem you used to read to me?" he asked suddenly. "Cliff somebody and the dinner? The wormwood?"

"Cliff Klingenhagen," Deborah answered. "I love that poem. 'Cliff Klingenhagen had me in to dine with him one day; and after soup and meat, and all the other things there were to eat, Cliff took two glasses and filled one with wine . . .' "

" 'And one with wormwood . . .' "

"And blah and blah, I can't remember, and then Cliff 'said it was a way of his. And though I know the fellow, I have spent long time a-wondering when I shall be as happy as Cliff Klingenhagen is.' "

They smiled at each other, she across the tops of their children's heads and he, looking down on all of them as if the only grown-up in the room, and for a moment, a pulse existed between the husband and wife that made it possible to believe in anything.

Deborah's voice was quiet, affectionate, amused. She had one hand on each child's hair, patting Caroline's braids and tousling Michael's curls, and she said, "I always think when people talk about whether the glass is half full or half empty that they're missing the essential point. I mean, what's in the glass in the first place—wormwood, wine, diet Coke—that has to matter more than anything."

He chuckled. "Or spring water or tap water or seltzer."

She said, "Oh yes, and is it of domestic or European origin?"

Michael giggled. "Or milk! It might be milk!"

"You guys are silly!" Caroline squirmed over and onto her mother's lap, her braids slapping onto Michael's thighs. He tugged them, grabbing hard with both hands so that she screamed. "Ee-aiow!" Caroline screamed. "Michael, you jerk, that hurts!"

He pushed her aside.

Deborah rolled Caroline further back and over, out of range. "You okay?"

Caroline burst out crying, her face flushing, pearls welling up and out the creases of each eye. "It's not fair! It's not fair! You always let him do anything! He's mean, he's mean!"

Chris's eyes went vacant. Without moving from his spot by the door, he seemed to Deborah to have drifted away, his corporeal person dissipating into vapor.

"Caroline," Deborah said. "I know Michael didn't mean to hurt you; you know he didn't mean to . . ."

"That's not true! He did! He did!" she wailed. "You know he did! He always does!"

Deborah looked up at Chris. His nose seemed longer and sharper, as if the effort to contain his anger was straining his skin taut, forcing his bones to jut forward. She remembered seeing a similar expression just once before, when they'd been racing home along the Long Island Expressway and Chris had been pulled over for speeding. Deborah, six months' pregnant with Caroline, had been furious at her husband for feeling the need to rush back from the obstetrician's office in Setauket to his own office, where there was a slim chance some emergency had developed. She'd wanted him to be with her that day, anticipating their child, worrying over the changes in her body, imagining the future. She hadn't wanted him to be so eager to return to the other side of his life, and when he'd been pulled over, she'd found a kind of justice there. Despite her annoyance, the carefully neutral way he'd dealt with the cop had been intriguing. She'd not been able to stop herself from asking about it after they'd been set free on the highway, ticket tossed at her feet.

"I've never been pulled over," she said.

"You haven't lived."

"No, seriously, I haven't. You know me, I follow rules. I have this thing about it. My sister used to say I suffered from terminal honesty."

He'd chuckled then, eyes still looking ahead, scanning the ribbon of road unwinding at the horizon. Oddly, the tension had been broken; she could tell he was no longer straining to return to work. He'd given up, she supposed, realizing that he couldn't possibly get back before the end of the day.

"Why were you in such a hurry? It isn't like you had patients scheduled this afternoon."

"I don't know," he mumbled. He was silent for a moment, but when he spoke, his voice was firmer and clearer. He said, "I like the idea of a baby, I really do."

She patted his thigh, admiring the lean line of it. "Are you worried? I'm not. We'll do fine, I promise you."

"I'm not worried."

At the western edge of the Pine Barrens, the sky overhead widened abruptly, spreading atop the landscape like an unfolding paper fan. The road seemed wider also, there, and the median grew from a series of concrete dividers to a generous expanse of wildflowers, a slim meadow splitting the bidirectional parade of Range Rovers and BMWs.

"Was that some kind of cop thing you did back there?"

He laughed. "What do you mean?"

"I don't know. You didn't look up at him; you weren't exactly friendly. You didn't talk much."

"It's the first rule of dealing with cops, didn't you know? If you talk to them, they ticket you. Especially if you try to explain. Keep your mouth shut and be polite; that's the only thing to do."

"But you got a ticket anyway," she pointed out.

He didn't answer.

"I'm just trying to understand."

Chris, looking exasperated, turned to glare at her briefly, before focusing back on the road. "It must have been the exception that proves the rule," he said.

She'd seen that "cop look" many times since then. In a small town, one often gets to drive by one's friends, neighbors, and acquaintances while they're wrestling with the law. Interestingly enough, the look did appear to work in Sag Harbor: Deborah had frequently witnessed the respectful silence with which the local boys in blue were greeted; she'd also had occasion to see those not so in the know as they tried to argue and negotiate their way out of a ticket. That strained near-death mask seemed to be the costume one wore to bedazzle figures of authority; and now here, the same expression was convoluting its way across Chris's face as he stared at his family. Which of them was he looking at? Deborah? Michael? Certainly not Caroline?

The doorbell rang, and Chris darted forward, toward them and to the left, opening the playroom door before she'd even registered that a visitor had come up the walk.

It was Martin Dunn. "Alice said you called," he stated defensively, as if wary of his welcome.

"I did, I did. It was me," Chris said. "Come in." He waved his arms wide, expansively, ushering Martin in as if to a huge and glorious cocktail party.

The master bathroom was a pale blue-green, extravagantly large, the kind of room where one could spend hours primping and posing. The mirrored wall was overwhelming, suggesting a level of self-interest Martin probably considered appalling. Chris was embarrassed having Martin in here; he'd not considered this aspect when he had the brilliant idea of calling Dunn's Plumbing about the leak.

Chris stood by the sink, at a respectful distance from Martin, who'd had to grunt in order to maneuver his heavy frame along the floor to the back of the toilet. Martin's manner had been cool ever since his arrival, as if he didn't particularly like Chris. Chris was determined not to be defeated by it. He had no intention of allowing himself to feel offended.

Instead, he offered to bring Martin a cup of coffee, and when the offer was refused, he made it again.

Martin said, "Honest. No thanks," and then said he was fine, nodding toward the door as if to indicate that he'd prefer to be alone.

"It's been running for a while, maybe a month. But the water down there, that leak must have started in the past few days."

"I can tell. The tile's not too stained."

"Oh."

Martin said, "Valve's off. I can handle it from here." Chris knew he was acting like a nervous giant, hovering over Martin and clearly making him uncomfortable. He couldn't help himself. Having arranged matters in this manner, he had to continue.

"Say, I hear Anna's coming back for Memorial Day weekend, Anna Downing. Mrs. Dunn told me when she was in last week."

"I guess that's right," Martin said, reaching behind to pull a wrench from his tool belt.

"She lives in Schenectady now, is that right?"

Martin grunted.

"Does her husband come with her?" Chris pursued.

Martin grunted.

"Does he? They have kids?"

"I guess."

"How many?"

"Look," Martin said, "if you let me fix the toilet, I'll be out of your hair in no time."

"There's no rush."

"I've got a business to run."

Chris turned the faucets on, began to wash his hands.

"Hey. If I can *hear*, I can fix it. I need to hear when the water stops running."

"Sorry."

Chris dried his hands on the blue hand towel Deborah had left by the sink. He swallowed and sighed. He stuck his hands in his pockets, jingling change and keys. What he was about to do was as unethical as what he'd failed to do with Alice only days earlier. Not telling her what he'd seen was a breach of his professionalism; now, broaching the same subject with her spouse was even more questionable. The person who was doing this, the man who kept betraying his own standards, whose judgment was suddenly so flawed—such a man couldn't really be Christopher Latham.

Something so strange was happening these days, and he didn't understand the why of things that had been utterly clear only a few months earlier. If he'd let himself think the words, he'd know that he was frightened, terrified, really, but of what? He had no idea. At the base of it, this was the problem. Too much was out of his control. He breathed in, deeply. "Say," he said abruptly. "How do you think Mrs. Dunn's been feeling?"

Martin looked up, the wrench grasped loosely in his right hand. Wedged there between toilet and wall, he looked like a huge, unwieldy kidnap victim, the kind that captors prefer to off without waiting for ransom, deeming them unsalvageable and of little value even to their loved ones. "What d'you mean?" he asked suspiciously.

Chris shrugged, turning back to the mirror over the sink. He picked up his hairbrush. "Has she had less energy than normal?"

Martin snorted. "She sits on the couch watching TV all day long. Has for the past twenty years. You tell me."

"Has she lost any weight recently?"

Martin snorted again. "Ha," he said.

Chris's skin took on a pale flush, hardly pink at all. He shrugged again, squaring his shoulders. He turned back to face Martin, who gazed up at him from the floor resentfully, as if conducting a conversation such as this from a position of inequality was utterly irritating.

"I saw something," Chris admitted finally.

"Saw what?"

"A corrugated patch on her tongue, probably nothing. Well, actually," he said reluctantly, "in this case, maybe something. I think she should see her family doctor. Get it checked out."

Martin squirmed and twisted, lurching uncomfortably to a seated position in front of the toilet. "Why didn't you tell her?" he asked. "Or did you?"

Chris shook his head, no. "I don't know." He looked down, but at his running shoes and not at Martin.

"You should have told her."

"I know. I just . . . I didn't want . . ."

"She could handle it," Martin interrupted, speaking quickly as if to reassure himself. "I think you should've told her. It'd be easier, hearing it from you."

"I just thought . . . ," Chris trailed off. Not even he was precisely sure what it was that he thought. He was confused by Martin's reaction, although he certainly wasn't clear on how he himself might react in a similar situation. "I'll call her," he said then. "I thought—I thought maybe you'd want to talk to her yourself."

"Well, I don't know," Martin said. "Aren't you her dentist?"

"I'm sorry," he said. "Maybe I should have . . . I'll call her."

"No," Martin said. "I was just pointing it out."

They were silent for a long moment, Martin eyeing the space behind the toilet and Chris trying hard to get Martin to look at him. "She should see your doctor," Chris said, finally, mustering up a more normal level of authority. "You used Bert Isen, right? That's what my chart says. I hear good things about his son Greg. He'd be a good person to call, has all his father's records. People seem to like him. Mrs. Dunn should see him as quickly as possible."

"Oh, I'll talk to her, don't worry. What do you think she's got, anyhow? Cancer?"

"No," Chris said, "but I think she's pretty sick."

Chris was watching closely, which was how he could tell that Martin's expression—exasperation—hadn't altered even the minutest amount. "What's she got then?" Martin asked again.

"I can't say for sure," Chris said finally. "But that kind of leukoplakia—those wavy lines on her tongue—that kind of oral hairy cell leukoplakia you don't really see in people, except when they have AIDS."

Martin snorted. "Right. Alice? Maybe you mixed her up with someone else? You had too much to drink the night before?"

"I wish," Chris said. "I wish. I did this training at NYU, at the dental clinic, that's the only other place I ever saw it. I just think, I mean, that's why I think Doc Isen should check her out."

Martin shook his head from side to side, as if he were questioning Chris's sanity. "About as likely as finding a goldfish in this bowl here," he said, amused.

"It isn't, though. She really needs to be looked at."

Martin shook his head again. "All right, I'll do it. I'll tell her," Martin said. "How about I run along now and do that? Paulie can come back this afternoon. He can finish up here in no time. Just don't use this toilet until he comes back. I left the water off."

Chris nodded, wanting to reach forward and help Martin to his feet. Instead, he watched as Martin struggled to his knees, heaving himself up with a grunt. If only Martin would look at him; then their eyes might meet. Perhaps he could communicate in that way how truly sorry he was.

Instead, Martin Dunn packed his tools back on his belt without ado.

When he tucked the wrench back into its place, it pressed aggressively through his jeans, into the soft flesh of his leg. He seemed to have nothing more to say, or perhaps he was distracted. That was probably why he failed to see Chris's outstretched hand, why he barely even nodded farewell. He didn't look to right or left, and certainly not at Christopher, who trailed him downstairs, past Deborah and the children, all the way to the playroom door.

21

"YOU KNOW, Viorica, he's not going to get easier. All we can hope for is that he doesn't get worse. I wish you could face it. I mean, Chris and I, we can't pretend anymore. It makes it worse. Honestly. It doesn't help anyone to pretend there's no problem, and it only makes it harder to feel that you blame us."

They were outside in the yard, seated on an old pink blanket, drinking iced tea. The temperature was in the low eighties, with little humidity. It had rained so much in the spring that they'd needed to have the grass cut more than once a week, a staggering accumulation of expense. The yard had looked beautiful, red tulips alight, the grass around them bright green and as soft to the touch as fabric. Now, it had turned into a summer Deborah Latham would always remember as the summer of wild sunflowers and glorious dragonflies. Colors all that July and August were brighter than normal, the air clear and dancing with butterflies, the evenings cool and cast with lovely pinks and purples that washed across the sky like paints. Their yard had been rich with scores of button-sized sunflowers and buttery cosmos. All the bushes had flowered madly in pinks and yellows and deep velvety lavender, a kind of paradoxical beauty that felt more reproachful than generous. It rained hardly at all that entire summer of 1997; the weather was balmy, never too hot or too cold, as if all the forces of nature were conspiring to render the world more enchanting.

Down at the far end of the yard, Michael had squeezed himself into his old baby swing; he filled it so tightly his thighs were squashed together. The swing hung down under his weight, hardly drifting back and forth. His eyes were open; he stared up at the cottony cumulus clouds, but the expression on his face was utterly blank. He'd been in that position since they'd first come outside, nearly an hour before.

Viorica sat with her knees pulled up to her chest, shoulders slumped forward and around, blonde hair draping over her face. Deborah couldn't tell if she was angry or defeated, and she felt exhausted at the notion of trying to find out.

Deborah said softly, "It'll be better once you accept it. It will."

"It's not that I don't believe—well, it's not that I don't suppose you have tried. If you had seen him there, what I saw back at the clinic, you would know that he will make it. I cannot give up. I cannot. You shouldn't either." Viorica's small, thin lips were drawn fiercely back.

Deborah sat up straighter, smoothing her jean skirt down over her knees. "My parents were emergency room doctors; did I ever tell you that?"

"No." Viorica's tone was resentful, as if she were wondering what Deborah's parents possibly had to do with her.

Deborah said, "I always felt as if I were on the brink of disaster, all the time, when I was a kid. And I always was, I think. At any moment, all through my childhood, my mother or my father—or in the worst of circumstances, both—would be called from the dinner table, from my birthday parties, from my bedtime stories. Always in order to cope with disaster—sudden, acute disaster. It was all so random, someone simply walking down a street and then a car plows into him and suddenly his whole life is altered. Ended. As if thunderbolts really are thrown out of the heavens, you know, the Greek gods playing some sadistic game of chance."

Viorica's gaze was on Michael, still and listless in the swing down at the end of the yard. He gazed up into the sky as if daring that thunderbolt to seek him out.

"So one evening, when I was about six years old, I remember my mother coming in with this cat, a gray and white beast of an animal," Deborah continued. "His name was Tiger, and he was extraordinarily large and beautiful, practically fourteen pounds with the biggest, deepest eyes. He ran around our house purring and purring, exploring everything. And my mother told me that the cat had shown up in the emergency room. Tiger'd walked in through the admitting doors, explored the entire ground floor, and then, as if he'd picked her out of the crowd, he'd strolled up to my mother, walked up her white coat, all the way up her body! He nuzzled into her neck and began to purr. So my mother felt as if it were fate, as if Tiger had picked her out and it meant something."

"Like Michael with me," Viorica muttered.

"Exactly," Deborah said. "But the thing is, Tiger purred for about a week. We thought he was wonderful. Then the next week came, and he was used to us. So he started clawing all our furniture and scratching me and my sister and peeing on all the rugs."

"Cats do that."

"I know. But he also would do this thing where if you were nice to him, say, if you petted him, he would purr and purr, and just as he seemed to be in ecstasy, then he'd lash out, really viciously, and scratch so hard he'd leave sores that bled from elbow to wrist. It was like he hated to be loved."

"Michael's not like that."

Deborah shook her head. "I'm not saying what you think I'm saying. All I mean is that sometimes things—cats, I mean, and people—aren't exactly the way they appear to be. The truth, what's underneath it all, isn't always so easy to see. Even if you're really good at seeing. That's all."

After a long time, Viorica took a sip from her glass. She swallowed with her eyes closed, her Adam's apple just the slightest bit visible. She said, "So what are you going to do? Send him back?"

Deborah, shocked, said, "Of course not! He's our son! All I'm saying is we can't expect miracles anymore. We need to deal with the son we have, not the one we keep imagining we'll have created when some magical transformation occurs. It isn't going to happen."

"So what will you do? What happened to that miracle worker you took him to? That homeopath?"

If she'd thought about it, she would have known Viorica would pull out all the ammunition. It was true that Emma Hollander had acknowledged that some cases are more difficult than others. Emma wasn't ready to give up, not at all. In fact, she felt sure she could keep peeling layers from Michael, exposing and stimulating his own inner healing processes to help him more and more. Emma's face had been pink with promise; she'd offered to speak directly to Chris, to help Deborah to convince him to go on with the healing.

But it hadn't been Chris who wanted to stop; it had been Deborah. She didn't want to risk anymore. She wanted the doors shut tight and locked.

She wanted hope to wither. Denying the truth, daring to dream, what purpose did it serve? She had tried, and only hurt them all, hurt them more. Now was the time to seal hope away and trust in endurance.

Deborah leaned forward and up, as if by straightening her back and sitting taller she might find herself in charge of the entire situation. On her left leg, just below the knee, where the ankle of her other foot was resting easily, a lumpy tracing of veins was visible. Viorica, gazing at the small deformity, smiled slightly.

Deborah placed a hand on the veins.

"Have you ever seen dragonflies like those?" Deborah asked eventually, pointing to an overgrown mass of sage and lavender that seemed suddenly infested by bright green and purple dragonflies.

Viorica shook her head. "We have nothing like that at home. But we have oak trees and beech trees, far larger than those here."

Deborah shrugged.

"I'm just saying."

"It doesn't matter," Deborah said. "The truth is, Michael's seen every expert, had every test. The only thing left is to put him on tranquilizers or something, but look at him. He looks like a zombie already."

Michael hung, stuffed in the baby seat, the weight of his body creating the only movement. His eyes, open and unflinching, frightened his mother. Viorica, on the other hand, apparently could not shake the belief that he was more alert and receptive than most of the other children she'd seen. She seemed to have little doubt that in another, better home, where the parents were less concerned about protecting their own way of life, Michael would thrive.

"*Servus*, Michael!" Viorica called. "*Ce mai faci?*"

His gaze veered toward her abruptly, angrily, and then melted into warmth when he realized who it was who had called to him. "*Nu înțeleg.*"

"What does that mean?" Deborah asked. "I didn't know he remembered anything. He was so young when he got here."

"He was one and a half. He's very bright; I've always said so."

"I know he's smart; I'm his mother. But to remember the language—that's impossible. What did he say?"

"He said he didn't understand me," Viorica said with a chuckle, seemingly charmed. She called out again, "*Îmi pare rău, scuză-mă!* Sorry, excuse me!"

"He never lets Mina speak Romanian at all," Deborah said quietly.

Michael scowled. "*Lăsați-mă în pace!* Leave me alone, why don't you?" He slipped himself out of the swing and down to earth, stomping back past them, into the house.

Viorica shook her head from side to side, amused. "He's such a boy, thinks he's so tough!"

They were silent for a long time, sipping iced tea, watching the dragonflies dip from leaf to leaf. Usually horseflies and dragonflies come together, one so viciously buzzing, the other so quiet and lovely, but today only the pretty dragons were dancing. "I should check on him," Deborah said. "I really should."

Viorica closed her eyes, and so did Deborah, feeling the sun warm on her neck and face and arms.

She could feel Viorica's breathing next to her, could sense a certain harmony in the way their bodies were aligned on the blanket, and she tried to tell herself the congruence was more than situational. "Viorica," Deborah said, "aren't there other boys like him? Aren't there other children with problems, who can't seem to become parts of the families they've joined? There have to be. Please tell me, can't you?"

Viorica opened her brown eyes, blinked twice at Deborah, and said, "I'd like to help you, I really would. You know that. But I continue to believe that your problems with Michael are not half as bad as you make them out to be. He's just a boy who needs a firm hand and a lot of love."

"I don't see how you say that! He isn't normal. He attacks his sister, this last time he really hurt her. And nobody will play with him. Whit Glennen left here in tears the other day, even a kid like him can't take Michael. He's not safe to be with; you have to supervise him every minute. It's exhausting, but it's a fact." Now Deborah's voice grew cold. "I think you refuse to see what is more than obvious to the rest of us."

"Have it your way," Viorica said. "Your mind is made up. The *sora şefă*—the head nurse at his clinic—she could tell you how many Americans wanted him, what a treasure Michael is. But you only hear what you want to hear."

Deborah's voice began to rise as she came to standing, the edge of the blanket catching under her white flip-flop. Later, when recounting this story to Christopher, she would admit that she'd felt fury first in her body, not in her mind, as if the heat rose up from inside, taking her by surprise. She'd not known, until then, precisely how ragingly angry she was. And it wasn't Michael who infuriated her, in fact, it was Viorica, the Trojan who had brought their gift so blithely and now so dishonorably refused to admit what she had done.

The glass spilled forward, ice cubes rattling against one another.

Viorica grabbed her own glass before it fell. Deborah lifted her toes high, letting the sandal flip away from her heel to free the blanket and then shaking her foot before stamping it fruitlessly on the grass. Her right hand curved, first into a claw and then a fist. She shouted, "I've tried, Viorica, I really have, to listen to you and hear your point of view! It's you who can't hear mine, ours. God knows we could be lying dead in our house, clobbered to death by that little devil, and you'd still be saying it was our fault, that if we'd only loved him a little more he wouldn't be so evil!"

Viorica stood to face Deborah, shoulders back, mouth wide and furious. Planted firmly on those sturdy legs, her chin was high, her fists up like a boxer's. "Don't try to pretend to me you don't intend to give him up! I can see that you do, and I'm the only person in the way, the only person brave enough to tell you how selfish you are! When you took him in, you said he was your son! You said he was part of your family, forever! Now you are looking for a way, an excuse! You can't fool me! I know! I know!"

"You're wrong!" Deborah shouted. "You are so wrong! We have no intention of giving him up or sending him away. If you'd stop fighting long enough to listen, you'd know we have a problem, in our family! That little boy, our son! How dare you! You can come over every other week and sneer at us, but why don't you try living here, day to day! Why don't you get the phone calls from the school, from the other parents, from the playground! See if you know what to do then!"

They were at the moment of choice, but it would take mutual agreement to back down and only one aggressor to move forward. Viorica's eyes were narrow with rage; even so, the sparkle, the love of the battle, was visible. Deborah couldn't even look at Viorica; instead, she tracked the course of the dragonflies: gold, green, and purple skittering through the air like jewels flung from a careless hand.

Fists clenched, Viorica stood unmoving. Deborah turned toward the house, toward Michael, thinking to end the confrontation without a conclusion. Her heart was beating so hard she could barely catch her breath; all she wanted was to get away.

Viorica made a small sound, half snarl, half cry. Deborah swiveled to face her, keeping her lips tight. She was terrified of what else she might say if she allowed herself the freedom.

In the next yard, a programmed sprinkler sprang into action; in the soft pulsing of the water, a rainbow hung motionless.

They stared at one another, panting as if they'd engaged in physical battle. Viorica opened her mouth, then closed it. She turned on her heel and stomped toward the driveway. As she opened the door of Mina's Subaru, she said, "I know what you're going to do, I do. And if you were honest, you'd admit it, too."

Deborah started forward, fists clenching. Her face was flushed, her eyes huge, her jaw wide. She couldn't help herself, had to yell. Words she'd held in for weeks now emerged like sandpaper, scraping the back of her throat. "Just come back here and say that! You selfish bitch! You just don't know how to admit that maybe you didn't know what you were looking at! You can't bear to admit you were wrong!"

"Believe what you want to believe," Viorica said coolly. "I obviously can't change your mind." With that, she inserted herself into the car and slammed the door purposefully.

In the yard, glasses and ice lay scattered over the blanket and on the lawn as if something far more violent had occurred. Deborah watched Viorica's car pull from the driveway. *Why had she ever wanted Viorica's understanding?* After weeks of fearing it, the rift between them came as a relief.

22

⁓

CHRIS, emerging from their bedroom the following morning, was surprised to see Deborah, still in her nightgown, quietly closing Michael's door. Her arms were full of soiled sheets.

"Is he okay?"

"Oh. You surprised me." She turned, smiling gaily. "You're up early."

"Same time as always. What's going on?"

Shrugging, she hugged the pile to her chest. "Nothing. Just picking up the laundry."

"You're getting started early today."

"Yeah. I guess."

"Smells funky."

"Yeah," she said. "Kids. They get so dirty."

23

"ME?" ALICE says, too stunned to shift in her easy chair. She tries to swallow, but fear has dried her throat completely, and the word comes out in a hoarse squawk. Martin moves toward her, as if to kneel by her chair, but they both know such an action is impossible. Alice waves him back, the flutter of her hand such a habit she can perform it despite the sudden numbness up her neck and jaw, and across her forehead, and down the back of her head.

24

"WHY does Michael get to stay alone with Mina?" Caroline asked, her tone as injured as it had been the evening before, when Deborah had first described the next day's plans to her. Deborah was washing Caroline's face with a white washcloth, carefully avoiding the seam now healing above her right eye. Caroline held her toothbrush with its neat line of paste, ready to begin on her teeth as soon as her mother was done. Even though they no longer needed to keep the stitches dry, they'd gotten into the habit of performing this cleaning ritual together, as if the accident had given Caroline rights to a certain level of regression.

The plastic surgeon had recommended they keep the stitches covered until the surgical tape fell off of its own accord, and Caroline had been obedient about keeping it dry. Now, ten days later, the cut on her forehead was healing nicely, although it remained fairly alarming to look at. They'd been to have the stitches removed, and even the tiny dots seemed inflamed—those spots where the needles had passed neatly through, sewing the raw tear in her flesh back together. The stitches had taken nearly an hour to put in, with Caroline's sobs audible even out in the waiting room, where Chris and Michael sat side by side, listening to light rock spewing from a portable radio and pretending to hear only the faintly complaining tones of love gone wrong. Chris told Deborah later that Michael kept playing with the dials on the radio, running through the stations as if the rise and fall in volume, the sudden changes in voice and song, might blur together, masking Caroline's cries.

Deborah, never weak of stomach, had been superbly strong this day; she'd held Caroline's hand throughout the entire painstaking fifty-three minutes of surgery. There had been so many stitches the plastic surgeon said it wasn't even worth counting for the insurance company—hundreds, he'd estimated. He'd had to sew up at least five layers of skin.

Today, Deborah and Chris were driving back to Connecticut, for another meeting with the doctor who had performed Michael's brain scans. It was Chris's idea, this appointment, and Deborah hadn't discouraged it; any attention paid to Michael by his father was better than the current level of mildly irritated disinterest.

The biggest problem presented by Christopher's desire to meet with Dr. Silver was where to leave the children. It was impossible not to worry about this. What if Michael got angry again? How could Mina be left responsible for guarding Caroline against such an extraordinary, unpredictable potential for rage? Leaving the children even with someone as trusted as Mina seemed so fraught with risk and danger that Deborah made plans for Caroline to spend the day with Ada Bloom.

"It isn't fair," Caroline had whined. "I never get to see Mina anymore. Ada's house is boring, it's so boring, and I just want to stay home. It's not fair!"

"I know, Baby, I know," she'd said soothingly, stroking Caro's hair with one hand as she rinsed the toothbrush with the other. "It's just this one time. We need to go have this very important meeting, all the way in Connecticut, and I think you'd have more fun at Ada's. Her mother's going to take you to the beach!"

Caroline's face had smoothed over; this was an interesting possibility. She looked into the mirror, smiled at herself engagingly, and then, with all the utter directness of a seven-year-old, said, "Next time I get to stay home and he has to go someplace else. I get a turn next."

"Okay," Deborah said, suppressing for the moment her certainty that there was no play date to which Michael could be so easily sent, not anymore. "Okay."

The doctor in Connecticut, the one who specialized in PET scans, was the man Deborah had hated the previous September. He'd held out so little hope for Michael's future; today, at Chris's request, he was going to be even more specific.

Earlier, he had told them that children who haven't been loved enough before the age of two often suffer from severe underdevelopment of the brain. "For the purposes of Michael's situation, it's best to try to think of the brain as a series of layers of growing complexity," he now said. "The bottom layer is the simplest—the brain stem—the area in charge of the most basic functions. Breathing, which we're born knowing how to do; and regulating body temperature, a skill our body rapidly gains control of in the very first months of life."

"I'm leaving out a lot," Dr. Silver said to Chris, apologetically. Chris nodded, making clear his lack of professional affront as he gestured toward his wife. Deborah gathered that they were there for her; there was something Chris already understood that he quite clearly wanted her to hear from an unimpeachable source.

Dr. Silver described the next region of functions, where sleep and hunger are regulated, and then, above that, the limbic region, in charge of sexual behavior and other instinctual urges.

"Over the entire pile, like a soft swaddling blanket, that's where we find the cerebral cortex," said Dr. Silver. "And that's the area of most concern when we look at children like Michael, of course. The area that separates us from other mammals, that makes us human. It's in this region of the brain that judgment and memory and reason are located. It's why we can live by rules."

On the phone, the doctor had said he intended to be blunt with them, a promise of candor Deborah had dismissed as self-bolstering cowboy talk. How much blunter could he be than he had already been? Almost a year ago, he had held out little hope for Michael's ever being amalgamated into the world in a normative way. What crueler statement could he make now?

Dr. Silver cleared his throat, running his hands to the hip area of his lab coat. He rubbed his palms against one another with a dry whisper. He seemed so uncomfortable around people; Deborah wasn't surprised that he spent his life placing children in coffinlike scanning machines. He wore no wedding ring, she saw, and she wondered if he even had a private life or if he spent all his time being proudly blunt for the benefit of troubled families.

Dr. Silver cleared his throat again. Perhaps he's nervous, too, Deborah thought, attempting briefly to see him as a bright young expert trying to the best of his ability to help them understand their situation. Once the doctor's stiff little speech restarted itself, however, she knew absolutely that she disliked him. "Michael, I suspect, lacks utterly the ability to love," Dr. Silver began. "He has no ability to connect, to be attached. He wasn't loved himself at an early enough phase."

Dr. Silver pushed his black-rimmed glasses back up his nose, looked over at Chris and gave a half shrug that seemed to Deborah not an apology but smug pleasure in his own words. Chris nodded back, wryly, signaling that he'd been expecting to hear such news. Deborah, the only one of them still seated, shifted her legs, recrossing them.

Dr. Silver pushed at his glasses again and sighed, as if disappointed.

"There's a critical phase for learning how to love," Dr. Silver said. "A window that closes for most children by the age of two."

"We got him at eighteen months," Deborah said, smoothing the yellow silk of her pants. She was wearing these pants the day she went to the airport to meet Viorica and Michael, the day she first gave her heart to the little boy and made him her own. She'd worked so hard to get ready for him, and not until she'd been in the car driving to Kennedy to meet the plane had she considered how different it might feel to receive a fully formed child, one she hadn't nurtured and dreamed of from nearly the first moment of conception.

She'd brought a stroller for Michael, she remembered, and a stuffed duck that had been Caroline's. With all the planning for his arrival, all the endless painting and rewiring and ordering of furniture, she'd forgotten to get him a welcome home present, but Michael hadn't minded, she could tell. He'd loved the duck, holding it tight to his chest for the entire length of the trip out of the terminal, and she'd loved him for that, immediately and absolutely, the desire to be his mother seizing her like a cramp and holding her without the slightest diminishing of intensity ever since. She'd been shaken by that first flush of absolute love; it was a relief to push his stroller from behind that first evening, reaching over occasionally to pat his head.

He seemed entirely engrossed in the scene before him, eyes shifting eagerly from a caftaned Arab to a chic young Frenchwoman. People milled, chattering excitedly and calling to one another in a cacophony of languages. Michael watched and stared and smiled, as if any one of these travelers might turn out to be a member of his new family. Two women clattered past in stiletto heels and miniskirts, and Michael turned to watch them appreciatively. Viorica and Deborah had exchanged glances then, rolling their eyes in amused recognition of Michael's incipient maleness, but Deborah also remembered how dull her own silk blouse and pants had suddenly seemed in comparison.

"The timing isn't exact," Dr. Silver said, and she started.

"Timing?"

"The window for developing the ability to love."

"Oh," Deborah said. "I'm sorry. I didn't realize."

Areas of Michael's brain were 25 percent less developed than in a normal child, the doctor continued. Not simply areas affecting memory . . .

"His memories must be horrible," Deborah said swiftly.

Doctor Silver turned to her with an elaborate show of patience. "Without memory, one can't learn. One can't reason. One can't judge."

"What do you mean?" She was flushing, not sure herself whether it was from irritation or embarrassment.

"It's very simple, Mrs. Latham. The ability to reason is based on the memory of experience."

"I don't understand."

Chris had turned from them and was gazing outside. They were so high up in the medical building that no other structures were visible, just clouds. Each time a plane droned past, the large, steel-framed windows rattled.

"Let me give you the most basic lesson," the doctor said, smiling professionally at Deborah, fingers toying with the metal band of his watch. "Remember the old story of the child who burns his hand on the stove and learns not to touch hot things? After one experience, or at most two, of finding his fingers on a too-warm surface, the child avoids not only the stove itself but also any other surface you describe to him as hot. Am I right?"

Deborah nodded.

"So let's say that this child simply cannot recall the lesson of being burned at the stove. Not only will he continue to head for that same hot surface, but he'll also have failed utterly at developing the ability to reason outward. He won't be able to judge the potential for *hot* elsewhere. He won't use his critical reasoning skills to understand that hot can be detected by touch, by similarity of shape or smell or sound, or by the express warning of an adult. He'll have failed to learn, failed to remember, failed to reason."

"It's not his fault, though," Deborah said.

"Of course not. But it is a reality. You have to wonder what he'll be capable of learning. Does he love *you*? Does he remember that you love him?"

Chris turned. "He asks me about forty times a day: Do you love me, Daddy? Do you love me, Daddy? Do you?"

"He isn't sure. He needs reassurance. He can't tell by the way you act with him."

"I tell him all the time."

"You used to."

His voice rose defensively. "I do!"

"He probably isn't exactly able to recall the sensation of being loved from moment to moment," said Dr. Silver. "He probably doesn't really know what it means. And if he can't comprehend it, he can't learn it or understand it or reason about it. I'm sorry. I suspect that even with a bottomless supply of love from you, Michael's always going to have a tough time understanding such a concept."

"I saw something on television recently," Chris said. "A Romanian boy, a lot like Michael, extremely bright but terrible in school, violent with other kids, charming, amoral . . ."

"He's not like that," Deborah interrupted.

Chris was watching the doctor, whose gaze in return was impassive and neutral, almost understanding. "Utterly amoral," he repeated, "and when he tried to hurt his sister, not so much worse than Michael's done . . ."

"How can you say this!"

"Because it's true. I saw it. And those parents, they decided to put him up for readoption, and someone took him, a woman experienced with very troubled kids. And he simply took this woman by the hand at the airport and looked up at her—they'd never met before. You should have seen this show," Chris nodded toward both Deborah and Dr. Silver, "and he took this woman by the hand and said 'Hi Mom!' and he smiled up at her like he'd loved her all his life. Then he turned and walked away with this little dance in his step. He never turned around, not once. As if the family that had kept him for five years wasn't standing there at all. He never even said good-bye."

Hushed, Deborah said, "That isn't possible, at least not with Michael. I don't know what's come over you. He loves us. He loves her. He loves me. He loves you, for God's sake. I know it. And I love him. No matter what you say, I love him. He's in our family, and I won't change my mind."

"What about the rest of us?" Chris asked quietly. "Caroline? You? Me? Don't we matter at all?"

In the car, almost as a welcome change of topic, Christopher confessed that Alice Dunn very likely was HIV-positive. He told Deborah that he had done the most horrible, unethical thing he could conceive of, that he'd failed to tell Alice what he had seen. He told her what a mess he'd made, how he had compounded matters by drawing Martin in. He said he could lose his license, he supposed, and probably would deserve to, except that he knew as well as she did that the Dunns were such decent people a problem would never arise. Chris spoke rapidly, telling the entire story in its ugly detail, his hands cramping on the wheel as he drove.

When he finished speaking, he turned to look at her for the first time. She didn't react at all. *God,* he thought, *she hadn't heard a word.* Her gaze was unfocused, vision diffused out on the series of cars speeding past them—Jeeps, Range Rovers, Toyotas, and Hondas—and her hands were on her lap, folding and pleating the yellow silk of her pants along the thigh. Her lips were so tight that five angry folds of skin pocketed the area. He could see a startling version of what she might look like as she aged. He picked up one of her hands, holding it as he continued to drive. She turned to him, still silent, and he noticed how limp her hand was under his.

"You know," Chris said, ashamed of himself again for another thing he had to tell her, a confession he suspected she would know immediately to be awful. "You know, in Sag Harbor, probably in all small towns, judgments are multiple. I mean, everybody knows everybody, all of us, I mean, the real families, the old families. It isn't just the kids who are judged when things go wrong. It's the entire family, as if the kid who smokes or drinks or hangs out in town or gets pregnant, or whatever, was taught bad ways by bad people. Parents, siblings, whatever."

"Ugh," she said, not turning toward him.

"Deb, come on. I love you. You know that. Can't you believe that maybe what I'm thinking is for all of us? That maybe it's best for all of us to throw in the towel?"

"No."

"Life is so hard, I swear," he said angrily, pounding the wheel. "But we can't help him. You heard the doctor!"

"No," she said, still gazing out the window. "I heard *you.*"

25

THE GASTONS hadn't exactly adopted Chris when his mother died. They'd taken Chris in long before; now that Mae Latham was gone, they kept him. The failure to undertake any formal legal work bothered no one. People in the Harbor were content to see the Latham boy taken care of; nobody doubted the practical good sense of having Joe and Eileen Gaston take responsibility for his upbringing. After all, the Lathams and the Gastons had been friends forever. Will and Chris had been raised like brothers, across the street from one another, of course, but in and out of each other's house moment by moment all day long.

Oddly, it was the presence, not the absence, of a father that loomed as threatening in Chris's memory. The risk was all in having him home, in the likelihood of his anger, his need for silence, his insistence on structure and routines and what he considered to be respect. The absence of a mother, on the other hand, was a loss beyond words, a terrifying black hole into which he could still recall tumbling.

The first time Chris had returned home from school, just days after his father's funeral, to find his mother seated by the window watching nothing and smiling with all the gentle sweetness of a dime store card of the Holy Mother, he'd not known what to think. She'd been herself earlier that morning, subdued as he—they were still reeling from his father's sudden death, after all—but certainly there'd been no indication of the embodied disappearance she was about to effect. That morning, they'd spoken of going up to Boston for a weekend, to see the sights, acknowledging that a change of scenery might benefit each of them. And that afternoon, at three-thirty, as he'd trudged home through the rare joy of an enthusiastic Sag Harbor snowfall, he had had no sense of his mother's disappearing, no tingle of intuition, no warning of her vigor abruptly going dry without taking her heartbeat, her blood, and her bodily functions along as well. He'd said, "Hi, Ma," as he walked past her to toss his schoolbooks onto his bed, to work his boots off his feet and throw them on the towel she'd left by the kitchen door, to search for chocolate chip cookies among the constantly replenished hoard supplied by friends and neighbors. She'd not answered then, but he'd not noticed it, not that very first afternoon.

He'd had the good sense to leave her alone that day, thinking she deserved a little quiet. It wasn't until the next morning, in fact, that he'd become first annoyed and then concerned. She wasn't soiled, or dirty; she'd obviously gotten up at some point and changed her clothes and brushed her hair, but she wasn't able, or willing, to speak, and that began to frighten him. Her laugh lines had smoothed over during the night; they weren't coming back, he suspected. More overwhelming even than the unthinkable concept that his father would never breathe was the realization that his mother might never share herself with him again. She had, without warning, closed up shop.

He was only twelve years old. Up until the past two weeks, his greatest worries had been about homework and the 1967 Yankees and why dumb Jud Leahey was always waiting and acting like they were friends for chrissake when everybody could see what a dweeb he was. Also, why all the girls were suddenly acting so weird all the time, like calling and hanging up and stuff like that when they used to be so normal. But now he'd have given anything to find that kind of normal again, anything at all, and instead his mother was sitting and staring out the picture window like he wasn't home, and it was weird as anything, it surely was.

On the second afternoon, he'd asked Will Gaston to come in with him, not explaining why. Will walked into the house, nodded at Chris's mom, looked at Chris, then scooted down the hall to the poster- and pennant-strewn bedroom, exploding into laughter as soon as the door shut behind them. "What's up with her? She turned into a zombie?"

"Ha ha ha. Very funny." Chris threw a pillow at Will, who caught it, decided not to toss it back, and settled back on the rug with it behind his head.

They talked about Miss Dunn for awhile; it was in her class today that Will had been reprimanded for shooting spitballs at Cynthia Stall, widely acknowledged to be the coolest girl in the seventh grade. She had her eye on Jack Dunn, Miss Dunn's nephew. Will was convinced that Miss Dunn hated him because she knew of his passion and wanted to make sure Cynthia continued to lust after Jack. "It's a family thing," Will explained, but Chris wasn't interested, not in the topic and frankly not in girls at all, not really, not yet at least.

Will blabbered on and on, covering multiple topics, including a family of box turtles they'd taken off the road the August before, his sense that his right arm might be longer than his left, and the question of whether people would actually be alive to witness the end of time or whether they'd all be dead first. "I can picture the sun *exploding* and all these people screaming, 'I can't see! I can't see!' What a bunch of dweebs! Can't you see it! All those bodies flying through the sky like a bunch of mummies! Cool. Don't you think that's sooo cool? Huh? Chris? Don't you think?"

Chris wasn't saying much at all. His head was on the other pillow, on his bed, and he was looking up at the ceiling at a poster of Mickey Mantle smiling dead-on, right back into his eyes.

"I heard some of the girls in the high school, Maureen Smith and what's her name, Amy Howe, I heard they wear their skirts so short when they bend over, you can see their stockings and garters and everything! Did you hear that? Des saw Lizzie Kane's, her thing, he said. She was wearing pantyhose, and she saw him see and she didn't even mind, she *smiled* at him, that's what he said. Can you believe it? What a slut!" Will said enviously. He was picking at the skin around his fingernails with sharp rapid pulls of his teeth.

Chris couldn't bear to watch Will. Something about him was so humid lately, so jumpy and anxious and damp, and Chris felt bothered and left out—also bored.

"Shut up, Will," he said.

Will turned, raising an eyebrow. "Stay cool, Man. Stay cool."

"Don't be a jerk."

"I forgive you, but only because your dad just died, that's the only reason, Man."

Chris didn't answer. In the ensuing silence, Will began to drum on his sneakers with two pencils, humming tunelessly. Eventually, Chris said, "Shut up a minute, will you? Don't bug my mom."

"What's with her anyhow?"

Chris shrugged, sitting up and swinging his feet over the side of the bed. "I dunno. She's been like that since yesterday."

"Crazy." Will shook his head.

"You know, I liked you a lot more before you got so groovy."

"It's a sign of the times, Buddy. You'll see."

But when Will went home late that afternoon, he said something to his own mother, who did speak to her husband, who did come over to try and get Mae Latham up out of her chair next to the window. When Joe Gaston left, the mission a failure, he told his wife he had no idea what to do about Mae.

"Thing is," he told Eileen, "when you go over there, she'll smile at you as politely as she ever did. She just won't say a word and she won't budge. That's all."

"I'll try it," Eileen promised, "as soon as I stick the chicken in."

And she did, kneeling at Mae Latham's chair and chattering away (she was definitely the one Will had gotten this trait from) about a minidress she'd seen that she'd never have the courage to wear, about the boys, even about Carl's funeral and all the casserole dishes they'd have to drive around and return.

"You're missing him, aren't you?" Eileen asked, kneeling, tracing one of the fragile peonies on Mae's skirt with a forefinger. Mae's brown hair was neatly pulled back in a ponytail; her nails were shaped and clean. Over her pastel flowered skirt, she wore an apron that said, "Mom's Kitchen." She looked for all the world as if she'd just stopped to take a rest before setting the table. Mae smiled sweetly, still not glancing down at Eileen Gaston, and she said, "No."

"Sure you miss him, Honey," Eileen said. "It's okay."

"No, I don't. I don't miss him. I told you."

"Okay, Mae, Honey, whatever you say."

They were silent for several minutes. Through the window, they saw Chris slam the Gastons' front door, jump down the three concrete steps, and gallop toward home.

As his footsteps pounded up the walk, Mae Latham said, "I see him. He's right there, waiting for me."

"That's right. Here he comes. Here's Chris."

"Not Chris, Eileen, that's Carl out there waiting for me."

Eileen chuckled uncomfortably. "Tell him to come back in a few years."

"I'd go now," Mae said slowly and distinctly. "I'd go as soon as he let me."

And so she did, although it took the better part of two long years, peppered with visits from neighbors and friends and village officials and psychologists and social workers. Eileen handled her grocery shopping, and Chris learned how to hold one-way conversations at the dinner table. But no one could shake Mae Latham from the torpor that had seized her, not even her beloved son. Eventually, Chris found himself spending afternoons, and soon evenings, and then all of his time at the Gastons, stopping in to hug his mother and sit quietly by her side for as many minutes as he could stand.

Years later, when Deborah heard Chris's version of this story, she'd said, "Why didn't you fight? Why didn't you yell at her? Why didn't you shake her out of it?" Deborah's cheeks had been red with fury, her brown hair springing up and away from her forehead in humid curls. "I can't imagine not fighting harder!"

They'd been out at Sagg Main, sitting on a shared blanket, watching the tiny whitecaps whipped up by the first warnings of a September storm. It was early evening, and one intrepid swimmer was struggling to do his daily lap up and back the entire mile-long stretch.

Chris moved closer to Deborah, putting his left arm around her and drawing her in. "It wasn't like that," he said. "We were respectful of her. We were. That's why we let her go."

"Didn't it hurt? Wasn't it awful for you?"

"Sure it was."

"How can you say that so calmly?"

"Well, first of all, it was twenty years ago, a long time ago, and I was young," he explained reasonably. "And secondly I still think she did what was right for her. She didn't want to live without him."

Deborah snuggled in, burying her head in the crook of his neck and shoulder, laying her face against the smooth beige cotton of his sweater. "I wouldn't want to live without you," she said. "But I could, if I had to. I couldn't throw myself on a funeral pyre."

"What an eighties thing to say," he'd teased her, trying to break the mood.

"Seriously, Chris, I mean it."

He sat up, pulling her forward to turn her face to his. His voice was low and serious, but one eyebrow was lifted—even at his most somber, he had to make light of himself—and he said: "All the family I ever had was good, even though whatever happened had to happen the way it did. I lost a lot, I know. But I'd kill, and I'm not kidding you, I'd sacrifice almost anything, to protect us. Because now that I have—now that I have you, I mean—I don't want to be without."

"Whew," she said, kissing him full on the lips. "Well, you don't have to worry. I'm not going anywhere."

At the time of his father's death, the beginning of his mother's slow evaporation, what Chris mostly felt was relief that the Gastons existed, that they loved him and wanted to care for him and that Will, odd as he was becoming, was still his best buddy in the world. Throughout the remaining years of high school—dissecting frogs in biology, playing football, working behind the soda fountain at Reimans and then caddying at the Maidstone, struggling to keep his grades up and work, work, work to save money for college—Will and his parents had been utterly welcoming and supportive. And everywhere he went in the Harbor, people knew he was the Lathams' kid—such a tragedy, that—and they looked out for him. He'd loved it here always, he really had.

He and Will hadn't always gotten along, of course. The worst phase the boys ever hit was when Chris and Cynthia got together midway through junior year of high school. Will had always, always had a thing for Cynthia—tall, blonde, self-assured Cynthia—but she'd never been remotely interested in Will. The truth is that Will had thought an awful lot about girls, ever since he was quite young, but girls hadn't paid much attention to him at all. He wasn't cute, and even though he was funny in a wiry, hyped-up way, he didn't have that ineffable element called *cool,* that slightly experienced aura that made some of the other guys attractive. He was too eager. It drove Will nuts that Chris wasn't all that hopped-up on girls. But Chris didn't get interested in women until late in high school, at least not so he'd talk about it. Still, most girls thought that was because he already had somebody, some girlfriend he had to keep quiet about because she was from the Maidstone, or maybe one of the beauties who summered in Noyac. Chris had mystery, all the girls thought.

When Cynthia Stall had turned her astonishing blue eyes on Chris, though, whatever had been lying dormant perked up, and Chris found himself embarked on an overpowering first adventure in passion. Toward the fall of senior year, he promised to marry Cynthia if anything happened when they, whatever, which Will assured him was so uncool as to be worthy of Liberace or Wayne Newton in these brave new days of love and the pill. Nevertheless, Cynthia was sufficiently reassured by this to proceed in precisely the direction Chris had hoped she would, and overnight, all Will's superior knowledge of the world at large became irrelevant.

That watershed did mark an increasingly noticeable degree of distance from Will, a slow seeping out of their early intense intimacy that was perhaps inevitable. Oddly, most folks in the Harbor continued to see Chris and Will as a twosome, far more than Chris and Cynthia, as if it were commonly and inexplicably understood that Chris and Will would stay friends forever but that Cynthia was fated to move onward and upward before settling down. (What she'd done, of course, was to move north instead of up, settling for seven years in Brattleboro, Vermont, before returning home with her husband and their three small girls, a tired, paler version of her former self.) Nevertheless, that slightly antagonistic sense of distance between the guys hadn't entirely dissipated, not even now; when Will came out from the city with his family, these days, he only rarely got in touch with Chris and Deborah. Still, they were best man at each other's wedding, godparents to each other's children; in point of fact, they were more brothers than friends, with all the ambivalence such relation entails.

The definitive sense of distance stemmed in large part from high school graduation. So much unthinkable stuff had transpired so abruptly during that one early summer night in 1977, including the event known only to Will and Chris and Anna Downing, a kind of event that later is never talked of because discussion would mean acknowledgment. The danger there was that all of them might be forced to face how cowardly they'd been. Even worse, others might find out as well. Des knew what had happened, maybe, but nobody expected him to speak up, and Jack no longer could. Cynthia had never been given the slightest detail of that evening's events; to her credit, an uncharacteristically acute sixth sense must have warned her of something, for after nearly two years of sworn undying love, she'd firmly parted ways with Chris the following week.

Such a disaster, and so few repercussions for the major players: drunken Des, weak Anna, dishonest Chris, and, in his own way, equally deceitful Will. And then those others who'd been so utterly without responsibility and who'd suffered so much: the Dunns. Jack, dead. Martin, well, Martin had been Martin before Jack's death, so perhaps his suffering remained constant, but Alice, oh, to survive a child's death! Chris knew on some level, simply from surviving his mother's slow demise, that Alice's injuries had to be total and irreparable. Now her inner destruction was being mirrored by a more physical one, fate having patiently bided for twenty years before attempting to catch up with her.

How the hell could somebody like Alice Dunn have contracted HIV?

Deborah Latham, normally so alert to the nuances of other people's situations, had completely failed to register the news about Mrs. Dunn that Chris had given her in the car. Therefore, she was slightly confused by Alice's somewhat shamefaced half shrug when they ran into one another outside the post office. Deborah, overloaded with two huge boxes of baby clothes she was forwarding to her younger sister in Philadelphia, at first thought Alice's discomfort had to do with the packages, that maybe the older woman thought the boxes were full of fancy items purchased from some expensive mail-order outfit.

"Hey," she said. "How are you?" Teetering slightly forward to balance both packages, she giggled. "Whoops, sorry."

Alice reached out to hold the edge of the cardboard box on top. "There."

"Baby clothes for my sister. It's her first, she's thirty-five. I thought I was almost too old at twenty-nine."

"I was nineteen in 1959; that's when Jack was born."

Deborah nodded sympathetically. "I'm sorry," she said. "Chris told me."

Alice shrugged, rheumy eyes watering. Her white cardigan slipped off one shoulder and down her back. One meaty arm lurched around to grab it, but failed. At the same time, the top package slipped off Deborah's pile to the ground, edges splitting, scattering worn pajamas and leggings and neatly folded sweatshirts over the pavement. A balled-up pair of yellow socks with black polka dots skittered across the concrete curb and into the street.

"Uh oh!" the women exclaimed in unison. Catching one another's eyes, they smiled. Deborah looked down at the mess at her feet. Alice began, awkwardly, to chuckle.

"Let me scoop this stuff up and I'll buy you a cup of coffee at the Paradise," Deborah said. "Mina, my baby-sitter, stays until four this afternoon. I was just, I was planning, I don't know what I was going to do. I can pick up a few groceries at Schiavoni's."

"Let me help you," Alice said, but she didn't move forward, didn't bend or kneel. Instead she stood above Deborah, watching as the younger woman's hands moved quickly, gathering spilled fabric, pulling reds and blues and grays and yellows into a pile so madly colorful, so ripe with the possibilities inherent in the very existence of even a single baby, that one's eyes could hardly bear it.

26

INSIDE the Paradise, Deborah moved automatically toward one of the booths on the right, turning to check with Alice just before sliding into the seat. "Oh," she said, "I'm sorry."

"It's my own fault for getting so fat. I wasn't always this big. I wasn't thin, no, not like you." Deborah smiled, tilting her head to the side in partial apology, and moved toward the tables, pulling a chair out for Alice, who continued, "But when my son died, I guess that's when it happened. I got a taste for my own cooking, you might say."

Deborah chuckled. "That could happen to me so easily you can't imagine. I love to eat."

Alice lowered herself into the chair with an expelled "huff!" She moved so slowly that even with her size she had a lumbering grace. Alice placed both her hands on the table and breathed out again with another huff of air and then smiled shyly at Deborah. "I haven't been here since they renovated the place."

"Really? I'm here all the time," Deborah said. "The kids love the pancakes."

"I love pancakes. It's just, I thought, it looks so fancy since they renovated, too downstreet for me."

"Downstreet?"

Alice shook her head from side to side. "Doesn't your husband tell you anything? Downstreet's been taking over the whole village, seems to me. Prettying it all up in such a nice way, it's good for business, but not exactly to my taste. Not as homey as it used to be. Downstreet taste isn't as comfortable, is what I think."

"You mean like downtown? Is that what downstreet means? Or upscale?"

Alice shrugged. "I guess."

Deborah had never seen their waiter before. He was no older than twenty, with a diamond stud lodged in the roof of his nostril and a distinctly purple tinge to his dark hair. A double series of pimples—some swollen with pus and others pink with overhandling—arched perpendicular to the line of his eyebrows. His smile was perhaps reserved for other customers, but Deborah saw and tried to be amused at the realization that she and Alice Dunn were utterly beneath his notice. Too old, too large, too unhip. She asked for tea. Alice, clearing her throat, requested decaffeinated coffee.

Neither woman asked for a pastry or muffin, and when the waiter halfheartedly offered to bring menus, both shook their heads, no.

In the silence that followed, Alice seemed to be searching for words. Deborah, too, felt slightly stymied. She liked Alice with the same genuine impulse each time they came face to face, and in a certain sense, this highlighted how few true friends she'd made in the years she'd lived in the village. She and Mina had, after seven years together, a relationship far more intimate than that of employer and employee; Elizabeth Bloom, the mother of Caroline's friend Ada, was certainly a close friend; and yet, Deborah rarely confided in either of them, or in her sister, about the struggles she was having regarding Michael. In point of fact, she trusted none of her friends or acquaintances to stand by her if matters with her son came to a head. If push came to shove, even gentle, cowlike Alice would probably turn her rheumy blue eyes, unable to empathize with Deborah's situation.

As a result, Deborah, who had instinctively wished to spill her soul to Alice, failed even to raise the one topic that was consuming her. Alice, perhaps equally doubting, pointed to a man walking toward her wearing a faded T-shirt sporting the legend "I survived Hurricane Bob."

"Look," Alice said. "Were you here then?"

"Oh yes! Caroline was just an infant!" During Hurricane Bob, seven years before, Sag Harbor had gone without electricity for three or four days, more in some areas. Deborah and Chris and Caroline had been lucky; their power was only out from Sunday to Wednesday, although it seemed aeons at the time. They were a threesome then, Caroline just a few months old, and Mina was such a new employee she'd been leery of imposing herself, even though that reticence had forced her to stay alone without electricity or company for several days. Funny, they hadn't known her well enough at that point to drive over and suggest she join them; now the idea of leaving her behind even for a ten-day vacation seemed unthinkable.

During the storm it had been just Deborah, Christopher, and Caroline. In the basement, Chris had found an unopened box of plumber's candles, and Deborah had remembered an old radio stuffed on the top shelf of the coat closet. Batteries came out of the television remote control, rendered useless already by the failed electricity, and only moments after the eye of the storm descended in blissful silence, they were finally able to make connection to the world at large, if only by eavesdropping on the adenoidal hysteria of the local disk jockey describing his own wind- and water-soaked circumstances.

Later that afternoon, when they'd heard conclusively that the storm had passed, Christopher and then Deborah ventured out into their yard, hoisting tree limbs to the curb, untangling a hose from the base of a Japanese cherry tree, righting the semiuprooted mailbox. Inside, people whose telephone service hadn't been severed were calling into the radio station, caller after caller complaining about the cable television provider.

"How're we supposed to get along without the TV, I'd like to know?" one angry caller said, her clipped tones disdainful of any cable company that failed to be one hundred percent prepared for natural disaster on this scale.

Chris had laughed at that, his strained expression suddenly relaxing. Watching, Deborah realized that he'd been holding his shoulders up tensely ever since the day began. "Sometimes I'm ashamed," he said. "You know as well as me that caller was Frances Dickson. What an idiot. You have to wonder how some of these folks ever survived without that big eye in the living room."

"I'm sure it's no better in Philly or wherever," Deborah said. "Television is not some kind of Hamptons phenomenon."

He snorted. "It's not that, it's just the idea that people could die in a hurricane—or have their houses destroyed, lose their businesses—and the minute they know they're okay, all they think about is cable TV. They're going to turn on and start watching the news, instead of going out to help. It's idiotic."

She smiled, which was still to him a form of magic. She was a dental fantasy, he said, mocking his own burst of affection. Her teeth were perfectly shaped, although not perfectly even, and so white she looked clean even first thing in the morning. She knew he still found her attractive; he'd said it so often, and she could tell by how often he reached for her, even now that the baby had come and they'd lived through all the delivery horrors and recovery and hormones and blood, the sleepless nights. He'd said it so often, she couldn't doubt him. Even now they wanted one another from some place so fundamental that even when she let him down, or he did her, they couldn't even mildly entertain the notion that they might not always be together.

"Let's go," she had said. "The ocean must be amazing right now."

And so they joined the small stream of courageous drivers out on inspection tours, making their way straight down Madison Street to where it turned into Sagg Road, across Montauk Highway due south to the nearly empty Sagg Main parking lot. Six cars were parked in the empty lot, lined up next to one another by the facilities building as if not merely people but also machines needed to band together in the hurricane's aftermath.

Carrying Caroline, Chris led the way up the wooden stairs and across past the bathrooms. There was no wind to speak of, just the wild roar of the waves and a kind of smooth cleanliness to the air and sand, as if the otherworldly janitors who'd sped through the community had brushed each individual molecule of oxygen, each grain of sand, as they whisked past.

Caroline had a hood over her bouncing black curls. Her hair had just begun to come in, and the first twists and waves of hair were so silky even strangers wanted to pet her head. She kept smiling and cooing, as if the booming thunder the waves made as they crashed was a friendly sound. The sand was damp beneath Deborah's toes, and as she stared out at the gray-green of the ocean, she could feel an easing of the tension that had contained her, holding her away from windows and doors, clamping her to a sturdy seat with Caro in her arms since six-thirty that morning; it was dissipating finally in the sharp clear end-of-summer air.

She'd knelt and then sat in the sand. Chris said he wanted to tangle with the waves, so she'd taken Caro and they'd sat watching him, shivering slightly, an audience for all his relieved exuberance. The blue of his jeans darkening as they became soaked, the gray of his sweatshirt, the ruddy tan on his face, had all been so brilliantly defined by the stormlight, a kind of clarity she'd never seen before; it had been as if

Christopher Latham were Adonis—that's how much she had revered his smiling good looks, his strong shoulders, the easy way his body moved through space. Just then she had loved him with such an entirety that she swallowed deeply, the childlike part of her hoping to hold such satisfaction whole and complete, and safe inside.

The Dunns, on the other hand, had spent that same day apart, each performing a role in the informal network of village support activities. Martin had gone in his car to check on the five elderly widows who were normally his responsibility to ferry back and forth from church. Those ladies, or at least the ones who could no longer rustle up a relative to visit, were always the Dunns' guests at Thanksgiving and Christmas.

"Weren't you scared?" Deborah asked. "Weren't you frightened for him out in the storm? I don't think I'd have let Chris go."

Alice snorted. "I couldn't stop that man if I tried. He's given his all to the church, that's the way he's always been. Even when the boys were small . . ." She paused, taking a sharp breath. "Even then, he'd be helping somebody out; he'd be too busy to get to Little League or home for supper. But he never missed a church service in his life. He's had his hands out helping others from the day I met him."

Deborah couldn't tell what she was supposed to understand from this. After a moment, she said, "What did you do? Did you stay home safely? I hope."

"No, I mean, yes. I stayed home," Alice answered. She wrapped her hands around the mug of coffee. "Did your husband tell you about me?" she asked abruptly.

"I'm not sure. What do you mean? We talked about you; we talked about you the other day."

"Did he tell you about my mouth?"

Deborah shook her head, aware that, in fact, there was some crucial fact she had been told but had failed to file in her mental lexicon. "He doesn't tell me about his patients, about their teeth."

"It isn't my teeth exactly," Alice began. "You won't tell, will you?"

"You can tell me," she said. "It's okay."

The waiter walked by, glanced down at their full mugs, hovered briefly and seemed once again to decide that they weren't worth his attention. Deborah grinned at Alice, who looked startled.

"It's a little confusing," Alice began. "I mean, I don't really understand myself what happened, but the doctor thinks . . ."

"Chris? My husband?"

"No. Excuse me. It's so hard to talk about this."

Deborah leaned across the square table, taking Alice's right hand in hers. Alice's fingers were soft in Deborah's hand; even her grasp was hesitant and doughy.

Alice cleared her throat, pushing her gray hair back behind one ear with her left hand. She looked up, straight into Deborah's hazel eyes, and she said, "Your husband found something on my tongue that made him worried, so he told Martin, my husband, that I should see Doctor Isen. Do you know Doc Isen?"

Sure, Deborah shrugged, her eyebrows lowering darkly. *Chris told Martin?* She couldn't imagine her husband behaving so unethically.

"So I went to see him, and what Doctor Latham had told my husband, well, it might be true. I have this leuko-something . . ."

"Leukemia?"

"No, no. I have this thing leuko-something on my tongue which supposedly you only get, doctors only see, with people who have HIV." The last words came out in a quiet rush, as if she had propelled them forward as quickly as she could, forcing the information out before she panicked and changed her mind.

"You? That's impossible. Isn't that impossible?" Deborah, startled, felt as if she were babbling. She could tell she was blushing.

Alice shrugged, one blue-shirted shoulder rising gently and lowering slightly back into place. Her shoulders were as fleshy as the rest of her, so padded one could imagine sinking one's head against her for comfort, even now, when she was so clearly asking to be comforted herself.

Alice said, "I have been thinking and thinking ever since the other day when Martin told me, and I can't imagine how, it's so silly even trying to think. I mean, the Lord knows, Martin isn't a sinner. It's his whole life, the church. But then Doc Isen asked me today . . ." She paused, breathing in again in that short, sharp manner. "He asked me about the kids, you know. We take in foster kids, and Doc Isen asked me, was there ever an accident, like did I ever find a needle? He said he was trying to figure out how I could have been exposed. I started laughing when he said that, I've been bled on so many times it's funny to even try and remember all the times. No needles, though, not in my house. But then, I remembered, I remembered something that happened back during that storm, that Hurricane Bob."

Deborah nodded, encouraging her to continue. Deborah's hands were still around Alice's, and she tried not to be aware of feeling slightly frightened by the contact.

"See, there was this family living in one of those camper things up in the woods around Mount Misery—you know where that is? That development back in the woods?"

Deborah nodded, yes.

"Well, back there it was just the mother, a kid about twenty years old, and her little boy, and the girl got so sick during the storm, and the father had just up and left them, and she struggled over to one of the houses in Mount Misery with the baby, and the folks there called an ambulance as quick as could be, but the truth is, it was too late for that mom. She had pneumonia, and she got taken before she even got to the hospital. And so the neighbors thought of us and couldn't even call because there wasn't any power. And right about the time the eye came overhead, the eye of the storm, they jumped in their car and ran that baby down to our house. We had diapers and cribs and clothes and everything, so it was just natural for us to say yes."

"So that's what you did during the storm, you took care of the little fellow?"

Alice nodded, yes, and then shook her head. "I didn't do so well with that boy, I guess. I was too scared myself, what with all the wind howling and being alone. I think I was sort of scared all alone with him. And I remember deciding to take him down to the basement, it'd be safer there." She paused. Deborah smiled encouragingly.

Alice took a deep breath. "And in our house, the stairs are so old, and I guess I wasn't watching where I was going and the next thing I knew, I fell, bang, and rolled down the stairs with that little boy in my arms." She looked up, into Deborah's eyes, and she said, "I don't even know that little boy's name."

"Was he okay? The little boy?"

"I guess. I mean, we both got knocked out. I hit my head on the railing, and he hit his head on the cement floor and we were lying there I don't know how long, and covered with blood, both of us. He'd cut his lip and so had I, funny that, now that I think of it."

She paused again, to take a sip of her tea. When she continued, her shoulders seemed slumped slightly, her elbows sunken beneath the table's edge. Along the knuckles of her right hand was a series of misshapen bumps, visible manifestations of rheumatism. She shrugged, looking back up at Deborah and then away. "So if I got it, it was probably then, that's what I told Doc Isen."

"The kid had HIV?"

"Yeah. I guess. We had a few that did. But that's the only time I really got cut myself, badly I mean. The only time something could have happened, so that's what I told Doc Isen. That must have been what happened."

"Does Mr. Dunn know about this? What does he say?"

Alice shrugged again. This time her shirt slipped slightly, revealing the broad tan strap of her brassiere. "He and I—we've been married a long time."

"You haven't talked about it?" Deborah asked, aghast. She took her hands back and picked up her napkin, wiping her mouth and fingers.

"He was the one who told me to call Doc Isen. But he hasn't asked since then, and I don't want to bring it up. I'm waiting to see. That's what I'm doing. The tests aren't in yet, and there's no way to know. So if he's right, well, we can talk about it then."

"That's true. That's true, isn't it?" Deborah was suddenly utterly relieved.

Alice smiled, her small, even teeth faintly yellow against the dull rose of her lips. "It's in God's hands, that's what I think. But I've dealt with enough already, I know I have. My guess is it's all a big mistake."

"Me too," Deborah said, smiling back. "Me too."

"So," Alice said, the syllable a small explosion. She heaved a huge sigh, chuckled, and shook her head. "Thanks for letting me talk."

"I won't tell a soul," Deborah promised.

"I know that," Alice said. "We don't have a friend in common, that's my guess. I think that's why I told you."

Deborah took a sip of her tea. "It would be so crazy. It wouldn't make sense. Who ever heard of anyone becoming HIV-positive like that, falling downstairs?" She chuckled. "Impossible, that's my guess."

"Yeah," Alice echoed. "Impossible."

27

"Why do you not tell them you speak with me, that you know our language?"

Michael turned slowly, tilting his chin to grin at Viorica, so that for a moment she believed he actually found something funny. "You keep secrets," he said.

"Of course I do. I learned how, when I was there. When I was at home."

He leaned back against his Power Ranger pillow; if she knew him less well, she'd have believed he was relaxed. "I keep secrets," he said. "Same as you."

She shook her head with rueful appreciation. "You're wild," she said, leaning in to brush the dark bangs back off his forehead. "My wild friend."

He grabbed onto her wrist, fingers gripping hard. "Don't go," he said. "Don't go back there. Stay here, with me."

She was silent, watching the line of his mouth stiffen as she tilted her own body away from his to regard him with quizzical affection. There was a way he needed her, she knew, that maybe no other male ever would, and she couldn't keep herself from warming to him, even when she knew her affection would no longer help him. She was leaving, after all; tonight she had come to say good-bye.

Deborah and Chris were out for dinner with the Blooms; they were trying a restaurant that had been the summer season's hottest, and even Mina had to admit they probably wouldn't be home for quite some time. Mina had been furious to see Viorica's rented car pull into the driveway and had only reluctantly allowed her cousin to enter the house. "They would be furious to see you here," Mina had hissed.

Viorica had only shrugged, tossing the keys into her left hand and raising her right palm like a traffic cop, making a joke of the fact that, if necessary, she intended to batter right through.

"You can't come in," Mina had said in that same furious hiss, pressing her face close to the screen door so that her face became a grid of shadowed squares.

"I want to see the boy. Let me in."

Typically, Mina had folded; she always would, Viorica knew. That same soft pliancy that drew the Latham children in also prevented Mina from protecting them the way their parents assumed she did. If Viorica and Mina's roles had from some accident of birth or situation been reversed, Viorica knew she would never have allowed Mina to tiptoe so discreetly into the sleepy little boy's room. If Viorica had been given responsibility for Michael Latham, she'd have tossed her body on the road before letting some forbidden person inside to talk to him.

If it weren't for Michael, returning home, even to the economic situation in her country, would be unmitigated pleasure. Only the thought of abandoning the boy to the confusing world she'd once believed was a gift—only that shameful situation made her consider the notion of staying in America.

"You are not wise, Little One. You must learn to love them. They want to be your parents. You make it much too hard for them."

Michael's head sunk deeper into the pillow, his shoulders sagging as he twisted over, onto his side, facing her. "I am a real American boy now. I'm okay here. I am. I'm okay," he said, tucking his left hand up and under his cheek. He looked tired—even his voice was weary—but she didn't think it was because she'd woken him up. He was exhausted, Viorica felt, by the effort he was making to be what he called a real American boy. Did he have any idea how badly he was doing, how little they appreciated his real worth? He was solid and strong, the kind of survivor her own brother had been. When presented with difficulties, Michael didn't whine and look for easy answers. He was so determined. The Lathams, spoiled as they were, simply couldn't see how hard his situation was. They didn't have any perspective. They didn't know what suffering was. They'd lost nothing worth noting, either of them. She, with her stories about cats and mothers. He, with his smug indifference. They had no idea what children like Michael endured, what it meant after living in darkness for so long to be propelled so carelessly into the glare and blare of American life. Of course Michael made mistakes, pushed too hard. He was confused. How could he fail to be?

His situation wasn't fair, she knew, but she didn't know whether to tell him so. Wouldn't it only make things harder to know that someone understood what he was up against? He'd been through so much, alone. He'd survived loss and abandonment, poor health and boredom, starvation and isolation, and he knew how to keep going. He was strong. She wanted to be careful. She didn't want to break that shell he'd built so well, that tortoise casing that kept him whole no matter what hell life kept carting him through.

He moved closer to her, snuggling in under the shelter of her left arm, leaning his damp hair against her white linen shirt. His legs, under the Power Rangers quilt, were so stick thin that the bed might still have been neatly made.

She loved him. She couldn't help herself. Viorica pulled him closer, drawing him in against her comfortable chest. "I wish I could take you," she said softly. "I wish you were mine. But you wouldn't want to go back there, not even with me."

He turned to her, twisting his neck so that his head arched back and his cheek lay against the triangle of skin at the opening of her blouse. In the glossy tar of his eyes, she saw a kind of wisdom, an elderly knowledge that was startling even to her. She held her breath.

Michael pulled his knees up, drawing the gaudy quilt up to his chin. He leaned back, studying Viorica's serious expression with what seemed to be puzzlement. "*Ce vrei să spui?*" he asked. "What do you mean?"

"When I go back, you'll be alone. With them. I don't want to leave like this."

"*Dar este bine aici!*" he said. "But it's good here."

"It's good?" she asked, surprised.

He nodded vigorously. "Oh yes," he told her.

"It's good?" she asked again.

He lay down, letting his legs disappear under the mounds of quilt once again. With the bedding up to his neck and those huge eyes glowing against his smooth skin, he looked so pure and sincere and healthy. Her own eyes, irritated and dry, wanted to drink him in.

"Really?" she asked. "Is it really good?"

"Oh yes," he said again, nodding with that same enthusiasm. "She is my mother. He is my father. I'm comfortable. I like it here. I do."

They were silent for some minutes, and Viorica could hear his breath coming slow and even as he drifted back toward sleep.

"It has to be better than what you had there," she said, more to herself than him.

His eyes opened, just the slightest bit, and then closed into the fullness of sleep, as if such a comment were so obvious it required no reply.

"It has to be better," she told herself again, standing to tuck the quilt more tightly around his shoulders. If she ever had a son, which she doubted at this point she ever would, she hoped he would be exactly like Michael, with all his artistic gifts and his toughness, his intelligence, and, above all, with that willingness to challenge and endure. Defiant and brave, Michael was built to survive.

One couldn't worry about him, she told herself. He would always make his way. It was only her foolish love, her stupid memories, her own fears, that made her doubt. Michael would be fine. "*Te iubesc,* Mihai," she whispered. "I love you."

28

THE SHEAF of prescriptions and directions from the doctor was ominously thick.

On the second visit, Doctor Isen hadn't beaten around the bush at all; he'd told her straight out, a sign of respect for which she guessed she should be grateful.

When he came into the room, he'd leaned in to take her hand and press it, very consciously, so that she'd know he wasn't frightened of her, but then he'd shaken his head grimly and said, "I'm sorry, Mrs. Dunn. Those tests we did two weeks ago were positive. You are HIV-infected. I treat HIV here, so that's no problem. Not every doctor does, you know."

Alice, her large form tucked into his plain pine chair so that her hips bellowed out beneath the armrests, nodded pleasantly, trying to grasp what Doc Isen was trying to tell her. The numbness that had prickled at her neck and shoulders on and off over the last two and a half weeks was suddenly back, spreading down even to her legs. The skin on her forehead tightened; dampness speckled the front of her white cotton blouse. She pulled the material away from the unevenly sized rolls of flesh at her belly. There was a question she knew she should ask, probably more than one, but she had no idea what they were. *All right then*, she thought, *I'm going to die.*

He was so serious he didn't nod back. Instead, he said, "There are some other tests we should do today. The T-4 and the PCR. We need to find out how your body is handling the infection. These two tests will give us blood cell counts and viral load figures to determine what treatment options are right for you."

"Treatment?" Alice managed to say.

He nodded. "The medication can treat the HIV virus, reduce the viral load, even make it undetectable. Taking the medicine is complicated, but not half as bad as it was even a few years ago."

She didn't understand a word he was saying, even though she knew it was important.

She closed her eyes. It was Jack's face she saw then, his eighteen-year-old's grin imprinted on the underside of her eyelids. He hadn't been an unusually good-looking boy—she honestly knew that—but he'd had such strong shoulders and sturdy legs, and such a gleeful smile. Anna had loved him for that, too, as much as she had, or almost as much. Anna, after all, had gone on to find a new love, make him her husband and have a family. Alice didn't blame her; in a certain sense, she applauded Anna's resilience.

"Mrs. Dunn? Mrs. Dunn?" Doc Isen was patting her meaty arm. He had hairy black tufts on the middle joints of each finger. Under other circumstances, she'd probably not have noticed them; today, she wondered if he'd ever considered shaving his knuckles. The hairs were sharply tipped, many at least a half-inch long, all glossy black. Oddly, his cheeks and chin had no five o'clock shadow, as if all the overgrowth were here, apelike, on his hands.

She tried to smile, to reassure him that she was all right, that she'd survive hearing such devastating news, that she was such a trouper he needn't fret about her. She'd endure it all; she really would. In a certain sense, she already had.

"It's okay," she told him. "Really. I'll be okay."

"The medicine," he said, "can help your immune system. The CD4 count often rises quite dramatically when taking it. But we'll talk more specifically about medication when we know your count."

Doc Isen wasn't very old. His father had been Alice's doctor for almost all of her forty-plus years in the Harbor; he'd died not long ago and now his son had moved to the area and was trying—an impossible task, most locals thought—to fill his shoes. He was younger even than Jack and Des would have been, probably no more than thirty or thirty-two years old. Alice felt sorry for him, such an innocent sweet boy having to spend his afternoon coping with the difficulties of a situation such as hers. How awkward he must be feeling.

"You know," he said, "I'll have to get a list of your contacts. It's obligatory, required, that they be informed."

"Contacts?"

"Sexual partners. You know. People you've had, uh, contact with, you know. Contact of a risky nature." He cleared his throat. "People who could have been exposed, uh, to the virus. Partners. Your husband and anyone else . . ." Abruptly, he stopped speaking and raised one tanned hand to his cheek. *He really was very young,* she thought. *Very young.*

Her right hand fluttered up, to her cheek and then to his arm and back down into her lap. "Not my husband, not Martin," she said. "Not to speak of, not for years. There's no call to say a word to him. I've never been much of a fan of all that business, though I don't know why I'm telling you."

Doc Isen looked so skeptical her heart sank. "Don't tell him," she said. "He'll just, he'll think, I don't know what Martin will think. I didn't want to have to talk to him, not about all this."

Even though he looked like he was about to, Doc Isen didn't shrug his shoulders. Instead, he turned and went to sit at his desk, effectively walling himself away from any impulse toward sympathy. "It's the law," he said. "We're under an obligation to notify anyone who might have been exposed. I'll have to speak to your husband about the risks of, of further contact. I really will."

Alice was silent.

"Hey," he said, "it's better that he knows."

Alice shifted slightly in the shallow chair. If she stood suddenly, the entire seat would probably rise with her, she thought, she was so tightly wedged in.

"How are you feeling now?"

"I don't know," she said. "Scared, maybe."

"I'd like to start you on a drug cocktail as soon as we have your numbers back. I think we might see an improvement, a real improvement in less than a month."

"I don't drink," Alice said flatly.

He stared at her.

"I never have, never have touched a drop in my entire life. I'm not going to start now."

"Oh!" He smiled, but grimly. "Not alcohol. I'm probably going to put you on Zerit—D4T. Have you heard of it?"

She shook her head, no.

"It can cause numbness and tingling in the extremities, so you should call me if that happens. But I'll go over all of this again with you next week."

"I don't feel bad now," Alice protested. "Why should I start taking things? I don't feel any different from normal. And I don't want Martin to be told, I really don't. It's my life. I should be able to tell him myself."

"I could give you a week or so," Greg Isen said. "But then I'd have to have him in for a follow-up discussion."

She was silent, staring down at the gnarls on her outstretched fingers.

Doc Isen looked down at his desk, moving two pens and several pencils to the top of his desk calendar. All the writing implements were imprinted with the names of drugs, names so long and complicated they barely fit on the whole expanse no matter how small the print. "Two times a day you take the Zerit," he said, returning to the medications as if directions for action made him feel more comfortable. "I've written it down."

Alice's left hand curled into a fist. She stroked it with her right, running her forefinger over the etched-in circle of her wedding band. She watched her hands. For a woman who had spent most of her life watching and reacting to the expressions of others, she was good at hiding her feelings, even from herself.

"Then there's Lamivudine," he said. "That's two times a day as well. Easy. And the last drug, that's Viramune, you'll be taking that also. Once a day for two weeks, then two times a day like the others. Viramune sometimes causes a general body rash. If you see a rash, you'll have to let me know."

She nodded.

"You'll take them all two times a day," he added. "Morning and evening. With or without food. But I'll go over this again next week, okay?"

Alice nodded again. She hadn't a clue what he'd told her.

"You must continue taking the drugs exactly this way. That's very important. Very, very important. You must take the drugs exactly the way I've outlined, exactly that way."

Alice nodded again, politely. "What happens if I don't do it exactly right?"

"Well," he said, shifting forward, leaning across the desk to make his point, "the virus reproduces so quickly. It makes, oh, probably a billion cells a day, really. And if you use the cocktail wrong, you can develop a resistance to the drugs. Very quickly, in a period of weeks. And that could be very dangerous."

"But I don't feel bad," she protested. "Why can't I wait until I feel bad? Maybe I can go on like this a long time; I'm sure some people do. Not everybody gets sick. Not everybody. I'm sure some people go on without—well, don't they?"

He shook his head. "The problem is vulnerability," he said. "You want to make the viral load undetectable. HIV is a chronic illness, like diabetes. It's not the killer it once was. But you have to treat it carefully."

"But I haven't any symptoms," she reminded him. "Maybe I'm not as sick as you think."

He shrugged his shoulders. "I've written it all out for you here," he said. "The instructions should be very clear. Read them over, and think about it. If you have any questions, please call. And next week, when you come in, I hope you'll commit to starting the regimen."

Alice nodded.

"And bring your husband in with you. It's important."

"Are you married?" Alice asked. She shifted forward on her chair and began to pull herself to standing.

"Yes," he answered.

"Children?"

"Yes, three. A boy, he's three. And twin girls going into kindergarten," he said.

"I had a son myself," she told him. "He was a good boy."

"I know. I'm sorry," he said.

"Me too," she told him. "Not a day goes by when I'm not."

"I can imagine," he told her, somewhat absently. He'd glanced at the clock and realized he'd taken twice the amount of time he'd allotted, not that he regretted it.

"What bugs me," she said, heaving herself up with a grunt and turning back to face him, "is how there's absolutely nobody in the world who would possibly, not even remotely, miss me the way I miss my Jack. Funny that. When I'm gone, he'll be gone, too. And I won't have lasted a moment more, not in anybody's thoughts. Don't tell my husband, though. He'd be hurt to know I know it. The poor man's got no idea how little his thoughts ever turn to me and that's just fine. It really is."

She nodded at him once and then pulled the door open. It wasn't until she was gone that he realized the papers—a whole pile of them that he and his assistant had carefully prepared for her the evening before: sample prescriptions, pamphlets, a typed list of medication instructions—were lying on the floor under the chair, in precisely the spot where her scuffed loafers had been so patiently placed for the past forty minutes.

He sighed, ran one hand through his short dark hair, and slipped the stack of papers into her chart.

29

ON THE same evening that Alice Dunn rejected the notion of a medical "cocktail," Caroline Latham threw the most alarming temper tantrum of her seven-year-old life. It began just before dinner, after a day that, for the Lathams, had been notably quiet and peaceful. Even Michael had been sweet and agreeable for most of the afternoon, and when Deborah went into the kitchen to make dinner, the two children remained in the playroom side by side. Caroline was reading, leaning against the couch, while her brother struggled over a five-hundred-piece crossword puzzle of a school of trout swimming, all shades of black, blue, and green melting together.

If only Christopher could see moments like this, Deborah had thought to herself as she chopped carrots and onions and garlic. *If only Mrs. Bennett or some of the teachers from the school could see him today.*

Chris burst through the back door a few minutes later, throwing his knapsack on the table. "Hey," he said. "Look at this!" In his hand he held a small plastic box; in the case was a dental crown.

"Thanks but no thanks," Deborah said. "I was planning fish for dinner."

"No, seriously," he said. "Guess whose mouth this came from?"

She put her knife down. "Whose?"

"Sammi Conway! She came to my office!"

"The actress? Wow, you're kidding! Was she nice? Was she as beautiful as she looks?"

"Oh, my God, she was gorgeous. She glowed, she really did. Everybody was lining up outside the office, pretending not to stare at the back of her head. I was glad I had the mask on; otherwise I'd have been so uptight the whole time." His face was flushed, and he was grinning with excitement. "She has no plaque, none at all, let me tell you!"

He rolled his eyes. "God, I sound like a dentist, don't I? It's embarrassing." She smiled, saluting him with her wooden spoon.

"Her regular dentist, in the city, he's on vacation in Europe, and get this: He's a friend of Will's, and I guess he'd heard about me from Will and maybe other people; I get referrals like that a lot, but Sammi Conway! She's a goddess!"

"You sound like a fifteen-year-old boy." She was grinning at his fervor, and he loved her for it.

He grabbed a beer from the refrigerator. "I was a fifteen-year-old boy the first time I saw her picture, I bet. God, what a day."

"What was wrong with her?"

"She'd been eating corn on the cob; her crown came loose. I had to move people around to take her, and Mrs. Dickson, Frances Dickson, she was sort of testy by the time I got to her, but oh! What a Hamptons moment!" He shook his head from side to side, disbelieving. "It was worth it," he said to himself.

"So did she seem happy with your services, my liege?"

He nodded. "She loved me! She said so! She's got a house in Bridgehampton—she said she's going to be out here most of the time now, with her new baby, and she will definitely be back. That's what she said. So I don't want to count on anything, but I think maybe Sammi Conway's on my client roster. That's impressive. Who knows? Maybe I'll raise my prices!"

"You're joking."

"Of course," he said. "You know me better than that. It's just nice that she loved my oh-so-gentle hands."

"Don't forget me. I'm the only one who gets to reap the real benefits from those particular hands. Don't share them, Buster."

"I couldn't and I wouldn't. Not even for Sammi Conway. Where are the kids?"

She tilted her head toward the family room. "Where else? They're playing so well today."

"I'm going to go say hi," he said cheerfully.

That warm, utterly contented feeling continued for another fifteen minutes. Deborah preheated the broiler, wiped the fish with olive oil, and then sprinkled salt, pepper, and paprika on it. She measured out a cup of dry orzo, browned it in a tablespoon of butter, and added two cups of cold water and a bouillon cube, covering the pot and lowering the heat beneath it. She set the timer and began to place plates around the table, humming to herself all the while.

She was at the stove, getting ready to stir the vegetables into heated olive oil, when suddenly Caroline's small form hit her legs from behind. "Oomph!" she gasped. "Hey, Little One, what is it?" She turned and knelt.

Caroline's face was red and damp; now she began to sob, gulping for air. "Momma! Momma!" she kept saying over and over again, first grabbing onto Deborah and then letting go, and finally throwing herself onto the ground on top of Deborah's bare feet, pulling at the bottoms of her jeans, so that Deborah had to stay herself not to topple over.

"Sweetie, what is it?"

"It's Daddy! Make him go away! I hate him! I hate him!" Caroline's voice was desperate and high; she clutched at Deborah's legs, her arms trembling. As Chris ran through the doorway, Deborah opened her mouth, ready to yell angrily. He shook his head, no, waving his arms, hitting the door jamb in his agitation.

"Look at her leg!" Spit had collected at the side of his mouth, dotting his lower lip. He was panting as if the run from the next room had been a timed dash. "Look at her leg!" he shouted, huffing for breath. Behind him, Michael quietly appeared and stood, unmoving, a spectator.

"What is it!? How did that happen?" The wound ran almost the entire length of Caroline's lower leg, raw scratches and broken scabs, oozing clear pus and pale blood. "Did you fall? When was it? Why didn't you show me?"

"Don't bug me so much!" Caroline yelled, slapping her mother's legs with both hands and falling backward onto the floor, her black hair splaying out across the worn oak boards. Her eyes were wide open in fury but seeing nothing, spittle shooting from her mouth as she screamed. *She's mad*, Deborah thought, *she's gone completely crazy and we drove her to it, not giving her enough, not helping her enough, focusing everything on him.*

Deborah knelt, trying to gather her daughter in her arms for comfort. Caroline kept hitting out with her fists wildly, kicking her legs and making strange grunting noises that sounded almost obscene. Deborah smelled urine. Sure enough, a damp patch was spreading around the crotch of Caroline's pink leggings. The bloody patch on her leggings that had first captured Christopher's attention was now tugged up almost to her knee; with her right hand, she kept reaching down, as if she wanted to tug the cloth back over the wound but couldn't control her hand enough to do so.

"How did you do it? What happened? Was it Michael?" Christopher was trying to keep his tone of voice under control, not to sound too angry, too frightened, not to alarm or agitate Caroline any further. Her back arched up, stiff between Deborah's arms; her eyes were so wild Deborah felt a rush of panic. *We've destroyed her*, was Deborah's only conscious thought. *We really have.*

Chris knelt beside mother and child, and put his hands on Caroline's legs, holding them so firmly she could no longer kick. She began to twist, hitting her mother in the jaw, screaming, "Keep him away from me! Leave me alone! I hate him! I hate you! Leave me alone! I don't love you! I don't love you! I don't love you!!"

Deborah pulled back, feeling the sore spot on her cheek and jaw. In Chris's eyes, she saw nothing but a panic that mirrored her own. No reassurance, no promise of a better day tomorrow, just fear. Caroline, the only one she'd never, ever felt a moment's true worry about, was showing her just how foolish that blithe attitude had been.

Deborah leaned back against the counter. Caroline, on the floor, began to writhe quietly, her screams muting to groans and low, soft whimpers. Chris lowered himself from kneeling to sitting, cross-legged. Michael stayed by the door jamb, eyes wide, face blank. One hand balanced him against the door; the other, in his jeans pocket, was clenched and still.

"It's infected, isn't it?" Deborah mouthed quietly to Chris. He nodded vehemently.

She moved forward, kneeling. She pulled Caroline onto her lap. This time, Caroline allowed it. She stilled in her mother's arms, breathing ragged and tearful. She lay there a minute, drawing great sobbing gulps of air at uneven intervals, and then, abruptly, she was asleep.

"I'll call Greg Isen," Chris whispered, and he slid cautiously backward and slipped quietly from the room. His footsteps, on the stairs, were hardly audible, not even to Deborah, who was listening closely.

Greg had been about to leave for the day when Chris's call came in, but he readily agreed to wait the five minutes it would take the Lathams to get down to his office. Deborah carried sleeping Caroline on her lap, ignoring any thought of seat belts. Michael, in the backseat, remained silent, as if engrossed in a difficult series of thoughts. Chris's hands were shaking slightly, and he drove slowly down Madison Street, letting every other car take precedence over theirs.

Chris knew Greg Isen fairly well, not because they were peers in terms of age, but because when Greg Isen had returned to Sag Harbor after his father's death, Chris had been one of the professionals who tried to reach out and make Greg's adjustment a little easier. He'd offered him advice when asked, but mostly he'd tried to make clear who was who in the village, a kind of informal training in the unspoken hierarchies of Harbor life that he knew Greg needed to go through if he wanted his practice to flourish. Deborah had offered to throw a party for Greg and his wife, early on, but Chris had said that wasn't necessary. The kinds of things Greg needed to know weren't social, exactly, although they had to do with social structure. But having been away as long as he had, what Greg Isen needed to know was whom to avoid and what to keep quiet about. Then he could figure out whom he liked and wanted to spend time with.

Deborah, on hearing this, had chuckled and shaken her head, walking back into the bathroom to rinse her toothbrush. "It's like a foreign country, the world you locals inhabit," she'd said, and he'd nodded, although she couldn't see him.

He was leaning back against the pillows of their bed, reading a new issue of *Sailing*, and he turned a page before he answered. "Every community is like this," he said. "You think because you grew up in a city that the rules were different, but they weren't. I'm sure the hospital where your parents worked was just the same way, and that over the years they chose which grocery store and dentist and hairdresser and everything else they wanted to patronize. They had choice about that. But there were also certain neighborhoods they didn't visit and people at the hospital they had to toady to in order to get along."

She looked in from the bathroom and nodded. In one hand, she held a hairbrush, and her face was freshly washed, he could see. "That's true, I guess," she said.

"So all I'm doing is warning Greg just a little bit about who's who and who matters, to make things easier. Because in a small town, if you learn a lesson the hard way, you can't forget about it. There isn't another grocery store to choose or another place to mail a letter. So it's easier to avoid the minefields up front if someone warns you. That way there's nothing to be surprised by later."

Those few clear lessons had clearly inspired a measure of gratitude in Greg. Now he came right out to the Lathams' car to examine a sleeping Caroline, gently probing at the deeper areas of the scratches until, of course, the little girl woke with a start. "Ouch!" she said, and she clung to her mother.

"We might as well get her inside," Greg said. "It's better than being out here."

Greg cleaned the wounds and disinfected them. As he taped the last bandage into place, he gave Caroline a hug. "You are a real trouper," he told her, "and now I'm going to give you some medicine to take to make sure that bad scratch heals right up."

Caroline nodded seriously. "Okay."

He knelt down to her eye level. "I'm wondering," he said. "I'm wondering if you scratched yourself because your leg itched."

She nodded, but then she paused and shook her head sorrowfully. "Not really," she said. "Not at first."

He put his hand on her knee and patted it. "I have two little girls," he told her. "They'll be starting school in Sag Harbor this fall. In kindergarten. I wonder if they'll like school here."

"I guess," she said, shrugging.

"I have a boy, too, a son. He's a little younger, he's three."

"Ugh," she said. "I have a brother."

"I saw him, out there with your father. Is he a pain?"

"I guess," she said, shrugging again.

In the silence that followed, even the ticking of his watch was audible.

"My brother . . . ," she began, but then she stopped, looking over at her mother.

Deborah looked down at her lap.

"She's not listening," Dr. Isen whispered. "You can tell me."

Caroline leaned toward him, pulling on his sleeve. "My brother is scary," she confided. "Like someone bad." Her right hand went to the bandage and rubbed it for just a moment before returning to her lap.

"Oh," Dr. Isen answered calmly. "Maybe we should talk to your mom about that."

"You can't," Caroline whispered. "She won't listen. All she does is worry about him. She thinks he's so special."

"Your dad? He might listen."

Caroline leaned close in, so that she was whispering straight into Greg Isen's ear. "If my dad hears any more about Michael, he's going to walk right out that door, that's what he told my mom, and he was so loud I heard him. So you can't."

Greg nodded. "Do you think maybe he might listen to me? Or maybe I could talk to your mother?" he whispered. "Maybe because I'm a grown-up, maybe I could help."

Caroline was silent a moment, thoughtful. Her legs dangled off the examining-room table, and now she leaned forward to study her bare feet. "I don't know," she told him. "Maybe my mom. You could try."

"I will," Greg said. "I think maybe I'll be able to help."

Caroline shook her head. "I don't think so," she said. "They never listen to me. All they do is talk about him all the time."

"Let me try," Greg said. "I'm good at getting parents to listen."

Caroline looked him straight in the eyes. "Thanks," she said, putting her right hand forward to take his hand in an utterly mature gesture of appreciation. "Thanks for trying."

Deborah, in the chair by Greg Isen's desk, had turned toward his window so she might wipe the tears off her cheeks without being seen. Now she nodded at Caroline and said, "Why don't you go find Daddy—let me talk with Doctor Isen for a moment?"

Caroline jumped off the table as if her leg wasn't even mildly injured and trotted from the room, a sense of relief already visible in the set of her shoulders and the height of her jaw. At the door, she paused, turning back to her mother. "Momma," she said. "Listen to the doctor. He's very smart."

Greg chuckled and turned to Deborah, lifting his hands into the air in an uncomfortable parody of amusement. "Kids."

"Yeah." She put both hands on her knees and stood. "She needs antibiotics?"

"Yes," he said. "And, as you heard, a little TLC."

"I don't get it. She's always so easy, I guess maybe I haven't been paying attention. Our son seems to take up a lot of space these days, behavior problems and all. He barely made it through kindergarten last year, and now I've just gotten a call saying they've decided he was too disruptive to the other students. The school is paying to have him tutored at home. And I guess my heart's just been breaking for that little boy . . ."

"Deborah," Greg Isen interrupted. "You've got to give that little girl some attention, spend some time worrying about whether she's okay. Because otherwise you're going to have another problem child on your hands."

She stared at him and lowered herself back into the chair.

"What Caroline did was to hurt herself, scratching and scratching at her leg until she drew blood and developed an infection. Nobody saw the scratches until they'd gotten infected. She wasn't getting proper attention. I'm being blunt because I count you as a friend, and I don't want this situation to get any worse. You've had a serious warning from your daughter. She's having a great deal of trouble getting you to notice that she's upset. I'm not a psychologist, I'm a family doctor, but I know the drill. I can honestly tell you, Caroline needs to get some help. She's asking for it, and you must pay attention. Otherwise, I can't even begin to predict what will happen."

"You can't mean that. She's so easy, such an easygoing child."

"I do mean it. I'm serious. I really am," he said, running his hand over his short-cropped hair. "Of course I am."

Deborah knew she wouldn't be able to stand again if she tried, her legs trembled so. She stared up at Greg Isen, wanting to say something else, to ask him something, to get some reassurance, but her lips felt stiff, her tongue like ice in her mouth.

"Take a minute," Greg said. "I'll go talk to Chris, if I can pull him from the kids."

As the door shut, Deborah closed her eyes tight, trying not to cry again, for God's sake. For some reason she remembered an afternoon when Caroline, in her high chair, had upended a bowl of vanilla yogurt onto her head and smeared it around with both hands, laughing and gurgling with such glee. Caro couldn't have been more than a year old, and never once, in those days, had it occurred to her mother that such a baby's life might ever be difficult. She was so easy, so lovely, so happy; how could anyone ever do her wrong?

Now, it appeared, not even a loving, genuinely devoted mother had noticed how deeply Caroline was suffering. If at this moment she weren't so desperately frightened for her daughter, Deborah knew, she'd be utterly despairing of herself.

30

VIORICA awoke abruptly, opening her eyes in panic, straining to locate any familiar object in Mina's living room. Blinking rapidly made no difference; even now, she could still see the twigs in the dark, woven and interwoven in a shape oddly akin to a crown of thorns. Her neck and forehead were warm and damp; under the light summer blanket, her cotton nightgown was soaked with sweat. What was it? What had she been dreaming?

She was winded; a knot of pain jabbed her side. She'd been racing. Michael had been there. They'd been running from a group of darkly garbed men in shiny boots, tall ghouls with nightsticks at the ready. Her breath came from the back of her throat in short, sharp gulps.

The street was long and dark, unlit by lamps, the windows on every house darkened by shutters. It had been raining, and each splashing footfall let their pursuers know the distance was closing. Michael, so serious, was panting, first behind her, then at her side, and then in the lead, his tiny feet moving so urgently. He wanted to live! She could tell how much he wanted freedom, to survive! He chose life! He did! Those horrid men—each of them had Chris's face; his tortured, angry sneer; his inability to love the little boy who only yearned to place his hand in his father's large, comforting palm.

In the dream, Chris's hands grew larger and larger, soft bowllike palms, until he could reach down casually to swipe Viorica and Michael, toying with them before clamping down. He would do that, she could tell. He didn't care enough; to him they were nothing. He could grab Michael in one hand and Viorica in the other, squeezing tighter and tighter until no room, no air, was left. But when his fist closed over Viorica, those thorny twigs around her head pricked at him, drawing blood, and he released her in a flash. As she fell, she called to Michael, or she tried to but couldn't form the words.

And as Viorica twisted and tumbled through the humid night, not knowing where she would fall or if she would survive, the fist around Michael drew tighter and tighter, closing him in, walling him off from the one person who truly yearned to help him.

In her pullout bed in Mina's living room, Viorica heard the sound of flies buzzing madly, bumping at the screens outside her window as if light had been urging them in. She kicked the damp sheets from her legs and lay there, panting, one arm twisted up and over to cover her eyes.

Awake now, she realized she was crying, a fact that seemed shameful even though she knew herself to be utterly alone.

One of the elderly ladies from church had fallen and broken her hip, and Martin felt strongly that Alice should move to her house to help Mrs. Phillips until she was more mobile. "It isn't as if you're doing anything around here," he'd informed her, and when she'd tried to explain that she had things of her own to think about, he'd shrugged and waddled into the living room as if there wasn't anything Alice could be considering that he'd deem a worthy reason for abandoning a neighbor in need.

She'd heard the click of the television, and she'd shifted her bulk in the armchair, trying to imagine how she might break her news to Martin.

Ellie Emerson's old Mercury Cougar sputtered and came to a stop just outside her biggest house, the one she cleaned on South Main Street in Southampton, as if the battered old thing had decided to lie down and die directly in view of the family Ellie most adored and envied in the entire world. Mrs. Hale's house had been one of the first, back when Ellie started cleaning in 1963, and the Hales had been extremely generous with Ellie and Gus over the years, giving them presents and clothes and furniture, and even the old Mercury itself back a dozen years before. Ellie hoped old Mrs. Hale wouldn't find a reproach in the Cougar's deathwatch at the end of her driveway; she wouldn't mind if Mrs. Hale decided to donate another car from her stable; she wouldn't mind it at all.

The only problem with the car's being out of commission was that now she had to trot up the street on foot to get to the dry cleaner. Mrs. Hale was giving a party. All her best linens had been taken out and inspected, and Ellie'd had the job of hand-washing the dingier ones and bringing them in for a special pressing. If they weren't picked up today, Mrs. Hale would start getting nervous about whether they'd be ready, and Ellie didn't want to come back into Southampton later in the week if she didn't have to, especially now that the car was acting up. Last time Mrs. Hale had thrown a dinner, which had to be two or more years before, Ellie had managed the wait-staff for her and made sure the ash-trays were emptied and the cocktail glasses were cleaned up. She didn't want that job anymore—she didn't like it—and so Mrs. Hale had asked the caterer to handle everything.

Those damn linens, though, they were Ellie's responsibility. She had promised to set the table before she left this afternoon. Luckily, it wasn't that humid, and when the house was up to snuff, she set off toward the dry cleaners. The air was sweet and pleasant, and for the first time in a long time, she realized how rarely she got to be outside. Her legs felt loose and easy, her arms swung at her side, and she held her head high, breathing deeply.

Once she crossed in front of the church at the corner of Job's Lane and Main Street, the sidewalks grew crowded, a typical shopping after-noon at the height of the Hamptons summer season. Without realizing it, Ellie's walk slowed. She couldn't help watching the other people, they were all so beautiful. Such lovely unmarked legs in short skirts; such simple, elegant hairdos; what clean, starched shirts! In her stained T-shirt and worn jeans, she herself wasn't worth a moment's considera-tion, but, oh, these women on the street—they were breathtaking! And their men, handsome in neatly pressed pants and crew cuts, or dashing with thin hair caught back in ponytails, sweaters draped around their shoulders, paper cups filled with cappuccino in their hands! Ellie walked slower and slower, admiring even a pair of towheaded children whining to their baby-sitter on the sidewalk outside the lingerie store.

A tiny blonde woman leading a huge Newfoundland headed directly for Ellie, failing even to notice her presence, and it was Ellie who moved to the side, murmuring "excuse me" to the dog, who stared back at her with bright, knowing eyes.

She was just remarking to herself, with a certain amount of awe and pleasure, how she'd lived in this area her entire life and still didn't know a soul walking the entire length of Main Street, when she stopped suddenly in her tracks. There, plain as day in front of her nose, was Des Dunn, twenty years older than he'd been the last time she set eyes on him and walking like a well-dressed peacock, arm in arm with a woman as remarkable as any other sauntering beauty on the block.

"Des Dunn!" she said, before she could even stop to consider not opening her mouth, and he turned, puzzled, to nod at her.

"It's me," she said. "Your Aunt Ellie."

The woman's hand tightened on his arm, as if she would like to pull him back and away. *Of course, I make her sick,* Ellie thought. *I'm a gnarly fingered, dyed-haired local with bad teeth. I bet I scare her.*

Des paused, put his hand palm up on the back of his companion's hand, and then nodded politely at Ellie. He did not step forward.

"You look wonderful, Des."

"Thanks," he said. "It's nice to see you." His posture was tall and straight; she hadn't remembered his being this handsome. He was still as slim as ever, but now he looked so poised and starched that he didn't seem underfed; he seemed elegant. His polo shirt was crispy white; his faded shorts were unwrinkled and hit his legs midthigh, revealing an expanse of tanned, downy flesh. His sneakers were so clean they looked new. His wedding ring glowed brightly, a thick expanse of polished gold.

"Are you—are you visiting? Alice didn't, I mean, I didn't . . ." She stumbled, aware that she was starting to flush pinkly.

"No." He looked down at the woman on his arm, whose face was now utterly expressionless. He nodded again. "We live here," he said at last. "This is Nina."

Nina nodded, the neutral line of her mouth immobile. Her hand, under his, was relaxed, the nails polished and pale. Her eyes did not seem to see Ellie, as if she were looking directly over Ellie's head in an excess of politeness.

"In Southampton?" Ellie tried not to sputter. "Does Martin—do they know?"

He shrugged. "It hardly seems to matter," he said, and then he leaned toward Nina and said, "The people who raised me when I was small, I've told you. They live somewhere in Sag Harbor, but I doubt you'd wish to . . ."

"Oh, no," Nina said. "I'd be delighted. I'd love to meet them, to thank them for all they did for you." Her tone was so bland Ellie couldn't tell if she was being sarcastic or genuine.

He shook his head. "I don't think so," he said. "But give them my best," he told Ellie. "I'd like you to."

She nodded. He began to move on, but Ellie stopped him. She was puzzled. "I don't get it," she said. "What happened to you?"

"Who knows?" he said. "The simplest way to put it is I figured it out. The way I was going wasn't worth it, that's all. I wanted more, and so . . ." He raised one arm in a laconic version of expansiveness, "and so I made it happen."

"What do you do? For a living, I mean?"

He smiled. "I buy things," he said. Nina, at his side, chuckled suddenly, light washing over her face and rendering it lively and endearing.

"And then he sells them," she said.

"That's right," Des agreed. "It's a fine way to live. You can tell that to Martin if you want."

"What do you sell?"

"Money," he said simply.

"Oh." Ellie stood for a moment. Then she said, "I wish I had some to sell."

"If you ever get any," he said, "I'm in the phone book." He reached toward her as if he would touch her arm or shoulder but he didn't quite finish the distance. Instead, he waved his outstretched hand just a few inches from her face and half-smiled so that, later, when she was telling Gus about it, she had to admit she knew Des was repelled by her.

As they walked on, arm and arm, neither Des nor Nina appeared to have anything to say about his encounter with his past. Ellie, on the other hand, couldn't move for a full minute or more. She was rooted to the sidewalk, her heart pounding, as if something momentous had just occurred. "And I can't for the life of me figure out why," she said later to Gus. "How come that murderer gets to walk around dressed up like some Latin movie actor, and me, I just keep scrubbing and scrubbing and nothing I labor over even stays clean a full week? How can it work that way?"

Gus was sitting on their top front step, drinking a beer, watching the cars whiz by down below on Brick Kiln Road; what he said was this: "If

Des Dunn is walking around looking like he's got a million dollars, I don't doubt he's got it. But if you ask me, he probably stole it. He was a bad little boy and a bad teenager, and I'm sure he turned into a bad man. People don't change. They don't ever change. And don't you forget it."

But Ellie didn't agree. "You may not like the thought," she said to Gus, "but if you ask me, anything's possible. Change is a basic fact of human life."

"There's change and change," he said, shaking his head before taking another swig from the bottle. His belly, even after thirty years of daily drinking, was fairly flat and lean, and she reached a hand down—the other was holding the screen door open—to run it over his T-shirted shoulders. "That feels good," he said. He took another swig. He belched, covering his closed mouth with his fist. He cleared his throat.

"People change," he said, "like they get older and crazier and cheaper and lonelier and grayer and sadder. That's how they change. Nobody gets better. Don't ever be fooled. I been around human nature so long I could write a book about it, and that's a fact. Nobody and nothing turns out for the better. If you just accept that fact, you'll do okay."

She shut the door and stood inside, watching him. "It's amazing I can still find a word of love for you, Gus Emerson," she said affectionately.

He turned and smiled cheekily at her.

"You're wrong though," Ellie said. "If you'd seen him, you'd know he was doing fine."

He shrugged, turning back to watch the cars. Beyond the road, a strip of water was visible through the trees, but he didn't look that far. "It's been a long day," he admitted. "Maybe you're right."

"Maybe," she agreed. "Just maybe. Dinner's ready when you are."

"I'll be right there," he said, but he didn't move. He sat, and as he did, his thoughts turned back to a group of little boys he'd never doubted would all become heroes, particularly the little boy who he'd once been. *Funny, even those of us who lived well,* he thought, *we none of us did blaze a path through the atmosphere. We none of us did fly to the moon. But we've been good Christians and that's what counts. When our reward comes, we'll have earned it right and well. I'm not ashamed of that, no, not at all.*

He took a last swig of his beer, setting the bottle carefully down on the step next to his feet. The cars whizzed past, Jaguars and Mercedes and Saturns, such names, such awe-inspiring names. He could barely hear the sound their tires made on the pavement, and yet he could smell rubber burning, the odor rising up the hill toward his small house with alacrity. He rubbed his eyes. Lately, in the evening, he was awfully tired.

"Ellie," he called, and she was there in a moment.

"You okay?"

"Yeah," he said. "I just, I don't know. I just wanted to say thanks."

"For what?"

He shrugged, leaning down to pick up his empty bottle. He grabbed onto the stair rail and began to lift himself to standing. "I don't know. For working so hard. For being such a good woman. For putting up with a grump like me."

She snorted. "Get in here," she said. "Dinner's getting cold."

31

CHRIS walked to work the following day, the Tuesday just before Labor Day weekend. Summer's end was palpably at the corner, lending an abruptly crisp quality to the air. He was musing about something Will had said on the phone the evening before, when he'd called to say he'd be coming out with Peggy the following weekend and wondered if they'd like to join forces for sailing and a picnic.

Chris had agreed immediately, even though he wasn't exactly sure what Deborah had cooked up. "She's upstairs now, putting the kids to bed, so I'll have to let you know whether Sunday or Monday would be better."

"Peg's pushing for Sunday. She wants to get back to the city early Monday morning, start the fall off on a well-rested note." They chuckled, each of them picturing the other as more busily managed by a controlling wife.

In the aftermath, they lapsed into a good-humored silence. Chris was thinking about how Peg organized all the food in her pantry: pastas arranged by box height; cans of tomatoes right next to cans of soup; cookies separate from crackers; and breakfast cereals on their ends so that the top labels showed to even a small child. Deborah made fun of Peg's obsessive organization behind her back; nevertheless, she'd defended Peg when Chris said her food shelves looked like a lending library. That had surprised him.

Through the phone line, Chris could hear the sounds of a drawer being opened and a piece of paper ripping. "Have you ever noticed," he asked, "how all women have something in common as they get older, no matter where they've come from or what they've learned or how they've lived?"

"Like what?" Will asked cautiously.

"I don't know," he said. "It's from having children or something, they all have stuff to talk about. My receptionist, she could talk to anyone, doesn't matter who, any woman, and within five minutes she knows who's had a hysterectomy and how much it cost to have her kitchen redone."

"So?"

"Well, I mean, they don't ever have, they don't—I don't know. They just tell each other stuff."

Will cleared his throat. Chris heard the sound of paper ripping once again; was Will opening his mail as they talked?

Chris began again. "You know, guys, like us, I mean most guys, the older they get, the less they talk about. I mean, golf and sailing and work and whatever, yeah, but there's lots of stuff you just don't say out loud. It's like forbidden territory, and it gets larger and larger, what's not okay to say." He paused, and then, hotly, finished in a rush: "That's what I think. Don't you think that's true? At least sort of?"

"I don't know," Will said. "Maybe."

More paper ripped on Will's end of the line.

Chris chuckled, a way of washing away what he'd said that wouldn't have been possible face to face. "I'm up for a sail," he said. "I haven't been out in weeks."

Will said, "If there ever was anything, you know, that you wanted to say, I could listen."

Chris breathed in, sharply, holding the air without realizing it until he was forced to exhale loudly. He opened his mouth, closed it, and opened it once again. His right hand, holding the portable telephone, tightened, so that the bony edges of his knuckles gleamed whitely under the overhead counter lights. He turned to look out through the door into the family room; Deb was nowhere to be seen.

"I've been wondering," he began, and then he heard the first foot-falls at the top of the stairs. "I've been wondering whether Peg could come over here and arrange our pasta in alphabetical order. You know, linguine then penne, then rigatoni, and *then* spaghetti."

"Ha," Will said. "Ha, ha. Then maybe Deborah can say some organic spells over it and we can all dance off into the New Age together."

Relieved, Chris feigned insult and signed off, literally putting all thought of the conversation out of his mind until the morning, when it occurred to him, as if from nowhere, that if he had to confide in someone, it would have to be Will. There was nobody else. In this world full of people he wanted to love him, only Will could hear him out and not lose faith.

When Chris arrived at the office, he closed the door to the lab and dialed Will's work number. It was too early for Will's secretary, he knew, but not for Will, who tended to leave for work before most people turned in their beds and began the restless journey to wakefulness. "Hey," he said.

"What is it, Sunday or Monday?" Will asked. "I gotta tell you, Peg's really pushing for Sunday."

"I forgot to ask her," he said.

"Oh."

"I was thinking," Chris said. "About that night."

He could hear the sound of Will swallowing, taking a gulp of coffee or of air, it was impossible to tell.

"You ever think about it?"

"Not really," Will said, but his tone was so uncomfortably neutral that Chris knew he was lying.

"Lately, I've been thinking about it a lot, I don't know why."

"It's so far in the past, I hardly even remember what happened."

"Right."

"Why dredge all that up? It was an accident. Completely. What good is it going to do to drag it up now? It's not as if we could change anything. It's not like anybody filed charges against him. Nothing happened to Des that wouldn't have happened anyway."

"You don't know that."

"Yes, I do. Des Dunn's been in and out of jail for years, that's what I've heard. Ask anybody, even his own parents lost touch with him. They wrote him off. He was trouble from the start, and you know it. It's not like he'd never bent the law, shit, Chris, he was into so much stuff. He robbed his own parents' house for God's sake! We didn't do anything to him. Not really. He was headed down his own path long before graduation. Long before that night, and you know it as well as me."

Chris had his back to the lab door. Someone began to rattle the knob. "It's me," he said. "I'm in here."

It was Rosemary, his assistant. "You okay?" she asked suspiciously.

"Yeah, I'm on the phone."

"Oh, sorry," she said, but he could hear the curiosity in her voice. Trust Rosemary to ferret out any deviation from the norm; she almost couldn't help herself.

"I'll be off in a second," he said. After a moment her footsteps began to move through the consulting room and back toward the front office.

"What brought this up in the first place?" Will asked.

"I don't know," he said, but then he added, "Mrs. Dunn, their mom, remember?"

"Of course," Will said impatiently.

"She's sick, real sick, and I don't know, it's bugging me. Part of me wants to tell her the truth, let her have some good news. Why shouldn't she know there was at least one thing Des didn't do?"

"What's she got?"

"HIV."

Will laughed. "Her?"

"Honest."

"That's weird."

"Weird stuff happens, I don't know. But she's definitely positive, that's what Greg Isen said."

"Why'd he tell you?"

"She was in the office, a broken tooth, and when I saw her tongue, I just knew. I've only seen oral hairy cell leukoplakia a few times before this, you know, when I did that dental clinic at NYU. This kind of presentation, it's pretty much a dead giveaway."

He could tell Will was shaking his head on the other end of the phone. "Wow. It's hard to believe. It's like thinking my own folks could have . . ."

Chris interrupted. "It wasn't sex, that's what she says. My guess is that Martin's been stepping out on her. He needs to be tested. Greg Isen hasn't had much luck reasoning with him. But what she told Deb is that she thinks something happened with an infected foster kid, some kind of freak accident. It sounded so far-fetched, I called Greg Isen back. He was really strange with me. I think he thinks I handled the whole thing pretty badly. Which I did. I screwed up all over the place. He could probably get my license suspended."

"Seriously? What'd you do?"

"Nothing really. I just couldn't bring myself to tell Mrs. Dunn. And I sort of talked to Martin about her. I was—oh, I don't know."

"Is Isen going to do anything?"

"No, I don't think so. I don't think he could, I've helped him too much. But he let me know he was pissed off. That he thought I'd been totally, you know, unethical."

Will cut to the chase. "Did you say Alice Dunn told Deb? What was Deborah doing talking to Alice Dunn?"

"At first I thought she was getting ready to start doing photography again, but I didn't say anything. I didn't want her to think it mattered either way to me; it was up to her. Now I can't tell. There's been some stuff going on with Michael, hardly worth talking about, but Deb's been having a tough time about it. And she and Alice, God knows why, they keep meeting for coffee. Two times now, and Deb was so upset when Alice told her what Isen said. I have no idea what the draw is. Deb just keeps saying she likes her. And it's been driving me nuts, because the more I hear about Alice Dunn, the more I want to tell her everything, get it off my chest."

"I am so opposed to that idea. I can't even think about it."

"Well, I wanted to tell you I was—oh, I don't know—I just wanted to say I'm thinking about it. That's all."

"Don't be a jerk. Don't do anything until we've talked," Will warned. "This weekend, maybe on the boat, we'll have time to talk then."

"Hey, you never told anybody, did you? Not Peg, not anyone?"

"Not even that shrink Peg made me see, the marriage counselor. She tried to pry out all my deepest darkest, but that one I kept for myself. I just made up stuff to tell that idiot, and after a few months Peg got tired of the whole thing." Will paused, cleared his throat. "Fact is, I don't think about it that much. I put it out of my head a long time ago; that's where it stays."

"That's how I used to be," Chris admitted, "but not anymore."

"You told Deborah?"

"Shit no, Pardner," he said, forcing a chuckle. He paused. "But I might."

"Tough for you, Buddy."

"I guess."

Both Chris Latham and his wife realized that they'd hit some sort of crisis, that their marriage was entering a skid of notable intensity. Deborah knew they were fighting about Michael, and she was afraid. On some unthinkable level, she was terrified that a pointed communication might result in an ultimatum. Chris would force her to choose between the two males in her family. To even consider this fork in the road was like the first chills of influenza, depleting enough to prevent a cautious step further.

Chris was beginning to believe that the tension stemmed from his own guilt about the past. While he thought about Michael fairly often during the day, and with some bitterness, he was coming to consider his son more of a physical interference, an annoying roadblock that might easily be moved with simple equipment. When the school called to say they recommended Michael be tutored at home for first grade, he merely shrugged at the news. His most specific thought had been that he'd probably start packing his lunch in that case or heading to the Paradise Diner for the soup and sandwich special. *Not that he'd dropped home for lunch in months,* he realized. *When had that changed?*

If Deborah had asked him what was bugging him, he'd probably have broken down and told her the whole damn story of the night Jack Dunn died, every single ugly detail, and watched as all the lovely softness of her gaze hardened permanently into disgust and then indifference. He expected that. Nevertheless, he knew he'd have to tell her eventually; otherwise, the curse he felt dogging him might never dissipate.

Until this summer, Chris Latham had always thought of himself as a decent, kind person, the sort of man who truly could congratulate himself on the rectitude—and the pleasure—with which he lived day to day. Lately, though, that image had been cracking. For years, he'd refused to face the fact that he was the sort of man who let people down: first his mother; then Jack Dunn and, by extension, so many other people, including himself; and now, of course, Michael. He'd truly failed to love Michael, and whether he was working or watching television, jogging or sailing or at the movies, he never ceased to know this about himself: That he had failed to live up to his own illusions.

While another man might have chosen to put the blame on the inadequacies of others, Chris knew better. In some way, he'd been on a path to failure ever since his father died, but he'd blithely ignored what he'd probably always known to be the truth. Now, with his sins exposed to inner review, it was only a matter of time before Deborah would see him for what he was. Such knowledge would surely shatter any faith she might have in him. The clock was ticking and he knew it.

At the same time, he couldn't bear his family the way it was, couldn't tolerate even looking at the sullen set of Michael's shoulders as he sat hunched before the television set, didn't want to rub his son's back and legs briskly with a towel before coaxing him into clean pajamas, no longer felt that hesitant pull of love when Michael closed his eyes and smiled as the covers were being drawn up to his chin. It was over, even the slightest urge toward loving his adopted son, and in its place was a kind of fury at the opportunities lost.

Were it not for Michael, he and Deborah would have had another child, a sweet boy of their own, he was sure, and the love between them would still be sturdy and unquestioned.

Sometimes Alice Dunn was more than just sweet, Deborah thought. Sometimes she could be surprisingly smart. There was something Alice had said only that afternoon, when she'd lumbered her way up the Lathams' driveway and hefted herself into one of Deborah's heavy kitchen chairs with a grunt.

"I was thinking," Alice had begun, even before Deborah had offered tea or made a move toward providing physical or social comforts of any sort. "I was thinking about something I wanted to tell you."

"Sure. Do you want anything? Water? Tea?"

"Whatever." Alice had fluttered her gnarled fingers up like butterflies before letting them fall, clasped awkwardly on her broad lap. "I wanted to tell you about Martin and me, how we met."

"Great, okay. When? Was it here?"

"No, that's the funny part. See, I was born in Shirley, just up the Island a ways, that's why I'll never be a local, not even after forty years. We met on a church youth group trip. I was pretty young, still in high school, and Martin was older, he was twenty-four and he had this business of his own, Dunn's Plumbing. It was already doing well, and he wanted to take me out, and my mother said go, a girl like you can't be too fussy, it's not as if you're pretty or good at much." Alice laughed and fluttered her hands once again. "I couldn't even cook, back then."

"I think you're pretty. That's ridiculous," Deborah said, turning from the counter where she'd just finished pouring boiling water into two pottery mugs. A zucchini bread was sliced into squares on a small white plate, and she was about to pull out some napkins. "How could your own mother say that?"

Alice smiled happily, as if Deborah's comment had erased, temporarily, this forty-year-old hurt. "No, I'm not, but that's nice. My mother, she was just saying what she thought. She was trying to make it all right for me, getting me tied to Martin. She didn't want me to be alone. So the thing is, I was so young, just seventeen when we got married. And I figured, if you get married, you must be in love. I was stupid, just like my mother said. I didn't know love was a feeling, I had no idea. I didn't understand that if you love somebody, you know it."

Deborah nodded, smiling, her cheeks pink. Her eyes filled, suddenly, with angry tears. She brought the mugs and plate to the table, placing a teaspoon and honey and a pitcher of milk before Alice, who simply ignored the entire tribute as she continued.

"So after a year, before Jack was born, I started talking to the pastor of my church a lot. I started saving up things to tell him. Fact is, I started knowing what it was to love somebody. I just had so much to say to Pastor. I loved listening to him. I liked him. He made me laugh and I trusted him."

Deb pulled out her chair quietly and sat down, hands around her tea mug, eyes glued on Alice.

"And one afternoon, oh, right before Jack started growing inside me, one afternoon I was speaking with Pastor and I had to tell him, had to tell him what I felt. Otherwise, well, I knew I'd burn just for the thoughts I was having about him. He was my, you know, my spiritual father, and the things I was thinking I knew I'd better be real clear about with him."

Deb nodded, once, tensely. Alice, looking up to meet her eyes, laughed uncomfortably.

"So. It makes me blush even now. So I told him, and he was, well, it wasn't what I expected. I guess I thought it would be all romantic and lovely, like in the movies. If he cared for me, which I pretty well knew he did, he'd take me in his arms and comfort me and tell me it was God's will we endure our feelings and help them to pass. That's what I thought he'd do."

"He didn't?"

Alice shook her head from side to side ruefully. "The one thing I didn't know too much about was"—she gestured downward, toward the huge expanse of her chest—"was these. I mean I always knew I had a lot down there. When I was in high school, boys used to tease me. But Pastor, he was grabbing onto me, with his eyes closed and him moaning about my . . . my . . . he called them such a word, I can't even say. It just wasn't what I thought would happen. And the way he was breathing, through the back of his throat—when I saw that movie *Star Wars,* the bad guy, Darth Vader, he made the same sound Pastor did. I had to get up and leave the theater."

"Did you yell for help? Or run? What did you do?"

"Well, Martin said it was my own damn fault, those were his words. You know. For spending time alone with a man. Young women shouldn't do that, it reads to other people as intentions, that's what Martin said. I mean, I led the pastor on, I know that."

"He was the pastor! In a position of trust! He should have been able to handle anything a parishioner needed to talk about, I mean, really, Alice, that's idiotic!"

Alice shrugged. "That wasn't what Martin said, not when I told him. See, after Pastor finished his—you know, his business—I got myself pulled together and out of there, and I was crying and crying, and later that night I tried to tell Martin what had happened, how mistaken I'd been. I never should have, he was so angry. And Martin, well, he said it was my own fault. He never said a word of complaint to anybody about that pastor, not for the whole next five years. That man baptized Jack and Des. He shook my hand every Sunday until he was transferred to New Jersey. And Martin stood by my side smiling. He figured, I guess, he figured that was my punishment."

"My God."

Alice picked up the milk pitcher and watched the tiny swirl spread and settle through the tea, turning the brown to milky white. She didn't look up, just kept holding her teaspoon above the mug. "The thing that bugs me is, did Martin marry me hating me, or did it come with time, from knowing me?"

Her eyes sparkled with tears. She forced a smile and said, "Zucchini bread, yum!" And then she sneezed, sweetly, like a cat, a surprisingly small sound.

"Why did you stay with him? I don't get it," Deborah said roughly.

Alice's sparse eyebrows lowered. "That's what people do, I think. They survive and endure. And then God gives them a gift, like I had my Jack for almost nineteen years. It was worth it, all of it, to have loved him. I was so happy when he was a baby! The way he'd wrap his arms around my neck and kiss me when he was two and three, oh! That was love! That was real love. Once I felt the way my heart loved him, I never wondered anymore about love."

"How about the other one? Des? Was that his name?"

"Des. Yeah. I loved him, too. He was a wild one. I loved him like he was my own son, at least I thought so. And then when Jack died, it was like I'd been in a fever all these years and the only cure there was, well, was more of Jack. He was gone, though. Des couldn't do it, couldn't make it better."

"So it wasn't the same kind of love?" Deborah's heart was pounding so hard, she had to speak louder to hear her own words.

Alice took a tiny sip of her tea. She wiped her mouth. She lifted the square of zucchini bread to her lips but put it down. "Funny, I'm just not so hungry this week," she said. "All this news has got me turned around. I'm all turned around."

Deborah brushed her fingers across Alice's wrist.

Alice said, "I've never really told anybody this," and she paused.

"It's okay."

"The thing is, when Jack died? Des was driving. The car, when Jack died. And he didn't even get a scratch. So the thing is, maybe sometimes I blame him for the one loss even though it brought me another. Because after Jack died, I didn't love Des anymore. But I didn't love anyone, ever, the way I loved Jack. I really never did feel that kind of love anywhere else." She shook her head again, leaning back in the heavy chair so that tears fell not onto the table but onto the wide expanse of her floral shirt, spotting the pale blue cotton.

"God," Deborah said, hushed. "I'd never thought."

"How could you?" Alice asked, smiling, even though the tears continued to fall, soft and constant, as if having opened the faucet, it would be difficult to stop this leak from running.

Chris's car pulled into the driveway.

"Oh! Oh! Is it that late? I've got to go," Alice said, and she pushed back awkwardly, spilling a milky pool of tea onto the table. "I'm sorry," she said, and those hands fluttered up, waving in the air before straightening her brown barrette and beginning to dig in her nylon bag for car keys.

"It's okay, there's no rush. Chris would love to say hello."

"Oh no. Oh no. It's time. I know doctors, they need peace and quiet when they get home."

"He's a dentist," Deborah said dryly.

Alice stopped and stared at Deborah for a moment, before starting to rifle through her bag again. "He works hard, Dr. Latham, he really cares about what he does."

"I never said he didn't," Deborah answered, her voice rising sharply.

"Some people might envy you what you have," Alice said, her voice so quiet Deborah had to strain forward to hear. "Not that you're well, not that. But that you have so much, your children, your home, him," she gestured toward the driveway.

"It's not, maybe, as good as it seems," Deborah said.

Alice nodded. "I figure. But you've got the chance to work it out; that hasn't been taken away. So maybe that's a gift you have to think about. Maybe, just maybe. Lord knows I made lots of wrong choices, and I haven't had all that much happiness, all in all, now that I'm starting to count it up. So what I'm saying to you is maybe you might want to do it, even for me. I'd like to know you didn't sneer at happiness when it stared you in the face. I'd like to know you stood up and went after it."

"How though? Where do I find it? I don't know what to do!"

Her posture was taller suddenly, and eager, leaning toward Alice with her wild brown hair splaying everywhere, her eyes so damp with trust, Alice almost wanted to kiss her. Instead, she pulled her keys from her bag.

"Here they are!" she said. "I'm just a stupid old woman, and I know it, but you'll figure it out. A pretty girl like you, you can figure it out a whole lot better than someone like me. I didn't even go to college . . ."

"Neither did I."

"Yeah, well," Alice said, and shrugged. "Someone taught you how to look like you did. Nobody'd ever think I was sporting a fancy degree. You'll be fine."

"I'm sorry," Deborah said. "I didn't mean to make light of you, of what's going on."

"You didn't."

"Good."

"Hey," Alice said gaily. "Make light of me! Then maybe I'll have room for that zucchini bread of yours!"

It was hard to tell who was joking about what, Chris thought, walking in the door. There they both were, smiling big as Barbie dolls, and the two of them panting, hard, like they'd run the middle distance since his car pulled to a halt in the driveway. Were they laughing at him? He didn't like it.

He didn't like it at all.

32

CAROLINE LATHAM hooked into her therapist, Dierdre, almost immediately. She hadn't exactly known what to expect—all her mom had said was that Dierdre was a special person who wanted to help her. Mommy had said it would be fun, but Caroline didn't believe everything her mother said anymore. That's why she'd been pleased to realize that all Dierdre wanted to do was sit on the floor and color. Dierdre was very small, and since Caroline was very tall, they were almost the same size, and that first day they were both wearing red shirts and blue-jean skirts. When Dierdre made a joke about that, Caroline giggled. She hadn't even minded when her mother softly said she was going to run down to Schiavoni's, that she'd be back in forty-five minutes.

Dierdre liked Caro's drawings. When she asked Caroline to draw a picture of her house, Caroline complied, sketching the renovated Federal the way it looked at Christmas, all covered with white lights. Caroline drew those using the gold crayon.

"I love this color," she confided. "Gold and silver and pink, those are my favorites."

"I like purple, too," Dierdre said, and Caroline nodded. She liked purple a lot as well.

"That's my brother's room," Caro said, pointing to an upper window on the right. "He's bad. I hate him."

"Brothers can be really difficult," Dierdre said sympathetically.

"See this?" Caro said, and she lifted her new bangs, revealing the knobby inflammation across her forehead.

"That must have hurt a great deal."

"My brother did it."

"Would you like to tell me what happened?"

"Not really," Caroline said.

"Okay. If you change your mind, feel free to tell me."

"Okay."

They drew for several minutes, each politely offering colors to the other and complimenting one another on drawing skills. Eventually, Caroline put her crayon down, pushed her drawing to the side, and said, "I like Christmas."

"Me too."

"It's happy then."

"Why is Christmas so happy?"

She shrugged. "Presents. My grandparents gave me an American Doll. Samantha. And now I want the bed and the chest of drawers. My other grandparents, they're dead. Otherwise, I'd get more presents."

"Do you miss your grandparents?"

"Oh no. I never knew them. My daddy barely did. They died when he was little. But that's why we have Michael, that's what my mom said. Because my dad didn't have parents, so he wanted to help Michael. So if I say one bad thing about him, they get all crazy. Or they just walk away like I didn't say a word."

"You must get pretty mad about that. Sometimes."

She nodded vigorously. "They think I don't remember," she confided. "But I do. It was nice before him. Daddy was funny. Mommy was happy. We had fun. I wish he'd just go back where he came from. I'm scared of him, and I don't like him, and I want it all to be the way it was. They think I don't remember. But I do. I didn't forget. Even though they think I did."

"It sounds like right now is a pretty tough time for you."

Caroline rolled her eyes skyward, picking up the gold crayon. "Nah," she said. "It's okay."

"Maybe I'll be able to help, if we spend some time talking. You'd like some help, I guess," Dierdre said. "Is that so?"

Caroline nodded. "Maybe," she said cautiously. "That might be good."

33

WEDNESDAY, August 27th, began with a humid grimness. The first of the season's tropical storms had narrowly missed the Caribbean Islands and was now headed north into the deep Atlantic Ocean. The Eastern coastline would surely miss a major buffeting from bad weather. Nevertheless, the air hung damply, and even before Ellie Emerson arrived at the Lathams', Deborah went around opening all the windows to let in any faint breeze. She didn't want Ellie to ask for the air conditioning; with Labor Day coming this weekend, it seemed too late in the season. Besides, once the rain began, it would grow cooler. It was definitely time for fall. The pale sundresses that had been flowery and lovely all summer looked dowdy and worn this week, even though darker clothes still seemed too harsh to pull from the closet.

Chris was heading to Stony Brook that morning for one of the professional seminars required for maintenance of his dental credentials. As a fellow in the Academy of General Dentistry, he was supposed to take twenty-five hours of continuing education courses every year. Normally, he liked to make this requirement into an excuse for a little junket to someplace like Aspen or Hilton Head, but this course, on medical and legal responsibilities in client care, had twanged a particularly sensitive nerve. The idea of avoiding the village for a day was appealing; he took his time getting dressed, giving himself a minivacation from responsibility. Knowing that both Ellie and Mina were coming meant that there was no pressure to help Deb get the kids up. He stayed so long in the shower that his skin grew pink and tender; if he could, he would have dressed quietly and made his way down the stairs and to the door without greeting any of his family. He was so tired of them. The notion of getting in the car and heading anywhere, even to one of these continuing ed things, was as close to heaven as he could fathom. He pulled on a pair of khakis and a white shirt, trying not to make a sound.

On Deb's side of the unmade bed, a book was open. She must have been reading by the early daylight, waiting for the children to awaken. It was *Dracula*. He picked up the worn paperback. She was already halfway done, he saw, and he was surprised that she hadn't mentioned reading this particular book. After all, Michael hailed from precisely the same part of the world Count Dracula did; had she been afraid of what he might think of her interest in such a story?

He turned to her page and read:

"'Oh, my dear, if you only know how strange is the matter regarding which I am here, it is you who would laugh. I have learned not to think little of any one's belief, no matter how strange it may be. I have tried to keep an open mind; and it is not the ordinary things of life that could close it, but the strange things, the extraordinary things, the things that make one doubt if they be mad or sane.'"

Outside the window, not a leaf was moving on a tree. The air, so still and damp, weighed on his chest and made it difficult to breathe. He shook his head, carefully replacing the book. As he buttoned first one cuff and then the other, he muttered, "Crazy. If you ask me, that's completely the opposite of true."

Behind him, Ellie Emerson cleared her throat. "Excuse me," she said. "I usually start in here, but I can do the kids' rooms first if you're going to be a while."

"Oh, no," he turned, smiling automatically. He bent to pick his towel up off the bed. "I'm done, I was just, I don't know, spacing out."

"I don't get much time for that," Ellie grumbled, moving past him to begin slipping the pillowcases off the pillows, throwing the linens into a pile near his feet.

"You're too good," he said. "That's why you're so busy."

She fought the smile, refused to lift her head, and continued stripping the bed. He threw his towel onto the dirty linens.

"Hey," she said suddenly. "You'll never guess who I saw."

He was already at the door, but he turned, one hand lifting to rest on the jamb.

"Remember Des Dunn? He was in your class, wasn't he?"

Chris lifted his other hand, steadying himself.

"You okay?" Ellie asked.

He grinned, his eyes looking just past her. She got the idea there was no emotion reaching his eyes at all.

Chris said, "I'm slow this morning. What did you say?"

"Des Dunn. Remember him? A dark kid, thin, with big eyes? He was Jack Dunn's brother. I know you guys played football together."

"Oh, yeah. Sure. I remember him; he was friends with Cal Stewart and some of those guys, right? Sure. Sure." Chris had turned completely, his back stiff against the pale yellow of the bedroom wall. His lips were flattened, pressed tensely over his teeth so that a jaunty dimple appeared on his cheek.

"He was in your class."

"Yeah. That's right. I remember."

"Get this," Ellie said, straightening. Last week's bottom sheet lay fluffed like a pale blue cloud in her arms. "I always thought that guy was headed for trouble, even his own parents did, at least Alice, his mother, Alice Dunn. She's a good friend of mine, has been for more than forty years. But you knew that."

Chris nodded.

"Thought he'd probably end up in jail. Truth is, I don't like to spread rumors or anything, but what I always thought was he had something to do with that whole accident, the way Jack died. Something fishy went on there; my Gus always said so, and he has a nose for trouble. Me, I don't like to get involved in other people's business, but if Gus says it's so, I got to believe him."

Chris wrapped his left arm around, bringing his palm into the comfort of his armpit. His right hand cupped his left elbow, the fingers stroking the cotton of his shirt.

"So anyways," Ellie said, expertly flicking the clean bottom sheet open with a snap and then floating it up to let it fall on the bed. "I saw him dressed to the nines the other day, walking down the street in Southampton, proud as a peacock and looking just as fine."

"What?"

"Damn," Ellie said, shaking her head.

"I'm sorry?"

"It's Mrs. Latham. I forgot. She asked me not to use the green sheets anymore, says she feels like she's sleeping in mold."

"Mold?"

Ellie lifted her right shoulder and her right eyebrow, letting both fall in a deliberate, slow shrug. "That's what she said."

"It's okay," he said, waving his right hand. "She must have changed her mind. Otherwise, she'd have gotten rid of them."

Ellie gave him a measured look, then shook her head. She pulled the green sheet up and off the bed, folding it expertly. "Guys don't under-stand their own wives," she said.

"Well . . . ," he began.

After a moment, she laughed. "Trust me, she doesn't want the green."

He shrugged.

"Give the lady what she wants, that's my motto," Ellie said.

He was still there when she came back with a neatly folded set of beige sheets. That seemed to surprise her, and he was equally taken aback to realize she'd forgotten what they'd been talking about. "I'm spacey today," he said, and made to move from the room.

"Hey," she said. He turned. "That Des Dunn, he looked like he hadn't paid one bit for what he did to Alice's real son. He had a beautiful wife, fancy clothes. His nails were clean. He looked like one of them, a city per-son. And he said"—she paused for effect—"that he'd been living here, I mean in Southampton, can you believe it? And nobody ever saw him! He lives right smack near this lady I've had since I started cleaning, I mean, twenty-five years ago I started with Mrs. Hale and now Des Dunn is her neighbor! South Main Street! Can you believe that?"

"No," Chris said, breathing sharply. "I can't."

"Des Dunn."

Ellie shook her head back and forth as if the shock were still hitting her afresh. "I looked him up in the phone book, he was right there," Ellie said. "Plain as day. Dunn, Des and Nina. Somewhere on South Main. And they had one of the old phone exchanges, meaning they've been here a long time. I don't get it."

"I thought . . . I thought he was in jail or something. That's what I heard."

Ellie sat down on the freshly made bed, shaking her head from side to side. Neither she nor Chris seemed to note the oddness of this behavior.

Chris ventured, "Selling drugs, that's all I can think."

"No," Ellie answered. "If you'd seen him, you'd have known he was on the up and up. I said what do you do, and he said he bought and sold money, so Gus says he must be in the stock market or something like that. He looked like a Ralph Lauren ad."

On the one hand, Chris was slightly suspicious that Ellie knew something, that she was making fun of him or taunting him for some purpose of her own. On the other hand, the notion of Des as a man of substance was so extraordinary, so overwhelmingly unlikely, that he felt sure it was true. He couldn't think further than that, though, as if the very nature of what Ellie had just told him had utterly destroyed the clarity of his thought process.

It occurred to him that the reappearance of Des Dunn at just this moment had to mean something. For the life of him, he couldn't imagine what new phase of his current disaster he might be entering; all he knew was that the worst of his past and the worst of his present seemed to be meeting head-on.

"Hey," Ellie said. "A real blast from the past, huh?"

Chris, rooted at the wall by the door, could only nod.

"Well, I've gotta get to work," she said finally.

"Yeah, okay. Well. Well, nice talking to you."

"Sure," Ellie said, gathering up the sheets and towels. "Sure thing."

In the hallway, he could hear the first distinct ploppings of rainfall on the patio stones. *Splosh. Splosh. Splosh.* The sound of each drop rang huge, hollow and false, pinging against the drainpipe and the deck chairs. Perhaps, he told himself, just perhaps, all his fears might ultimately be rendered fantastic. He hoped this more than anything.

Deborah felt calm. She had woken this morning with a renewed sense of purpose. The moment Chris's car pulled from the driveway, she gave way to the pleasure of his absence. She was eager to focus on Michael, newly certain that the way to handle him was to acknowledge more fully the difficulties of his position.

Something Alice had said two days ago had really struck Deborah: that even if Michael had been taken from his mother at birth, he'd still have a memory of being inside her body. For nine months, he'd grown there and been nurtured there; he had his first experience of loving care there. He must have known her rhythms, the way she smelled, the sound of her voice. And he'd been with her in his early infancy, before her death, so he even knew the feel of her hands and how she hugged and danced him back to sleep. He'd lost so much.

He'd lost time as well, suffering in the dull day-to-day of life in his Braşov orphanage. The photograph Viorica had first brought to them, the one that had so touched their hearts, had shown a little toddler with dark patches of exhaustion pouching his huge dark eyes. On Michael's tiny, skinny frame, those eyes had loomed even larger, windows on a soul Deborah had been immediately certain she would come to love. He was dirty and small, seated in the center of a crib, in a row of similar cribs, in a crowded, dreary room. It was his eyes that so compelled Deborah to want to be his savior. People adopt kittens for the depth of the soul they see staring back at them, and Michael was a person, a person with the deepest, purest, straightest gaze one could fathom, living under circumstances unacceptable even for an animal. His eyes had told Deborah all she needed to know: how much he needed them, how much they could help.

And they had helped, they really had. There had been far more improvements than setbacks, if one could only keep perspective. She honestly believed it. He was just eighteen months old when he came to them, and he was in the habit of pulling off his diaper and wiping his feces all over his crib. She'd found him that way dozens of times, covered in shit, his eyes narrowed, eager to get a reaction from her. She hadn't let him see how much it bothered her, not once. She hadn't even rolled her eyes or sighed. Instead, she'd matter-of-factly stripped the sheets from the bed and plopped him into the tub for a good scrubbing, making sure to give him a whole lot of hugging later in the morning, when he couldn't possibly connect one event to the other.

Cleaning feces from the walls in Michael's bedroom was something Deborah had handled on her own. She didn't want Ellie Emerson getting hold of the knowledge; the way Ellie so constantly insisted she wasn't a gossip just before spilling some revelation or other made Deborah certain she couldn't count on her discretion. The truth is, she hadn't discussed the shit question with Chris either. He was so quick to judgment where Michael was concerned that she didn't dare reveal this to him.

The fact was that over the years, Michael had grown better. Once in a great while, there was a morning when she found shit in his bed or thrown on the floor in a sad cold lump, but it was so rare now she really felt she'd made the right choice saying nothing, keeping this one problem to herself. As long as she got to Michael's room in the morning before anyone else, nobody would ever have to know. In an odd way, it was a secret they shared: His dark eyes would link right into hers when she entered his room, and she'd know immediately that the challenge was on. It would be her job to find the gift he'd deposited before anybody else did, a task she shouldered without expression or comment.

Actually, there had been only one or two incidents of this nature since the summer began. Michael had been happy at home this summer, away from the school, away from the indifferent world of the village. He had been pleased to hear he wasn't going back to school—having a tutor come to the house each morning sounded special. Of course, trying to balance the needs of both children was going to get trickier this fall; Caro was no longer willing to have Ada over to the house, and her other friend, Sarah, wasn't calling at all. There had to be a safe space for Caroline to play, and that meant keeping Michael away from her friends.

When Mina arrived that morning, Deborah brought up the subject. "I'm thinking that maybe this fall, once school starts, we might make an arrangement where you come over a couple times a week and stay with Caroline and her friends or take Michael to the park. If we split them up, then maybe she can get some play time in without, you know, being worried."

Mina shrugged, placing her beige crocheted bag on the counter by the door. "That's fine," she said. "Okay."

They were silent for a moment. Deborah looked down at her ripped sweatpants and faded T-shirt. "I should take a shower," she said. "Do you want him or her?"

"It doesn't matter. I can handle him. I can handle them both for a few minutes. Don't worry."

Deborah had been smiling, her face lit in friendliness and greeting, her entire posture up and calm and resolute, but at Mina's words she crumpled unexpectedly.

"God, Mina, I can't help it. I don't think I can leave them alone anymore. I feel so scared."

Mina's eyes softened. She patted her own brown hair gently and then pulled it back into a high ponytail, using the elastic she'd had around her wrist. "It's getting worse, I know."

Deborah turned back to the counter, away from Mina, placing both hands on the scarred oak surface and leaning down onto her elbows. "God, I'm sorry. I thought . . . today . . . I really thought I was doing better today, with Chris gone, and them playing nicely in there. And all I had to do was see your face, I'm sorry, it just seems as if you're the one friendly face, the only person who isn't pushing at me for something I can't do."

"What can't you do?" Mina asked, moving halfway across the room, toward her employer, but then stopping at the table to rest a hand there. "Give him up or keep him?"

Deborah began to sob without tears, gulping air in pained gasps, her shoulders lifting. "We aren't even talking about that. We aren't."

"Yes, you are."

"No, we're not. Honestly."

Mina's plump arms went around Deborah, who collapsed, sobbing, against her. "I'm not," Deborah managed to say. "I want to keep him. I have this idea. I think if I try holding him more, just holding him calmly, that . . ."

"That he will be well? That he will learn to love? That you can turn him from the path he already treads?"

"It's my obligation; I took him on. I committed to him. I love him."

They were speaking in whispers. Rain made a plinking sound on the metal deck chairs. Deborah lifted her head. "Eeew," she said, her voice abruptly matter-of-fact. If someone were listening from the living room, she would have sounded entirely normal. "Do you smell that?"

"Yes, it's awful, what is it?"

"The septic system I think. Chris was going to call somebody. It's terrible, worse today than yesterday. With this humidity, I don't think I'll be able to bear it."

Upstairs, Ellie Emerson switched on the vacuum cleaner and began to run it loudly across the master bedroom floor. Each time she hit a chair or dresser leg, there was a loud thump and then the low dragging sound of the machine being pulled across the wood.

"Why don't you ask Viorica if she will take him back? Back to Romania when she goes?" Mina's voice was so hushed Deborah wasn't sure if she imagined the words. She turned. Mina's eyebrows were low and level, hovering over serious brown eyes; her lips were pursed. For the first time, Deborah noticed that Mina's skin was thinner, her cheeks no longer pink with sprightly zeal. Lines darted from the outer corners of her shadowed eyes. Across the center of her forehead, a dreary crease was settling in.

How long had she been with them, nearly eight years? Most of her twenties had been given in service to the Lathams. What did Mina think of this? Did Mina regret her choices, wish she'd given her youth for something else, for someone else?

"Do you, excuse me, Mina, but do you wish—no, nothing."

Mina, misunderstanding, said, "Do I wish he would go away? Yes, I think. I love Caroline so much, she's a little bit mine, I think, I've known her since she was so little. I mean, you must see—do you see how she's changing?"

"Of course I do, I'm her mother. But part of it is a natural part of growing up. There are struggles growing up and unhappiness. Part of this is due to that. I don't want to blow it all up and out of proportion."

"You can't mean that," Mina said, shocked.

Deborah nodded. "I do. I know she's going through something tough right now. I'm doing what I can to help her. She saw Dierdre again on Monday, and it was great. She's really good. Dierdre swears Caroline is unlikely to hurt herself again. Believe me, Caroline is a survivor. She's a strong, smart kid. I don't worry about her. She'll do just fine."

"Deborah, I don't know how to say this, but what's going on is bigger than that. She's having a really bad time. Her friends don't call anymore; she doesn't call them. She just sits around with Michael, and they, they don't talk to each other. They hate each other."

"No, they don't."

"Yes, they do."

"Look at them now, they're in the playroom. It's quiet. They're doing fine."

"As long as they just watch television. Otherwise, something always happens. She never laughs anymore. Look at her hair—those beautiful black curls have lost their shine. Can't you see how unhappy she is?"

"Mina," Deborah said stiffly, "I appreciate your concern, but this is my family. I'm doing what I can under very difficult circumstances. Sometimes the best interests of the individual have to be sacrificed to the best interests of the entire group. It's a fact. That's what's happening right now. We need to get Michael calmed down and back into a school setting. I have this idea, I told you, about holding him more. I think it will help. We need to settle him down, and then she'll be okay. And that's that."

Mina shook her head. Her cheeks took on a dull reddish cast. She turned so that she was looking directly up at her employer, and she said, "I am the only person who can tell you this, I think, even if it makes you angry. Even if you tell me to go. But look at you. Your hair is dirty, your face, your skin is covered with pimples. I'm going too far, I know, but when is the last time you and your husband were together, you know, made love?"

"Mina."

She raised both hands in the air, pushing the sleeves of her blue shirt past her elbows. "I tell you this because I am a woman, and I know your family very well. I have been part of this household for many years. You will lose him, I can tell. Another woman will want him, and take him. That's what happens. What you are losing is not just him but all of them. Nobody wins. Not even Michael. The whole family loses. And there you will be, you and Michael, for he will take Caroline with him. He will leave to save her. And you will be alone with that boy, I promise you. It will be the end of happiness for you."

"I'll stay with him, I don't care," Deborah said automatically.

Mina moved closer, as if to take Deborah in her arms, but the older woman flinched, drawing back. Mina said, "I'm telling you now, don't sacrifice your life for him. He cannot be saved."

"How can you say that?" Deborah hissed.

Mina's voice was low and calm. "I know it. You know it. Give up and save your daughter. Save your marriage. That little boy is what he is. He cannot change. I promise you. I know."

In the next room, Caroline began to cry, small, mewling high-noted sobs, more misery than pain. Deborah did not move.

"I'm coming, Little One," Mina called. She turned back to Deborah, saying, "You love her more than you remember. Come to your senses. Send the boy away. Please."

When Ellie Emerson clattered down the stairs with the vacuum some five minutes later, she found Deborah cross-legged on the kitchen floor, leaning against one of her hand-burnished antique fir cabinets, eyes closed.

"You okay?" Ellie asked, curiosity mingling with concern.

"Oh. Yeah. I'm fine."

"Need a hand?"

"Oh, no," Deborah said, but she didn't move. "I'm fine."

Ellie hauled the vacuum over to the storage closet and began to wind the cord up and around the two hooks on the door. "Well," Ellie began doubtfully, "if you need a hand . . ."

"She's fine, Mrs. Emerson," Mina called from the playroom. "I'll help her upstairs in a moment."

Ellie, startled, looked through the doorway Mina and back to Deborah again. Mina was picking up puzzle pieces. Deborah was still.

"Should I start on the kitchen, then?" she asked Deborah.

Deborah began to wipe beneath her eyes with both hands. "Oh, I don't know," she answered. "Do what you want."

"Well. Well." Ellie seemed rooted to the floor over by the storage closet, aware that she was on the track of some fascinating gossip but unsure as to how to proceed. Mina came through the archway, passing Ellie as if she weren't there, and leaned over to help Deborah up.

"Here we go," Mina said softly. She placed one hand beneath each of Deborah's armpits before hauling her to a partial standing position and then moved one hand to Deborah's back to support her body weight. Although on her feet, Deborah couldn't stay upright. Her entire torso keeled slightly backward and to the right.

"She's not feeling well, Mrs. Emerson, that's all."

"Oh," Ellie said.

"I was feeling great," Deborah protested weakly. "I really was."

"I know, Deborah," Mina whispered. "I know."

Even though Deborah was a good five inches taller and some thirty pounds heavier, Mina was clearly able to handle the weight. She pulled Deborah's arm over and around her shoulders, arching her back visibly to take more of the burden. "Hey," she whispered, and her voice was a loving whisper, a light flutter in the air that only Deborah could hear. "I will help you. It will be okay."

Not until then did Deborah really begin to cry, helplessly, loudly, as if the very act of leaning had freed her of the need to carry herself with dignity against all odds. "Oh, oh, oh," she moaned, the sounds rising up with an awful musicality, her eyes closed, her head against Mina's. "Oh, God, oh, oh, oh."

Mina's eyes, meeting Ellie's, disclosed nothing.

"Come," she whispered into Deborah's ear, "Let's get you upstairs."

34

Thursday, September 28th, 7:17 A.M.

CHRIS, emerging fully dressed from their bedroom, was surprised to see Deborah quietly closing Michael's door.

"Is he okay?"

"Oh," she said, turning. "You startled me."

"He's all right?"

"Oh. Yeah. He's fine," Deborah answered, hugging the soiled sheets to her chest.

"What's that?"

"Nothing. Just laundry."

"Smells funky."

"Yeah," she said. "I know."

35

WILL AND PEG weren't thrilled about taking the kids out on the boat, Chris could tell. There wasn't a choice, though; Mina was taking Viorica to the airport, and there really was no one else to ask. It had been Will's idea to spend Sunday night anchored at Coecles Harbor. His own children were staying with friends; they were older and hardly interested in wasting their time with grown-ups or little kids, and Will had not considered the fact that the Latham kids might have to come along.

There had been a long silence when Chris said this, and Will had sighed before he said, "Ah, hell, I had little kids once. I can take it. So we'll have to watch our mouths a little, who cares? Let's do it anyway."

"I've got to talk to Deb, see what she says."

Deborah, uncharacteristically, hadn't thrown up any roadblocks about the idea. She was too spent to consider all the difficulties such an overnight might entail, but Chris didn't realize this and read her indifferent acquiescence as enthusiasm. Caroline was so excited at the thought of sleeping on Uncle Will and Aunt Peg's boat that she packed her own knapsack, remembering to put in two bathing suits and an entire assortment of Beanie Babies but neglecting to include a toothbrush or hairbrush.

On Sunday morning, Deborah spent a quiet twenty minutes in Michael's room, organizing and packing his knapsack. She looked tired;

even her faded gray T-shirt seemed to sag across her collarbones in exhaustion. Her skin had taken on a putty-colored hue, and her hair was pulled tightly to her head in a ponytail, revealing the rather startling size of her ears. Michael sat on the bed, watching her. "It's going to be fun," she told him. "We'll swim from the boat and spend the night listening to the waves. You'll love it."

"I guess," he said. His fingers, the nails chipped and dirty, were thrumming at his knees nervously.

"Are you scared about the boat?"

"No," he said. "I don't get scared."

"I didn't think so," she said calmly. "But if you do, I can come and sleep in the bunk with you. I won't mind."

He didn't answer.

"You know, sometimes I don't know what to expect, I mean, when I'm about to do something I haven't done before," she offered.

He was silent.

"Well, that's done," she said. She patted the knapsack as if pleased with her own efficiency. "If you'll bring it downstairs for me, I'll go get my stuff and Daddy's."

Michael nodded.

"It'll be fun," she said, and he looked up. His dark eyes were unreadable, the black of the pupil merging so neatly with the cold circle of the iris. She chose to see agreement there, nodding at him pleasantly.

After she left, he sat for a long time, looking at the knapsack and then at his knees and then nowhere in particular. He was thinking about the sea, about how big and empty the water seemed when he stood on the wharf looking out. He wondered what the water would look like when he was on the boat, and it concerned him. It scared him, actually, and he hated being scared. He hated it more than anything. When he was home, he was always happy. He knew where everything was. Nothing surprised him. Nothing changed. That was good. He really wished they were staying home.

Down at the dock, Will and Peg had already stowed their own gear, opened the portholes, and put ice in the fridge. Since Labor Day weekend meant crowds on the water, they wouldn't raise the sails until they were out of the harbor.

Chris shouted, "Hey, Captain!" He was standing at the slip, smiling, his arms loaded down with cloth sailbags and a string sack taut with four bottles of wine.

"Come on board, Landlubber! Where's the rest of the live ballast?"

He shrugged, handing packages down to Will. "On the way. Deb's going so slow this morning, I just thought I'd come down and start taking orders. Hey, Peg." He leaned in to kiss Will's wife, a spiky woman who emanated nervous energy. She had extremely short dark hair and wire-rimmed glasses that softened the severe stretch of her narrow-lidded eyes.

"Nice to see you, Chris. Now excuse me, I've got to get our stuff organized below," Peg said, disappearing in a rush.

Will rolled his eyes. "Don't say it."

"I'm not even thinking it, not me, Buddy." They slapped hands, smiling broadly at one another.

"How're you doing?" Will asked.

Chris turned, looking around for a job. "Fine. Better. What say I take the covers off the sails?"

"Great."

They worked in silence, the sound of Peg's movements below echoing up with an inconsistent clatter.

Will said, "Hey, there's your guys. Hey, Deb! Hi, kids!"

Caroline, like Chris, seemed to be shining with anticipation. She bounced as she ran toward the slip, waving giddily. She wore pink shorts and T-shirt. Even her baseball cap was pink, and under it, her black curls bounced and fell soft as fleece. Deborah and Michael walked more slowly. Their legs moved in lockstep. She had one hand on his back, guiding more than pushing him forward.

"Hey," she said, her smile a visible effort. "Where's Peg? Organizing?"

"Ha. We're always shipshape, the envy of the high seas."

"She's down below," Chris said.

"I heard that!" Peg shouted. "Hi, Deborah! Need help with the kids?"

"Hey, Peg. Thanks, we're fine. Okay to come aboard?"

"Give me a hand, Baby," Chris said, extending his own hand to Caroline.

"Let me," Will said, elbowing Chris aside. "She's my goddaughter; don't I get to hug her?" Caroline giggled delightedly, stepping down and into Will's arms.

"I can come aboard myself," Michael said.

"Hey, Michael," Will said. "Where's my hug?"

Michael shrugged, then scrambled past his godfather. Will glanced up at Deborah.

"It looks like rain," she said, scanning the sky. "Has anybody listened to the weather?"

"It's supposed to stay like this the whole day," Will answered. "We'll be fine. And it sure is humid enough. I can't wait to get out on the water."

Michael snorted, as if some aspect of this comment were utterly foolish. Will didn't appear to have heard the sound. When Chris turned to reprove his son, the little boy was already seated aft, gazing calmly out at a handsome sloop docked in the next slip, his face devoid of expression.

Caro pulled at the hem of her father's shorts. "Daddy, Daddy! I've never slept on a boat! I can't wait!" Her face shone up at him, her eyes small diamonds glowing so fiercely he could almost feel their warmth prickling at him. He knelt, taking her in his arms and squeezing her with a pressure borne of affection, his love made greater by the general lack of pleasure daily life had lately contained. He closed his eyes, inhaling the sea odor along with the scent of clean soap at her neck together. For the first time in several weeks, the smile that came to his face felt enlivening, and he stood, still holding his daughter clutched to his breast, and began to laugh with a giddy, unfamiliar sense of pleasure. He kissed her neck and her hair, and when he opened his eyes, she was smiling at him, too.

"Daddy," she said. "Daddy, I love you."

"Me too, Baby, I love you too," he whispered. He kissed her cheek and then her hair, and he set her down sweetly on the deck. "Go help Mommy," he said, patting her toward the companionway. She disappeared below with an obedient grin. He could hear Peg greeting her and the sound of another giggling hug.

Chris stood, stretching his arms in an unaccustomed gesture of well-being. Even his lungs felt different, softer and more accepting than before. He had to smile; for the first time in a long time he wasn't tethered by fear.

Michael, behind him, sat hunched against the stern cushions, glowering. No longer pale, his eyes had taken on an electricity all their own. Will, still unaware of all but the most minor tension in the Latham family, looked up, saw Michael's face, and shivered. He had been about to ask his godson to join him at the wheel.

Later, he would say he'd felt foreboding in the air. At the time, however, he simply raised his shoulders and shook his head. "God, I must be getting old," he said, wryly, to Chris. "I can feel the damp in my bones."

They cleared the harbor and raised the sails, Will skippering and Peg a predictably efficient first mate. They got under way easily, and soon they were cruising along at a jaunty clip. "I can't remember the last time we sailed together!" Chris shouted.

"Years," Will said. "It's been years!"

"High school even? Did Anna Downing's brother work on somebody's boat, right? Remember? And we went out, you and me, and Claudia and Anna?"

Deborah cleared her throat in mock resentment. She and Peg were seated side by side on the cushions, backs to the wind.

Caroline half-sprawled across her mother's lap, smiling into the sun and sea spray. Her long legs hung down, nearly touching the ground. Chris couldn't take his eyes off his daughter. How slowly those first two years of her life had gone, and now time seemed to be moving so quickly it was as if they'd transferred from bicycle to jet. She was going to be grown and gone before they could blink.

Will shook his head. "Not me, I wasn't there. That was back in the days when you two almighty jocks did everything together. Or almost everything."

Chris mock-glared at Will.

Will turned to Deb and Peg, smiling sourly. "Did you know your husband was such a jock, one of the big football players at Pierson?"

Deb shook her head. She was patting Caroline's curls with one hand; the other elbow was supported by the boat, curved up and into the wind, as if she were greeting the salt spray.

"Yeah, we were big," Chris joked. He leaned toward Will, as if trying to draw his attention away from Deborah. Will continued smiling that odd, cocked, unhappy smile.

"Pierson's never had a football team," Will told her. "The school's too small, there isn't enough land. But Mr. Big here, he and Jack Dunn, they traveled all the way to East Hampton, every afternoon, so they could handle the pigskin."

Deborah literally had no idea that tension was rising. Across the boat, her entire body cooled and relaxed by the rushing air, she simply couldn't read that Will was peevish or that they'd strayed close to a topic that made Chris uncomfortable. She had no way of knowing and neither did her hostess. Peg was planning dinner, imagining how she'd drop the grill over the stern and light it out there, planning what she'd ask Deb to do and what she'd handle herself, and already thinking through how leftover grilled salmon might be stored until morning.

"What about homecoming weekend? The big game?" Deborah asked. "I always see the sign in front of the high school."

"Oh, that," Will said. "It's volleyball or girl's hockey or something. No football. Not ever."

"That's kind of cool," Deborah said. "You'd never think of Sag Harbor as being so progressive."

"It's not exactly progressive, Deb. It's just the old ways, the Harbor ways. Make do. Don't let anything go to waste. Don't use more than you need to. They'd never think of it any other way but as making use of whatever decent materials are at hand."

"Meaning what exactly?"

"Meaning why waste effort and money on a football team when we couldn't have won anything," Chris said dryly. "There were only about six kids over a hundred pounds in the entire upper grades."

"I resent that," Will said, and Deborah still thought he was kidding. He leaned toward her, twisting at the waist, and offered her the wheel. She declined.

"Peg?"

"Only if you want me to. I'm relaxing," she said, and Chris rolled his eyes to Deb, who grinned back delightedly. As far as she could tell, they were in Paradise.

Martin Dunn was also happy—overwhelmingly, deliriously happy—although he couldn't precisely put his finger on why.

To add to his glee, now he'd gotten the word about Des from Ellie Emerson. Alice hadn't reacted at all when Ellie marched into their living room like a blown-up balloon just waiting to explode. Alice had sat and rocked a little bit forward in her chair and then leaned heavily back, as if she couldn't rev up enough energy even to acknowledge the thrilling nature of the news.

But Martin found the thought of Des exhilarating, as if it meant his life was worth something after all. Des had survived it all, made something of himself, and that showed Martin once again that the Lord was paying attention, that all their good works hadn't come to naught.

For months now, he'd known that something big was coming, and here it was. Dunn, Des, and Nina. Right there, in the phone book, plain as day. It was hard to believe, a small miracle of the sort that renews energy and vigor with remarkable efficiency. "Do you remember me telling you about the murder my father saw? Down at the watch factory? Did I ever tell you that?"

Alice nodded. "Yeah," she said. "You told me."

"Ellie doesn't know, I'm sure. Want to hear?" He leaned forward with a forceful heave, so that Ellie found herself nodding despite herself, not really wanting to hear any story of Martin's at all, but somehow not being able to say no. *How typical of Martin,* Ellie thought. *All he ever wanted to do was blab about his boring family.*

"My father worked at Fahys when he was a kid. He ran errands for Mr. Fahys and the Deans—you know, Dean married Mr. Fahys's daughter; they lived right next door to the big house and sometimes my dad worked for the Deans and sometimes he worked for the Fahys."

Ellie nodded. Alice watched Martin, her expression sulky and resentful, her hands unmoving on her lap. If he'd paid attention, he might have wondered where her usual anxious smile had suddenly disappeared to, but he didn't watch her, never really did look at her. He knew what she looked like; after all, they'd been married forty years by now.

"So one day," Martin continued, "my dad was in the men's room, and there was an Italian guy in there picking on a Swede. Calling him all kinds of names, that kind of thing. So when the Swede comes off the throne, if you know what I mean, he starts heading for the Italian like he's going to box him one. So the Italian, he picks up a spittoon and he heaves it, and it clocked the Swede right in the head. No blood flowed from the cut. My father always said he knew right then and there the guy was dead, because if there's no blood, the heart isn't working. And when the cops came, the Italian was gone, run straight into the woods to hide, and he didn't come out for three days. My father had to testify at the trial."

"Did the guy go to jail?" Ellie asked.

Martin shrugged. "I don't think so. That's what my dad said. But the other thing he always said was that the defense lawyers made it sound like my dad was the murderer, not that Italian guy. And the rest of his life, no matter what my dad saw, he always acted like he didn't see a thing. He didn't ever want to go back to court again. And he saw plenty, let me tell you. He saw plenty."

"Martin's father ran a speakeasy," Alice said spitefully. "Down by where the American Hotel is now."

"My father worked for Angelo Sciabba, down at the pool hall. He used to make twenty, twenty-five bucks a night unloading hooch," Ellie said. "Everybody ran hooch one way or another. It's the only way we survived the Depression."

"I didn't know that," Alice said.

"See, you never will be a local, not ever," Martin said, running his large palms over his thighs.

Ellie rolled her eyes, slapping her hands down onto the arms of her chair. "Well, I gotta go," she said. "Just thought you'd be interested to hear, about Des and all."

After the screen door slammed, Martin said, "I remember something my father used to say. That when he was a kid, he'd walk by the funeral parlor with his friends, and he'd see Mr. Osborn out front sitting on a bench waiting for the next bit of business to come his way. And he'd always say, 'Hi, Mr. Osborn,' and Osborn would lift one hand and wave, and he'd take the cigar out of his mouth and smile big as a bell, and give a wink. And then he'd say, 'I'll get you one of these days, Luther Dunn. I surely will.'"

Martin's head turned, pivoting just a few degrees on his thick neck, and he said softly, "And he did, of course."

In the silence that followed, Alice cleared her throat. She opened her mouth to speak, then closed it. When she opened it again, Martin raised one thick hand. "You don't have to tell me," he said, and his voice was almost kind. "Doc Isen called a few days ago."

She looked down at her lap.

Martin picked up the channel changer and turned on the television. As the dark images flickered and grew brighter, the cheerful tones of *Jeopardy!* filled the room.

"Well," she said.

"Well, we'll see," he answered.

Her hands fluttered up, almost as if they would fly across the darkening living room to brush against him. She wiped her eyes and turned her palms over, studying the liver spots that dotted hands and wrist. "Well," she said again, but he was smiling, following a commercial for camera film with rapt attention.

"I suppose you'd be happy if I died," she said softly.

He turned to look at her, clearly surprised, although whether it was at her honesty or her intuition was unclear. He opened his mouth, then closed it, eyeing her speculatively.

"Well?" she asked sharply. "I suppose you'll be glad to get rid of me after all these years, won't you?"

He shook his head thoughtfully. "I never thought of that, you dying," he said.

Was he about to say something kind, admit that after forty years together he truly did love her? She drew in breath unobtrusively, watching his face as he worked through what was obviously a difficult train of thought.

"If you get there before me," he said eventually, "to heaven, I mean, you better keep your big mouth shut when you see my son Jack. He's my boy; don't make him listen to all your poison."

She was speechless.

He picked up the remote control again and flicked the volume louder, as if to drown out whatever she might think to say. After a long time, maybe even five minutes, he turned back to her and said, in his most reasonable tone of voice, "Who's to say you'll be heading in that direction anyways? The good Lord might see what I see, you never know."

She rubbed her eyes with pressure, running her hands across her cheeks and down to her neck. The fingers lifted again like wings, floating nervously from shoulder height down to her lap. A pointed shiver ran the length of her spine and faded across her shoulders. Her eyes closed and opened. She sneezed twice, sweetly, like a kitten, and closed her eyes again. The back of her throat felt prickly and dry. With the abrupt quality of surprise, every molecule of Alice Dunn's overextended body was suddenly—and fundamentally—exhausted.

36

"IMAGINE living on the water."

"What a dream," Deborah answered him, smiling with such pure glee that he could almost feel his heart leaping across the boat toward her.

"How often do you guys go out?" he asked.

Will shrugged. "Pretty much every weekend we can. The kids like to take her out, too, and the weather isn't always great. But this summer we haven't missed a weekend. You guys should come with us more often."

Peg, seated next to Deborah, nodded in agreement.

Michael made his way to the companionway, gait rolling slightly, and disappeared below.

"Is he okay?" Peg asked.

"He's fine," Chris said swiftly.

"I should show him where everything is down there," Deborah said, but nobody answered, and she was so comfortable and the sun beat down so warmly on her shoulders and it all felt so good that she didn't move. Not, of course, that she could have stopped the next sequence of events; nevertheless, later, this was the one moment that grew in intensity in her mind, the place where she'd failed to perform her maternal responsibilities as expected. If she'd only . . . well, if she had, who knows what else, what worse event, might ultimately have transpired?

"Come sit by me." Chris motioned to her lazily. It was Caroline, however, who got up and ran to his lap first, and though he smiled ruefully at his wife, he did nothing to burst the little girl's bubble.

"Hey, I heard a funny story," Deborah said. "From my cleaning lady." No one moved. Except for Will, everyone's eyes were closed. "This guy who went to high school with you guys, the brother of Jack Dunn? Apparently, he's some Wall Street wheeler-dealer now, living in Southampton with his wife for the last ten years or so, and his own parents didn't know he was living in the next town. Can you believe that?"

Will turned, letting the wheel spin freely. The boat began to keel. "Oh, God, sorry, whoops, we're okay." He grabbed the wheel and came back on course.

Chris came to sitting and then to standing. He walked over next to Will and put a hand on his back. "Hey," he said. "Want me to take over? I remember what to do."

"Did you know this? About Des? Why didn't you tell me?" Will's face was mottled pink and pale, his eyes narrowed in confusion. *I don't know him,* Deborah thought suddenly; *I really don't. He's not familiar in the slightest.*

Chris shrugged. "I heard a couple days ago."

"You did?" Deborah asked, surprised. "From Ellie?"

He nodded.

"Why didn't you tell me?" Will's entire body was skewed toward Chris, even though his hands remained on the wheel, gripping whitely, as if he were having trouble keeping himself from leaping forward.

Chris shrugged again, turning toward Deborah with a faintly apologetic lift of his shoulders.

"Why didn't you tell me, Chris? If Des Dunn is around here, wouldn't you think I should know it? Me, of all people?"

Sometimes when Will Gaston spoke, it was easy to see what an anxious teenager he must have been; when he failed to monitor himself with adult dignity, he gave his whole body—particularly his arms, chest, and neck—to conversation, so that he began to sway and bob toward Chris in a jittery combination of speed and curiosity, a series of movements that Deborah found so fascinating she almost lost the thread of his words.

Chris, on the other hand, stood rooted, his clean white sneakers solid on the deck as if no movement of the boat could throw his balance. He gazed at Will, and for the first time, Deborah observed a slightly superior, even disdainful, air to her husband's behavior with his lifelong best friend. The two men stared at one another without speaking for a full thirty seconds, until Chris broke the silence coldly, saying, "Less than a week ago you said it didn't matter."

"Come on, Chris!" Will said, and his tone was pleading.

Chris glanced at Deborah, who was watching both of them alertly. He turned back to Will, shrugged for the third time, and said nothing.

"It's a pretty amazing story, isn't it?" Deborah ventured casually.

Peg stood, stretched her arms, and went below.

Will, glancing at the top of his wife's head as she disappeared, had the dazed expression of someone who's just been in a fight. Chris put his hand on Will's shoulder again.

"Hey," Deborah said, and she stood up. "What's going on? Are you guys okay?"

Will looked at her as if he'd heard her speak but didn't know the language.

"It's fine. He's fine," Chris said firmly.

The wind, which had felt so gentle and balmy when she was sitting down, had now taken on a damp, piercing quality. She shivered, wrapping both arms around herself. "Is there something I don't understand going on here?"

Will said, "No," loudly, just as Chris turned to her and nodded yes. Chris took his hand off Will's shoulder, starting to move toward her, his eyes pleading, his arms beginning to open, as Will said, again, "No."

"Deb, I . . . ," Chris began, taking her wrists in each of his hands, and then Peg moved swiftly up the companionway, her voice clipped and tense, saying, "Excuse me, Will, you've got to drop anchor. Now. Chris, can I see you below?"

Again in the aftermath, another question Deborah would ask was why it was Chris Peg selected to bring below deck and not her? Because if she'd been the one to go downstairs and pull Michael out of the bathroom, well, perhaps it would have gone differently. Perhaps. But who could ever know? Events play out only one way in real time; once a hand is played, one rarely gets the chance to pick up the cards and think matters out again.

The head on the *Ericson* was no bigger than normal, but it was generally spotlessly clean, bathrooms being one of the areas in which Peg's compulsiveness ruled with complete sovereignty. Above the head was a small sign asking all users to have consideration for others, to flush fully, to leave the room spotless. The sign itself was typical of Peg: neatly lettered, framed under Lucite, centered with care directly across from the septic unit so that no seated user could fail to miss it.

Now, though, it was smeared with feces, the marks of Michael's palm smudged across the wall and over Peg's carefully lettered sign in chalk-brown shit, the smell shocking, overwhelming in its intensity. His filth was everywhere, streaks of brown on the plastic mat just inside the door, along the walls, across the head, in the sink, and even on the outside of the door and along the white walls of the cabin, as if he'd produced an outrageous, putrid excess for the occasion.

Peg held her palm out to Chris. There was fecal matter staining the outer mounds of flesh, a semicircular stencil her fingers curled out and away from in horrified disgust. "I didn't see," she said, her voice quavering. Her narrow shoulders were high, nearly grazing her jaw, her mouth pursed tightly, her nose wrinkled. "I didn't see," she repeated.

"What is it?" he said stupidly. "What's that?"

Peg couldn't say the words. She held her hand toward him, stuttering, "It's . . . it's . . . it's . . . ," and abruptly, he understood.

"Oh, my God, Peg, oh, my God," he said, and then he looked down. Michael's shit was on Chris's sneaker. "Where is that little bastard?" Chris's eyes were so taut, thin with fury, he could barely see out of them. He could barely breathe. He didn't have a thought in his head; his brain was so crimson with anger he could feel its pulsing, could feel himself propelling forward, his hands rising into fists, his shoulders widening and pushing forward, his stomach clenching. He gave a growl of fury. "Where is that little bastard?" he yelled.

Peg pointed, her finger curving toward the V-shaped forward bunk. There was a stripe of brown across the shutters.

Chris screamed in fury, "Get out here, you little runt! Get out here, right now!!" Deb's footsteps clattered down the companionway and stopped.

Michael did not emerge, but it didn't matter. Chris was already pulling the shutter so hard it bent a hinge. He grabbed the boy, no longer caring what he touched or how, not even smelling the awful odor rising off his son's shit-smeared face, not even seeing the terrified expression in his eyes. In his mind, later, Chris would recall Michael's look as smug, as if his father was finally doing what the little boy had always expected he would. At the time, though, Michael's slight body was only air, weightless under his father's fury, ethereal enough to hold and shake, and shake and shake and shake until he couldn't even feel his arms moving, or hear his voice yelling, or know who he was. He wasn't separate from the little beast. He was him. He was what Michael had made him into—they were one and the same—joined in filth. All Christopher Latham wanted to do was kill the evil in himself, get it out of his life forever, if he had to shake it and shake it and shake it until it flew, humbled, from his grasp. He didn't care, he didn't, and he held Michael's shoulders and twisted him over and began to hit, hitting hard, seeing that piercing demon light pulsing in the boy, feeling the softness of his shit smeared everywhere and hardly caring, just wanting to get rid . . .

And there was Deborah, screaming and pulling at his shoulders, scratching his back, anything, screaming, "Stop it! Stop it!! You'll kill him! Chris! Chris!! You'll kill him!!"

Peg held Caroline on her lap, seated on the bottom step, unable to see a thing but well able to hear.

And Will, his own face taut with disgust and rage, grabbed Christopher's arms from behind, holding him, the two of them panting synchronously like lovers. Michael, sprawled in his own filth, lay humped up on the bunk, crying and mewling, mouthing a series of angry growls that arched into wails and back again, his own sounds, no words to speak of.

"I don't care," Christopher Latham said calmly, wiping sweat and feces from his forehead with a dirty hand. "I don't care. You know as well as I do I can kill a person. Christ, Will, I could kill him and you know I could. I hate that little bastard! I hate him!"

In the cabin, there was hardly any sound, no slapping of line or sail in the wind, no drip from the faucet, no splash of a wave against the bow. The smell was putrid, the air still and noxious, and only Deborah's gulping attempts to breathe were audible. Will sighed, drawing his arms tighter around Christopher. He said, "You didn't kill Jack. I did."

Deb knelt, taking Michael in her arms, allowing him to kick at her without complaining. She did not look up.

Chris began to cry—huge, throaty, gulping sobs, his shoulders shaking as a storm of tears overwhelmed him. He sank to the floor, one hundred and eighty-five pounds of fallen armor, across from Deb, not looking at her or Michael, blind with tears.

Will repeated, "It was me, Chris. I'm the one who did it. I'm the one who unhooked the jesus clip."

Neither Deb nor Peg looked up or at each other, or in any manner acknowledged the discussion that was now taking place. The term *jesus clip* was a mystery, but asking about it would mean admitting to an interest in the rest of the topic; to Deb, and apparently to Peg, such a venture was absolutely unthinkable. Maybe Peg, too, was already on overload.

Chris shook his head from side to side. His throat was too tight. He kept gasping, trying to breathe; he could feel his heart pounding in his chest so hard it threatened to burst through. The smell of shit was so awful he could barely take air in, and then, once he allowed it , the odor burned like poison down the back of his throat. "I hate that little bastard," he said again, staring at Michael with cold, furious eyes. "I hate him."

Peg and Caroline hadn't moved. They sat quietly, drawing no attention to themselves, not even visible to the others. Caroline's eyes had been closed the entire time; she was leaning back against Peg as if she were an infant being rocked. Later, Peg told Will that although she'd been terrified throughout Chris's rage, she didn't think the little girl had noticed. It was as if Peg's thin body felt as soft as pillows, so soft, in fact, that part of Caroline's seven-year-old soul yearned to fall asleep in Peg's comfortable arms.

Michael made a series of mewling, moaning sounds, his body starting to quiet. His gray T-shirt was wet, ripped at the neck and left arm. Blood trickled down his neck in two timid streams. Deb, holding him, did not look up.

37

THANK God for outdoor showers, Deborah thought, having finally gotten both children cleaned, dried, read to, and asleep. Caroline had been utterly subdued, submitting to the shower without whining for a bath as she normally did. She'd allowed Deborah to dry and dress her, listened quietly to her story, and gone to sleep before the sun even began to set, so exhausted was she by the day's events. Michael had gone from his shower into pajamas, but then he'd headed out to his baby swing and rocked there from seven until eight-thirty, when Deborah finally emerged from Caroline's room. Chris, of course, was nowhere to be seen; he'd stayed down at the dock helping Will and Peg, and now she imagined he was at the Corner Bar or someplace similar, losing himself in the company of old acquaintances and beer. It was what she'd have done in his shoes, she thought, and she couldn't imagine that he was still with Will. They'd barely managed to hobble together enough syllables to organize cleaning the cabin, neither man even glancing at the other despite the fact that they were scrubbing side by side. She and Peg had scrubbed down the shutters on the forward bunks and wiped down each of the couches, trying not to shudder at each new revelation of Michael's disgusting display. Caroline sat quietly on the stairs, where she'd been since the entire scene began. Michael, told he had to clean the head himself, had sat on the floor rocking back and forth, occasionally pounding his forehead against the wall with a loud exclamation; at the same time he moved a rag back and forth over the mess, spreading it more thinly over the white surface of the wall. No one bothered to chastise him; they were all too broken, too frightened, to make the attempt.

Once Will's half of the cabin was done, he moved wordlessly into the head. He turned on the shower and manipulated its nozzle to spray the entire space clean, water splattering out onto the companionway and Caroline, who didn't seem to notice or care.

In time, with no further discussion, the last bucket of filth-laden seawater tossed back overboard, Will came around and headed back to the harbor.

Deb, the only one who attempted a stuttered apology, and Peg, the only one able to think of accepting one, grasped hands tightly and almost hugged before shepherding the children off the boat. Later, once the kids were in bed, that moment of communion—that woman-to-woman acknowledgment of how what we deem dearest in the world so often destroys us—was like a talisman she wanted to grasp in her fist and hold to her heart, a bauble of reassurance and sympathy that glowed brighter as the sun began to set and Chris still failed to return home.

She was glad he wasn't in the house when she put Michael to bed. Normally, the little boy seemed to go into a submissive, apologetic phase after one of his major displays. Tonight, he didn't seem able to calm down. His legs twitched and kicked when she told him to get out of the baby swing. He resisted until she peeled his hands from the ropes and slid his stubborn torso forward. Even when she held him, he continued twisting and kicking, starting that infernal mewling again, so that no matter how sweetly she hummed and sang, she couldn't get his attention, couldn't distract him from his misery.

Once she finally had him tucked into bed and was beginning to open one of the Dr. Seuss books he adored, Michael took a deep, raggedy breath and said to her, "Does Daddy love me?"

It was the question of it that broke her heart. Usually when children are mad or upset or hurt, they take such definitive stands on the source of the trouble: *Daddy hates me. You're not fair. That story stinks.* But he asked her, "Does Daddy love me?" and the timid quaver to his voice was one of the saddest sounds she'd ever heard. It resounded, amplified, repeated itself: A question she'd hear over and over, every night for the rest of her life, she thought, every single solitary time she walked past his door. "Does *Daddy* love me? *Does* Daddy love me? Does Daddy love *me?*"

"Does Daddy love me? Mommy? Does he?"

She leaned toward him, brushing his silky brown hair away from his eyes. "I'm worried about Daddy," she told Michael, refusing to lie. "He seems to be having a horrible time of things right now. But I'll help him to figure it out. I promise."

He took her hand, bringing it toward his lips as if he would kiss it. *He needs me*, she thought. *He needs me so much.*

Michael's lips brushed the back of her hand, softly, a dry, sweet whisper of a kiss. She leaned closer, about to kiss his cheek. He turned her hand over, taking her palm so that her thumb angled toward his mouth, and then he opened his lips, bared his teeth and bit down, hard, gripping her thumb so viciously that she could feel individual teeth piercing the skin, hitting bone.

Her scream, sharp with shock and pain, did not wake Caroline but would surely have brought Chris running.

That is, if he had been at home.

38

"Hey."

"Hey yourself," she said, rolling over to a seated position, gathering the covers in front of her as she squinted. She pulled two pillows up and placed them against the headboard. When she leaned back, lowering her head, her curls settled around her shoulders with the majestic air of an eighteenth-century magistrate's wig. "Turn off the light."

"Sorry," he said, turning the three-way switch to low. He wasn't drunk or disheveled; she had expected him to stagger in as a parody of male distress. Instead, his eyes were open and forthright. If anything, he seemed more pulled together than she had seen him in months, a purer version of himself. He'd come to terms with something, she could tell.

"How are you?" she asked, patting the white-on-white embroidered quilt invitingly. He sat down on her side of the bed, his back to her, and sighed. When he leaned forward to rest his elbows on his knees, the back of his T-shirt came untucked. She extended one finger, running it along the knobby path of his spine.

He shrugged.

"That seems to be all you do these days," she said, shrugging back in imitation.

He twisted to look at her, arching one eyebrow, and then he shrugged again, leaning in for a kiss. "We'll be all right, won't we? You and me?"

She lifted her left hand to his cheek, so that the sleeve of her cotton nightgown fell back loosely, exposing the long line of her arm. She ran her fingers down his cheek. "Not if you don't get the septic system fixed. I thought you were going to call."

"Sorry," he said. "But seriously. I'm really sorry. I really am. I don't know, I didn't mean—I never thought . . ." He paused. He opened and closed his mouth twice, and then he said, "I could have hurt him."

"You did hurt him."

"No, I mean hurt him badly. Seriously. I'm not kidding. It scares me."

"Where did you get cleaned up? Will and Peg's?"

He shook his head. "No. I went down to Tyghes Beach and dove in, with all my clothes on. I must look like hell."

"You don't," she said. "I couldn't even tell."

"What time is it?"

She pressed the button on her watch. "Two-thirty-five. It's late."

He nodded. "We've got to talk," he said. "We've got to do something. He's destroying us."

"Seems like he's destroying you," she said, and she leaned back against her pillows. He couldn't tell whether she was angry or not.

"Deb," he said. "I hate him. I wish it was different, but I do. I can't help it. I hate him. He's hurting Caroline and you and me. He's not getting helped by us either. We're not helping."

"How do you know that? He's doing so much better, most of the time."

He drew her hands from beneath the quilt; she pulled her right arm back before he could see the gauze and first-aid tape bandaging her thumb. Holding onto her left hand, he said, "When we took him in, we said he was ours. I know that . . ."

"Our own child. Under the law, in every way. He's ours, our responsibility. What do you want to do, turn him out onto the street? I hope you understand that's no different from turning Caroline out of the house—you're as bad as his own parents were, worse, because you're taking a child you knew and telling him you tried to be his father and he was too awful, too horrible, for you to endure it. How do you think he'll feel to know that? How much worse can things get for him?"

"Deb, I've talked to the lawyer who handled his adoption," he began desperately, but her hand rose up as if she were about to hit him and he stopped.

"You did what?! When?"

"A few days ago," he admitted. "I had to call. I can't take it anymore. She told me this happens sometimes. Some families can't handle the children they take in, for whatever reason. We wouldn't be the first, not by any means. So we're not without options."

"I can't believe that we're even talking this way," she said, but she didn't stop him from continuing. From the heat trapped in the upper rafters, a small gray-brown spider suddenly danced down on a long string of web, coming to a sudden stop only inches from Christopher's head. Deborah breathed in, sharply, inhaling a whiff of Michael's sour odor that still clung to Chris. Her gaze flickered, toward the spider and back to her husband, and she suddenly remembered—what?—a small snapshot of a morning, the three of them around the breakfast table and Caroline's toddler mouth opened wide with giggles, her sweet white teeth aglow, half-empty bowls of oatmeal before each person, Caro's spoon held high with delight. They'd been happy; they really had. They'd been so happy, they'd been foolish. They'd been so happy, they'd been willing to share. They'd been so happy, they'd been sure there was enough glee in them to rub off on someone else, like the little plastic transfers of rabbits and stars that Caroline loved so much—her tattoos, she called them.

But Michael's surface hadn't been open to the magic; the love hadn't stuck at all. Whatever they were made of—their chemistry, whatever joy they had to give—was out of his reach. Michael with them—it simply wasn't right. They couldn't reach him, but he could certainly reach them. Day after day, hour after hour, he was reaching the Lathams. Like a virus, he was infiltrating every cell of the organism that was their family.

And it was killing them.

"We have options," he repeated. "We can work with the orphanage in Braşov, see if they'd be willing to take him back, but that's pretty unlikely. He's an American citizen now."

"I can't believe you did this without talking to me," she said evenly.

"I had to. For us. For Caro. For me. For you, too, if you'd only see it." He wiped one of his elegant hands across his face; in the lamplight, his exhaustion was concretely visible: Small lines were etching their way out from his eyes in delicate fans, digging from his nostrils to the edges of his mouth, crossing and recrossing his forehead.

"What did Emily Conway recommend?" she asked at last. She hadn't moved; was this a first concession?

He looked at her gratefully. "She didn't know that much. She said she'd never handled a failed adoption before. So I asked her to do some homework. Turns out it would really be no different than putting him up for adoption in the first place. I mean, he's older, of course, so it might take a while. It could be really difficult to place him, he's almost six."

"He'd go to another family? Just like that?"

He shook his head. "Actually, he'd go into foster care. And part of that might mean us having to work with the foster care family. The state would want to see us make an effort, you know, to patch things up with Michael."

"Why not just keep him here then? Are you trying to threaten him? To let him know this is the last straw? Is that it?"

"No," he said evenly. "I don't want him. I want him to go."

"If he goes away, then what happens to him?"

His hands were in his lap, and he looked down at them. He was close, he could tell, and so he was frightened. The pounding of his heart underscored it. "Well, there are foster families who take in tough kids all the time. There happens to be a family in Suffolk County that's very highly thought of. They've helped a half-dozen kids and then sent them to good homes. And the word is that now they're looking to adopt, so if he got in with them, well . . . you know," he said.

He paused before finishing in a rush. "It could be perfect."

"So he'd be right here, right near us? That would almost be worse."

He looked up, but not at her face. In a moment, his gaze was back on his own still, dependable hands. "Emily learned that there are agencies who handle difficult adoptions. There's a clearinghouse in Rochester, she said. So if the placement up the Island didn't work out, he'd go on, to a family that was right for him. We'd go through the state, through Social Services. Of course," he added wryly, "Emily suggested counseling. Like it was a new idea."

"Mina says Viorica might take him, for herself, I mean. I haven't spoken with her, though, not in a long time. I hate to think of calling her, even for this," Deborah said quietly. Her hands were back under the quilt; he couldn't see her gently fingering the bandaged thumb.

"No," he said. "I understand. Besides, she's gone, remember? Mina drove her to the airport."

He didn't smile, didn't want to appear to have won anything. Instead, he brushed her hair off her neck, placed his palm softly on her cheek, and waited.

She'd grasped it fully now, what they were about to do, and she leaned forward and into his arms, so that he half-sprawled across her legs, holding her as tightly as he could, and she began, quietly, to weep. He stroked her hair, his fingers widely splayed and gentle, making a cap with his hands and then moving down to her cheeks and mouth. He could feel her breath on his own face, could feel her fingers capping his knee. He could barely breathe with the relief of it.

What they didn't do, as much as he wanted to, was to make love. If he'd made one further move in that direction, she'd have acquiesced willingly, even gratefully. But he didn't. He couldn't. For whatever reason, such an act seemed completely inappropriate.

Across town, Alice Dunn was wide awake. Her nose was stuffed, her chest hurt, and Martin beside her was snoring so loudly she could hardly bear it. If she weren't a Christian woman, she wouldn't have minded holding the pillow over his head so she'd no longer hear the *glub-glub-honk* of his breathing. She wouldn't mind it at all.

The good Lord could make no mistake about why she was so wrung out tonight, that's for sure. What a day it had been. When Martin got Des on the phone like that, first time dialing, she had to think she was losing her mind. How that boy could have done what he did, moving right around the corner practically, married and comfortable as could be, and never even coming back to say a word—she had to wonder. She was looking forward to telling Deborah Latham this latest news about Des, she certainly was. She liked talking to Deborah; when she did, she had the idea that she, Alice, hadn't wasted so much of herself as she sometimes figured she had. She didn't know why that was, but Deborah made her feel good; that was just the way it was.

The boy hadn't been in jail, not once, is what he told them, at least not once since that last time they knew of, the trespassing and breaking-and-entering charge. He hadn't served much time, just four months. After he got out, he moved to Manhattan. He got a job as a clerk in a brokerage house, the Lord only knows how. Funny thing of it, he'd proven to have a knack, and so he got promoted to broker and then he moved over to become a fund manager and then a partner; finally, he'd sold his interest in the firm, retiring at the age of thirty-five. Retiring.

And he and Nina, his wife, had moved to Southampton, to their summer house, and they were thinking of having children. And why hadn't he called? He hadn't answered that one.

But the thing he had muttered, as soon as Martin said, "Hello, Son, it's me. Your father," was: "Oh, hi, Martin. I've been thinking I'd be hearing from you."

That was funny. Like he'd known they'd be calling. Like he'd waited for his own reasons, whatever they were. He was polite, but he wasn't very warm; that's what Alice thought.

What made Alice angry was when Martin suggested they all get together, said they'd like to meet Nina and get reacquainted, how Des hadn't even cleared his throat, he'd just answered that it wasn't a good idea. She hadn't been listening, exactly; she was standing near the phone and so she knew what Martin had said and she heard enough of Des's answer to know what it meant.

Martin went blank-faced for a moment when Des spoke. His whole face sagged, but then he put his shoulders back and played his trump card. "Well, you should know, your mother's dying; she's very sick and probably going to die real soon, the doctor told us, and maybe it makes sense for you to say good-bye."

The statement was so patently untrue it made Alice furious, so mad she grabbed the phone away from Martin. "Hi, Des," she said. "Don't listen to that old man. He's lying."

Des laughed, not a happy sound. He said, "That's exactly why I don't think I'll come by. You're probably as healthy as the stockmarket."

"I don't know about that," she said.

"Well, I do," he answered, "and I'm sure you're fine."

He wasn't going to see them, she could tell. "Actually, I am sick, a little," she admitted then. "Just a little."

"How so?"

"I don't know," she said. "Not as sick as he makes out. Probably it's nothing. But I'd sure love to see you."

"Oh." A silence fell.

She said, "Des? Maybe you hate us. Maybe you're right. Maybe we didn't do for you what we should have, but we tried to do right. We really did. And I would love to look at you for myself just once, just to know you're okay. I really would."

He didn't say anything for so long that she began to wonder if he was still on the line. "Let me think it over," he said eventually. "I'll call you back."

He'd hung up then, and though she had waited by the phone the entire length of the afternoon and evening, it hadn't rung again. Sooner or later, he had to call, she thought at one moment, and then at the next she knew he wouldn't. If he'd meant to, he'd have done it of his own accord. She had to get used to the fact that even though he was around, he didn't care. Whatever good she'd done for him meant nothing. And she'd better get used to the idea that having lost him once, she'd not found him again. Even though for the first few seconds of the phone call it had almost looked like she had.

And so now she was awake and feeling a little bit annoyed with herself for bugging Des like that, embarrassed really, and also entirely stuffed in the nose. The truth was it had been another horrible day in a series of them; the sad part was how long this particular series had been going on.

39

THE NEXT morning, Labor Day itself, Deborah awoke with a guilty start, as if she'd overslept and missed a critical appointment. Chris lay on his side, facing away from her, his breathing placid. It was possible she'd dreamt the entire previous day and night; the house was so calm—perhaps she'd imagined all of it. But of course that was what people always wish in disaster's aftermath. She knew better. They had given in.

Could she possibly have agreed to it? She reached forward, about to shake Chris by the shoulder, to turn his face toward hers and tell him that she'd changed her mind, that giving Michael up was impossible. What stopped her hand was knowing Chris was right. *Call it quits, Deborah*, she told herself, feeling with surprise that she remained capable of the thought.

The humidity was already so high this morning that the air outside their window was tinged with gray. She got out of bed and headed for the bathroom. Both children would be awake soon. She didn't relish it, but the day would have to run its course. In the shower, she decided that she would take them to Southampton to buy shoes. Yes, shopping. No discussion, none at all. Caroline and Michael both needed sneakers.

The children seemed subdued at breakfast, as if they, too, understood that change was in the wind. In the car, they sat leaning away from one another, silent as strangers. On Scuttle Hole Road, Deborah suddenly thought of Alice and wondered whether she'd like to make the trip with them. She pulled to the side, turned around, and headed back toward the Dunns' house.

Alice didn't look right. She was seated in her armchair, as usual, but her face had slimmed down so dramatically in just the last few days—it had been Wednesday of the previous week when they last saw one another—that Deborah hardly knew how to greet her. Was it right to acknowledge how different she looked?

Alice herself didn't appear to be aware of any dramatic changes, although she did complain that her chest was a little achy and her nose stuffy. A little bug coming on, she suspected. She was taking it easy today.

But when Deborah offered to take her into Southampton, Alice's eyes opened so wide she looked like she was about to pop, and she nodded, yes, vigorously, and said she'd be back in a moment, she just wanted to change her shirt. "Oh, and if Martin comes in—he sometimes does midmorning—don't tell him where we're going, okay?"

"Why? I doubt he'd want to join the ladies, would he? It doesn't seem like his style," Deborah said, smiling as she twitched Chris's white cotton shirt away from her skin.

"I'll explain," Alice said, and she heaved her doughy frame from the chair, lifting her hands in a hallelujah of eager promise before she lumbered down the hallway toward the dark bedroom she and Martin shared.

It was Deborah who insisted they find his house. Alice, who wanted to be convinced, protested that it would be an intrusion, that Des hadn't returned her call, that it really wasn't considerate. She also said that she wasn't dressed properly, as if the red and white checked shirt she'd hurriedly pulled the tags from in her bedroom weren't the best new blouse she'd ever had, as if the denim skirt weren't her favorite.

They were on the bench just a few steps down from the shoe store, and the afternoon was so warm an optimistic shop proprietor might easily convince himself that the summer season might not be ending in only a few short hours. Nevertheless, the town of Southampton was already beginning to empty out, car after car heading west toward Manhattan, stuffed with a summer rental's worth of bedding, towels, faded swimsuits, and puckered, deflated beach rings.

Deborah swallowed the last bites of her chocolate chip ice cream cone, gathered the plastic shopping bags containing the children's old sneakers, and asked for Des's address, dismissing every single one of

Alice's protests with a kind of tense hysteria that someone who knew her better might have found alarming.

"I don't have it," Alice said helplessly. "It's somewhere on South Main Street."

"Let's go to the village clerk!" Deborah said feverishly. "This isn't even a challenge. You can track down anybody!"

Village Hall was closed, of course, for Labor Day, as would be the post office and probably the Southampton Press as well. Deborah, defeated, seemed to sag at the door to Rogers Memorial Library. She sat down on the steps, and Caroline sat next to her, placing her head in her mother's lap. Michael paced back and forth behind them, and after waiting for a moment to see if the exercise were worth it, Alice lowered herself carefully to the step, leaning her weight back onto her thick arms before sitting.

"God, it's hot," Deborah said, shoulders slumping forward so that her lower arms and practically her entire torso hugged the length of her thighs. Her elbows rested on her knees, and she lowered her head to her hands with a sigh. "I thought it would be so easy to find him. Wouldn't it be so nice? So nice for you, I mean, to see that he's turned out well. You know, that it was worth it after all."

Behind them, Michael added a kick to his pacing. First one door and then the long measured steps to the other, with another thudding kick before turning and heading for the first door again.

"Worth it?" Alice snorted. "Worth it?"

"You don't mean that."

"I don't know," she said. "I don't know. Loving Jack, that was worth it. The rest of it's just been surviving."

Caroline shifted, turning her head to look at Alice with a curious combination of apprehension and understanding. Deborah watched the cars heading west down Job's Lane, her hand stroking Caro's back. Michael kicked and turned to march toward the other locked door.

"But you helped him, you must realize it. You helped Des. Otherwise, how could he have turned out the way he did?"

"My thought is maybe he was always going to pull out of his skid. It wasn't our doing at all. Look, he doesn't think we did anything—he can't possibly or he'd have wanted to see us. So what difference does it make, even if we did help?"

"There's a difference between helping someone and having them know you did it," Deborah said reasonably. "Like a guardian angel or a benefactor, or even the parent of an adolescent who's always angry and resentful."

Alice touched one of the red checks on her shirt with an affectionate finger, then pulled at the blouse to loosen it from the folds of her belly. "My whole life, I've worked so hard," she said peevishly. "And that's the entire story. He doesn't think I've earned a thank-you and neither does Martin, and I suppose if I watched that little boy for you all day long, stood over him to make him learn his letters and cleaned every last poo-poo he swiped on the walls—oh, yes," she said, turning knowledgeably to Deborah, "I know his kind. Des was like him, so like him you don't know, except there was a place in Des I could reach because I rode him hard, I held the line with him, and I see you don't do that. And if I take him in, like you're thinking I might, I'd help, I guess, but . . ."

"I wasn't . . . ," Deborah began.

"Oh, yes, you were. You don't let yourself think the thought, maybe, but it's true. What else would you want with an old lady like me? Took me almost a month to figure it out. I was having so much fun, hanging around with your kind, feeling so great having a downstreet kind of friend, but just now, I knew it. You wanted something from me all this time, and it's a fact. And if I took him, you'd disappear like Mrs. Downing's coffee cake at Bible study. Before the first head was bowed in prayer, you'd be gone. What a blind old lady I am, not realizing that until just five seconds ago. I swear, Martin's right, I am dumb as a post."

Caroline sat up, eyes bright, two pink spots flaming on her cheeks. "She'd thank you, I bet. She would. And I'd thank you every day of my whole life." Caroline reached across her mother to take Alice by the arm. Michael, behind them, had stopped pacing, but his breathing sounded like movement, a harsh, scraping sound that nearly whistled with intensity.

"Caroline."

"It's true, Mom, I would."

"Well, it's not going to happen," Alice said stoutly. "I've been saying yes to everybody, every single day of my whole wasted life, and I'm going to die sooner than I meant to if Doctor Isen is right, and he's poison, that son of yours; I say it to his face. I'm not taking on anybody else's problems, not one more time in my life. Nobody's jumping to help me, that's the Lord's honest truth. So that's my choice. I can tell you straight out, because you aren't from my people and never were. You're one of them, one of these people here, and I won't ever see you again, I bet. We don't walk the same streets, we don't have the same friends, we don't live the same lives. I'm not going to bring you into my church, and you sure don't have a church for me to go and visit, so let's just admit the truth and you can take me home. That can be your one real favor to me."

Alice, who hadn't stopped for breath or looked toward them the whole time she was speaking, now inhaled deeply, as if the air had gotten sweeter and she wanted more. She sneezed delicately, placing a bent forefinger beneath her nostrils for just a moment. She closed her eyes. *Surprise. She wasn't crying, nor was her skin warm with the effort to tell the truth. Something had snapped. It had been easy to say what was really between them, so easy she knew she'd be able to do it again, to Martin, and even to Des if he came calling. All this time and all these years, when she'd been holding her tongue and telling folks what they wanted to hear, maybe she hadn't had to. Just maybe, she could have said what was on her mind all along. What a surprise that thought was. What an absolute, pure, glorious thing to know!*

Opening her eyes to look straight into Deborah's shocked gaze, Alice gave a broad smile. "What the heck," she said, shrugging her shoulders so high that even her heavy breasts rose with the creaky air of a dumb-waiter shelf. "It doesn't hurt to have the cards out on the table after all."

"I'm sorry," Deborah said stiffly. "I mean, I don't agree with you at all, but if anything I've ever done or said led you to believe I had some purpose in mind, some incredible plan . . ."

"Oh, no, it's not that. I don't think you meant to feel the way you do. I don't think you meant to be in the situation you're in. But I understand how it happened. Everyone knows the Dunns take in kids, everyone in the Harbor knows about us."

Michael, who had been completely silent during this entire exchange, now came leaping down the single step and along the landing, toward Alice, his teeth bared in a hideous, wolflike grimace. For such a lumbering woman she moved with an incredible burst of speed, snatching his arm and pulling it down with the grace of an adder's tongue so that he fell to his knees, groaning, his head collapsing forward. "No, you don't," she said sternly. "Not with me."

In the silence that followed, Deborah wished only to be transported from this spot to any other, any place at all; even prison, even hell, would be a relief. She'd been caught as red-handed as any villain, and she knew it with a hideous certainty. Worse yet, she'd not realized her true purpose any more than Alice had, not until this precise moment. She hadn't respected Alice. She hadn't liked her. She'd wanted to dump her troubles on her, as if Alice Dunn had handled so much garbage in her painful life that one more load of human trash could hardly tip the balance. It was true.

After an eternity, Alice said, "Help me up, then, would you, Mrs. Latham? I'd be grateful for a ride back to my house." Her tone couldn't have been gentler, nor her words, but Deborah was cut through, shame like an actual flare of fire licking hotly at her heart.

40

THE STRIPED bass were incredible this year, and there were more fluke than most people had caught in ages. Scallops weren't plentiful, but at least the hauls were better than recent Septembers, no brown tide having corrupted the spawning grounds. No one knew for sure what the brown tide was or where it came from, but most locals blamed the murderous algae growth on the pesticides used to maintain grassy lawns at fancy summer residences and golf courses. Today, though, no one was complaining. Chris's patients chattered happily all morning about the way the fish were running, and as a result, he himself was running late. He must have removed the mirror from half a dozen mouths to let their owners continue bragging about fantastic catches from the depths of Gardiner's Bay and Block Island Sound.

It wasn't until nearly two that Rosemary insisted he pause for lunch. "I called the Imhelders and told her you were running half an hour behind. You look like you need a break," she said, and if they hadn't been standing out near the waiting room where anybody might walk in, he'd have hugged her just for noticing him. All day, he'd been feeling as if the protective mask covering his mouth were also temporarily obscuring visible distress, but not a single patient had blinked when he removed the mask to say good-bye. Only astute Rosemary, his assistant of more than sixteen years, was sensitive enough to see any sign of trouble.

He didn't want to say anything to her, though, certainly not in public, but would any place be private enough to confess what they were about to do, he and Deborah? They were returning the boy; at least, they were finding him a new home. It was decided. Oddly, he'd been working so hard to get Deb to agree to the end of Michael's tenure that he hadn't paused to speculate about how difficult it might be to inform his friends and neighbors. As shaming as Michael's presence had been, admitting to such a notable failure was equally humiliating.

After lunch, he walked down to Malloy's and took a look at Will's boat. It was shipshape as always; nobody would ever be able to tell what a disaster had taken place there only two days before.

He retraced his steps, heading back toward the office. At the last minute, he didn't use the crosswalk between the Bay Street Theater and the Corner Bar. Instead, he kept on walking, up and over the bridge to North Haven, imagining that Rosemary was at the window to his office, waving for him to come back to work on Mrs. Imhelder's mouth. He trudged over the bridge, marveling as always at the way such a solid structure actually swayed beneath his feet. He marched past the estates that lined Ferry Road and past other, less pretentious houses in which he had dined, danced, and chatted with fellow villagers on many occasions over the nearly four decades of his life.

He wondered why it was that he, of all his classmates and acquaintances, had failed to move on, had failed to leave the Harbor behind? Others of them had left, many for ten or twenty years, and were only now deciding to move their families back to this place that memory had re-created as an idyllic location. He, though, had been the least connected of anyone—except perhaps Des Dunn, of course—and he'd had the least possible reason for staying here and calling Sag Harbor his lifelong home. He'd failed somehow, he thought, to grow up and away, to make it on his own without the blind backing and acceptance of the Harbor. Maybe this was the only place he could have survived, he didn't know.

He came around Dead Man's Curve, and there was Peerless Marine and, curving off to the water, Fresh Pond Road. *God*, he thought, *the tree. It's gone.*

It was, too. The huge oak that had taken Jack Dunn's life was gone. Not even a stump was in its place, as if the loss were no longer an absence but merely a lack of existence. No marker here for Jack's end and for the rest of them, he and Anna, Will and Des: No headstone, no memorial, not even a bunch of flowers laid on the grass by the side of the road.

Once, several summers ago, he and Deb had made plans to meet the Blooms for a picnic dinner at Long Beach. Les Bloom was coming from his office in Southampton, and he'd been delayed so long that first the children and then the grown-ups had begun to sample their cold chicken and sesame noodles and salad. Finally, after more than an hour, Les had pulled up in his Lexus, announcing breathlessly that he'd been held up by the most awful accident! A man on a motorcycle had been hit by a delivery truck and killed. His girlfriend, riding behind him, had been thrown to the side of the road, her leg completely severed. The leg itself had risen through the air like a boomerang, flashing high and then falling with a huge splash directly into a group of paddling toddlers at Trout Pond. Imagine the screams, Les had exclaimed, and they'd been horrified to think of the children, the woman, the man.

Deb had poured another glass of wine for each of the grown-ups. Ada and Caroline went down to the water's edge as if the story hadn't registered. Hunting for shiny jingle shells to string on thread for necklaces, they chattered sweetly. Michael, near but not with either group, played in the sand, digging hole after hole and filling each one up as soon as he hit water, an exercise that occupied him completely that evening.

The thing of it was that at a dinner party the following winter, Chris had told the story to one of the emergency room doctors from the hospital. He and Dr. Dyson had been trying to place which night the Devon Yacht Club fireworks had been, and he'd used that evening as a reference point because he was sure it had been the next night. But Dyson had stared and laughed, shaking his head. "You certainly got taken," he said, reaching for his red wine. "I wonder where the guy actually was."

"You mean that didn't happen?" he asked, and he poked Deb on the knee to get her attention. She was laughing with Lois Adler, a local attorney, and when she turned toward Chris, her mouth was open and her eyes alight with enjoyment.

Dyson shook his head. "Believe me, I'd have heard about it. No spare legs flying into Trout Pond, no dead motorcyclists on Noyac Road. Not last summer. No way, no how."

Deb turned to Chris, shocked. "Of all people," she'd said. "I'd never have expected Les Bloom to have the imagination to make that kind of thing up. And why? I hate to think."

Even though Chris didn't know what Les had been doing, he certainly understood the impulse to embroider. There were so many careless carvings in the totems of his own creation that he sometimes wondered what it was he'd intended to manufacture in the first place. Whom had he made himself into and from what flawed raw material? The young boy, scared and guilty, who'd first begun sneaking across the street to Will's to find dinner and who'd later called the Gastons' home his own—who had that little boy been? Where else might he have gone, what might he have done, given the possible other circumstances another fate might have laid at his feet? And now, here he was, his future no longer a matter of free choices but of a narrowing series of options closing in to leave him only one clear move.

He had to tell her. He knew it. Whether she left him or not, whether she loved him afterward or never again, no longer was the crucial point. If he didn't tell her, he'd be Lester Bloom, bigmouthed befuddler of reality. He couldn't be that kind of man. Even being silent, at this juncture, was a version of a lie.

Chris sat on somebody's lawn. It was no longer the Drummond's— they had moved to Florida and whoever bought the place used only initials on a neatly painted sign to self-importantly trumpet a desire for anonymity. He gazed over at the spot where Jack Dunn had lain, crushed and dead, in the wreck of Anna Downing's '65 ragtop.

In truth, he wasn't a dentist, though that was what he'd spent his adult life calling himself. He was a murderer. Christopher Latham, murderer. No other title, no other degree, would ever be as well earned. For with one practical joke in his eighteenth year, he'd destroyed so many lives he could barely track the numbers. His own, Jack's, Alice's, Martin's—those were obvious. But how many others? What path had Des Dunn been diverted from? And Michael himself? Deborah? Anna Downing? Who else? Who knew? By ending the entire road that forked under Jack Dunn, he had closed off host upon host of possibility.

The power he had briefly held, that one awful night, had brought him little pleasure. All he wanted was absolution—from Deborah. If she could look him in the face, after knowing, and still love him, well, he might be saved, after all. If she couldn't, he'd know he'd been brave enough to try.

He hoped it wasn't foolish—he knew it was unmanly—to hope for her forgiveness.

Alice spiked a fever on Tuesday evening. She was shivering and sweating, and after he failed to offer of his own accord, she asked Martin to call Greg Isen to let him know she'd picked up a little flu.

Martin didn't answer her, but he did go to the phone and look up

Isen's number, and he listened to the message to find out how to contact him in an emergency. When the phone rang with Greg Isen's return call, Martin quickly sketched in the situation, dispassionately reporting that Alice's fever was hovering around 102° and that she was coughing and sneezing, having chills and nausea, and generally feeling awful.

Dr. Isen sighed and said, "There's flu in the area with exactly those symptoms. She'll be fine. Lots of times, people who are HIV-positive think they're going to die when there's just a bug going around. She'll be fine, I promise. But when she's better, she's got to think about starting that medication. Please tell her."

Martin knew his ground on this one; he was utterly solid about his position, and he answered, "I don't have a say in what she does, why should I? She's got the right to make her own mistakes, same as me."

"She could fight the virus," Greg said, and his voice cracked. He cleared his throat. "Lots of people with her illness do okay, live fairly normal lives. And I do need to see you in my office as soon as possible."

"Is she going to die soon?" Martin asked, and even Greg could hear the yearning for it.

"I don't know," he answered, wanting to hang up the phone and be free of Martin Dunn. "I suspect that's up to her."

"Would you explain to me why Martin Dunn contacted Butler and Pantera?" Ellie Emerson asked the following morning, swishing her string mop back and forth across Deborah's tile bathroom floor. "You know him, right? He does your plumbing."

Deborah nodded. She'd already gotten the Advil bottle from the pharmacy cabinet and had thought she would get out of her bedroom unnoticed, but she'd underestimated Ellie's need to talk. When Ellie had a story, it was hard for her to go even half an hour without retelling it; the truth was, she didn't care if Deborah knew the Dunns or not. This news was so unbelievable she could barely keep herself from hopping on the Lathams' phone to call Nan Downing. All she'd done was go out to pick up Mrs. Latham's mail and she'd heard the news from one of the kids who helped the Butlers out. Turns out Martin Dunn had called the previous evening to inquire about the cost of a modest funeral, for his wife, no less! And Alice didn't have a darn thing wrong with her, just a touch of the flu was what she'd told Ellie on the phone only last night.

Ellie was so excited she barely moved the mop in one lazy circle the whole time she was talking. For the first time, Deborah noticed how truly strange Ellie's eyes were, yellowish irises like a cat's that seemed so focused, on the one hand, and so oddly indifferent at the same time. It was hard to look away from her and equally difficult to know how to react. What did Ellie know?

"What do you mean?" Deborah asked, as indifferently as she could. "She's sick? Mrs. Dunn, I mean?"

"Do you know her?" Ellie asked, curious for just a moment until her brow uncreased and she waved the hand without the mop dismissively. "Oh, yeah, she's a patient of Dr. Latham's. Of course. Well, I doubt but that there's one thing wrong with her, I really do. It's that husband of hers, he's crazy as a bug in a jug. All she is, she's a little under the weather. She told me herself, and Alice Dunn's been my best friend more than forty years. Anything was wrong with her, you bet I'd be the first to know. And let me tell you this, Mrs. Latham." Here Ellie's eyebrows lowered darkly. "If something happens to her, I'll sure know who to blame."

Deborah blushed hotly, opening her mouth, but Ellie continued without noticing. "It'll be that Martin Dunn, pushing his wife over the brink if anybody ever did. That man hasn't done one kind thing for his family, not ever. But he's good as gold to the church, so it's hard for me to judge, I guess. It certainly is." Ellie's mop swished forward and back, once, with a snap, as if reminding its master of the task they were supposed to be performing.

Deborah stepped toward the door, planning to head downstairs, away from Ellie, in order to telephone Alice. She was going to call Alice and make sure she was all right. No, she was going to drive right over to the Dunns' house and check in person. Deborah Latham would be bigger than her shame; she was going to prove herself a decent person after all.

"Hey," Ellie called from the bathroom. "There's never been a murder in the Harbor. Not one. Not ever. But if Alice Dunn dies, I'm going to bring the cops in on this. I swear I am."

For a moment, Deborah savored guilt, as if Ellie Emerson had been accusing her of murdering the plumber's wife. She scurried downstairs. Michael and his tutor were working quietly in the family room. As she headed out the back door, she actually heard Michael giggle. If thoughts could moan, hers would have. *Oh, God,* she thought, *he's happy. Maybe he can stay, maybe it will all turn out right.*

In the car, she didn't allow herself to think, just drove as if she were embarked on the most natural of errands. At Alice's driveway, she turned off the ignition and let herself out of the car, striding up the path determined to endure whatever humiliation might be before her, all in the name of allowing Alice the assistance and support she so surely needed. So determined was Deborah that she failed to note the silver BMW parked down at the road, as if the driver had come this far and no further before needing to pause and take stock of the errand he was engaged in. He hadn't been able to park in the driveway, couldn't bring himself to that level of commitment.

Deborah opened the door and let herself in quietly. Alice wasn't in the bedroom, though; she was seated, pale but hardly sick looking, right in her usual chair in the living room, chuckling sweetly and holding the hand of a sloe-eyed Hispanic man in his late thirties.

It was Des, it had to be.

"Oh, I'm so sorry! I didn't mean to interrupt; I just wanted to see if you were okay," Deborah babbled, an idiotic flush burning its way up her cheeks. She slapped her right hand helplessly against her blue-jeaned leg and turned, intending to let herself out.

"Wait," Alice said. "Look here. It's Des, returned home to see me."

Deborah's upbringing occasionally had its uses; she could easily track back from humiliation to social enthusiasm without blinking. She leaned in with a wide smile, extending her right hand. "Hello, I'm Deborah Latham. My husband went to school with you, I think."

Des smiled. His smile was odd—it had no pleasure in it—but his teeth were white and strong. A series of small whiteheads dotted his forehead, just under the curve of his dark hair. If Alice hadn't been pushing it back affectionately, this small imperfection would never have been visible. "Chris Latham's wife? Funny. I've been thinking about him a lot today."

"You have? Huh. I could call him. I'm sure he'd love to see you," Deborah said, hardly aware that she was offering something Christopher would be furious about, no matter who the high school friend. He hated being disturbed when he was at the office. The last time she had called him during the day was when Caroline had to go to the emergency room. Luckily, Des wasn't eager to take her up on the offer.

Alice said, "Des has been explaining why he hasn't been to see me before."

"I should go," Deborah said.

"Oh, no." Alice waved her to Martin's empty chair with a flick of her gnarled fingers. "Sit down. We don't mind."

Deborah couldn't move. She felt compelled to stay, even though she suspected Alice was just being polite. Des watched her with a kind of supercilious amusement that made her feel even clumsier than normal. As she dropped into Martin's chair, he leaned closer to her, pushing at the floor with his feet so that the ottoman he sat on slid in her direction and he could grab her by the hand. "Christopher Latham's wife," he said thoughtfully. "You aren't what I'd have expected."

Alice's house was dark and awfully stuffy. From the depths of her chair, Deborah could smell Martin's lingering perspiration laced with the sour odor of yesterday's pork chops and onions. On top of it all, one couldn't ignore the heavy bodily perfume distilled by Alice as her body temperature maintained its rise.

Des shifted back again, smoothing his hands down the crease of his khakis. His white cotton shirt was crisply ironed, buttoned all the way to the collar. Seated next to Alice, no trace of relationship was visible, not a similarity in posture or movement or outlook or appearance. He practically glowed in the gloom, teeth and whites of eyes and well-buffed nails all clear and bright with health. He matched nothing in his surroundings, not a thing.

Des peered at Deborah through the dusky light, returning to her previous statement. "You think so? Chris would love to see me?"

"Of course," she said stiffly, not sure what he'd been implying by saying he'd expected a different kind of wife for Chris. Martin's chair was so deep she felt lost in it, as if she'd be unable to get up with even a semblance of grace. The cushions were thinned from supporting his weight, and a spring coil kept jabbing the back of her right thigh. "Why not?"

Des looked at Alice, who looked at Deborah, who watched both of them with a certain sense of confusion. "Why not?" she asked again.

Des chuckled. It was easy to imagine him as the villain in a silent picture, top hat on his head, greased mustache he could twist evilly as he sneered. "My guess is that husband of yours doesn't want to come face to face with me. He'd feel too guilty, don't you think?"

Alice's face was wary. Deborah said stiffly, "I don't really know what you're talking about. Alice? Is there something I don't know?"

Now it was easier to see that Alice was ill. Her skin had blanched a pale white and her smile was weak. As the conversation took an uncomfortable turn, her eyes seemed damp and distracted. "I don't know," she answered. She coughed, a thick, croupy sound, and then she shrugged uncomfortably, lifting her hands and lowering them to the arms of her chair.

Des smiled as if he hadn't heard the rattle in his mother's chest. His teeth gleamed in the dusk of Alice Dunn's cramped living room. He lifted his right hand and patted Deborah on the leg, failing to notice the way her muscles tightened in dislike. "What the hell," he said. "I bet I have a good story for you."

41

MARTIN DUNN walked that morning. He still took his walk every day now, even though little Shane had gone to a permanent home nearly three weeks earlier. Martin liked the walking; it made him feel as if nothing had changed, as if Shane were still around, as if Jack were still around, as if his own father were still around.

He'd asked Gus Emerson only a few days before about the trees, about remembering how the trees had been so small back when they were kids that it was possible to see from the ocean to the bay if one stood near where Gus's house was now. Gus had laughed when he said that, shaking his head back and forth like Martin was some kind of fool he'd never seen before. Gus had said the widow's walk on the tallest Main Street whaling mansion was too low now even to see the short reach to the bay. He'd bet it hadn't been possible to see the ocean ever, not in a hundred years or more. Martin didn't know what to make of that. He'd been sure that as a small boy, nine or ten or so, he had been able to see all the way to the waves splashing in the Atlantic and all the way back to the bay slapping against the beach. Gus had just laughed again and said it never could have been that way.

Martin hated Gus—not because of any particular thing, like his leaving Martin after nearly thirty years together and acting like in his new plumbing business he had reinvented every damn thing Martin'd done all his life. It was more because Gus was the kind of man who could do that, could just get up and say he didn't want to live the way he did and make the change. Martin couldn't imagine shaking off all the ties that bound him to regular life. He couldn't.

Rounding the first curve on Noyac Road, Martin stopped short, his toes in the fancy new walking sneakers suddenly cramping painfully. The Other Stand was gone! In its place, a razed field, a new wooden fence, the beginnings of a pasture. The farm had disappeared, between last week and this, its owner having surely decided to give up the struggle and sell his valuable farmland to the highest bidder. True, another farmer was comfortable now, after struggling for generations to make ends meet, but that didn't make Martin feel even the slightest brush of sympathy. Instead, he thought of Gus Emerson and all those others who were taking on the new ways, the ways of Them, and giving up on the values that had kept Sag Harbor stable for so many generations.

He trudged on, rounding the corner where Sauer's farm had been. Long gone, its acreage was now devoted to summer residences and artist studios. But when his father had worked for Ed Sauer back in the late 1920s, it had been home to a goodly percentage of the hooch Lucky Luciano ran through the Harbor. Oh, the stories his father had told about those days! How the village had honored Luciano and his men! They welcomed the rum-running because the money was needed so badly. Mr. Sauer had his chicken coops stuffed full with bottles of Scotch that had sailed down from Canada. He stored it all for Luciano, and when he wanted Martin's father to load a truck, he'd ask him to load up the Rhode Island Reds or the Orpingtons or the Speckled Sussex, and that would be the chicken coop Luther Dunn would head for, so he could find the hooch he was supposed to throw on the wagon.

There'd been no temperance folks in the Harbor, not the whole time of Prohibition, and he supposed that was because not one villager ever conceived of rum-running as a crime. Until Lucky showed up, there hadn't been a single stable way to make a living in more than sixty years, not since the whaling trade fell off. And once Lucky brought business to Sag Harbor, things really changed. A guy could make twenty-five bucks a night unloading hooch—if he had a truck, that is. And if he didn't, he could still haul in a tenner or so, enough to take care of his entire family.

Luciano had changed the Harbor's luck all round. Even after Prohibition was repealed, well, that was when the factories started coming in, and all of a sudden there were jobs, real jobs! And after the war, once lots of folks got ahold of those cheap Ford cars, that's when the tourists had started to flock in, big time. Martin didn't mind the tourists, not like some people did. They were people, same as he, and if they paid their bills, they put food on his table. He couldn't fault them; they were God's people, too. At least, most of them were. But now, things had gone too far.

He trudged on, toward the beach, and suddenly he remembered a story he'd heard from George Walters, the village historian and an old friend of his late father. When George was around twenty-one, he'd been working down at Marine Park as a tree surgeon, and one afternoon his boss came over to him and said, "George, weather's coming up real bad. If I was you, I'd hurry home." And what George did was he hightailed it up Madison Street in the wind, and as he passed the old Presbyterian church, he heard a loud whooshing noise, and a bang, and then a bell ringing loud as the Judgment Day. He looked up and saw the entire steeple of the church rising up in the air like an umbrella and then sailing toward him, across the old graveyard. It fell not fifty yards from George, and what he always said was, "That hurricane of 1938, I thought the world was coming to an end, I really did. I was so glad to wake up the next morning and see I was still around, that nothing else could ever scare me again."

Martin had been five years old during that hurricane. He didn't recall one second of the afternoon. But years later, whenever the wind came high, he always did like to keep busy, like if he stopped and settled down, waited for it all to be over, he'd rise up just like that steeple and crash forever to the ground.

He wiped his face. All this remembering was making him warm and a little sad. His father had been sad all the time—that's what Martin thought—so sad he'd needed to sample more than his share of Southern rum and Canadian Scotch whiskey. He used to pass out in town regularly, and Martin had to go pick him up. He'd loved his dad, but he hated that particular errand. Once, when he was about ten, his mother had ordered him to go downstreet and get his dad, and he'd taken his time wandering down to the bank. He'd meandered, if he faced the facts, but he couldn't put it off forever, and when he got there, there was his father, stretched out proud as Jesus on the ground in front of the bank, shouting, "This is the place where I want to die, right here! This is the place!"

That was back in the early 1940s, before the hordes of tourists started coming in. Every single one of the folks gathered around his dad was a familiar face, which sort of made it easier to haul him up and slip a shoulder under his arm and begin to help him home. And as they were starting to make their way uneasily toward Madison Street, one of the Gilmans had leaned in and quietly asked, "Hey, Luther, why here? At the bank, I mean. Why d'you want to die here?"

Everybody seemed to slow down, waiting to know what it was made this particular spot so special. Luther Dunn had thought about it, too, before he mumbled his answer. He'd waved one arm drunkenly through the air, not minding that he hit his own son as he did so, and he said, "What a place to die, what a place! So close to the money!"

Martin reached Long Beach, trudging along, his thighbones pounding sorely against his kneecaps so that each step was followed by a searing exclamation point, a reminder of how poorly he himself had used his body. He'd never drunk a drop of liquor in his life—he wasn't his father's boy that way—but he'd eaten all he wanted and sat unmoving and knelt without thinking and overslept and underslept, and he'd done some things with women he maybe shouldn't have. Now his body knew it.

Alice was about to be gone, too, after all the years together. She was dying fast, no matter what Greg Isen thought. He wouldn't miss her, not a whit, if he confessed it. Still, the thought that she'd be seeing their boy before him—that bothered him more than he liked to admit.

It wasn't Christian of him, he knew it, but it was as if she were about to win the last battle between them. He hated to think that. He hated it.

If he had the courage, he'd like to go before her, he really would. He wanted to find Jack first. Jack would understand. Boys understand their fathers, it's the way of things. As long as their mothers didn't get in there, bending ears and twisting stories around so folks got all confused, well, boys and their fathers had the easiest, simplest love.

They had respect for one another, that's what it was. They accepted each other, warts and all. No carping. No complaining about how things had turned out, about the disappointment of knowing one another deep down. That was liking. That was love. That was respect.

He was panting, not just with exertion but with resolve. He was going to beat her to it. If it had to be today, so be it. He'd step in front of a truck. He was going to Jack, and that was that.

"This is the place I want to die, right here," he whispered, feeling the light bay breeze whisper over his shoulders as if it wanted to nuzzle him. "This is the place I want to die."

No one was on the beach, not a single soul, despite its being such a warm afternoon and only the middle of September. The first steps, the ones that dampened and then soaked the legs of his beige pants, they were the hardest. By the time he reached waist height, he was determined and no longer thinking of his physical self. First one meaty arm and then the other struck the water, and he was swimming, remembering the bay when he was a boy and the fish were everywhere, tickling his knees and arms as he slashed through the water. In those days, the fish had kissed him with every stroke; they'd shared the clean blue-green water and the white hot sun when it was bright and the sweet, constant rain when it wasn't.

His pants and shirt were clinging, impeding his strokes, and when he slipped them off, he knew he meant it. A Dunn would never appear in front of others in his Skivvies. He wasn't going back.

Martin Dunn turned once and then again, rolling over like a small, swollen dolphin. He wasn't happy, precisely, but he was calm. He knew where he was going, and he was fine with the thought. He was going to Jack, and it was more than time to do so. "This is the place," he whispered, beginning to swim smoothly out, into the bay. "This is the place where I want to die. Right here."

And he did.

42

THE LAWYER didn't like him anymore, Chris could tell that. She wanted to treat him professionally, but the idea of what he wanted to do disgusted her. When he'd first called, behind Deborah's back, Emily Conway treated him as if he were having the kind of problem that a little talk therapy might cure. She'd actually humored him, trying to distract him with talk of Caroline and Deborah and if the family intended to go on vacation that year. When he didn't respond, Emily had suggested he take her to lunch, and the way her voice softened as she said it had shocked him. He hadn't dreamed of coming on to her.

He'd told her he was kind of busy these days, going to the gym at lunch when he didn't go home for a quick break. She'd taken it gracefully, finally acknowledging the purpose of the call. And when she called him back a week later, she was solidly up to speed on the appropriate areas of the law.

"The truth is," she'd said, "you can't technically return the boy. It's been more than four years after all. And he received his American citizenship last year. In the eyes of the law, he's your natural child, yours to protect. I read the papers, and I do know that some adopted children have a very difficult time. Attachment disorder, that's what they call it. As you know, I don't handle lots of adoptions. I only did yours because we had mutual friends and because private adoptions are basically so simple to arrange. I've certainly never handled what they call an adoption disruption before. That's what you're talking about. I suggest you contact the agency that did your home study. Social Services will require you to do so, and it can't hurt to get the process started. Besides, they might be able to help you solve the problem without," and she paused, "without actually removing the child from your home."

He swallowed. The social workers at New York Children's Morning had been wonderful with them, had gone out of their way to provide support and invite the Lathams to therapy meetings. They had sent monthly mailings updating the family on all the services that might benefit them. Deborah and he had both scoffed at all the well-meaning interventions in the beginning; they'd been above such notions. And he remembered how Nancy McLean, their social worker, had once informed them that adoption wasn't a service; it was the beginning of a long and often difficult process. She was a deep-voiced woman given to blue jeans and paint-stained sweatshirts, the kind of person who dropped papers on the ground without noticing and constantly misplaced her glasses. He'd not taken her as seriously as he might have. In her third visit, the one in which she'd congratulated them and said they'd been approved to adopt Michael, she'd stood by the door, tapping the frame with a beringed forefinger, and then she'd said, "Lots of folks go into adoption with wonderfully fuzzy pictures of how easy it will be to integrate the child into their lives. In a parent-initiated adoption such as yours, we won't necessarily do as much follow-up as we might, so I hope you'll come to us. You really can lean on us when things get difficult."

Deborah had fluffed her curly hair up from underneath, exposing the long line of her neck, and then she'd made what was almost a bow in Nancy McLean's direction. She'd said, "Of course we will, and I thank you," and her tone was so formal that even Ms. McLean probably knew Deborah had no intention of relying on the agency's services.

Still, Ms. McLean hadn't seemed willing to leave. She'd gone outside, closed the screen door, and leaned in. It was fall, just growing colder, the same time of year as now in fact, but it had been far more wintry that year. Her skin was pale under her purple chenille cap, and the end of her nose had a nearly imperceptible turn to it that was slightly pinker than the rest of her face.

She said, "I'm an adoptive parent myself, not just a social worker. My child is Romanian, like yours will be. And I know a lot of parents have difficulties, real difficulties, with their adoptive children. Don't give up. I promise you, it will be worth it. I have such a happy story, so many of us do. Please don't expect it to be easy, and don't give up just because there are difficult times."

"We won't," Deborah had promised her. "I can assure you of that. We aren't like that."

"Everyone needs a shoulder to cry on, that's all. Every parent, of any child, but adoption can be particularly intense."

"You're scaring me," Deborah said, smiling awkwardly, moving toward the door as if to push Ms. McLean on her way.

"People always talk about the difficult placements. The truly horrible ones sell newspapers and magazines, so you hear about those all the time. And parents start the process expecting little angels who will be eternally grateful for what's being done for them. It's angels and devils, that's all people can ever imagine. But the truth of the matter is something in between. I love my daughter. I'm so glad I have her. I'm so proud of what I've done for her. But it isn't—oh, I don't know," and here she shrugged, and began to turn from the door, so that the small wire checks made by the screen door no longer dotted her face. "It isn't pretty or romantic all the time. I want you to know that."

Deborah was genuinely puzzled, as was Chris, and both of them found the social worker's comments vaguely distasteful and thoroughly unnecessary. They had no doubt they would succeed with their little boy. Hadn't he been handpicked by Viorica after all? Hadn't he been chosen just for them? Of course there would be difficulties, they weren't fools. They had no doubts, though, that they'd be able to surmount any rough spots in the road ahead. After Nancy McLean left, they'd giggled about her, about how with an attitude like hers of course everything was arduous and painful.

Now, calling her seemed like the ultimate humiliation. He knew it had to be done; how else could they begin the process of sending Michael away? Unless he could get Emily Conway to handle it for them.

"There are support groups for parents, you know, that I understand are very helpful," Emily said. "There are chatlines on the Internet that I've read about. And, of course, there are qualified therapists who work with troubled children; they can be very helpful."

"We've done all that," he said tiredly. "It didn't help. Not us."

Emily's voice took on an edge. "It helps most people. Most adoptions work out."

He knew they had failed at something, and he hated her for making it so clear. Deborah wouldn't be able to handle the defeat of this process.

If she made one phone call, she would change her mind. Chris was certain of it.

He repeated, "There isn't a thing we haven't done. Support groups, therapists, chat groups, brain scans—we've done every possible thing, talked to every expert. Now our daughter is having terrible difficulties as well; this whole summer she's been going downhill so fast it's scary. And Deborah, my wife, she just refuses to understand . . ."

"Mrs. Latham may be more willing to shoulder the burden, to take on the challenge," Emily Conway had said, but he'd cut that line of conversation off sharply.

"She thinks she is, but it can't last much longer. She's not sleeping; she herself is in terrible shape. The stress is too much for us. We're worried—scared, too, honestly—all the time."

There had been a long silence on the other end of the line, and then Emily Conway had softly cleared her throat. "Excuse me," she said. "I've honestly never dealt with a situation like this before. I do think you need to contact New York Children's Morning. It's the correct next step."

"Can you? Can you call them for us? I mean, if we decide to go ahead?"

"Of course," she'd said. Meaning, it will cost you, but I'll do it.

That had been in August. Today, after Mrs. Imhelder left the office, he locked himself in the lab and called Conway and Seltzer, Family Law Practitioners, at their Riverhead number. Emily wasn't available, so he left a message with her secretary saying that the situation was no longer tenable and that they'd definitely decided to act. As he was hanging up, Rosemary knocked loudly on the door. "Sorry to bother you, Chris, but something's happened at your house. Deborah's not home, and Michael and his tutor are having some kind of problem. It sounds like you better get over there."

43

IT WAS the smell of the house that brought the past rushing back for Des, that compacted odor of accumulated dirty diapers and evening meals. Walking through the ragged screen door, before he had even seen Alice, his senses had responded, raising memories that hadn't scurried through his mind, he was sure, in years. Here, there was always some just-this-side-of-too-old cut of meat slowly cooking, chopped into a casserole to stretch a pound to feed two growing boys and two expanding adults. That was the scent of his childhood, the aroma he had never wanted to inhale again.

Martin had always had a hankering for fresh air, and she sometimes inched a window briefly up to accommodate him, but Alice preferred the house shut tight and always had. Odors accumulated in the stillness, no matter how diligently she cleaned the floors and scrubbed the counters. Since she did not leave the house very often, she probably had no idea how stuffy the old Colonial was.

The house was set atop a steep hill, on a large piece of property that had hardly been this unkempt when he was a kid. Under strict orders from their father, Des and Jack had spent countless hours manicuring that rolling lawn and its plantings. Back when the boys lived there, nobody would ever have said an unkind word about the Dunn's home or their garden. Nothing looked wrong, not in those days.

What Des and Jack knew, the secretly humiliating aspect of life at their house, was how much their parents hated one another. The poison of Martin and Alice's mutual distaste didn't ebb and flow, or alter with the seasons, and neither boy had even an inkling of what early event might have begun the deterioration of their parents' marriage.

One thing Jack always said to Des, and it was true, was this: "Funny thing is, you should have been their real kid, not me. You're the kind of apple that would fall from that tree." Des didn't mind his saying that; there was almost nothing Jack had ever said to him that he didn't take at face value. That was the tie they had. Growing up in that house, they'd had no choice but to trust one another completely.

Another thing Jack said was: "You can tell how much they like hating each other. They go out of their ways to do it." Des could even recall the night Jack had noted this, just days before high school graduation in 1977. Martin had failed to come home for dinner, even though he had called from a client's house to say he'd be back in twenty minutes. Alice had held supper for him until seven o'clock when Jack, who had a movie date with Anna, had simply gone into the kitchen and dished himself a portion of macaroni casserole. He sat down, hunkered both elbows onto the table, and began to scoop huge forkfuls into his mouth. Des waited a moment, eyeing Alice's shocked face, and followed suit. It was an unthinkably grave violation of Martin's rights as head of the family.

Alice's hands had fluttered up as Des seated himself and began to eat. "Oh!" she managed to gasp, and then a more thoughtful, "Oh." After a moment, she spooned out a serving for herself, pulling out her heavy oak chair with a scraping sound. None of them spoke; the only sounds were the coffeepot burping steam at the back of the stove and the occasional glint of fork on plate. It was as if everyone were waiting uneasily for Martin's car to pull up in the driveway and settle just outside the front door.

He never did arrive home that night, at least not until long after the boys had headed their separate ways, Jack to the movies with Anna, and Des out . . . , well, out doing stuff he oughtn't to be doing. But the next morning, the half-full casserole dish was sitting on top of the garbage can instead of by the sink, the challenge to his authority utterly rejected.

It was because of Martin's anger—and his impulsiveness—that anything ever changed at all in the house. He was out and about all day, and he usually did the grocery shopping. Even Des had figured out that his father liked to keep Alice on a short financial rein. He would show up, fairly often, with a cast-off chair found by the side of the road or an old television a client was throwing out. He bought from television ads—a set of knives, car wax, a home canning set—and when the products weren't what he thought they'd be, he sneered at Alice as if the suspect choice had been hers.

Alice did occasionally embark on small, low-energy rebellions. Once she left a broken vacuum cleaner by the front door for more than a month, never telling him it needed to be fixed. He didn't say a word about it; he merely stepped over the vacuum corpse night after night, morning after morning. It was Jack, of course, who mentioned the machine at breakfast one day, and when Jack wondered who would fix it, Martin and Alice actually worked out how it would get to the dealer in Southampton and who would pay for it. A miracle.

The house itself was both grand and unkempt, a hodgepodge of old family heirlooms Martin's ancestors had treasured for generations and cheap new furniture purchased or bartered decades ago and now falling apart at the seams. Jack hated to bring his friends over to the house, and Des would have been a fool to bring his wild companions, so most of the boys' social lives took place where Sag Harbor teens' social lives had taken place for generations: on stretches of beach found down hidden lanes that only the locals knew about.

Most weekends, someone would bring a keg or two out on the back of a pickup truck and leave the radio on until the battery died and a pal had to jump-start it, and a crowd of kids would drink and dance and laugh and make out until the following morning. Since everyone's parents had done the same thing when they were kids, nobody seemed to have trouble getting permission to sleep at the beach with a crowd of teens. It was as if the parents had washed their hands of anything that happened down there by the water, and that was fine with most kids. There were couples who had sex down there and kids who smoked dope or dropped acid; there was lots of beer drinking and, occasionally, a fight, but somehow, it always stayed contained. It was actually fairly harmless, if not entirely innocent. Certainly, no adult ever had to interfere.

The night Jack Dunn died began like any beach party night. June, full moon, beautiful deep sky, and high spirits all around because it was graduation night. Suits and dresses had been discarded for shorts and sweatshirts by now, but there was a serious party in the air because this was such a big night for so many people. Jack, Des, Chris Latham, Will Gaston, and most of their friends, including Jack's and Chris's girlfriends, Anna and Cynthia—a whole knot of personalities that had filled the high school—were passing out of the confines of family life and into the greater world.

Jack and Chris were heading off to Stony Brook together that fall. Each of them had superb academic records, a shared football captaincy for the East Hampton team, and histories of jobs caddying at the Maidstone on top of working dawn to dusk for anyone who would proffer an invitation. No wonder Stony Brook had extended free-ride invitations to the pair; they were clearly going places few Sag Harbor boys had ever tried to go. Jack's guidance counselor had suggested he apply to other schools, even mentioned the possibility of the Ivy League, but Jack didn't want that. Sag Harbor has a way of holding onto people, and secretly he was leery of the great world outside, as much as he wanted to discover it. He intended to stick by Chris; leaving was going to be hard enough without a friend by his side, or so he confided in Des.

That night was a great night for Des, too. He'd graduated from high school, along with his brother and everyone else. Given his spotty record of attendance, his history of brief incarcerations for petty crimes, this was a miracle. He was high as a kite, buzzed as a bee, proud as can be. He didn't have to drink that night, simply did not have to. Pride's elation was good enough, for once.

It was a night of switches, that's for sure. Des did not drink a drop, and Chris and Jack, who rarely even had a beer, got drunk as lords. Celebrating, that's what they were doing. Celebrating the closing of one door and the opening of another. Gleeful at getting out; relieved, though such weakness would never be revealed aloud, to be doing it together. They were doing shots of beer around the bonfire and playing a game called Thumper that they'd learned on their overnight visit to Stony Brook. Long before midnight, Jack lumbered down to the bay and sat, *kerplunk*, with his feet in the water and his shorts growing damp in the sand. He stared at the moon and the softly lapping waves, and seemed to be thinking very deeply.

Cynthia Stall sat between Will Gaston and her boyfriend, Chris Latham. Chris and Cynthia had been together a long time. It was understood that one day they'd marry; everyone knew it. After that night, however, they didn't speak again for years. Strange how nobody ever mentioned that, as if focusing attention on that breakup might mean the aftershocks of the supposed accident had headed out in far more directions than most locals wanted to notice.

Cynthia was a perfect height, not too tall, not too short. She was slim and had a broad smile, long blonde hair, and deep blue eyes. She was so beautiful it scared older men. When she walked into the grocery store and asked for six lamb chops for her mother, the counterperson looked away so as not to be caught with hunger in his eyes. Wherever she went in the village, people seemed to avoid seeing her. Nonetheless, when she exited a room, every person looked after her, man or woman, yearningly. It was impossible not to. Will Gaston had thought of Cynthia day and night since the fifth grade, with a passion that even he couldn't fathom the depths of. He'd never touched her, not more than a brush of hand when giving her a piece of paper during art class or letting his fingers pass over her hair as if by accident. Tonight, though, was slightly topsy-turvy; she was more than a little sloshed from the beer she'd been drinking, and Chris, sitting by her side, seemed actually to have his arm around Anna; was that possible? Chris's hand was creeping around Anna's waist, circling toward her breasts; Anna had to realize it, and she wasn't doing a thing.

"Hey," Will said drunkenly, leaning in toward Cynthia. "I want to show you something. Come 'ere." He hauled Cynthia unevenly to her feet, supporting her with his arm as he walked her over to Anna's car, the Golden Goddess. His heart was pounding heavily; as stewed as he was, he could feel every pore in his skin open up to receive Cynthia's touch, the weight of her back on his arm, the flow of her hair and its nearness to his face. He twisted around, toward her face. He kissed her. She kissed him back. The oceanic blue of her eyes was obscured by lowered lids; her lips were full and responsive. His pants grew tight and uncomfortable.

They sat down against a tree by the car, and soon they had slithered down, and her shirt was unbuttoned. Will couldn't allow himself to think about what was happening, because he'd go off, go mad, finish before he started. His own best friend's—his brother's—girl, but who cared? Not tonight. It was the end of the beginning, and no rules held true. Not tonight. Hadn't Des Dunn proclaimed just that at the beginning of the evening, holding his diploma high above his head in glee?

Suddenly, Cynthia gave a snore, deep and ugly, and he opened his eyes. It was true, dammit. Shirt unbuttoned so that the white swell of her right breast was revealed to its matching goddess—the moon—arms thrown out in abandon, left leg splayed open and right leg bent slightly in, she had passed out against a scrub oak at the edge of the beach.

"Shit. Wake up, will you?" he said, shaking her gently. She only snored again, lightly this time, and settled back against him, bringing her hands together to lay them sweetly across her abdomen.

"Hey," Chris said above him, quietly. Will turned, cowering, as if expecting a punch to the jaw.

"Ssh," Chris said. "Don't wake her up. Listen, do me a favor, will you?"

"Of course. Anything."

"Real quietly, can you get under the hood of the Golden Goddess? On the side of the carburetor, there's a throttle linkage. It's held to the side with a jesus clip. Unhook that clip and lay the throttle between the linkage and the accelerator rod, and just close the hood as quiet as you can."

"Why? What'll that do?"

"They won't be able to get any juice from the Goddess. It won't hurt the car, just puts her out of commission until we get back. It'll give us some time. You know? I'm taking her over to Long Beach in my car, okay? Anna, I mean."

"Sure," Will said, and then, gesturing to Cynthia, still prone against the tree, "Hey, I'm sorry, okay?"

Chris shrugged. "Tonight, who cares? You know? Don't even think about it. I won't."

"You don't know any of this," Deborah said angrily. "You've made it all up."

Alice, who had fallen asleep the moment Des began talking, as if she couldn't bear to hear any story he might tell about that night, now sighed heavily in her sleep, settling back into her chair with a childlike contentment that was almost immediately punctuated by a series of sniffles and coughs. Despite the irritation, she didn't wake.

The phone rang. Des turned toward his mother, who did not stir, and then back to Deborah. He shrugged one shoulder. Deborah blinked several times. "Are you going to answer it?" she asked.

He raised the shoulder again, cocking his head. "Are you?" he said. "God knows it's not my house."

"Why did you come back?" she asked him. Des's shoulders stiffened under the soft cotton of his shirt, hands snapping into tight fists. His eyes narrowed, as if he were about to say something terrible, but when she sat calmly, not flinching, he closed his mouth and began to run his fingers down the pressed surface of his khakis. He looked down at his trousers, and oddly, the vision of his clean beige slacks seemed to calm him. When he looked back up at Deborah, only seconds later, his expression was good-humored.

"Why did you come back now?" she asked again. "And not before?"

"I liked to think of all of them, her . . ."—he jerked his head toward his adoptive mother, without turning to look—"Martin, everyone, so pathetic their lives. I liked knowing I could live just a few miles away and never even come in contact with any of them. My world is a stratosphere away from theirs, from yours and your husband's, mark my words. And I was under their noses all this time, I liked that. I liked knowing that if anyone bothered to search for me, they'd be looking down, for a loser, a druggie, a thief. Not one of them would even dream of looking for me where I've been all this time, and I liked that. I liked that a lot."

"You could have run into anyone you knew any day on the street," she said. "It wasn't like you wouldn't be recognized."

He shrugged those slim shoulders again. "You think not," he said. "But I've been here for years. And every single day, every time I left the house, I thought, maybe today I'll run into Chris Latham. Maybe today, that bastard will find out how little it matters what he did to me. Maybe today. I can wait as long as it takes, years don't matter to me. And I was right. Here we are."

Deborah crossed one arm over the other, pulling them tightly against her waist, rocking forward. Her heavy brown hair dripped forward, over her shoulders, and she shook her head as if the movement would flip it back. Des reached his right hand toward her, taking a spray of curls gently between his thumb and middle finger. "This hair," he said. "It's softer than I'd have thought."

In the silence, Alice's breathing resonated with harsh purpose, bitter intake marred by a thin high whistle and then a slight moan as she exhaled. A warm flush spread across Deborah's cheeks and down her throat. She didn't move, couldn't bring herself to wrest the strands of hair from him, as if such a gesture might add present insult to past injuries.

She could feel the warmth of his breath on her lips and chin and neck. His eyes moved down her face, to her throat and then her breasts. Even though she didn't like him, her nipples reacted. She pushed her entwined arms higher to cover where the small, hard knots might be showing through the cloth of her shirt. His gaze dropped past her arms, down her body and the length of her legs. He took in the scuffed grime on her sneakers, and then he looked directly back to her face, not bothering to glance over her form again.

"My wife," he said, dropping the hank of hair. He leaned back with an odd smirk. "She's a friend of Sammi Conway's, you know her? The actress?"

Deborah nodded. Despite his clear disinterest in her, or maybe because of it, her breath was coming faster. Her heart thudded against the inner wall of her ribs. He smelled better than she would have imagined, a sour-sweet lemon scent. She'd never breathed in such a compelling aroma before; bottled, the market for it could be enormous. Des was utterly dislikable; she understood that completely, yet she wanted to lay her head against his neck.

"My wife used to model, before she met me," he said. "She's so beautiful people stare at her in restaurants."

Deborah nodded again.

Des said, "My wife loves me, though. Only me. She's mine."

"Do you have children?" Deborah managed to ask. The disdained lock of hair had settled on her left shoulder. She could feel it tickling her skin but could not lift her hand to brush it back.

He closed his eyes, sighed, then opened them again, very wide, as if to assure her of his honesty. "We're enough for each other, just the two of us. I doubt we'll ever have kids. But my wife, she's young enough . . ." Here his eyes ran down Deborah's body again. "She could change her mind," he said.

The phone rang again, a series of double trills that went on for eight sets, nine, then ten, before cutting off.

"It's not for me," Des said sarcastically. "That's for sure. Maybe it's your husband, looking for you."

"Oh no," she said, shaking her head. "He's at work."

"Good old Chris Latham, king of the Harbor."

"He's a dentist," she said.

"I know."

"What in the world did he ever do to you that made you hate him so much?"

Des smiled thinly. "That's what I was starting to tell you."

"I don't know," she said doubtfully, rubbing her thumb over a freckled area on her right thigh, avoiding his gaze. "Maybe this is something I should hear from Chris."

He shrugged. "Please yourself. If you think he'll ever tell you. How long have you been married, and you haven't heard a word about a murder? A vicious stupid murder that your own husband committed?"

The phone began to ring again, but this time neither of them even glanced toward it. "That's ridiculous," Deborah began weakly. Des put his right hand up. Her eyes moved toward it as if it were a trident she was under oath to follow.

"I don't think you should . . . ," she began again, but when he shook his head, his eyes and mouth clearly indicating that protest only amused him, she leaned back and looked toward the picture window. The short run of blacktop at the driveway's crest was glistening silver in the hot sun, and the air was thick and gray. She could leave, she knew, he wouldn't stop her. But she wouldn't. She wanted to stay, to seem to have heard him out. Nothing this complicated creature had to tell would be the truth; nevertheless, she would listen. She wanted to give him the benefit of that. Such a small gift for someone so replete with the trappings of wealth, yet it was the only prize she had to proffer that he would take. And she wanted—for Alice, for Chris, for herself, she wasn't sure—she wanted to give him something.

Jack Dunn had gotten really drunk; his blood alcohol level was off the charts when they examined the body, which is probably why nobody ever did look too closely into what happened. Even though almost everybody in the Harbor believed Des Dunn had been driving the car, Jack's blood was practically all beer, and that had a great deal to do with the decision to let matters rest with the corpse.

When the drinking game had first started, hours before, Des hadn't participated. He had been an observer that night, a role so unlike him at the time that later it almost seemed as if his life course had been changing all day with a gradually increasing velocity. But Jack and Chris and Will, and the girls, and everyone else down by Fresh Pond that night had been drinking up a storm, heading toward the ragged edges of one another's possibilities at an alarming clip. It happened all inside people, that night; outside, the sky was beautiful and clear, millions of stars twinkling benevolently above. The June air was balmy and warm, still in the high sixties even as the clock was rounding past midnight.

Down the narrow strip of beach, couple after couple was settling on blankets or under them, pale white legs wrapped around other legs, clothing piled or thrown in sloppy abandon.

Jack and Des Dunn sat by the water's edge, feeling the lap, lap of the icy cold bay against their calves and the backs of their knees. Neither of them spoke. It was one of the most peaceful moments they had shared in years. They rarely spent time together any more, except when they worked on Anna's car, the Golden Goddess. That car, a '65 Chevy Impala, a ragtop, was what held them together. They spent hours fooling with Anna's car, and there wasn't a gasket they hadn't removed, replaced, polished. It was the Golden Goddess that showed them they were still brothers, still buddies, connected forever.

After the longest while, Jack got up and headed back to the bonfire. No one was there at that point. Everyone who hadn't paired off had scuttled on to other pursuits—home, to the village to lap town a few times, out to the back roads to uproot a few mailboxes, whatever. The fire was dying slowly, and it no longer gave off much light. The moon, however, glowed brilliantly, and he could see all the way up to Anna's car, parked by the edge of the dirt road, and so he knew his girl was still somewhere around. He stumbled drunkenly toward the Goddess, and that's where he found Will.

Will Gaston had almost been having the night of his life. Cynthia Stall remained dead to the world, her lovely head on his shoulder; her blouse unbuttoned; her mouth, unfortunately, wide open and emitting a series of grunts and snores that might have dimmed the glory of the event for a lesser man. When Will closed his eyes, he imagined a whole series of beautiful pictures involving the rest of Cynthia, the parts still unrevealed, and when he opened his eyes, well, he had taken the opportunity to kiss her a few times, to sneak a few more looks at her unresisting beauty, to move the cloth of her blouse ever so slightly farther aside. He knew he would regret not having explored her sleeping form further; he knew this to be one of the great opportunities of his life, yet he also knew himself to be a coward. Not here, not with the possibility of humiliating discovery. After a period of bliss, Will had, in fact, forfeited the decision and dropped off to sleep, his head slipping down to rest on top of Cynthia's.

"What the hell?" Jack Dunn was standing over him drunkenly. It had to be hours later, Will's shoulder and jaw felt so stiff. "Where's Latham? What the hell? Where's Anna?"

Will couldn't think what to say, he was so sleepy and he couldn't remember what Chris had told him to tell Jack. His brain was pure fuzz and static, no news coming in. "Uh, uh . . . ," he began, waking Cynthia with his jerky effort to sit up.

From Jack's point of view, it was obvious Will Gaston knew something he wasn't eager to say. He was too drunk to think of words to use to ask Will questions, and so he leaned in and pulled skinny Will up and began to shake him, hard, not even noticing how Cynthia had slipped to the ground, her cheek scratched by a tree root. She lay still, watching the scene as if she understood nothing, and that was probably true. It was probably not even until the next day, when she thoroughly sobered up, that she completely grasped how many of her dearest friends had betrayed her that evening. And then, of course, she made the decision to walk away from all of it, telling no one what she must have known.

Will's neck flopped and jerked beneath Jack's thick hands. Such rough handling was terrifying. He'd been lucky to be under Chris Latham's protection throughout his teenage years. He really hadn't had to pay the price most guys of his build and brains usually did, so this punishing treatment was not the kind of thing he'd ever learned to endure with fortitude or to extricate himself from with brilliant wit.

"Where is she? Where's Anna?" Jack's eyes were wide and bloodshot, his mouth a snarl. As he shook Will, he kept shouting, "Where is she? Where's Anna?" and spit shot out of his mouth with the words.

Will's arms flailed up in the air and then down repeatedly, as if he were made of stuffing and cloth. His neck, though, must have been in agony, on the verge of snapping with each lurch forward, each vicious shake back. Jack was beyond caring what he did to Will. No telling how painfully this would end. It was to save himself that Will sputtered the words, "Long Beach." He must have known his best friend Chris would understand the need for betrayal. At least, he hoped he would.

"She's at Long Beach? With who? Latham?"

Will nodded.

"I'll kill the bastard! I swear, I'll kill him!" And Jack dropped Will against the tree, against Cynthia Stall, without a further thought, leaving the two of them panting next to one another until Cynthia rolled herself out from underneath Will's legs. She stood, buttoning her blouse without a glance downward. She turned silently and began to trudge out through the scrub oaks, toward the dirt road. Her feet were bare, and the ground rough, but Cynthia didn't turn back to the bonfire circle where her sandals still rested; instead, she headed home with a sturdy, purposeful trudge.

Will let her go without a word. His moment was over.

Jack Dunn crashed over to the Golden Goddess, started scrabbling around on the floor mats to find the keys. He was too drunk to grab them, though; his big hands kept pushing all the wrappers and cans and discarded towels back and forth, and by the time he had finally snared the keys, Des was in the car, pushing him over, saying, "Let me, I'll drive, let me."

Jack pushed his brother back, shoving Des against the inner passenger side door with a roughness he'd rarely displayed toward him. Jack snarled, "Back off! I'll do the fucking driving! I'm going to kill that fucking Chris Latham! I am! Get out of my fucking way!"

But Des stayed right there, watching over the only person he'd ever really loved in the world, determined and sober and intending, with some satisfaction, to help his brother kill Chris Latham. Without Chris around, it would be Jack and Des again, happy all the time, like when they were kids. He had no seat belt on, had no inkling of where they were headed, besides Long Beach, of course. He just wanted to be with Jack, to back him up. That was all he ever wanted, really.

The Golden Goddess bumped slowly up Fresh Pond, past the ghostly outlines of the few lone houses lining the road. Jack was pumping and pumping at the gas pedal, but it seemed like it wasn't working. He couldn't get any pressure, no matter how far to the floor he took the pedal. "Shit, shit, *shit*! This goddamn beast! Shit!"

Shouting didn't change anything: The Goddess couldn't get up past five miles an hour. It took forever to reach Ferry Road. "This fucking car! What the fuck! What the fuck's going on with this fucking car?" Jack yelled over and over, pumping at the gas pedal in fury.

Suddenly, as Jack's foot pressed down, the gas pedal stuck wide open. At first he grinned in triumph, allowing the Goddess to come up to speed, but as she passed fifty and kept going, the grin on his face went still and soft. Des didn't even realize what was happening, sober as he was, because Jack didn't say a word.

Jack pumped at the brakes with the same passion he'd been using to pump the gas. He couldn't get anything from the brakes, not anything; they were useless. His face went white under the moon's glow, and his smile went broader then, sweetly, almost like he knew. The car sped crazily up and out onto Ferry Road, bumping, the broad back end winging ever so slightly up and to the sides, tires singing on the paved surface. That smile, that was the last thing Des saw of his brother alive, that weird fixed smile, and the high-pitched scream from his throat, the way the last words Jack Dunn ever said were "I hate your fucking guts, Chris Latham! Rot in hell. I hate you!" It happened that fast. And the car crumpled in, hitting a huge tree that had rested by the side of Ferry Road for generations, just waiting for some boy to come along and die, crushed and moaning, between the gnarls of its unearthed roots.

Des himself, flung up and out of the Golden Goddess, landed a full twenty feet away, in the deep welcoming arms of some huge, sweetly scented lilac bushes. He wasn't even scratched, not Des, but he couldn't move. He lay suspended in the air for what seemed hours, listening to sirens and shouts and Cynthia Stall's moaning tears, breathing in the incredible perfume of the flowers, wishing it were he rising up to heaven, not Jack, and knowing that forever, unless something changed, his own life was over.

"Why?" Deborah asked.

"Obviously, because they all assumed I did it, that I was driving and I ran away. My parents are sure, and so is everybody else, that I killed my brother. My brother Jack, he's stone dead. And I suppose it doesn't matter what anybody thinks, except what I know is it wasn't me. I didn't do it. I wasn't even driving. It was your husband, and Will Gaston, who killed my brother, and look what's happened to them. They sure didn't pay much of a price, now, did they?"

Des was crying, a tiny begrudging tear spotting the corner of each eye, so unwilling was he to show any feeling, even anger, even well-deserved, long-nurtured fury. In his lap, his well-manicured fingers had clenched into fists so tight that the nut-brown skin on his knuckles had paled into patches of white.

"What a terrible thing, and you were all just kids," she said. "But what makes you think your brother's death wasn't an accident?"

"Well, it was, I mean technically." His emphasis on the last word was strong and sarcastic. "But Will Gaston and your husband, they fooled around with Anna's car. They messed with the throttle and they killed him. That's the reason Jack died."

"You don't know that. You're just guessing. It's just your own jealousy that makes you want to believe all this."

"I know it. You don't understand. I knew the Golden Goddess so well she could have been me. I know what happened. What Will Gaston did was, he unhooked that clip and laid the throttle rod in between the linkage and the accelerator rod, thinking he'd keep me and Jack stuck down on the beach while Anna was off with Chris. But the damn fool put the air cleaner assembly back on, and my guess is it gave the Impala just enough pressure to keep us going, pumping the gas like that until the throttle got pulled wide open, and that's what killed him."

"Why in God's name would Will have done that? Didn't he know how dangerous it was?"

"Probably not. Not Will. He was a dickhead back then, and he's still one now, I bet. Besides, they were all too drunk. And every soul in the Harbor knows Will Gaston had been after Cynthia ever since elementary school. My guess is Will was thinking of his own self, planning how to make his way into Cynthia Stall's pants finally, after so many years of yearning to get there. So Chris was screwing over my own brother, and his own best friend was planning to do the same thing to him. And I was the one everyone thought was no good."

"But I don't understand," she insisted. "They obviously didn't mean to hurt him. It was all so adolescent, really. And a sad, pointless accident, but hardly the result of evil intentions."

He didn't like the way she thought. She was honing too sharply, focusing on intention as if it were as important as effect. He didn't think she understood what they'd done.

"An accident, wasn't it? They didn't try to hurt Jack," she repeated.

He nodded reluctantly. "Yeah. I guess. If you look at it that way. But my thought is that it was your husband who told Will what to do, how to unhook that clip, and it's your husband who was off with Anna in the woods, and it's your husband who didn't speak up. He let me bear the brunt of everything, so that even my own parents couldn't look at me, thinking I'd done something to kill the only person I ever really loved in the world. You know, when the cops did all their forensic work on the Golden Goddess, they couldn't figure out what happened, not for sure. But I knew. I knew that car so well, I knew everything about her. I'd have been charged, I bet, if the cops had figured out what happened. Not your husband. Not that little worm Will Gaston. You have to admit it wasn't a very decent thing for Chris Latham to do. He left me hanging out to dry. Not too great for such a decent upstanding kind of guy. That's what I think."

"But nothing happened to you. How do you know what he'd have done? Besides, he was just a kid," she said. "And look what he'd been through himself."

"I knew you'd defend him. People have been defending Chris Latham every day of his entire life."

"How do you know any of this? You're just imagining it, the whole scenario."

He shrugged. "It's true," he said stoutly. "Believe me."

"And maybe my husband deserves help, deserves to be defended now and then. That's not so wrong."

"What about me?" he said, and his voice was almost a wail. She didn't know how to answer, she suddenly realized, because in the long run he wasn't a person she loved or ever could love. Who could worry about Des Dunn? He was beautiful, alarmingly so, actually, but it was all external. Inside, he was awful: whiny and self-pitying despite all his supposed success. She didn't begrudge him anything; she simply wasn't willing, after all, to parse his past in a way he'd find satisfying.

He shrugged, looking away from her, out the grimy eight-paned window to the right of her chair. "Maybe Chris deserves sympathy. I guess you think so. Doesn't make it any easier to take the fall for him."

"But did you? Who blamed you, really?"

"Really?" He mocked her. "Really? Everybody."

She was winded, thinking about this kid, this horrible kid blaming Chris his whole life for something pitiful and tragic, and hardly any person's fault. When Des smiled at her, his brick-hued lips were so thin and cruel that she wanted to cry. He was hateful.

"Look," she told him, "I am not saying you didn't have a tough time of things. You obviously did. And so did he. And so do many people, whether they live or die. And I'm not being unsympathetic to you, not in the slightest. But it's twenty years ago now. It's time to put it all away. He didn't kill your brother, even if he was a jerk in high school. You sound like you were pretty awful yourself, frankly, and you managed to do quite well by anybody's standards. So what's the point? It's not as if you're suffering. And he isn't sitting in a bed of roses every day, if that makes you any happier. We have problems of our own you have no idea about. If this is what he did to you, and you didn't speak up about it, you've got only yourself to blame."

"Nobody would have believed me," he said resentfully.

"That's not true. It isn't." She gestured toward Alice. "She's a good person. She'd have done anything for you. I know it."

He sniffed. "You don't know anything then."

"Maybe," she said, "just maybe you are so full of every damn bad thing that you were ever victimized by that you haven't the slightest idea of how many wonderful gifts you've been given. This family took you in and loved you. They weren't perfect, but who cares? My family wasn't perfect, but they loved me. They tried to do the best, and so did she. Look at her. You can't tell me she didn't do everything she could possibly imagine to help you. And later, my God, some company believed in you despite your prison record. A woman loved you. What in the world gives you the right to wake up every morning hating? Maybe it's not all been perfect, but you've been pretty damn lucky. What the hell more could anybody ask?"

"You don't understand," he muttered. "I couldn't expect you to."

44

THEY HADN'T heard his footsteps running up the steep driveway, and when he banged the screen door open, they jumped, flinching back from one another. Deborah's knee banged against Des's. *Her husband? What was he doing here, appearing without warning like a furious cuckold at a motel room window?*

And he wasn't seventeen at all, even though she'd been thinking of him that way for upward of an hour. He was a sturdy man, nearing forty, angry with the heat, the effort to find her, even fear. His hair, plastered to his head, was the color of mailing paper, pale and limp compared to Des's glossy cut. Des by contrast seemed too shiny; unbelievable that only a short while ago his touch had electrified the hair on her arms.

Not rising, aware she couldn't lift herself from the seat if she wanted to, she grinned nervously up at Chris.

Sweat beaded his forehead; his face was red, his mouth open and furious. "Jesus Christ, why the hell didn't anybody answer the phone! I've been driving around the goddamn village for almost an hour trying to find you. What the hell are you doing here?"

She opened her mouth. He kept yelling, not waiting for an answer. "Jesus Christ! Ellie didn't know where you'd gone; the damn tutor, he bit her in the fucking hand! Michael bit the tutor! Ellie's got him locked in his room! How the hell could you leave them alone like that? What the hell is wrong with you?"

He turned abruptly, noting Des. Recognition came to him immediately, a shutting off of one light, a turning on of another, and he said, "Oh, my God. Des Dunn. You're here."

"Just trying to make your world complete," Des said.

His hands, tucked on either side of his thighs, had drawn into tight fists. *He's scared*, Deborah realized, *scared of Chris*. She wouldn't have predicted that. And Chris, too, had the look of someone who'd been confronted with the very worst of horrors. *They're frightened of each other*, she thought, *two dogs poised to begin marking out turf.*

Alice shifted in her chair, snoring loudly, then drifting back to deep sleep. Perspiration stained her chest and the armpits of her blue blouse, Deborah saw, and a sheen of moisture glistened across her plump, unlined forehead. Neither man turned. *Like dogs,* Deborah thought again; *one of them will start to growl at any moment.*

Chris turned to his wife. She'd never seen that stiff-lipped smile on him, but it was a familiar look all the same. It was the expression Caroline wore when asked to greet a visitor or thank an adult for a glass of juice or a present. So unable was she to take even the smallest action under the scrutiny of a stranger, it was as if all the life drained out of her.

Chris lifted one sneakered foot—still childlike, he seemed about to stamp petulantly—but then he replaced it precisely on the carpet. Instead, he swung one arm out and toward her in a demiarc and then away. The denim of his shirt bunched, twisting into a long line across his back and side. His arm fell heavily. A small circle of sweat appeared on the lower portion of his shirt, just over his belly button. "He told you, didn't he? About Jack?"

"Yes," she said, sitting straighter in the chair. She placed her hands on her knees but did not stand, still not trusting her ability to do so. "You mean it's true?"

"That we fooled with the car that night?"

She nodded.

He nodded. "Yeah," he admitted. "We did."

She was silent, studying him.

"I've wanted to tell you for the longest time."

"God," she said quietly. "I didn't really believe it, believe him." Chris took a step toward her and stopped, both hands raising up as if he were about to fall at her feet.

She stood.

Chris dropped his arms to his sides.

"I'd do anything to take it back, make it happen differently." His voice was so neutral, his expression so rigid, that she couldn't fathom what he was actually feeling. Her heart beat so fast she could feel its reverberations against her skull, a padded drumstick thrumming with such constancy that one note did not die before the next began. *God, it was hot in Alice's house. Did the Dunns ever open a window?* Her hair was a sodden towel against her neck.

"Why didn't you tell anyone? You could have saved my skin a thousand times over," Des hissed furiously. He had come to standing, but now he sat abruptly down into the chair Deborah had just vacated. His slim form sank into the unresisting cushion, raising the seamed edges up to curve against his thighs. He glared up at Chris.

Chris opened his mouth and closed it, staring at his wife with a dazed expression.

Deborah, who with her long limbs rarely felt graceful, had the notion that she was participating in a previously choreographed piece, that every movement she was making was predetermined and imbued with practiced agility. She lowered herself onto the small handworked ottoman next to Des. But then her knees knocked into his, too aggressively. She shifted, avoiding his glare. August air billowed dankly throughout the cramped living room.

"I didn't think . . . ," Chris began, but Des interrupted, pitching forward in the chair so that his slim belly rested on his thighs, his chest arching up to pull his neck into a long, surprisingly thick column. *Like a circus contortionist,* Deborah thought, wanting to giggle. The thought of laughing made her cheeks and jaw feel stiff and unnatural.

"Of course you didn't think," Des snapped. "You couldn't think. You'd have to admit you traded my life for yours. Stony Brook wouldn't have ponied up a scholarship for someone like you, now, would they? Not if they'd known."

"No." He said it quietly, staring at her all the while, as if any explanation belonged not to Des but only to Deborah.

"But what did you *do*?" she asked. He was acting—they were both acting—as if he'd actually murdered Alice's son, as if he'd planned some vicious crime. The man she knew had shown himself capable of cruelty—look how he'd been with Michael—but he had always had such integrity, such an ability to reason. She'd never thought of him as young enough before—young enough to be so dumb.

"I killed him. It was my idea to toy with the car, and worse, it was me who went after Anna that night. I'm such a jerk. That's why Jack died."

"You should have come clean. You should have told the truth!" Des cried.

"Of course he should have, but what difference does it make now?" she snapped, glaring at Des, her face chalk white, rage thrumming through her, elating and violent. She'd been numb for the longest time, at least since Michael threw the rock at Caroline back in early July, maybe even longer. She hadn't had a notion of how delicious it might be to grow furious, to want something, to protect someone—yes, that was it, to protect a person who truly might grow better because he knew she loved him, because she could summon up enough love to defend him!

She'd been head-down, slogging down a path as if any footstep might send her tumbling into hell for so long now; thinking she was fighting hard for something valuable, she'd missed another battleground of equal importance. Chris didn't trust her to stand by him and probably never had. With all they'd been through, her love for him had never actually been tested. He needed her. He needed her defending him. He needed her angry, not at him but for him. For the first time in their decade of marriage, she understood.

Des shifted ever so slightly to the right, so that his legs no longer touched hers. He ran his fingers neatly down the perfect creases of his pants. He did not look at her. Instead, he turned toward Chris. "I heard your wife was a major bitch," he said.

Chris blinked, shook his head slightly. Deborah said, "What? What did you say?"

He shrugged. "Word has it that Chris Latham married a good-looking woman from away, a girl with money of her own who lives like she doesn't care about it and runs him like a houseboy."

"What do you mean?" Deborah asked, still confused. "Me?"

"Funny," he said, shaking his head. "I don't think you're so hot to look at. You're too tall for my taste."

Chris didn't move.

Deborah said, "Why would you say that to me? How can you say that to someone?"

Des stood, as if he now knew his exit line. His khakis remained uncrumpled despite the stint in Martin's chair, but his small mouth was twisted so tightly one could easily imagine the marks of his disdain would be permanently etched there. "Not *someone*," he said spitefully. "I'm saying it to *you,* to the bitch who saddled Chris Latham, the lucky bitch who gets to find out just how pretty her husband is, on the inside. Everybody loves Chris Latham, everyone thinks he's so fucking great, but now you know what I know. You know what a true shit he is."

Chris hadn't moved; he was staring out the filthy window as if he'd seen something there, but when Deborah turned, breathing hard, to look, she couldn't see anything but the first blush of red tinting the leaves of Alice's one large oak and the hot sun glinting on the roofs of their cars, side by side just above the crest of the high driveway.

"Do you think I'm like that? A bitch who runs you?" She was seated still, her entire frame collapsed on the stool so that, for the moment, she could have been a much smaller woman.

Chris shook his head. "No," he said, turning to her. "No. Actually, I love you."

He stepped into the tight space between Deborah and Des, kneeling so that he was at her eye level, wedging Des in, forcing Des to shift even farther toward the window. "I'm sorry," he said.

"It's funny, I can't look at you," she said. She hadn't even dared to try. Instead, she'd watched her own hands still upon her knees and marveled at the way her own body could look so calm, could fool its owner and everyone else, when all it wanted to do was scream furiously, in an outrage she knew she'd never, ever express. And when she spoke, her tone was calm and quiet, nearly matter-of-fact.

"The stupid part is that if you had told me, if I had known this all along, it might have made sense to me. But now, the idea that you've been carrying this around for ten years, living with me and loving me and making a home and family together, and all the time, you've had this thing inside you—this poison—I don't get it. I don't see how you could look at me, and swear love to me, and live your life day to day not ever feeling how wrong it is to have something this huge inside you that you don't share. It makes me feel I don't know you. Like I never knew you."

"I didn't think—for the longest time, I didn't think about it, not at all. As if it never happened. At least not until you started hanging around with her—with Alice, I mean." He jerked his head toward Alice, who was still fast asleep, face damp, jaw drooping open, snoring lightly.

"How could you put it out of your head? I don't understand how."

He shrugged. "I don't know; it wasn't easy, it wasn't hard. I just did it."

She shook her head. Her fingers toyed with her wedding ring; she watched the gold glint on the band as the circle turned. "How could you?

How could anyone live through a death like that, a sense of responsibility for it, and not need to talk about what happened?"

He shrugged again. When his shoulders lowered, much more of his shirt was damp with sweat.

"You hate me now. You do."

She shook her head. "It's the not telling I hate."

"You mean, what I did, it doesn't bother you?"

She shook her head. "It does, but not the way it bothers you, not as if a moral lapse is the same thing as a murderous impulse. You were a kid, for God's sake, acting like a kid, and something happened you obviously weren't actually responsible for. What I hate is knowing you didn't, couldn't, tell me. That you would keep something so important a secret. I thought we could share anything. Everything."

"We can." He said the words softly, flushing red as he did so. She wondered what he could possibly be thinking of.

"I know the type," Des said spitefully, turning back toward them. His lips pursed viciously. "You get in their pants and they try to take over your head."

"Shut up," Chris said, not turning from his wife. A bead of sweat dripped down from his chin, onto her bare knee, but neither of them looked at the drop as it flattened and disappeared over the knob of her kneecap.

Deborah started to laugh, suddenly; a high-pitched giggle rose inside her throat with all the force of bile. One hand waved in the air like a flag of surrender. Chris leaned away as her laughter grew and widened, catching upon itself and swelling without humor, into a larger, deeper guffaw that began to thin into vapor even as its successor began. The laughter seemed bigger than she was, as if something had exploded and now could find no other way to burn itself out.

Des watched blandly. Eventually, she trailed off into a hiccuping trickle of giggles. Her neck bent back, and she looked up at the ceiling, still giggling. "He's right," she managed to get out, knowing that from his point of view it was most certainly true. "I *am* a bitch. That's just what bitches like me are like."

She turned to Des. Her eyes tingled; she could feel how hot her face was and that the sweat was collecting on her neck and chest, but she didn't care. She wanted him to know that. She truly didn't care.

"I'm not afraid," she told Des. "That's what's strange about me. What you can't make sense of. I make no claim to be perfect, no matter what you think. I make no claim not to be trying just as hard as anyone else to do right, to be a good person, to take care of the people I love. But I don't have to be soft and compliant for you. I don't have to roll over and refuse to fight to help my children or my husband. I don't have to be the kind of woman *you* would like. I never could be. And if that's being a bitch—if being strong enough to have an opinion and ask questions and try to get things done makes me into a bitch, then so be it. I guess I don't fit your mold of a perfect little girl grown up. I guess I can't let that keep me up at night."

His face didn't change; not even his eyes shifted. He didn't get it. Surprising how she wanted him to know, how much she wanted him to know she didn't care what he thought.

And then she started to laugh again, another series of high peals that seemed to feed on one another as tears collected at the corners of her eyes and then fell directly onto her knees, leaving small dots of water on her skin. Chris watched without moving; Des merely tightened the snide sneer his lips had flattened into. Deborah's shoulders shook with wave after wave of laughter. She caught her breath, finally, wiping at her eyes and shaking her head back and forth. Her shoulders were high, as if by keeping them raised she might forestall another fit of giggles. Eventually, she no longer hiccuped with the effort.

The room was quiet.

All three of them were still, arranged neatly in an unintended triangle, Chris kneeling at her side, Des angled in toward her as if there were something between them, perhaps some treasure resting on the floor.

After a long, long time, knowing it to be only half the truth, Deborah quietly told her husband, "It's okay, you know. It really is."

Chris blew out his breath in a long sigh.

She said, "You know, I never wanted to be that kind of person, the kind he . . . ," and here she tilted her head toward Des, "the kind of woman he thinks of. And I don't mind being stronger than you, about some things. I don't mind that at all. But I need us to be friends. I need to know we can talk, that you can trust me."

"I do," Chris said. "You're my best friend. I trust you completely. Especially now, especially now that you know . . . "

Hollow words? Maybe not. He trusted her, but what about her faith in him? Convincing herself again of what she'd believed until now to be true would take some unknowable gesture from him. She'd assumed, all these years, that he could never be other than who he was: good, kind, bright, generous Chris Latham, the man with whom she shared her life, her heart, her children. The man, in a word, to whom she had entrusted everything.

"I want to believe in you, I do," she said. She remembered suddenly an evening years before, when they'd only barely begun to be together. They'd been on the beach as the sun went down, sharing a bottle of wine, and Chris had confided in her, for the first time, about his mother's death. She recalled how sad his eyes had been, the way he hadn't been able to turn to her after he admitted that his mother had loved his father more than him. The breeze at Sagg Main had been low and constant that evening, and just as the sun dipped below the horizon, it disappeared completely; they leaned back against the dunes and began to kiss, holding each other with an intensity she could still feel, just thinking of it, even all these years later. He'd told her then that he could never leave anyone he loved, that for him caring like this was a permanent condition, no more alterable than the passage of time. She had wanted to tell him that she wasn't like that, to confess to the weakness of this part of her character, to the way love had so frequently bloomed and faded under her care. But she hadn't. She had been silent. For him, with all his goodness, she had taken a quiet vow to be more constant, more loving, to see the whole thing through.

Against the dunes that night, they had made love quietly, sweetly, rolling themselves inside the plaid beach blanket, not eager to be caught by evening strollers or dog walkers or, even worse, a village cop. The sex hadn't been great—they were both too anxious about being seen—but the feeling had been wonderful. She'd felt so tenderly toward him that night; his goodness and honesty were lodestars drawing her to him as if he were the center of the known world. She had wanted more than anything to be worthy of him.

"I'm sorry," Chris said to Des, "I really am. If you knew how many times, how often I've thought of you. I was so glad when I heard about you, just the other day, so relieved that things have turned out okay for you."

"She says I should thank you, that because of the shit you pulled, I straightened out my life," Des said, his chin lifted slightly, the set of his spine impeccably straight and elegant. His hands lay relaxed at the edges of his pockets, as if he might scoop out a tip at any moment. "I have to thank you. Because you left me hanging, I figured out I'd be the fall guy for every damn thing that ever happened around me for the rest of my life. It taught me a huge lesson. I didn't want to be that guy, but I would have been. That's the way the world is."

"Yeah," Chris agreed. "That's true." Chris smiled, extending his right hand.

Des did not extend a hand in return. It was here that his veneer utterly failed him. "Well, all I can say is, you should see my house," Des said abruptly. "But I won't invite you. And you should see my wife." He looked Deborah up and down dismissively. "Yeah. I guess the truth is I didn't catch up to you, I surpassed you in every way. So suck on that, Chris Latham, if you can."

Chris shrugged. "If it makes you happy." And then he turned to Deborah. "I'm sorry," he told her again. "Can we go home now?"

When she nodded, his shoulders slumped just the slightest bit in relief, and he took her by both hands. She didn't look at him, but she let him help her from the house. As they headed down the slope of the high driveway, she put her hand against his back, leaving another damp spot on his shirt. He put his arm around her shoulders, drawing her closer, ignoring the heat.

"You told me," she whispered. When he tilted her face up, she kept her eyes closed, and then he saw: She was weeping quiet tears. She had heard his story, he saw, and they had survived, but at what cost? He couldn't tell. He tried to kiss her, but she turned away.

"I'll be okay, you know, and so will you," she said then. "We're adults, have been for long enough we don't have rights to moan and groan about the past. But think about Michael. Look what you're carrying around like day-old news you can't shake. Think what he'll have to grin and bear. He might as well be dead for all his life is worth."

"So we can't help him, I admit it. I'm not man enough, is that what you're saying? I run away from what I take on? I'm sorry, Deb, I really am, but I'm sure I gave him my best shot. Lots of things I've done I can't claim to be proud of, but not this. The boy. I tried. I couldn't do it. And that's as far as it goes. If someone else can help him, I welcome them to try. I know my limits. God, I know my limits."

"I wish I'd known them," she said bitterly, and then she reached for the door handle of her car. "I wish I'd known my own," she said. "I feel like dirt."

"You?" he asked, surprised.

"Don't you get it?" she snapped. "Me. I'm the one who couldn't pull it off." She stepped into her car and slammed the door shut. She was about to start crying again, and she didn't want him to see.

Des didn't move until both the Lathams' cars had disappeared around the corner. He stood rooted to the same spot, in front of the ottoman, his back to the woman who had raised him and his face utterly unreadable.

After a long time, five minutes or more, he put his hands into his pockets and headed for the screen door. He'd not glanced around the room once or turned to gaze at the only mother he'd ever known.

As Des opened the rickety door, his mother snored lightly. Her hands lifted several inches into the air, gracefully, before settling back against her thighs. She sighed.

It was warmer now, the heat rising with that two o'clock enthusiasm that generally announces the onset of a cooler evening. Somewhere a lawn mower kicked into action. Across the street, Sid Carcopino's battered truck ambled to a halt, but Sid failed to emerge. He'd been arriving home with just that lackluster energy for a good forty years; the truck had to have changed, of course, but it appeared identical to its predecessors. Des tapped his foot and swiveled, marching back into his childhood home.

He didn't wake Alice, nor did he kneel at her feet. He moved cautiously, as if by disturbing even the air he might raise some unbearable matter. When he leaned in toward his mother, his knees bent only slightly. No tears, no words, not even a shiver of affection playing across his face, and yet his lips were gentle on her cheek. He kissed his mother, once. He smoothed her damp hair with his opened palm. And then he straightened.

Again, and finally, Des was gone.

When Alice woke, almost a full hour later, her fever had broken. She'd remember only that she dreamt of seeing her adopted son once more, that she distinctly felt his lips against her cheek. Later, when the police arrived to tell her about Martin's drowning, she wondered if the vision of a loving, well-settled Des had come to her as a warning or a sign. And when the undertaker left, and before Ellie and Nan showed up with their bustling grief and their solicitous affection, she made the phone call to Greg Isen, telling him she was feeling slightly better. In fact, she informed him, she'd decided to take those pills after all. If he wouldn't mind phoning in the prescriptions, that is.

45

ONE OF the Allans from the tackle store had told Chris the blue crabs were still plentiful, and when he mentioned it to Deborah, her eyes brightened immediately and she insisted they take Caroline crabbing. The past month had been such an endurance event that something special was needed to turn, as it were, the tide.

Elizabeth and Ada Bloom came along, too, so of course Chris was the unlucky fellow in charge of tying the chicken heads onto every one of the lines and tucking a rock inside each lifeless beak for weight. Deborah had fretted in the car on the way to Sagg Main Beach, but Ada and Caroline didn't seem to mind the sightless chicken heads in the slightest. It was Elizabeth and Deborah who found them repellent, squealing and backing off each time Chris pulled another gardening stake out of the bag, tied a line, and threaded it through a beak or neck.

The girls ran back and forth between the salt pond and the ocean, dampness and sand creeping up the legs of their jeans. Deborah was wearing sweatpants and fishing boots, her curly brown hair clipped up on her head so that Chris joked that she looked as if she were posing for a crabbing brochure. Elizabeth, more practical, was barefoot and in shorts and a heavy sweatshirt. This was the first easy evening they'd spent with Elizabeth since Les left, the first time she hadn't been sobbing or red-eyed or blustering with anger. It was just too beautiful to focus on rage this evening, too warm, the air still fuzzy the way it is in early fall before the winter light sharpens and it becomes difficult to peer directly toward the sun.

"It's so warm. It's so beautiful. I can't believe it's the end of October," Elizabeth said, gazing around at the wide sky, the scattered clouds, the expanse of wind-swept, unmarred sand. A few hundred feet away, two women and a man shared a plaid blanket and a rope-bottomed jug of chianti. Their dog kept galloping toward Chris and Deborah and Elizabeth, but before he reached them, one of the women would stand and yell out, "Brandy! Get over here!" Brandy would turn reluctantly and pad back to the blanket with a slow, defeated air, but he wouldn't give up for long. He wanted a chicken head of his own, it was clear; eventually, Chris opened the plastic shopping bag to let Brandy nose one out and take it proudly back to his owners.

Chris placed the gardening stakes at two-foot intervals just a few steps into the water. As the chicken heads sank to the bottom, the lines went slack. "What do we do?" Deborah asked eventually. Her eyes glittered with excitement. This was what true villagers had done for their meals for centuries past. As living history, it was much more than a simple distraction; it was a thrill.

"Watch," Chris said, and he pointed. Two of the lines were straightening slowly, as eager crabs grabbed onto the chicken heads and tried to take them back to the depths of the pond. Chris picked up a net and steadily pulled at one of the taut lines. He lifted it and quickly netted the crab hanging off the sodden chicken head. Banging the net on the side of a bucket, he loosened the unwilling crab, who skittered against the metal and then stopped, accepting its fate. "Come on!" Chris said. "Grab a net! There goes another one!" He pointed. Elizabeth lifted her net and began to raise a line carefully.

"Okay! Here goes!" Elizabeth, who had spent much of the last weeks since Les left her in tears, looked giddy. They were actually catching their dinner, she giggled, and Deborah wanted to hug her. It was such a relief to see her smiling.

Deborah, too, began to laugh. The girls came running back across the sand.

"You got one! Daddy! You got one!"

Elizabeth hauled in her line and snagged two crabs at once, and then the first line grew taut again, and then another a few feet away, and soon they were all in the water, drenched to their knees. The crabs kept coming in, their blue backs glistening with water as they rose, netted, in the evening air. With their claws snapping, they clutched fiercely onto one another in the bucket. Later, when they were cooked, it was shocking to realize how many crabs had sliced off each other's claws on the trip from life to death.

Deborah couldn't stop laughing. The wind picked up, the sun lowered rapidly in the sky, and it grew chilly. Her boots filled with water. The girls trilled gleefully, counting the crabs as they fell reluctantly into the container. There were at least thirty, they counted. As the sun dropped, Chris pulled in one line that had three huge crabs on it, clawing at one another so cruelly it took a full three minutes to loosen them from the net. They were the king crabs, the girls proclaimed!

Nancy McLean, the social worker at New York Children's Morning, had called Deborah just that afternoon to plead with her one more time. Social Services had taken Michael and placed him in foster care, provided the Lathams paid the monthly foster care expenses themselves. Chris hadn't minded; he'd thought that was exactly right. He was more than willing to support Michael, but not at their home.

"I really think you should see him," Nancy said. "He's doing so well. And the therapist the Reisers are taking him to wants to meet with you."

"I can't," Deborah had said. "I *can't*. And Chris won't."

"Why *can't* you?" Nancy had asked, imitating Deborah's insistence.

"I don't know. I don't know if I can imagine he even still exists. The truth is, I've tried several times to call him. I've heard Linda Reiser's voice saying hello, and I just haven't been able to ask for him."

"Why not?" Nancy asked.

"Because whatever is happening, whether he's happy or sad, I can't change it. I can't take him back."

"If he could just hear your voice . . ."

"He might think I was coming. I don't want to mislead him, not for a second. You saw how Chris didn't even want to meet the Reisers. He's done. And Caro's so fragile . . ."

"So is Michael."

"It's time now," Deborah said firmly. "We tried. We were honest with him. He's got to go on now. He does. I'm not pretending I feel good about it, or clean, or that I don't doubt myself."

"Well, if you doubt . . ."

"Not the way you think, Nancy. Honestly. We aren't ever going to take him back. For his own sake and for ours, it has to be a clean break."

"Well," Nancy sighed heavily, "I'll let you go then. But if you decide you need to see him . . ."

"Of course."

Chris would never agree, Deborah knew that. He'd refused even to be in the car when she brought Michael to Riverhead. In fact, the Reisers had offered to drive out to Sag Harbor to pick Michael up, but Deborah had known better than to accept. She didn't want the Reisers to see their house or how they lived, the huge yard, the pretty rooms. From the outside, the Lathams looked precisely like the kind of people who should have been able to do everything for Michael. She couldn't bear to see in the Reisers' eyes how inadequate her family had been.

Even looking at Nancy McLean had been difficult enough, when she had driven out to plead with them face-to-face. Nancy had admitted that many of the Eastern European children were having more difficulties than other children, that she'd seen an alarming increase in failed adoptions in the past several years.

"In two decades, our agency had no more than twenty calls about disruptions," she admitted, glancing nervously over at Michael and then away. "Before the last four years, that is. This year alone, we've had twenty calls. But adoption is difficult under any circumstance. Raising a kid, any kid, is never simple."

"We know that," Chris said, and Deborah was grateful that he took responsibility for saying the words. "And maybe we didn't understand how hard it would be, how unwilling we were to cope with the problems. It's just been so much harder than we expected. We thought it would get easier, that we could help him."

"It takes time," Nancy said.

Chris shrugged, raising his shoulders, hands, and eyebrows at once as if to indicate a complete sense of helplessness, that the Lathams had run out of time. On the floor, Michael fingered a puzzle piece, one of the few remaining shapes not placed in the large photo of the planetary system that he'd been putting together all that morning. He picked the piece up, waited as if expecting someone to speak, and then began to turn the black shape against the puzzle, trying to find the place in which its jagged edges would fit.

"We—I regret the way we did your home study, to tell the truth. Because you seemed so set on the boy, so sure of yourselves, and the circumstances were so perfect. I should have asked you more questions. I broke my own rules, didn't spend as much time with you as I normally do.

I have never—in twenty years of doing this, I have never cut as many corners as I did with you people. I'm furious at myself about it. He . . . ," and here Nancy McLean nodded toward Michael, who continued working at his puzzle as if all his concentration were focused on the project, "he didn't deserve this. God knows this is hardest on him."

"He shouldn't be in here now, while we're talking," Chris said.

"Oh yes, he should," Nancy answered firmly. "He has rights, too. He'll need to understand what's happening. He has to be here, so that he'll *know*."

"Don't make it worse than it already is!" Deborah cried. "Please don't!"

Nancy's eyebrows lifted with a gently mocking air.

Deborah didn't know what was most difficult to take: Michael's calmness, Chris's matter-of-factness, or the way bile kept rising in her throat, a sour reminder of how weak she had been, how she had failed to live up to her own expectations, how she had entered into the entire adoption process with such arrogant self-confidence and failed so shamefully, hurting all of them with her irresponsibility.

"Please don't make this harder!"

Nancy stood, walking swiftly to Deborah, to the side away from Chris. She knelt by the couch. *Her mouth looks soft enough*, Deborah thought, *to say the most caring, empathetic things.*

"Will you try again then? Can you at least consider it? We'd do more, help more than we have. We've been remiss, not followed up with you as much as we normally do. And when I saw you in Hampton Bays, at the meetings, you always seemed to be doing so much better than anyone else. I never thought, you see. We're understaffed, and you, well—we didn't know. I've never had a family be this quiet for three and a half years and then request, you know, what you did. To send the child into foster care. Usually, people contact us much sooner. We can try to work with you. We have so many resources available. If we'd only known, you see. Honestly, I feel we could work with you."

Deborah, about to cry, merely shook her head back and forth. No. They had tried. They had. Clearly their best effort had not been enough to help Michael, but they had done what they could, more than they could. Perhaps some other family would succeed where they had failed.

Nancy McLean dropped to her knees, next to Michael. His breath drew in sharply, although he did not look at her. He continued to turn the puzzle piece in the air above the remaining spaces. It was a piece of the Milky Way, vapor dotted with glowing stars in a vast dark sky.

Nancy's voice was soft. "Michael," she said. He paused, eyes still focused on the puzzle.

She put one hand on his arm. "Michael," she said again. "You must feel sad and angry right now. I know *I* do. And your mom and dad do, too. We all wanted this to work out. But this is not the only adoption that ever failed. We know what to do and we will help you."

He did not move. It was hardly apparent that he was even breathing. His chest in the black T-shirt—his arms, his eyes—were as tensely still as a rabbit's.

Nancy spoke again. "I will find you another family. I'll make sure you have a mom and dad to take care of you. You won't be alone, I promise."

"I'm always alone," Michael muttered stiffly, his voice so quiet Deborah had to strain to make out the words.

"It's okay to feel that way," Nancy said. "It certainly is. But I will work with you, do whatever it takes. I promise you I will find a family that works for you. I promise."

Michael shrugged, eyebrows, shoulders, and hands in the air, his helpless expression a perfect mirror of his father's. Chris, however, didn't see the gesture. He had slipped from the family room when Nancy first began to speak to Michael. His footsteps were faintly audible overhead, sound diminishing as he walked down the long hallway to the bedroom where Caroline lay quietly atop her pink quilt, reading a Dr. Seuss book she'd long ago outgrown, and waiting.

The foster care family was to meet them at Social Services; that's what Deborah had asked for. Earlier in the day, Christopher had decided that he and Caroline would say good-bye to Michael at home. "It's going to be hard enough," he'd said, and Deborah certainly couldn't disagree.

Once Michael's suitcases were in the car, along with the trash bag full of bedding and stuffed animals and the three liquor-store boxes filled with soldiers and puzzles, they'd all four stood awkwardly in the driveway. The moment they had been focused on since early September had arrived. Michael wore his new red sneakers; they were already scuffed and one lace trailed over the driveway gravel, but no one bent to tie it.

Chris cleared his throat. *Kneel!* Deborah thought fiercely. *Tell him good-bye! Hug him! Wish him luck!*

"Well," Chris said. "Uh, Michael," and he did kneel, drawing Michael into an uneasy embrace. Michael's neck remained straight on his spine; he did not fold himself into the hug. *Like a dog who'd been kicked once too often,* Deborah thought.

Caro stood by her father. When he knelt, her knees bent slightly down and she leaned in toward Michael, but she didn't touch him. When she said "bye," the syllable came out so softly that only her mother, who'd been watching, knew that Caroline had mouthed the word. If the little girl felt some sense of victory, it didn't show.

Michael seemed focused elsewhere. Deborah guessed he was worrying about the Reisers and what the future might hold, but as she opened the car door for him, he asked her, "Can we stop at McDonald's?"

"No. There isn't time."

"Oh," he answered coolly. Then he said, "I can do my own seat belt."

Chris stepped in front of Caroline. Deborah couldn't bring herself to say "see you later." She merely nodded at them and switched on the engine.

As they drove out the circular driveway, Chris and Caroline stood mutely, not waving, not turning away. Michael didn't see them. He was gazing forward, out the window.

Deborah remembered Chris's description of the television program he had watched months earlier, about the family that gave up their boy for adoption. That child had gone off easily with his new foster mother, as if the family he had called his own for four years had not had the slightest impact. It was what Deborah hoped for, that Michael hadn't felt them at all, hadn't appreciated that they were the Lathams and not the Smiths or the Millers. Then she'd be able to tell herself it really hadn't mattered, that Chris was right, that they'd meant no more to Michael than anyone else could have, that he was beyond saving.

He'd known, though; once they were safely away from the house, away from Chris and Caroline, he wept. He'd been so quiet, she almost missed the way the tears slid down his cheeks.

He didn't pay the slightest bit of attention to her the entire forty-five-minute trip. He stared out the window at the desolate line of gas stations and delis and hardware stores that lined Route 58, and then he stared at the trees that took their place. As they pulled into the parking lot at the county building, he was still staring out the window.

"We're here," she said.

He didn't answer.

When she opened his door and unlatched his seat belt, he didn't move. When she reached a hand out to take his arm, he flinched and drew back, as if she'd been the aggressor all along. He pulled himself inward and low, so that his weight on the seat could not be budged.

"Come on," she said. "This isn't going to be easy no matter what we do."

"You never loved me," he spat at her, turning in the seat so that his relentless gypsy vision assailed her. "A real mom, you said you were my real mom, and now you're giving me away."

He was right.

Behind her, a young couple chattered about going to the movies as they hauled a neatly dressed two-year-old girl with careful pigtails between them. Each parent hoisted her by the arm, high into the air, without bothering to count one-two-three. A game they'd played so often, so completely understood by all three players, that it no longer required full attention. The little girl giggled gleefully each time her Mary-Jane'd feet rose high.

"You didn't love me. You didn't love me. It's not fair!"

"I did!" she wanted to shout. "I did!" But of course, she no longer did.

She hadn't for weeks. She had tried so hard not to feel anything for this child who had been her son. She'd stopped allowing him in, she supposed, from the very afternoon he mauled Mrs. Nowicki, the tutor the school district had hired to help him. It was the ultimate sign, she believed, the clearest indication that no matter what was done for him, he was only going to get worse, become more violent, hurt more people. She didn't want him anymore, didn't want to love him. He wasn't hers. No child of hers could be capable of such things. Her love hadn't withered and died; it had wiped itself away with the same efficiency she'd used to clean Caroline's wounds: dab, swipe, no more blood. The willingness to care was simply gone.

"I'm not going," Michael said stubbornly. "I'll run away. Nobody cares."

"That's not true," she began, and then she reversed tiredly. "You know, Michael," Deborah said, and it was the last gift of her mothering. "It's up to you, too, to make people care about you. You can give up on your life. You can admit defeat. You're only six years old, just six, and you can say it's all too hard. Or you can try with the Reisers. You can do your best to make it work."

"Make it work? Will they keep me? Are they my parents now?" He was curious, trying to understand her. Nobody had ever denied that he was smart enough to get the whole picture; it was his refusal to do so that was so frustrating.

She could picture the Reisers: a rubbery couple with firm biceps and slow smiles, who'd run nearly a dozen difficult children through their home in the past five years. What were they looking for? Was there any child they would want to keep forever? It was impossible to know. She shrugged. "Come on, get out. Let's go find them. You never, ever know what life is going to bring next."

"You're stupid," he said bitterly. Nevertheless, he let her take his arm and gently help him from the car. And he let her hold his hand all the way into the office where the state social worker and Nancy McLean waited with bland expressions. Nancy avoided looking at Deborah, not even a glance to serve as absolution. She focused completely on Michael.

Michael shook hands politely with both Mel and Linda Reiser, and allowed Mel to pat his brown cheek. The six of them stood in silence for an awkward moment, and then Mel said he supposed it was time for them to be moving along home. Michael nodded, started to walk away. He took two short steps and turned.

She knelt and held out her arms, all the love she'd placed in cold storage surging forth for one last time. He flew into her arms, clutching onto her so tightly she could feel each finger digging into her shoulders. His breath, hot on her cheek, smelled like good clean spring dirt, and she breathed in deeply, suddenly wanting more than anything to remember precisely this scent. His two arms around her neck were more than a hug. They were a vise grip that nearly knocked her from kneeling, a clutch of fear and anger and, oh yes, love. He had loved her; she couldn't pretend he never had. He couldn't stop himself from hating hand in hand with any love he felt, but that didn't mean he didn't love. Michael Latham wouldn't forget. He really had loved his mother.

She'd never, ever be able to deny that.

When she tried to explain it to Chris, later that same evening, he didn't understand. He didn't want to. The first time she began to whisper to him, in the kitchen, he acted as if he didn't hear. Instead, he called to Caro in the living room. "Hey, Little Princess, drop that book!" he shouted cheerfully. "What say I push you on the swings?"

Later, they put Caroline to bed, the two of them together tucking her in for the first time in more than three years. Fast asleep, her expression was oddly careful even now, even when she could believe that her life would return to normalcy. In the hallway just outside Caroline's closed door, Deborah, so exhausted by the day that she could barely stand, nevertheless couldn't contain her anger. She stopped her husband with a tap to the back, and she asked, simply, "Why?"

"Why what?" he asked defensively.

"Oh, why anything?" she mocked him, her tone shrill and rising.

"Why make me take him alone? Why give up before we knew we would fail? Why be so deliberately opaque, pretending to be true and clear? Why? Why are you not who you promised you would be?"

Chris didn't turn to look at her. He remained facing the staircase, only the abrupt sagging of his shoulders revealing he had heard. Her hands were on her hips; if he had swiveled to face her, he would have seen the rage knotting her brow, her tight, furious mouth. Instead, he stood, caught, until the sound of a neighbor's Mustang, its engine revving past the front windows, broke the silence.

"What's going on in there? Who are you?" she said then, impatiently.

"I don't know," he answered, his tone slow and puzzled. He ran his right hand through his hair, shook his head, and began his usual shrug. Only then did he twist to look at her. His eyes were so sad, so darkly brown, so deeply guilty, that she lost any desire to press the point.

"I don't know," he said again, and he began to cry, a pained barking that was unbearable to hear. She thought she'd faint if he didn't stop, but she couldn't move, couldn't shout at him, couldn't speak. He was gulping, gasping; he wanted to tell her something but couldn't get the words out.

She wasn't aware when her arms stretched out for him. It was as if her fingers wanted to extract his words from the space between them.

"I . . . let . . . you . . . down." Each word washed out on a single sob. He was forcing himself to tell her, forcing himself, finally, to feel ashamed. "I . . . let . . . you . . . down," he repeated.

His eyes never wavered, nor hers, and yet the few feet of hallway seemed to have stretched, the distance between them uncrossable. She would never know him, she realized. Never.

"I . . . let . . . you . . . down. I . . . always . . . do."

Drooping head, he moved toward her, just one step, and then he waited. She had never seen how weak his chin was, how when his shoulders slumped he was not half as large a man. When she put her arms around him, he slumped against her, his torso heavy against her chest. He smelled like fear, sour and musty, and she was reminded suddenly that the odor out by the septic tank had been gone all afternoon, ever since she'd returned from Riverhead. Chris sobbed again, quietly, and a frisson of shame ran through her body.

There weren't words for what he needed. She held onto him. Arms enclosing, heart pressed to heart, she willed him to know that she would make everything right, a power she no longer possessed, and eventually his sobs, and his shame, seemed for the moment to die away.

She hadn't been enough for him, nor he for her, at the crucial moment. Yet could anyone have done more? She doubted it. In the long run, they were better than most.

Back at home, Deborah and Elizabeth spread newspaper over the kitchen table while Chris rinsed the crabs. The girls were upstairs playing, and even though it was a school night, no one protested that it was growing near eight o'clock and they hadn't had any dinner. One by one, Chris lowered crabs into two huge pots while the women sprinkled them with Old Bay Seasoning. They were drinking beer and talking rapidly, the way people do who are coming off a high moment and yearning to stay aloft.

After the lids were on the pots and there was nothing left to do but wait, Elizabeth said, "This is the real Sag Harbor, isn't it?"

Chris shook his head, swigging from his beer bottle at the same time. "There is no Sag Harbor, not anymore."

The women laughed uncomfortably. "Yeah, right," Deborah said. She picked up the sponge and began to wipe the counter.

"Really," he said. "I mean, the Sag Harbor I knew, growing up, the people who all cared about each other and took care of each other . . ."

"You can't deny that's still true," Deborah said, but he shook his head again, no.

"It isn't," he said. "Sag Harbor hasn't existed since the 1970s, not really. Not since all the local families sold their worthless old houses to the people from away and moved out to the developments outside the village. The people who live in the village now, they think they're living in Sag Harbor, but what they're living in is their version of the village. They come here with an idea of village life that's really part of wherever they come from—Germany, Vermont, Manhattan, Aspen—and that's what they bring. It's a fantasy village, now. It used to be real. It's over."

"That's funny," Elizabeth said. "I have a friend who's an anthropologist. She studies Sicily, and the other day she called me and she said she was thinking of changing to another line of work. She said there is no Palermo anymore. Twenty years ago there were no hotels, and you had to know someone to find a restaurant; now there are hotel chains and tourist buses and everything else. She said there's nothing to study, that indigenous culture is dissipating into some global commercial mess. She was starting to wonder if there was anything left to study in the world. The minute you start loving a place, you destroy it. That's what she said."

He put his beer down. For a moment, it seemed as if he would walk toward Elizabeth Bloom, take her by the arms and what? Hug her? Hit her?

Deborah cleared her throat. She had never told Chris the worst of it, and she never would. She would never recount to him how Michael had cried out for her, how she had tried to turn cruelly away. It would be impossible to explain to anyone, even Chris, how the failure to be Michael's mother had altered her. She had built the whole solid castle of her self-confidence so carefully. She had known herself to be strong, wise, and good-humored, and she had not been ashamed to know it.

Now, she no longer read the world strictly in black and white; moral terms were fuzzier. There were reasons people did what they did, fell where they fell, arose abruptly and with determination. She no longer felt certain of what those reasons were. It was difficult to live with that knowledge, much of the time.

It was hard to imagine what Chris saw now when he looked at her. Did he forgive her for turning out to have less fortitude than she had promised? Did he even allow himself to think of Michael? She suspected not. She would never tell him about the phone calls she had tried to make to the Reisers. And if she ever had the courage to stay on the line and ask to speak to her little boy, well, she knew that Chris could never hear a word about it.

Nevertheless, both separately and together, the Lathams were okay. They were in it for the long haul. They would even, she believed, be happy again.

Chris shook his head for the third time. He didn't say anything for the longest while; they were all silent, and then he said, "Back when I was growing up, there was a nickname we had for ourselves, for the Harbor. People didn't say it out loud much, at least not to anyone from away. But we used to call Sag Harbor 'Old Skinemandcheatem.' It was the attitude, that the people from away would come, the Time-Life writers and photographers and all the other folks who saw us as a resort rather than a village. And we'd take everything they had from them, happily, and throw away the carcasses. We were poor and they weren't, and we were willing to take advantage of what we could. And somehow, in all the profit making and selling up and cleaning up and taking 'em to the cleaners, well, we all lost."

Deborah's affection for the village was grander than Chris's, she guessed. She didn't believe its soul could be destroyed, couldn't imagine what it was he was missing. He'd never lived in a city, maybe that was it. With all his fear and guilt, he'd held himself so rigidly to his rules for living that he'd not experienced the alternatives to village life. What he supposed to be a loss of soul might really be an evolution—partly better, partly worse, net equal. It was the illusion of innocence that he was losing, that was all. No more, no less.

In the ensuing silence, the timer stopped its clicking and began a tinny whistle. The crabs had lost. Mallets and picks to the ready, it was time to feast on their remains.

46

ONE morning, before school, Caroline Latham rooted around in the closet in the spare bedroom, searching for her tennis racket. She'd taken the free tennis lessons in the park the summer she was six but hadn't taken them the previous summer because she hadn't felt like it. She hadn't done much of anything last summer, but things were different now. Her life was so much better. It was, she told herself, almost as if the bad part hadn't happened. Most of the time, she could believe it never had.

Today, she and Ada were going over to Mashashimuet Park with Ada's mother, Elizabeth, after school, and even though it was cold, the girls wanted to hit some tennis balls. She'd need to borrow Ada's mother's racket. Hers was nowhere to be found, not even in here. She hated this room and entered it only as a last resort. There wasn't much in the closet at all, just a baseball glove and a down jacket, some books, and a box of foreign-language cassette tapes.

Her parents avoided this room, too. It was the only place in the house that still held any flavor of his essence, and she knew her parents felt the same way. The bed was gone, replaced by a sleep sofa that her grandparents used when they visited. The walls had been painted white, the carpet lifted and replaced by three bright throw rugs, the blue curtains metamorphosed into neutral blinds. Still, this was the spot where Michael had lived; it was the only place his specter could still be awakened.

At school, only a couple of kids had asked her about Michael, where he'd gone. Most everybody seemed to have forgotten him so easily, even her parents didn't talk about him much. When Dean Stewart, in her class, learned that Michael had been given up to foster care because he was so bad, such a mean kid, well, Dean blinked a few times and his whole pudgy face went tight. You could tell he thought about that one for a while. After that, he was always real careful to be nice around Caroline, which was just fine with her. She never did explain to him that it hadn't been her decision, Michael leaving, and for the rest of second grade, Dean Stewart was awfully quiet. If the other kids had known why, they'd have thanked Caroline Latham from the bottoms of their no longer apprehensive hearts.

During second grade, Caroline read so many books she sometimes got confused about what was real and what wasn't. She loved to read. One thing she thought she might want to be was a writer. She'd written some poems, and her mom sent one in to a children's literary magazine contest; the whole family was so happy when she won! The poem went like this:

> *This little puppy was cute.*
> *He didn't know what to do.*
> *So he felt that he was growing up.*
>
> *This puppy was a newborn.*
> *This is very odd!*
> *The next day, he was a dog.*

When her dad read the poem, he smiled so big it looked like his eyes were closed. He hugged her and hugged her, and he laughed, too, and that made Caroline feel happier than happy. Her mom made a special cake the night she got the letter about the prize, and it was like having an extra birthday.

Caroline's mom read to her every night, but most nights Caroline read some more after her mom kissed her and closed the door. She worked her way through the stories of Nancy Drew, the Moomintroll books, and any other stories Mrs. Kiernan at the John Jermain Library recommended. Her favorite was called *From the Mixed-Up Files of Mrs. Basil E. Frankweiler,* and it was about a girl and her younger brother who run away from home and live secretly at the Metropolitan Museum of Art in

New York City. There was a line in it that Caroline loved; she read it over and over like it would disappear if she didn't memorize it, because the words described what she'd been feeling ever since November.

"Happiness is excitement that has found a settling down place, but there is always a little corner that keeps flapping around"; that's what the writer had written. It was exactly what Caroline felt. She was happy again, happy enough to play tennis and have friends and love school. Happy enough to move her arms and legs and pretend she was flying through the backyard; happy enough to make angels in the snow last January and not imagine she was dying; happy enough to laugh even when nobody said something funny. But some other part of her was like that little flapping corner, a little bit afraid to be cranky or have a bad day or get annoyed with anyone. The little fear just didn't seem to go away.

The fear took all kinds of shapes, some of them scarier than others. There were bad men who tried to take her away and monsters under the bed, but the worst fears were so scary they set her heart to pounding. No matter how hard she tried to breathe, she'd feel choked, perspiration dotting up under her black curls while her skull numbed and the back of her neck locked stiffly. It would pass in time, but it never disappeared completely. She was frightened of real things, possible things, and she wondered constantly if those possibilities loomed the way she thought they did. If it wasn't Michael, returned to them by some fluke of fate, it was her parents, who hugged and giggled and went out to dinner with friends again, but might easily dissolve and separate with as little warning as Ada's had given.

Sometimes, listening to her father's complaints at dinner, she feared for the village itself, which never seemed to her to be changing, until her father pointed out another boutique or a traffic snarl or a craftsman put out of business, and then she knew Sag Harbor to be changing, becoming different every year. Her dad liked things the way they were, and Caroline agreed with that, even though her mom threw up her hands like her dad was silly when he griped about the village. It was hard to know where right was and where wrong was, and that scared her, too. Most of all she wondered about herself. She, Caroline, what was she becoming? Who would she turn out to be? A teacher? An actress? A brilliant scientist? A tennis pro? She could so easily grow breathless with the glories awaiting her! Would she succeed? She could not, oh, she hoped she would not fail!

More questions than answers, of course, and there always would be worries that danced and disappeared like the sun's streaky hands wiping across the deep green of the bay at sunset. Looking forward, into the future, most of what Caroline Latham would ever see were memories, pictures of her own lived life trailing like ribbons. Before and after this moment of remembering, there would be a thousand other half-lived instants of knowing fear and no longer knowing why. The bruises wrought by Michael were as permanent as paint, defining her substance, the essence of the woman she would so soon become. It was the truth, though she would never really know it: He had made her, just as grit creates a pearl.

ACKNOWLEDGMENTS

I AM VERY grateful to dentists Allan Goodstein and Glenn Heinze, to doctors John Oppenheimer and Jeremy Halfhide, to attorney Meg Rudansky, to homeopath Anne Marie Minicucci, psychologist Bettina Volz, and to my Romanian friend Ileana Popeanos. Also village historian George Finckenor and John Jermain Library local historian Suzan Habib and librarian Pat Brandt; as well as Del Dordelman and Joe Hanna, all of whose memories of Sag Harbor's past are sprinkled throughout these pages. I am also grateful to Southampton College at Long Island University for the use of the John Steinbeck Room; to my writers' group: Robin Dorsty, Hope Harris, and Lou Ann Walker; to the many friends who read this manuscript in progress; and to Tom Dyja, Suzanne Gluck, Gail Winston, and, especially, to my husband, Jim.